ALSO IN THIS SERIES...

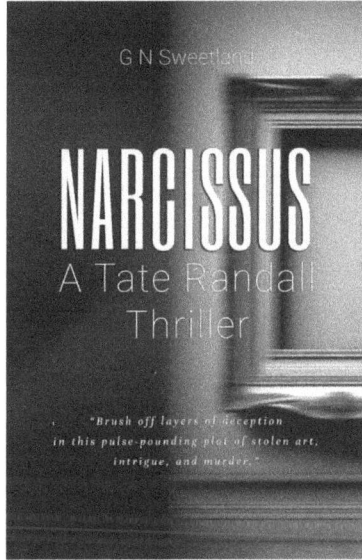

A Stolen Masterpiece

Mysterious Macabre Murders

And a new nemesis named NARCISSUS

When a stolen Caravaggio painting is rumoured to have resurfaced in London, DCI Tate Randall of the Arts and Antiquities Investigation Department is tasked with locating and recovering the artwork. When a number of potential buyers are found murdered and their corpses mysteriously posed, the case takes an unexpected turn and Tate must confront the skeletons of his past and recover the stolen artwork before the Narcissus claims another victim.

ISBN: 9781800946323 | Paperback | Hardback | eBook

G N Sweetland

NARCISSUS II
The Seven Acts of Mercy

A Tate Randall Thriller

First published in paperback by
Michael Terence Publishing in 2024
www.mtp.agency

ISBN 9781800948921

Michael Terence
Publishing

Ness… for your endless inspiration.
And the belief that keeps me on the right page…
Forever more… x

Nothing emboldens sin so much as mercy...

Timon of Athens
William Shakespeare

This book includes media links...

Explore artworks, locations and more.

Go to gnsbooks.com (Interactive) or scan the QR code
to unlock images, maps and facts as you read.

29th October 1606

Pio Monte Della Misericordia

Via dei Tribunali

Naples, Italy

PROLOGUE

Caravaggio appeared from the squalor and insalubrity that festered within the shadows. He hastened his stride as he crossed the roadway. His reckless urgency very nearly became his undoing as he stepped into the path of an approaching carriage, narrowly missing a collision with the flanks of the harnessed horses. Leather bridles cut into the horses' mouths as the coachman pulled heavily on the reins to stall his steeds. The carriage came to an abrupt stop. Each horse exhaled heavily through flared nostrils and the coachman hollered some choice words in return for his quick thinking.

Caravaggio lumbered forward, oblivious to his close encounter, before once again being swallowed into the shadowy world that penetrated the deepest recesses of the street. He pulled his cloak around his shoulders as he hurried along the cobbled walkways. His chosen path hugged the stone facades of the encroaching buildings, their walls providing a sense of security and protection from an unexpected ambush or chance encounter. He periodically glanced over his shoulder to alleviate the constant gnawing feeling that he was being followed. He was constantly on edge but had plausible reason to be concerned for his safety.

Rumours abounded within the whisperings of local hostelries that men looking to take his head in revenge for the killing of a brother had followed his trail south and had been seen within the walls of the city in recent days. His hopes of an early pardon from the Pope for his misdoings had also floundered and it now seemed his life in exile would continue beyond what he had initially expected. Over the previous few months, he had questioned his faith on more than one occasion; the accidental killing of Ranuccio had caused him great grief and continued to torment his mind. The taking of another man's life for whatever reason, whether it be deliberate or unintentional, would be something that any living soul would find difficult to reason with for the remainder of their years. Caravaggio had already encountered many sleepless nights as his conscience fought to question any rightful reason to justify his actions. But none came and the suffering continued.

He checked over his shoulder once more for signs of anyone on his tail and his toe caught the edge of something bundled within his path. This caused his forward momentum to stop abruptly at his feet but continue from the waist upwards. He toppled forward and found himself sprawled across a bony mass enshrouded in threadbare rags. A head appeared from within the pile of clothing. Its face was riddled with ulcers and pox; its mouth was locked in an ugly, toothless scowl. Flustered and unnerved, Caravaggio writhed as he struggled to pick himself up. The sight of the disease-ridden woman made his skin crawl, and once standing, he vigorously brushed down his clothing to rid himself of infected spores and contagion. A grimy hand appeared from the bottom of the raggy bundle, and the toothless scowl looked at Caravaggio and attempted to smile. Disgruntled, he swore under his breath and reached into his pocket. He dropped a coin toward the upturned palm and curtly strode away.

As he ventured deeper into the poverty-stricken quarter of the city, he found himself constantly stepping over and around a multitude of beggars and bodies littering its many gutters and alleyways. Naples was quickly becoming the most overpopulated city in Europe as its streets filled with the sick and needy. Immigrants had followed trading routes to its shores and rural farmworkers whose crops had failed and who could no longer provide for their families flocked to the city in search of salvation. The city had become engulfed. Rickets, scurvy, dysentery, and severe malnutrition reared their ugly heads at every turn of the street. However, a number of shelters, hospices and confraternities supported by churches, brotherhoods and affluent donors were beginning to bring hope to those affected by these debilitating afflictions.

Caravaggio hurried along as it was with one such charity that he was due to meet, and he was already late. He should never have succumbed to the offer of more wine and should have departed the taverna when he had originally intended. But the devil's nectar had always been his greatest vice and the root of many of his troubles.

He turned the corner and the facade of the Cathedral loomed above all else. Its grand entrance shadowed the smaller, recently constructed church on the far side of the street. Caravaggio fussed as he sought to find an entrance to the smaller of the two places of worship. A small door to the side of the main entrance presented itself and a gentleman of notable attire stood at its opening. As Caravaggio crossed to the door, the man stood forward and offered his hand.

'Signor Caravaggio. Welcome to chiesa del Pio Monte della Misericordia.'

Caravaggio accepted the handshake. 'It is entirely my pleasure. I am eternally grateful to be afforded the opportunity to offer my services to such a great cause,' he replied, still looking up and down the length of the street for unwanted pursuers. Noticing Caravaggio's unease and sensing a stale odour of alcohol upon his breath, the gent stood to one side and extended an arm towards the inner sanctuary of the church.

'Come, come. Let us loiter no longer. Please, let us step into the safety of God's house.'

With one final backwards glance, Caravaggio stepped past the gent into a long, stony corridor lit with sconced candles. The gent closed the door and followed Caravaggio along the passage to a large open plan room with a long table at its centre. Seven chairs circled the table.

'Please,' he gestured once more, 'sit yourself. I will bring wine and water.' While the gent busied himself on the far side of the room, Caravaggio gazed at several paintings that adorned the walls.

'I am a bit of a collector myself,' remarked the man, returning and noticing Caravaggio's interest. 'They are fine works, but none to parallel your great acclaimed masterpieces in Rome. Your reputation precedes you. There is much talk within Naples of your talents and many who would wish to commission such genius.' The gent took a chair opposite and poured two golden goblets of wine. He offered the first across the table to his guest.

'I, too, recognise the finesse of the artist's stroke,' remarked Caravaggio, gesturing his hand towards the works on the wall. 'The one to the left, I believe, is from the studio of Caracciolo, is it not?'

'You too have a good eye, Signor Caravaggio,' declared the gent before drinking from his goblet. The two sat in silence while Caravaggio continued to observe the paintings.

The gent eventually spoke. 'Forgive me, for I have not introduced myself. My name is Giovanni Manso. I am one of the seven founding members of the Pio Monte.' Caravaggio raised his goblet in recognition. 'May I firstly take this opportunity to thank you for taking the time to honour us with your presence. I know I can safely say on behalf of the other members of our brotherhood that we are truly honoured at the prospect of a commission by your fair hand.' They both drank from their goblets. Caravaggio removed a clay pipe from within his cloak. 'May I interest you in the background and history of our confraternity?' enquired Giovanni.

'Please do. It will afford me an insight into your cause. It could provide a direction for any work I may undertake for you and your brothers,' replied Caravaggio as he thumbed some tobacco into the bowl of his pipe before reaching across the table for a candle.

Giovanni guided the candlestick in the direction of his guest before continuing. 'At first, we numbered just seven. Seven young aristocratic men who would meet each Friday at the Hospital of the Incurables to provide, feed and tend to those less fortunate. We wished not only to offer support through prayer but to provide hands-on care.' Giovanni paused to sip at his wine and Caravaggio tilted the candle's flame to light his pipe. 'As our numbers increased, we were able to spread our wings and establish a foundation. From there, we could offer further provision of food, shelter and clothing for the sick and needy.'

Caravaggio continued to listen, occasionally nodding his head or tipping his pipe in response to a particular remark. He said little but listened and absorbed all that was said. He helped himself to more wine and suckled on his pipe.

Giovanni continued. 'Our cause has since received the recognition of Pope Paul V and our church has been sanctified in recent weeks. As the seven founding brothers, we have discussed the need to commission a magnificent work to sit at the high altar of our newly completed chancel.' The exhaled smoke from Caravaggio's pipe clung to the air and mixed with the soot emanating from the candle flames. Together, they created a smoggy atmosphere within the area where the two men sat. Giovanni needed to continually sip at his wine to moisten his lips and suppress a discouraging cough.

'We have conversed over many possible artists to approach for such a commission, but upon hearing of your arrival in the city, we believe God has provided us with our answer.'

Caravaggio exhaled a plume of smoke, removed the pipe from his lips and used it to gesticulate as he spoke. 'I have just one other commission but do not see any foreseeable reason why I could not carry out such a work.'

A gratifying smile crept from the corner of Giovanni's mouth as he fought to contain his delight. 'Our initial thoughts are for the work to bring together the corporal acts we as a charity provide, united with a depiction of "Our Lady of Mercy", descending from above to bless those in need. Of course, we are open to your judgements and propositions.'

Caravaggio nodded.

Giovanni was keen to broker a deal.

'Should you wish to produce such a piece, I have been entrusted by my fellow custodians to offer you the sum of 400 ducats.'

Naples, Italy

Present Day

1

The large iron key engaged in the lock and the heavy-set doors moaned as the weighty oak strained inwards against the reluctance of the centuries-old hinges. The priest stepped across the sacred threshold as he had done for as long as he could remember and always as the bell tower rang out the six chimes of the early hour. He turned, lowered the hood of his robes, and secured the entrance behind him. He slid the key back into his pocket and crossed to a much smaller door on the far side, from which he retrieved a large broom, a mop and a galvanised bucket. The priest then followed a colonnaded walkway to the inner sanctum of the building.

The church of the Pio Monte della Misericordia was originally built at the start of the 17th century within the walls of two previously constructed buildings. The small central church is still surrounded by galleries, a library, and various associated rooms that are all part of the confraternity's trust.

The priest entered through the vestibule. He crossed himself with water from the holy bowl carved into a pillar before continuing into the nave. He placed the mop and bucket to one side and began to sweep the floor between the rows of congregational chairs.

Simple in its design, the octagonal nave is enclosed on each side by six lesser altars that together surround a grand high altar. Lines of polychrome marble transect diamond-shaped terracotta floor tiles, each radiating out across the floor from a central motif to one of eight supporting pillars. An octagonal baroque cupola rises skywards. Its inner vault culminating in a single oculus. Hanging in pride of place overlooking the high altar is Caravaggio's painting of the 'Seven Acts of Mercy'. The six side altars are also each home to works by artists such as Azzolino, Onofrio, Giordano and Santafede. Each painting further depicts the charitable acts conducted by the institution.

The priest continued to clean the aisles between the chairs. Dust from a long, sweltering summer and sand from nearby beaches had been deposited by the soles of worshippers attending yesterday's unusually busy evening mass. It was proving to take him much longer to clean than usual. Movement in the corner of his eye caused the priest to stop mid-sweep. He looked up in the direction of where he thought the movement had come. He was half expecting to see a pigeon or a dove. Both were regular visitors who would endlessly flap up and down the walls in a bid to escape into the dawning sun. However, the scene that revealed itself was one he had not expected.

A solitary young woman was sat upon the central red carpeted runner of the steps leading up to the high altar. She was slouched sideways on one hip and rested to one side on the elbow of her right arm whilst her long, slender legs reclined behind her. Her focus was towards the Caravaggio altarpiece. The woman's beauty and recumbent position reminded the priest of Titian's 'Venus of Urbino'.

The woman did not hear the priest approach and did not move as she remained transfixed on the picture above.

The priest crossed the transept and gingerly approached the altar's early visitor.

'Signora, I am afraid the church is currently closed to the public. I am also in a quandary as to how you have gained entry at this hour?' He was certain he had locked the main doors behind him.

'Oh, I have been here for quite some time, Father,' replied the woman. She did not turn round or avert her gaze from the picture. The priest suddenly had a concerning thought. Perhaps the woman had been locked in overnight. Had Giuseppe missed her when he had locked up the previous evening?

'My child, please do not tell me you have been here all night?' Finally, the woman turned to the priest, and he could see her face for the first time. She was equally as beautiful as the Goddess Venus.

'But how long have you—'

'It is not a question of how long,' interrupted the woman, 'or how I got in; all that matters is that I am here.' The priest could not decide which was the worst scenario, the woman being mistakenly locked in overnight or the possibility that she had broken into the church.

'May I ask who or what you seek?' enquired the priest nervously.

'I wish no harm to either you or the church, Father. I only wish to spend some time with those closest to me.' The priest looked perplexed as he cast an eye over the nave for signs of further visitors. He could not see, hear, or sense the presence of another soul. As his eyes continued to wander the circumference of the church's inner sanctuary, an isolated thought emerged from the periphery of his mind. Perhaps the young woman had relatives laid to rest within the crypts that ran below the church.

'Forgive my lack of understanding.' The priest paused, anxious of his inquisitions. 'To whom do you refer as those closest to you?'

The woman sat up and leant back on her arms. She stretched out her legs, extended her neckline and rotated her head, easing any tightness and tension in her muscles. The priest noticed her movements and again worried that she may have been here much longer than intended. When the woman spoke again, she had a heartfelt vibrancy to her voice.

'I am the last in a long bloodline. A bloodline leading back to the artist your forefathers commissioned to create this majestic representation that graces your grand altar.'

The priest looked up at the imposing picture that towered above them. His eyes moving between the figures depicted within the scene. As he did so, he mulled over a train of thought and considered whether it could be feasible.

'You are a direct descendent of Caravaggio?' The woman stood to face the priest.

'He is my paternal ancestor, and the woman whose face he used to portray your "Lady of Mercy" is the progenitor of my family's maternal lineage.' She picked up a bright red Louis Vuitton clutch bag from the floor near her feet and removed an ornate, silver-plated case. It contained a small square of aged paper. She carefully unfolded a picture before handing it to the priest. 'This is Maddalena Antognetti, the maternal mother of my bloodline. Her face can be seen in many of Caravaggio's works. He drew this sketch of her the night before he fled Rome, just a few months before he came here to create this magnificent work for your forefathers.'

The priest studied the picture and contemplated the importance of what he now held in his hands. A simple pencil sketch that few may have held and whose existence is unknown to many. He carefully handed the delicate picture back to its rightful owner with the utmost care.

'The church will not open its doors to the public for some time. Yet, you have my blessing to continue your vigil in the peace and solitude of the moment. Please, Signora, feel free to stay as long as you wish.'

'Thank you for your extreme kindness and warm-hearted generosity, Father,' she replied with a gratifying smile. The priest reciprocated the gesture and turned to continue his chores.

'Forgive me,' he declared, 'for being so ill-mannered. I did not introduce myself. My name is Father Salvatore.'

'And I, too, must apologise, Father. It's been a pleasure to meet you. My name is Lena.'

Gwynver, Sennen Cove
Cornwall, England

2

The two surfers duck-dived the wave, one emerging briefly before the other on the far side of the swell. Without hesitation, each surfer arched their back and paddled towards the next set of breaking waves. Both paddled hard with long, powerful strokes to maximise their forward propulsion, enabling each board to glide efficiently through the water.

With the next breaking wave bearing down upon them, both surfers adjusted their upper bodies to position their weight slightly forward towards the nose of their boards. The surfers looked across at each other and took a deep breath. In unison, they grabbed the rails of their board and thrust the board's nose deep into the water before sinking the tail with their back foot. Keeping as much forward momentum as possible, each surfer pulled their body down onto the board and as the turbulence of the wave passed above them, they angled their boards back towards the surface, and the natural buoyancy allowed them to rise upwards to simultaneously emerge behind the spilling wave.

'Wow. That one had some power,' said Jonathan, looking across at his friend while flicking his wet fringe back from his eyes.

'Yeah,' replied Tate, 'looks to be rolling in at a constant three to four foot. Good intervals between the sets and the light offshore breeze should hold it up nicely.'

DCI Tate Randall, the head of the Metropolitan Arts and Antiquities Investigation Department, and partner and friend DS Jonathan Harvey were surfing the early autumn swell like they had done every September since meeting as first-year university art students.

Having cleared the breaking sets, Tate and Jonathan continued to paddle out across the rise and fall of the approaching swell lines. Happy that they were beyond the line of the breaking waves, in an area referred to by the surfing community as 'Outback', they straddled their boards and looked out towards the horizon for the next approaching swell. Many surfers enjoyed the serenity and tranquillity of sitting 'Outback'. It pervaded an atmosphere where one could clear one's mind and, for a while, not have a care in the world.

Tate looked across the line of the incoming swell. 'Not too many in today,' he commented, in reference to the lack of other surfers sitting in the line-up waiting for a potential wave.

'That's a good enough reason to keep coming back to Gwynver. It doesn't get busy like the beaches of Porthmeor or Polzeath. That and the cottage only being ten minutes away along the coast path.'

They had rented the same cottage year after year. When it was put on the market several years ago, they invested in a joint purchase agreement, and it now provided them both with tidy second incomes from the holiday rental market. However, the cottage would always be their bolthole for the last two weeks of September.

'This one's got my name all over it,' said Jonathan as he slid to the tail of his board and spun it around toward the shore. He laid down and began to paddle, occasionally looking over his shoulder at the encroaching wave. He continued paddling and as the wave drew level with him, he momentarily disappeared before popping up again seconds later. He tracked the wave to the right, riding his board up and down the cascading face before disappearing again. This time in a cyclonic barrage of foaming white water.

A few minutes later, Jonathan reappeared as he paddled over the crest of a wave and the unbroken swell of the following two. 'Caught an edge and ended up going over the falls and straight into the washing machine,' declared Jonathan in his best 'surf speak' as he approached Tate, who was still sitting astride his board in the 'Outback' zone.

Tate smiled, amused at his friend's anecdote. 'You may be known as the "Tin Man" because of your greying hair and lack of heart, but it appears you surf like someone who has rusty unoiled joints too,' laughed Tate at his best friend's expense.

'At least I'm chasing waves. It beats just sitting around on your butt out here.'

'It's nice sometimes to embrace the opportunity to take a moment and reflect, and there is no better place to do it.'

Jonathan noticed his friend's repose. 'What's swimming around that never-tiring brain of yours?'

'I was contemplating all that has happened over the last twelve months.'

'How's things with Harriet?' enquired Jonathan with one eye on the approaching swell. Both surfers allowed the full set of yet-to-break waves to pass beneath their boards.

'We're taking each day as it comes. We both have heavy workloads but try to steal as much time together as possible. The important thing is that we are enjoying each other's company again.'

Tate had just rekindled his relationship with DI Harriet Stone after they had been thrown back together when their separate investigations had crashed head-on last summer in the hunt for a serial killer known as the Narcissus. London's art community had been thrown into turmoil when the corpses of prominent art collectors were discovered across the city. Each body had been seemingly posed to replicate the works of Caravaggio.

The case was still an open investigation, the Narcissus having escaped after a confrontation with Tate and Harriet on the rooftop of London's Battersea Power Station. The aftermath had all three of them dealing with their own issues. Tate with the discovery that his investigative partner, Lena Johnson, had, in fact, been the Narcissus and both Jonathan and Harriet dealing with the loss of someone close to them by the hand of the same killer.

'Things have certainly been different and, at times, difficult.' Jonathan cupped his hand across his forehead to shield his eyes from the low autumnal sun peeping from behind the altocumulus clouds.

'Sometimes it takes a dramatic turn of events to point your life back in the right direction. Not in my wildest dreams would I have imagined Harriet and I together again. But here we are. And the three of us being here, just like old times, is as good a medicine as anybody could prescribe. What happened has meant changes for all of us, but we will get through it. What are friends for if not to support each other through difficult times.'

'You can always count on me, *Amigo*. You know I've always got your back. And on that note, I believe this one is yours,' declared Jonathan enthusiastically, pointing to the first wave in the next approaching set.

Tate had also noticed the increased size of the swell and turned his board towards the beach. He looked back at the wave and decided that the face would likely break to the left. He angled his board slightly in that direction and began his take-off paddle.

As the wave reached its peak, Tate propelled his board forward with three large final strokes before thrusting himself upwards and popping up onto his board into a crouched stance. He rode the shoulder of the wave, staying just in front of the breaking water, tracking along the face by applying alternating pressure to his board's toe and heel edge. The wave continued to peel away from its crest and Tate continued to ride his board up and down the water's glassy surface. When he finally dropped off the back of the wave he could only just pick out Jonathan's silhouette at the other end of the beach.

Pio Monte Della Misericordia
Naples, Italy

3

She wore a black pencil skirt with a figure-hugging narrow cut, finishing just below the knee. A simple ruby red classical cardigan complemented her ivory full-length buttoned blouse. Her legs were naked but shone with a bronze Mediterranean tan. The look was finished today with her customary pair of red heels, courtesy of Jimmy Choo. A mane of jet black hair cascaded across her shoulders, her face framed within its layers and held back by a pair of oversized Bvlgari sunglasses pushed up to her forehead.

Lena had spent the earlier part of the day perusing the shops on the Via Toledo. She had stopped at a traditional *trattoria* in the Quartieri Spagnoli and eaten a light lunch of pasta al pomodoro. It being her final afternoon in Naples, she had spent some time, firstly at the Capodimonte Museum viewing Caravaggio's 'The Flagellation of Christ', before visiting the Palazzo Zevallos Stigliano to spend some time in the presence of Caravaggio's last known work, 'The Martyrdom of St Ursula'. At both locations, she had found herself absorbed in thought and ruminating over her own real-life creations of each picture. She replayed each chain of events in her mind. The killing of the model with a crossbow bolt to the chest. The flogging of the art dealer Jeremy Grayson after crucifying him to the chimney. Each brutal act she had committed had a reason. Each life she had taken had been justified, and each victim was answerable for their downfall. Their temptation and greed were the root of their iniquity and a pathway into transgression. They had no one to blame but themselves. Lena held no remorse. She felt no repentance, and her faith was untarnished. She showed no sorrow for the righteousness of her actions. In her eyes, the sins had been committed and needed to be paid for.

Being in the presence of both pictures had further instilled belief in the courage of her convictions, but Lena found she had felt a greater bond with 'The Martyrdom of St Ursula'. She believed that in producing what would be his last work before his death, Caravaggio had once again used a likeness of Maddalena in his depiction of the face of St Ursula. Had Caravaggio kept hold of and used the pencil sketch she now had in her possession as a reference? This attachment to her distant relative's image was why she found herself in the gallery until much later in the afternoon than she had first anticipated. By the time she eventually pulled herself away, the warmth of the afternoon sun was blazing a trail straight up the Via Toledo and she still had one last stop to make.

She stood at the bottom of the stairs and waited for a tour guide and her snaking line of sightseers to file past on their whistle-stop tour before they returned to one of the many cruise liners moored in the bay of Naples. She reached the *Il Coretto* as the last of the visitors jabbered and fussed to capture one final snapshot of the church's interior; they neither knew the name nor the significance of its inclusion in their 'Naples in Ninety Minutes' tour. Lena stood patiently to the rear of the little choir balcony that overlooked the nave towards the grand altar. She picked at the nail bed of her thumb with her index finger. It was one of those repetitive behaviours that had become a compulsive habit in moments of quietude. She stopped picking and started polishing as she rubbed her thumbs across the line of her nails while checking the condition of the dark red varnish coating their surface. The nonsensical prattle had subsided as the tailenders hurried away and a single voice broke her reverie.

'Back again?'

She looked up to be greeted by the affable smile of the priest from the previous day.

'Father Salvatore. So lovely to see you again.' She took a step forward. 'May I again offer my heartfelt thanks for your generosity and understanding yesterday.' The priest stepped closer and proffered his hands towards Lena. She held his hands within hers. The skin was cold, aged and papery, but she could sense a warmth from within. Father Salvatore held her gaze. His piercing cerulean blue eyes had an enchanting allure she had not noticed the previous day.

'You will always be welcome here, my child. You can without fail find comfort in the hands of God.' He clutched her hands. In that briefest of moments, Lena felt contentment in the priest's offering. For the first time in a long while, she welcomed acceptance.

'As it is my last day in the city, I could not leave without spending a few more precious moments here within your church and enjoying the magnificence of my forefather's work one final time.' Father Salvatore released her hands, and they stepped to the front of the small balcony.

Very few people were in the church as the afternoon drew to a close, and a stillness filled the air. They both looked towards the Caravaggio.

'This is the best position from where to view the picture,' declared the priest, raising his arms forward in a similar manner as one would in an offering to God. They both stood in silence and took in the majesty of the picture. Neither stirred nor spoke for several minutes. Each had viewed the picture numerous times, the priest almost every day, but both were drawn into the deep shadows and the raw humanity of the scene.

Father Salvatore was the first to speak. 'I believe it is traditional for the seven charitable acts to be depicted on individual canvases, and at the time of its creation, there was also a suggestion to the possibility of an altarpiece and two side panels. However, the brotherhood was intent on portraying our cause on a single vertical canvas.' Lena continued to study the intensity of the picture's setting and the numerous figures crowded within its frame.

'I believe Caravaggio has truly captured the reality and brutality of the Neapolitan street as it was beyond our doors 400 years ago,' continued Salvatore, his depth of knowledge unparalleled after a lifetime with the brotherhood. 'He once again used the world around him to bring true realism to his work while capturing true-to-life human behaviours in his depiction of each of our charitable acts.' Lena momentarily turned her focus from the picture to Father Salvatore. She could hear the fervour in his words and feel the belief he held for the church's cause. The picture held a special meaning to Lena and she could sense it meant as much to Father Salvatore, if not more. She looked back to the altar where 'Our Lady of Mercy', flanked by angels, cast down a leading light from the top of the picture onto the exchanges between the needy and their saviours.

'Tell me, Father, do you believe that those who have sinned should be granted mercy for their wrongdoings?' asked Lena, this time without diverting her gaze from the picture.

'God is inclined to show mercy on those who themselves have exhibited clemency and forgiveness to others. God will judge us according to how we have judged others, whether we have sinned or not.'

'Are some not beyond judgement, where their behaviours and misdoings have become merciless?' Lena turned to Father Salvatore and the priest took her hands once more.

'Remember, God's grace will be granted upon the merciful. Ask yourself. How would you wish to be judged?'

Gwynver, Sennen Cove
Cornwall, England

4

The fiery, burnt amber eye of the setting sun was well on its way towards the western horizon when Tate and Jonathan finally emerged from the foaming waters of Cornwall's North Shore. The sky was fast becoming an explosion of burgundies and crimsons. Splashes of coral orange and tints of ochre and saffron illuminated the trailing whisps of the high cirrostratus layer. The sun reflected in a glittering path across the crests of the ocean as if Helios had unleashed a blazing arrow towards the shoreline.

The fading sun still provided sufficient light for Tate and Jonathan to negotiate the twisty inclines of the narrow coastal path that crept across the headland. Both surfers had stripped their wetsuits to the waist and carried their boards under one arm. Jonathan followed Tate's lead while remaining several steps behind to avoid unnecessary collisions with his friend's board.

'You've had that wetsuit for about as long as you've owned the Land Rover,' joked Jonathan as he briefly looked up to check Tate's progress before diverting his eyes back down to be sure of his footing on the gravelly path. Tate still wore the handmade 'Second Skin' wetsuit he had purchased over 25 years ago.

'I'll take that as a compliment and a testament to retaining the body of a twenty-something well into my forties,' retorted Tate as he straddled the short stone wall into the rear of their property. 'Unlike someone I know, who insists he changes his suit each couple of seasons to benefit from the latest technologies but refuses to admit to the real truth behind the matter being a passion for good food and an ever-expanding waistline.' Both men laughed as they passed Tate's vintage Land Rover and stood their boards against the rear wall of the cottage. A hardtail mountain bike was propped to the side of the back door.

'Looks like Harriet's back.'

'Smells that way, too. If that passion for good food is not mistaken. I believe the aroma escaping the kitchen window is one of roast potatoes.'

'And if my ears are not deceiving, that's 'Jacob's Ladder' by Rush, I can hear.' Both men laughed again before removing their wetsuits and throwing them over a fixed washing line in the rear garden.

Tate and Jonathan sat in reclining chairs, each chugging a beer before Harriet exited the cottage's front door. She wore Jersey beach shorts, an oversized chunky knit jumper and her hair was wrapped in a towel turban. A glass of rosé wine hung from the fingers of her right hand. She leant over Tate from behind and kissed the top of his head.

'Hey, you,' he looked up, 'how was your ride?'

'Yeah, really good, thanks,' she moved between the two chairs and squatted on the grass looking back at the two boys. 'I went as far as Botallack Mines and back via Kenidjack Castle and Cape Cornwall. Mostly on the roads, just being out and about in the countryside was great. How about you? How was the surf? It looked good from the cliffs at Porth Ledden.'

Jonathan swallowed his mouthful of beer and beat Tate to a reply. 'I've got to admit, the old man's still got it. He had some super long rides today. The conditions were calling out for it.' He held his bottle high and saluted it in Tate's direction. Tate returned the gesture. Harriet could not help but smile.

'Were you listening to Rush's *Permanent Waves* album earlier?' enquired Tate as he took another mouthful of beer.

'If you say so. It was whatever was in the player. Once I had found the correct button, I just pushed play. The singer has an awfully high-pitched voice.' Both Tate and Jonathan could not contain themselves and burst out laughing. 'You guys!' bemused Harriet as she shook her head in disbelief while fighting an escaping smirk from appearing across her face. 'Some things will never change,' and she, too, raised her glass as the merriment continued.

'Well, we have been lucky once again,' said Tate, seizing the moment to speak as the laughter subsided. 'The last two weeks have delivered an unusually good persistent swell. What with that and the Tin Man managing to survive the whole fortnight without denting himself or his board.' All three shared their laughter, each smiling at the warming company that goes with good friends. 'As always, it's been refreshing to leave the worries of the job and the city behind for a while. Although we must return in a few days, it's been great to recuperate and briefly forget all our worries and tribulations.' Tate stopped and they all respected each other's silence for a short moment. 'I believe buying the cottage when we had the opportunity was one of the best ideas and the most sensible suggestion Jonathan has ever made.' The laughter erupted once more, with each of them nodding in unison. They each fought to gain their composure but to little avail.

'Gwynver keeps on giving,' declared Jonathan, grinning from ear to ear. 'Here's to many more years, clean surf, stunning sunsets and best friends.'

The merriment continued as all three looked to the west and raised their drinks towards the final remnants of the sun as it crept below the horizon.

'I have fixed a simple salad and some marmite-roasted potatoes. If you fancy lighting the barbeque, there is some honey and mustard marinated belly pork.' Tate took that as his cue and raised himself from his chair.

Jonathan remained in his slumber. 'And mine's another beer as you are getting up!'

Knightsbridge
London, England

5

She curled her toe around the ornate tap to stop the water flow into the free-standing roll-top bath. Interlinking her fingers behind her head, she stretched her neck back to rest on the rim. She closed her eyes and exhaled slowly. Minutes passed as Lena lost herself in the tranquillity of the moment, allowing the warm water and the therapeutic essence of the bath oils to relax her body and soothe her mind. She opened her eyes and fixed her gaze. All the while focusing on her breathing pattern, ensuring each inhalation and exhalation was measured and controlled. This, along with the calming effect of the bath oil, eventually had its desired effect, and Lena soon found herself heavy-eyed and nodding in and out on the fringes of sleep.

She awoke to find that she had succumbed to a state of slumber; the bath water was now on the tepid side of warm and daylight outside the window had been replaced by streetlight. She extended one leg forward and felt for the plug chain with her big toe before pulling it free to release a small amount of the cooled water. As the bubble line receded, Lena slid deeper into the water, replaced the plug with the ball of her foot and once again, toe to tap, refilled the bath with hot water.

After relishing in the revitalising sensation of the rewarmed water, Lena grasped the sides of the roll top, raised her knees to her chest and sat back into the curve of the bath end. She puckered her lips and deliberated as she looked across to a small bath side table, where a single-cut crystal wine glass stood alongside a 2008 vintage Pouilly-Fumé cocooned in a silver ice bucket. Reaching for the neck of the bottle, she allowed the icy water residue to drip back into the bucket before half filling the glass with the pale straw coloured liquid. The first sip moistened her lips, the second awoke her taste buds, and by the third, she savoured the wine's light flowery bouquet and the slight smoky afternote. In juxtaposition with the warmth of the bath's water, the frosty chill of the ice cold wine caused her to slide once more into the deep foamy layer. She held the glass forward, turning its stem through her fingers as she stared through its tulip shaped bowl and cast her mind back over the previous few days.

Lena had bid farewell to Father Salvatore and thanked him for his benevolence and consideration during her visits to the Pio Monte before dining at a *ristorante* overlooking the Castel dell' Ovo. She had then retrieved her checked luggage from the bell boy at the hotel and headed straight to the Stazione Napoli Centrale, where she had caught an evening train from Naples to Rome.

Most of the following day had been spent whiling away the hours and losing herself in the numerous galleries and chapels which housed the capital's vast collection of Caravaggios. With many of his most important works commissioned by wealthy aristocratic families and holy places of worship within the city walls, one third of Caravaggio's existing catalogue can still be found within Rome. The first stop was the Galleria Borghese and its world renowned collection of six works by the artist's hand. A fleeting visit to the private galleries of Doria Pamphilj had followed. Its collection included one of Lena's favourite works by her ancestor. The 'Penitent Magdalene'. She had stopped briefly on the Piazza Navona and admired Bernini's famous fountains while eating a simple Risotto ai funghi lunch. Visits to the churches of St Luigi dei Francesi and St Agostino had allowed her to view four more Caravaggios en route to the Galleria Nazionale d'Arte Antica. It was here that she would spend the most time that day. Lena had viewed the picture of 'Judith beheading Holofernes' and like she had done the previous day in Naples, she played over in her mind the moment she had severed the neck of the art collector Sir Christopher Roebuck, leaving his corpse posed in her own representation of the scene. She had also spent considerable time reflecting on Caravaggio's depiction of the Greek mythological hunter known as the Narcissus. The name which she had chosen as a signature for her murderous works and the moniker the British press had attached to the perpetrator of a series of art-related killings across London during the summer of last year.

Lena had then made one final stop before boarding an overnight train service to Paris. She had attended evening prayer at the Basilica di Santa Maria del Popolo and had briefly viewed the two Caravaggio altar side panels on her exit from the chapel.

On her arrival in Paris the next morning, she had pre-arranged an early check-in at a small boutique hotel just off the Champs-Élysées. However, she would spend very little time in the hotel room. Just enough time to change her appearance.

Her name, passport details and profile picture were flagged at international borders as a 'red notice', a request to law enforcement agencies across the globe to provisionally arrest an individual pending extradition to the country where their crime had been committed. She had changed her appearance and travelled on numerous false papers over the past year, but this would be only the third time she had risked a return to the UK.

A couple of hours in front of the mirror in the nondescript hotel room, a wig and a change of hair colour, a new set of blue tinted contact lenses and some carefully applied liquid latex around the cheeks and the eye sockets. This was an artform she had fine-tuned with practice over the last few months, coupled with some precise transformational make-up and she had exited the hotel with an altogether different appearance. She would be travelling from Paris to London on the passport of Madeline Archer.

Madeline Archer had sat outside a small café in the shadow of the Arc de Triomphe, where she had sipped espresso, ordered a *croque madame* for brunch and happily watched Parisian life wander aimlessly by before she had needed to depart for the Gare Du Nord railway terminal. She had planned her departure from Paris and her arrival in London to coincide with the border patrol's busiest periods of passenger footfall. Times when a fleeting glance at a passport photo was more than enough at a European border. Her journey aboard the Eurostar had gone without a hitch, and a little over three hours later, she checked into her new hotel, ran a bath, and had room service deliver a bottle of wine.

Lena swallowed the last of the wine and sat forward, placing the empty glass on the side table. She poured a refill but left it next to the ice bucket and instead reached for her phone. As she sat back into the curve of the bath, she tapped an app on the screen. She would have to wait as the anonymous mail software bounced between several untraceable servers across the globe before she could continue. Retrieving the wine glass with her free hand, she took a sip, pausing thoughtfully and allowing the glass to rest on her puckered lips. Zesty aromatics drifted across her nostrils as she pondered her next move. The phone pinged and the screen illuminated.

It was time.

Lena thumb-typed with one hand and occasionally sipped her wine with the other. The content of the message was brief, but the recipient would fully understand its meaning. She continued sipping wine and smiled pleasingly to herself as she re-read the words several times.

Satisfied that the message would have the desired effect, she hit the send button before kissing the phone's screen as if bidding a fond farewell to the message.

As the untraceable email scrambled, encrypted, unscrambled and zipped between various worldwide VPNs, Lena placed the glass and the phone to one side and eased herself from the bath's foamy waters. As she stood, her gaze caught sight of her reflection in the room's full-length mirror. Lena turned her shoulder as a cloak of soapy bubbles dissipated from her neckline to her waist.

Inch by inch, unveiling the outline inking of a full back tattoo.

Gwynver, Sennen Cove
Cornwall, England

6

He raised the blade above his head, carefully eyeing the limb that lay before his feet. The axe swung through the air in a downward arc before plunging deep into its intended target. The wood splintered and the log fell in two. Perfectly spliced through the heart of the wood. Tate placed a second log on the chopping stump and raised the axe again. The recently honed blade of the axe head was razor sharp and very little downward force was needed to split the kiln dried logs. A crescent moon had replaced the sun and the odd star was beginning to peep through the few remaining feathery clouds. However, the north easterly wind that had provided the ideal offshore conditions that surfers so often relished was now bringing an unwanted chill to the autumnal evening. Not wanting to waste the opportunity of a beautiful starry night, Harriet had asked Tate to light the fire pit to provide some warmth so they could stay outdoors for a while longer. Tate looked down at the quarter full basket to his left and decided that half a dozen more logs should do the trick for tonight. He was mid-swing on his second to last log when the pocket of his shorts vibrated and his phone pinged. He ignored the message alert and split the final log into multiple pieces to provide a small amount of kindling to get the fire started.

When Tate rejoined his friends at the front of the cottage, Jonathan handed him a fresh beer as Harriet relaxed into the chair where Tate had previously sat. Jonathan helped Tate move the circular fire pit closer to the chairs before they built up layers of kindling and newspaper in the bottom of the steel bowl. Tate had just lit the edges of the paper when his phone pinged a second time. He ignored it again, assuming it would be one of his parents wanting to finalise plans for the five of them meeting for lunch in St Ives the following day.

The dry kindling caught quickly and it wasn't long before Jonathan put the first of the logs onto the fire. Tate had taken the other chair beside Harriet when his message alert sounded for the third time. His curiosity got the better of him and he reached into his pocket. The first two messages had been from his mother, but the third instantly put him on edge, and a sense of unease spread through his body. Tate did not need to open the mail, he instantly knew who it was from. It had been sent to him from his own email account in the same way a series of taunting messages had been sent last summer. In the very same way as the messages he had received from his ex-partner during her killing spree. Each was signed by the assailant, now known as the Narcissus.

Tate looked to each of his friends, both of them in turn, noticing the sudden change in his demeanour and the apprehension on his face. Finally, he opened the email.

Tate Randall
Tate Randall
26th September, 20:34

Take forth the quest of flesh and skin
Lay bare the souls of all man's sin
Casting judgements upon the meek
Salvation promised for all who seek
Yet time and tide await no man
As flooding waters rape the land
The Raven's return is a merciless sign
Destiny's message for all mankind

Narcissus

Perplexed by Tate's silence, Harriet and Jonathan wordlessly gaped at their friend. Tate said just two words and handed the phone to Harriet.

'Lena's back.'

Camden Town

London, England

7

The figure stood in the shadows of the alley, drew heavily on a cigarette, and looked up at the light emanating from the small back bedroom window. Three extinguished butts lay at his feet. He had frequently watched the routine of the flat's occupant over the last few weeks and had become familiarised with their daily regime. The light should go out in the next ten minutes and then the occupant would head off to work at a popular wine bar on Camden High Street. They would not normally return until around 2 am.

On cue, the light went out and the figure moved to the other end of the alley from where he could observe the occupant exiting the front of the property before watching them cross the road and follow the canal path to the top of the high street. Just as they did habitually every evening from Friday through to Tuesday.

Moments later, the figure dressed in dark overalls scaled the fire escape at the rear of the property and made light work of opening a fairly rotten fire door at the top of the stairs. He entered the flat. All was still and quiet. The smell of jasmine and sandalwood hung in the air. He checked each room to ensure he was alone. However, it was not the flat where his interests lay but the small art gallery on the property's ground floor.

As ever, he had done his homework. The Lockkeepers Collection was a small traditional gallery recognised for selling affordable works and prints by British artists of the 19th and 20th centuries. The gallery was at the far end of a parade of shops adjacent to Regent's Canal. Just two visits had been made to the gallery itself. Each a month apart, each when the gallery was at its busiest, and each time inconspicuously dressed with a slightly different appearance. There had been no reason to chance recognition or to create any unnecessary suspicions. It had been during one of these covert visits to check for the installation of alarms, the presence of CCTV cameras and other security measures that he had noticed the chimney stack snaking up the exterior gable end of the building. While perusing the gallery's display space, a discrete tap of the interior wall had returned a hollow echo and the presumed existence of a false stud wall over an old fireplace.

He eased the door into the flat's living room, and a short-haired tabby inquisitively raised its head from within a sea of plump multicoloured cushions strewn across a throw covered sofa. The cat purred quietly and paid little more attention as the man placed a bag on the floor and removed a small prybar. He nodded a gratifying approval to himself. There was no false stud wall in the flat. He stood looking at the surround of the original Victorian fireplace. A small decorated wooden panel covered its firebox. Tonight's job had just become a whole lot easier.

He moved the occupant's oil burners and candles to one side and made quick work of removing the panel concealing the opening to the chimney flue. Within minutes, he was shimmying down the inside of the chimney, applying opposing pressures between his knees and his back as he edged his way towards the ground floor. He broke through the single skin of plasterboard with relative ease. A couple of solid strikes with the heel of his boot and he soon stood within the gallery's main display room. Immediately after exiting the chimney, he activated a remote frequency jamming device, overpowering the signal transmitted by the room's digital security cameras and disabling any further recordings.

Time was now on his side, although it did not take long to locate the intended targets of tonight's heist. He could have carried out his raid several weeks ago, but persistent scrutiny of the gallery's website and patience for the right moment had paid off. The online announcement of a pair of signed first edition Lowry prints due to be displayed as of yesterday had caught his attention. 'Punch and Judy' and 'Market Scene in a Northern Town' hung on the wall to his left. He nodded and tutted to himself. Could it really be that easy. An in and out job, just the way he liked it. During one of the reconnaissance visits, he discovered that works within the gallery were not individually alarmed and no further security measures were in place. Just the simple task of lifting the pictures from the wall and securing them safely in a canvas portfolio case.

If life as an art thief was always this easy, he might consider making a living from it, he thought, cheerfully chuckling to himself as he tied a length of rope to the handle of the case. He then retraced his route back up the inside of the chimney, reversing the method he had used on the way down. He emerged from the upper firebox, panting and damp from the extra exertion. The climb back up had been far more strenuous and the cramped space had felt far more restricted. He caught sight of himself in the mirror above the fireplace and chuckled once more. His face had blackened and rivulets of sweat ran through the sooty mask. He paused, trying to remember the name of the actor in *Mary Poppins*. When it didn't come, he shook his head, untied the end of the rope looped around his belt and gently pulled the canvas portfolio up from the floor below. He lifted a cuff and turned his wrist to see his watch face. Less than an hour, in and out. Job done.

Ten minutes later, he was ready to leave. He had reattached the wooden panel as well as he possibly could and replaced the items around the hearth. There may be a sizeable hole in the gallery wall below, but there was no reason to cause any more disruption than necessary to the occupant of the flat. However, every handle and surface within the property would probably be covered in fingerprint powder by midday tomorrow.

He removed his gloves and rolled them into a ball before tucking them safely into his overall pocket. The cat looked up and purred as it arched its back and rubbed its head against the man's legs. He tousled the cat's head.

'Van Dyke,' he smiled, 'Dick Van Dyke.'

Gwynver, Sennen Cove
Cornwall, England

8

The eyes looked up at him, pleading for help. Two words escaped the lips as the face silently mouthed the two syllables. Each was easily recognisable.

'Save me.'

Although dead, her skin waxy and ashen, she still looked beautiful. However, as the mouth spread into a smile, the image of beauty was shattered, and the lips parted to reveal broken decaying teeth through which a forked tongue, like that of a mythical serpent, appeared. Suddenly, the open wounds of the neck erupted and an entanglement of snakes emerged from the gaping flesh. Each writhed as it coiled, crawled and fought its way to the surface. The snakes began to twist and entwine as they slithered around the severed head. Occasionally, one would draw back into a serpentine coil before striking forward to spray its venom.

The Medusa began to laugh.

The sound now audible.

Cackling and grinning like a possessed witch. The laughter escalated to a howl before pitching into an ear piercing scream.

Jonathan woke suddenly.

He sat bolt upright and gasped, drawing heavily on his lungs as he fought to capture a breath. He clutched the sweat-soaked bed sheets as his brain adjusted to the reality of the situation. Eventually, his eyes began to conform to the new world before him, his body still shaking and perspiration drenched his skin. He looked across to the bedside clock. It was once again just before 3 am.

Night after night, his sleep had been disturbed by vivid, tormenting nightmares. For over a year, they had become a regular part of his sleep pattern. Fortnightly therapy sessions were doing little to manage the burden of the tortured aftermath of his girlfriend's severed head being delivered in a box and his subsequent hospitalisation from a venomous snake bite. How long would these terrors invade his sleep? Could his body tolerate the suffering and anguish of countless sleepless nights?

As he lay back down, he adjusted the pillow behind his head to sit more upright and pulled the crusty fragments of sleep from the corners of his eyes. Eyes that were drawn and heavy with dark shadowed bags from the constant nights of broken sleep. As he had become accustomed, he knew that he would fight with his mind and battle with its gnawing questions as the next few hours would hold little more sleep. He would then stare mindlessly at the walls and ceiling until morning came.

St Ives

Cornwall, England

9

Tate, Harriet and Jonathan had risen early, although none of them had anything like a decent night's sleep after learning of Lena's possible return. Each had read through the email received by Tate several times, and all three had discussed the ramifications and subsequent actions that would need to be taken. Harriet had contacted her chain of command back at Bethnal Green CID. She had talked extensively with her superior officer, DCS Leslie Gibbs, as the Narcissus murder enquiry was still an active case. At this stage, he had agreed it was unnecessary to curtail her holiday and return to London. She had agreed to meet with him on her return in a couple of days. Tate had emailed his team and advised them of the situation. He had also returned his mother's messages and arranged to meet with them around midday.

The unseasonably warm, dry weather had seen an influx of day trippers and holidaymakers flocking to Cornwall's seaside towns and beaches. St Ives had always been a popular destination and crowd-puller. Today was no exception, it was packed to the gunnels as Tate, Harriet and Jonathan meandered through the strings of parents desperately clinging to small children, carefree couples aimlessly wandering hand in hand and the throngs of happy-go-lucky tourists who had escaped the cities in search of fresh air and Cornish cider.

As they sauntered along the harbourside, the salty scent of the ocean, alongside the aromas of fresh shellfish and fast food, wafted on the breeze, enticing those easily swayed to succumb to their cravings. The boundless joviality of the crowds was occasionally disrupted by the horrifying scream of a startled tourist whose ice cream or cone of chips had disappeared with the single swoop of a divebombing seagull.

The three friends made their way along the Wharf before turning onto Back Road West. As they rounded the corner onto Porthmeor Hill, Jonathan stopped and looked over the wall.

'That's why we don't surf here,' he declared, pointing out the scores of shoaling surfers sitting in the line-out of the beach below.

'Come on. No time to linger,' replied Tate, 'we're already late, and you know how my parents are always early.' He tugged at his friend's shirt sleeve. Jonathan reluctantly turned away from the view of the incoming waves and the pair caught up with Harriet, who had stopped at the bottom of some large steps leading up to a stone rotunda.

St Ives had always attracted artists to its coastline for the unparalleled natural light and dramatic landscapes. In 1988, the Tate Group had acquired the site of a former gas works with the vision of creating what was to become its second regional gallery. Since its opening in 1993, Tate St Ives has continued to celebrate the legacy and work of its local artists while showcasing numerous exhibitions of modern and contemporary art from further afield.

Tate walked out onto the café's terrace. His mother instantly noticed him and raised a hand. Harriet and Jonathan took the cue and followed Tate to the corner table.

'So lovely to see you,' his mother beamed as she stood and kissed Tate's cheek.

'Dad,' nodded Tate as he turned and shook his father's hand. Harriet was greeted in much the same way, with Tate's mother retaining her hold on Harriet's hand as she expressed her joy.

'I am so happy to see you together again. I'm sure it will do you both a world of good.' Jonathan passed on the pleasantries and just hugged both of Tate's parents before they all took a seat.

'I was only just saying to Joseph how lovely it would be to see both our boys in happy relationships again,' declared Olivia, beaming from ear to ear. 'I had lunch with Turner just last week. He told me he had met someone via the Friends of the Gallery website. If I remember rightly, I think he said her name was Sarah. Apparently, he is going to arrange to meet her for dinner one evening.' Like Tate, his brother had also acquired a Christian name that reflected their parents' artistic passions.

Harriet continued to chat to one side with Tate's mother while Joseph Randall caught up with his son and best friend. They talked for several minutes, discussing the past two weeks at the cottage, and Tate asked his father about an exhibition he and Olivia had recently attended. Eventually, Tate's mother, who had been bending one ear to the other conversation, could no longer suppress her inquisitive nature.

'Did I hear you say you were returning to London today?' Tate shifted in his chair to address his mother. Harriet and Jonathan glanced at each other before tentatively looking to their friend to answer.

'Something has,' he hesitated while deliberating over his choice of words. 'Something has come to our attention that may be of concern.' Olivia glanced fleetingly at her husband before returning her attention to Tate. A look of concern was etched upon her face.

'Is it Lena? I told Joseph, you mark my words… she will return one day to haunt you.'

'It's a possibility. But at this stage, it is just speculative. It's nothing to worry yourself with.' His father could sense the apprehension in his son's reply. A father's intuition of sorts. They infrequently discussed Tate's work. They didn't ask, and Tate divulged very little. His father was extremely proud of his son's position and all he had achieved, but still, he would rather have had his boy follow a similar path to the one both he and his wife had chosen. Before their retirement, Joseph and Olivia Randall had both been curators at the Tate Britain in London.

Joseph knew better than to delve deeper and unnecessarily question his son. He handed a menu to Olivia.

'Shall we order?'

Wardour Street

London, England

10

Ripper Tattoo's presence at the northern end of Wardour Street is easily distinguishable by its 19th century raised letter, fairground-style signage. Its single full-length window frontage and set back Edwardian door are nestled between a Vietnamese street food café and 'Knee High', a bespoke boutique leather shop. An etched glass logo adorns the centre of the door, and beyond, the space offers an open plan, airy feel. Rough-sawn wood panelling and reclaimed bare brick walls purvey an industrial age appearance. Vintage advertising mirrors and embossed enamel signs hang from the walls. Two blood red leather Chesterfield wingback armchairs and a black leather chaise longue provide a small waiting and consultation area to the front. An open vaulted ceiling is hung with a plethora of butchery chainmail, meat hooks, barbed wire and strings of heavy chain links, all interwoven with bare bulb-cabled lighting to form an elaborate geometric cobweb. Two vintage Marshall speaker cabinets hang in each of the room's rear corners. Blondie's 'One Way or Another' was currently playing at a low volume. Three antique dentist chairs and two surgeon's tables with black leather mattresses create a spacious workspace. Each area subtly separated from another with Victorian bi-folding room dividers.

The tattooist swivelled his stool and turned to the stainless steel surgical trolley. Numerous inks, needle cartridges and sterilising equipment were laid methodically across his workstation's top tray. He squirted a small amount of flesh tone ink into a clean pot before adding two drops of white to the mixture. He mixed the ink with a sterile needle. He then added a little more white, one drop at a time, until he was satisfied he had the exact tint required to colour the next area. The tattooist changed the cartridge on his machine, selecting a larger needle configuration to better suit the next section he was to block in.

He turned back to his client and with the fingers of his spare hand he stretched out the skin around the part he was about to colour. He worked in small circles, packing colour into the darker areas and blending out the tones as he pulled the colour towards the edges. He continued to work a small section at a time, wiping any excess ink away with a sterile wipe. The tattooist worked a series of skin toned inks. Each colour was vital to obtaining the correct shadowing and contrast. All the while, he referenced a colour print of the original artwork.

Lena had now been lying on the tattoo couch for over four hours. The straps of her red La Perla bra dangled helplessly to her sides and her black hair, loosely tied, cascaded across one shoulder. She tensed slightly as the tattooist worked more ink into a sensitive area between her shoulder blades. But the pain was welcoming. It heightened her senses, brought her inner torments to the surface and provided the mental release she longed for. It provided a distraction from the painful emotional state she had locked away for many years. The pain satisfied the gnawing guilt she held in denial of her own misdoings. The pain was her flagellation, the scourging of her own sins.

'Sorry,' said the tattooist, noticing her discomfort, 'I am just trying to pack in some deep shading and it just so happens to be in a place high on your collarbone that is a little more susceptible to pain.' He wiped a sterile wipe across the area. 'Just a few more minutes and I should be done.'

'Sometimes we find pleasure in pain. I am actually finding the whole experience de-stressing.' Lena turned her head slightly and gave the tattooist a sly smile. 'It has given rise for me to question all that has come before and to all that is yet to come.' The tattooist paused to clean his needle cartridge and took the opportunity to take a break for a few minutes.

'You talked during your initial consultation about your reasons for wanting such an extensive tattoo, especially since it was your first. If I remember correctly, it was about creating a bond.'

Lena lifted her chin to look directly at him. 'I was looking for something to provide a connection between myself and two significant family relatives from the distant past.' She paused, noticing the tattooist had rested a buttock on the corner of the mattress, crossed his arms and was attentively listening. He was a good listener. It came with the job.

Lena continued. 'The angels are my guardians and embody the paternal nature of providing protection. Whilst the Madonna cradles me in her arms, conveying the maternal instincts of comfort and reassurance.' She placed a hand on his knee. 'I will feel safe in the challenges that confront me and secure in all that my destiny holds. All the while, comfortable in the knowledge that someone close is watching over me.' The tattooist nodded, recognising the importance and spiritual significance that the tattoo would hold. Lena looked up once more and held the tattooist's gaze with her eyes.

'As each figure is added to the tattoo, it will symbolise a judgement has been made and a rite of passage has been taken. Each marking the end of an act and the next step towards self-fulfilment.'

Bring the pages alive…

Explore artworks, locations and more.

Go to gnsbooks.com (Interactive) or scan the QR code to unlock images, maps and facts as you read.

Tottenham
London, England

11

Dusk had settled and the night would not be far behind. The nights were drawing in and the streetlights were beginning to come to life earlier and earlier as each week passed. The younger children of the street had been called in by their parents and would now be cleaning teeth, fighting with dressing gowns and, for those fortunate enough, settling down for a bedtime story. Although these days, most would have to suffice with half an hour alone upstairs with an iPad or tablet whilst mum and dad conversed downstairs over a bottle of Shiraz and a lukewarm ready meal for two. Those slightly older were still hanging out in teenage groups on street corners, parking their backsides on garden walls and street signs. Their faces were illuminated in the glow of mobile phone screens as they all perched, stooped and slouched as they frantically thumb-typed messages to other teenagers on similar street corners. None looked up, none said a word, each immersed in the solitary silence of their own small corner of the social media universe. The serenity of the street was only disturbed by the occasional whining of a passing food delivery scooter.

All was different at No.53. For there were no children there. No parents discussing the antics of Mrs 'What's her name' at No.34 and no habitual teenagers transfixed in the zombie stare of a hypnotic X-box. The only sign of occupancy at No.53 was a soft yellow hue luminescing through the smoke stained net curtains of a small bedroom to the rear of the property.

To passersby, No.53 appeared to be no different than the other Victorian terraced houses that lined the suburban street just north of the football ground. A low wall, come teenage bench, fronted a modest lawn and a brick façade of two windows and a door. However, unlike the other neighbourly families on the street, No.53's occupant was somewhat reclusive. He kept himself to himself and only ventured out after dark. Ask the other occupants of the street about the man at No.53 and nobody seemed to offer any insight or knew very little. The man at No.53

preferred to be an unknown entity; he did not wish to be the subject of small talk and street gossip and did not need nosey neighbours prying into his business.

The owner of No.53 was William O'Connor or 'Billy the Owl' as he was known amongst the rogues and rapscallions of East London. He had lived in the street for as long as anyone could remember. Few knew his name and fewer knew of his true vocation. A cat burglar was not the type to shout to the heavens or advertise what they did for a living. His trade was slowly becoming a dying vocation of years past. The thieves of the 21st century now wished to work from a desk as they stole from the unsuspecting in the dark web world of cybercrime. However, William still craved the rush that went with breaking and entering. The intoxicating frisson that went with the chance of being caught red-handed. But he had also changed with the times. Jobs these days were fewer but far more lucrative. He could be choosier and wait for the best opportunities to arise. And wait is exactly what he had done with his last outing. He had watched the gallery's online presence, carried out his reconnaissance work and then patiently waited for an appropriate artwork to appear. Within weeks, a pair of pictures by the same artist had been advertised on the gallery's website. Patience had been a virtue and good things had come to he who waited.

William stood in the small back bedroom. A single bare bulb hung at the end of a flex that emerged from a hole in the laths and plaster ceiling. The room's only furniture was a single dining chair, a small kitchen table, and two easels. A small battery powered radio sat on one corner of the table. The radio was transmitting at a low volume. 'Paint it Black' by the Rolling Stones was currently being broadcast. Pinned the length of the longest wall were detailed architectural plans of a building and an additional plan of its internal vents and ducts. There were also photographs of the building's exterior and further plans of the neighbouring streets, sewer systems, and tunnels that ran below the surface. Pictures downloaded from a private equity firm's website were spread across the table. Each of the two easels held a painting. The pair of Lowry prints from the previous heist currently had his attention.

The print on the left easel was entitled 'Market Scene in a Northern Town'. The original oil painting had been produced by L.S. Lowry in 1939. It captured a bustling town market set in the backdrop of an urban landscape. The numerous figures in the picture's foreground are characteristic of Lowry's widely known 'matchstick men'.

The picture to the right was produced several years later, in 1947.

Entitled 'Punch and Judy', it is a typical example of the artist's work. A simple town square with Lowry's stylistic figures mingling around a traditional puppet show. Both pictures were signed first edition lithograph prints. Even as a print, each still demanded a respectable price on the open market. William hoped to achieve a reasonable return for his efforts after the heist went so smoothly and there had been no heat from the investigative authorities in the first twenty-four hours. He was sure he had contacts who could move the pictures on quickly. At the end of the day, you don't get rich without the money in your pocket and William had no love for art.

'Billy the Owl' led a solitary existence. He had not only lived alone his entire life, but he also preferred to work that way too. No partners in crime and no gang members to be reliant upon. He watched his own back, and with very few known associates, he had little reason to fear being sold out to the law.

William had grown up on the street, living in the same house his grandparents had bought when they moved across the sea from Ireland in the 1920s. Now knocking on the door of his late fifties, he had not done an honest day's work throughout his entire life. Starting as a pickpocket's decoy and purse snatcher while still at school, he moved on to breaking and entering crimes in his late teens. His misdemeanours manifested into more lucrative looting throughout his life of crime. William was a man of short stature, just shy of five foot two, with a thin, wiry frame. His physique would have warranted that of a good jump jockey. His diminutive build had its advantages. When he ventured out at night, dressed in a hoodie with his head down low, he looked like every other teenager prowling the streets after dark, and his lean, willowy body enabled him to crawl and sneak through the smallest of spaces. A beneficial asset to a cat burglar.

William moved his attention from the stolen works to the maze of maps and drawings collated on the wall. He moved his fingers across various outlines on the maps, each time tracing a route or following a particular course or direction. Each path was firmly embedded in his memory, stored away until it would again be needed to instigate part of the plan he was formulating in his head. With the strategy firmly planted in the forefront of his mind, he turned to the table and assembled a list of items he would need to retrieve from a lockup across town. He had always kept the tools of his trade in a different location. Therefore, there was less chance of any connections should he ever be investigated.

He looked out through the small rear window. The night was closing in, and soon he would venture out. His window of opportunity for this next job would be within the following couple of nights. The restructuring of the internal layout of office space two floors above his intended target offered a probable way in and out while the works took place. He had no need to wait for favourable circumstances on this job as the quarry he sought was a permanent fixture on the company's office wall. It could easily be seen hanging in the background of several photographs within the company's online profile.

William had changed into a set of more appropriate clothing and placed his mobile on the mantle above the fireplace downstairs. He did not need his movements being traced if something untoward should happen. He opened the front door and looked towards the skies before giving himself a nod of consensus. He stepped out onto the street.

As he walked towards the corner where the teenagers had gathered earlier with his head down and his hands in the hoodie's front pouch, he failed to notice the figure in black sitting astride the motorbike as it slowly started to follow him.

12

He ran a hand through his hair, tussling it to remove the final remnants of shampoo. Beads of water ran down the contours of each defined muscle between his shoulder blades.

'Looking good, *Mon Ami*,' said Jonathan, peering through the fingers of his hands as he rinsed his face in the flow of the shower head.

'You better not be shower perving,' Tate retorted as he closed his eyes and tilted his head back into the full flow of the water. He welcomed the invigorating sensation of the shower as it cascaded across his temple. He remained, eyes shut, head back, allowing the water to revitalise both his mind and body. If it was for only the briefest moment, it still had the desired effect.

'Can't a man comment on his best buddy's physique these days?'

'Yes, but preferably not when he's standing three feet away and covered in soap suds.'

Jonathan laughed. 'Looks like the hours you're putting in at the climbing wall are paying off.'

Tate answered, but his eyes remained closed. 'It beats going to the gym, hands down. I can happily spend a couple of hours on the wall, whereas I find myself bored within twenty minutes at the gym.' He stepped out from under the shower head and reached for a towel, wrapping it around his waist before returning to the locker room.

'And the athletic constitution wouldn't have anything to do with a certain young lady re-entering your life now, would it?' Jonathan looked up, realising he was now alone and talking to himself. He looked left, looked right, shook his head and tutted before grabbing his towel and following his friend into the adjoining room.

Unlike Tate, Jonathan wandered through the corridors of lockers, towel drying his hair, completely blasé to the nakedness of his body. He was heedless of the elderly gentleman tying his shoelaces who he passed with his nether regions at the bowing gent's eye level. Tate was partially dressed in his shirt and trousers and was sat astride a bench with one foot up, drying between his toes when Jonathan rounded the corner. He noticed his friend's state of undress at the periphery of his vision and did not look up. He had learnt over the years to accept the over gregarious personality; no one would ever change Jonathan, and that was not such a bad thing; he liked his friend just the way he was. However, the traumatic events of last summer had definitely put a dent in the Tin Man's armour. Having your girlfriend's head delivered in a box would present significant psychological issues to even the best of men. Jonathan had been attending post-traumatic stress therapy sessions for several months now. The MET were strongly suggestive to any individual who may have encountered an injurious situation to attend talking therapies before resuming their position within the force. Jonathan had returned to work on the understanding that he would continue attending his twice-monthly sessions.

'Back in the saddle today then,' implied Jonathan, referring to their return to work. 'We'll soon be waist deep in canvases, ceramics and silverware. And before you know it, Cornwall will dissipate into the distant forgotten past.'

'You're not wrong there. A fortnight never seems long enough when the swell is so consistent,' Tate declared as he slid a foot into the first of his socks. He'd welcomed the chance to unwind and leave the stresses of the job locked away in the bowels of the city. He had looked forward to sun, sea and clean air as they both did each year. It allowed them to reflect on the things that really mattered, to focus on the more important parts of life and to leave behind, if only for two weeks, the gnawing questions, the uncertainty in decisions and the stresses of the 'What Ifs' that life consistently threw at you. They had managed to relax, recuperate and recharge until that evening when the message arrived.

And then everything changed.

'So, have you—'

Tate paused, slightly apprehensive about approaching the delicate situation at the forefront of his mind. Now that they were back in the city, they would each have to address a change in circumstances since the Narcissus appeared to have resurfaced. Twice, unable to sleep, Tate had been awake in the early hours of the morning during their Cornish break. On each occasion, he had heard his friend's night terrors. The anguish that disrupted Jonathan's sleep and burdened his mind. Upon hearing the torments, he realised for the first time how much his friend was still suffering from the aftermath of the brutally murderous actions of the Narcissus.

Tate thought it easiest to tackle the awkwardness of the question by being open and light-hearted. They were best friends, after all, and Jonathan would not take offence to his inquisitiveness. He would know that Tate just had his best interests at heart.

'How have you been since Lena raised her ugly head?'

'Ugly is one thing Lena is definitely not.'

'Yes. Wrong term of phrase, I'm afraid. But seriously though, how are you doing?'

'I won't lie. Since you received the email, a whole plethora of mixed emotions has bounced around inside my head. I really thought I had turned the corner for the good and was on the positive side of dealing with it. But "it" is now attempting to fight back.'

'I believe all three of us will have to address our state of mind in our own different ways now that circumstances have taken a turn.'

'Yeah. It's probably just a blip in the recovery process. Honestly, it's nothing I can't deal with.' Tate knew all too well that Jonathan was putting on a brave face and hiding behind his armour. He would be reluctant to reveal his true feelings. Seeing it as a weakness, he would prefer not to disclose it for fear of denting his bravado and swagger.

'Do you have a therapy session this week?' asked Tate.

'Yes. Thursday morning. Rosie…,' he corrected himself, 'Dr Young's sessions are proving to be productive and beneficial. She has an aptitude for recognising what triggers negative thoughts and emotional reasoning. She quickly sees ways to guide the mind into the neutrality of a given situation. You know, turning negatives into positives and all that.' Tate picked up on his friend's misnomer. He furtively smiled to himself. Perhaps the therapy had proved more beneficial than he had first imagined. He hoped that the damage was only a chink in the Tin Man's armour. And maybe Rosie would be the answer in more ways than one. Tate was about to question his friend's intentions but was beaten to it as Jonathan changed the subject.

'What are your initial thoughts about the Lena situation?' enquired Jonathan, still naked and towel drying his back. The old man had just departed and they appeared to be alone in the changing room. Both men were still in a state of undress as their attention had briefly focussed on their conversation and not the task at hand.

'Harriet and I discussed the implications and possible scenarios when we arrived home yesterday evening. The case is still active, albeit with a smaller team at present. Harriet has a meeting first thing this morning with her Super. They will probably discuss the best way to proceed, given that the email I received is the only lead to Lena's whereabouts or her current status that the case has had in a little over a year. I imagine they will start with border patrol camera footage in case she has decided to re-enter the country and, if they haven't already started, attempt to trace the source of the email.' Tate moved across the walkway to a mirror on the wall, flicked his fingers through his hair and continued to talk to Jonathan's reflection. 'They probably won't pull Harriet back onto the case until they have something more substantial. She is still SIO on another homicide case they have been working on for the last three months. The suspect is apparently in custody and has been charged; they are currently working with the CPS to assemble the case material and prepare the prosecution witnesses.' Tate knew all too well that Harriet could carry the workload of both investigations, and she would not let the Narcissus case drop until Lena had been apprehended and was in police custody. A day when all three could once again lay their minds to rest.

Tate turned from the mirror just as Jonathan pulled up his briefs. He felt a whole lot more comfortable in continuing their conversation than before. Jonathan pulled on a pair of chinos before turning his back and reaching into the locker behind him.

'You've read the email several times. What do you think?' Tate asked as he watched Jonathan spray his entire upper torso with deodorant. 'What is she implying this time? Each of the previous messages was indirectly accusatory and each was used to provoke a reaction. The timing of the message must be important, but why now?'

Jonathan spoke as he buttoned his shirt. 'If I remember correctly, the first four lines reference "Judgements" and "Salvation".'

Tate nodded in agreement.

'And she mentioned "go forth" and "lay bare".'

Tate nodded once more.

'Maybe she is alluding to her return. The "casting of judgements" may imply a return to unfinished business, and she sees "the promise of salvation" as her redemption in return for...' He paused, allowing himself a moment to remember. '"the souls of all man's sin".'

Now fully dressed apart from his socks and shoes, Jonathan leant against the lockers behind him. 'The lyrics, like before, are from a Neptune's Finger album, a band you admire and whose album artwork adorns your office wall. Again, both are facts that Lena is fully aware of. However, this new message is from the band's second album, *After the*

Flood, and the section of lyrics she has chosen is from a song called 'The Return of the Raven'. The song tells of an alternative fate of man if the raven had returned instead of the dove.'

Tate, who had been listening intently, his hand grasping his chin, motioned to Jonathan and interjected. 'Maybe the using of lyrics from the second album is Lena implying her own second coming, and the use of the line "the Raven's return is a merciless sign" is insinuating that she is the raven and in her own twisted and deluded way she sees the fate of man is at the mercy of her own hands.'

Jonathan continued the speculation. 'Maybe choosing the album *After the Flood* also references a return. A return to where the devastation was inflicted the first time.'

Both Tate and Jonathan were intelligent enough to surmise that the message would mean one thing for certain.

Lena was coming or was already in London, and further bloodshed was inevitable.

13

There were eight, all armed and ready, crowded as one along the kerbside. Each jostled to maintain their position. Where there had once been solidarity and playful banter within the pack, it had now been replaced by a rapacious dog-eat-dog appetite and the camaraderie had vanished as each fought to gain the best vantage point.

Steve held his camera up and forward as far as his arms and the shoulder strap would allow. His feet pushed as far forward into his boot's toe as he fought to gain the all-important extra inch to obtain the clean shot the papers would pay good money for. His *en pointe* would be the envy of royal ballet dancers. Others within the scrum of paparazzi hustled and grappled to maintain their footing as the gravity of anticipation escalated due to a development behind the doors on the opposite side of the narrow pavement. The pack pulsated and undulated as each photographer awaited the VIP they all stalked. An entwinement of arms flailed forward like the tentacles of a giant octopus feeling for its prey.

Behind the restaurant's closed doors, Myles Harrison, celebrity presenter, thanked the maître d' and exchanged pleasantries while a cloakroom assistant retrieved his jacket. Myles had met with his agent for brunch at Yopo @ the Mandrake. They'd had much to discuss. Myles had been the talk of the town since the announcement of his engagement to pop starlet Anusha Dupree.

A doorman held the decorative scrolled door to one side, and a sporadic burst of camera flashes erupted. Myles stepped out to a barrage of shouts from the awaiting paparazzic hyenas and a volley of cameras clacked while the blaze of flash guns flared in the exiting party's direction.

Steve held his camera high and rattled off a series of shots. The articulating screen of his DSLR was angled downwards so he could be assured his lens was pointing in the correct direction. He could think of one thing and one thing only. Getting that all important shot. The one shot that would help pay this week's bills. Elbows and forearms collided as a confusion of cameras moved along a parallel trajectory as their celebrity target moved towards the waiting Mercedes. The ensuing scrum advanced as Myles neared the car. Steve anticipated the move and was in the first row as the pack began to encircle and flank the vehicle. Camera lenses adhered to the rear windows, hoping to gain one last shot. The driver cautiously edged the car forward as each photographer clamoured to get the final moment of the celebrity's attention.

As the Mercedes rounded the corner onto Eastcastle Street, the hunting pack began to disperse and Steve moved away in the direction of Rathbone Square before parking his backside on the corner of a raised planter. He checked the images he had captured on the preview screen of his camera. He would need to send the best images straight to each of the papers in the next few minutes, as all of his fellow 'paps' would be doing the same. First in, first to get paid. Missing the 2-minute deadline could make a difference in getting paid or not. He was still reviewing the images when his phone started to ring. He retrieved it from an inside pocket but did not recognise the caller's number. He looked at his camera in one hand and the phone in the other.

Decisions, decisions.

He pushed call accepted.

'Hello Steve, my name is Lena. You may also know me as the Narcissus.' He stood dumbfounded, not knowing quite how to respond. So he said nothing. With the murders of high profile art collectors all over the headlines last summer, Steve had a pretty good picture of the caller in his head. She was still wanted on four counts of murder and one of attempted murder. He knew exactly who she was. But again, he had no words.

'I am going to offer you the scoop of a lifetime. The papers will be queuing up to purchase your photos. You will most probably have a bidding war on your hands.'

'How did you get this number?' were the only words he found.

'How I got your number will pale into insignificance compared to the proposition I have for you. I wish to leave a legacy. I wish to complete the work I began. I want to offer you a commission. The responsibility of capturing my work and presenting it before the eyes of the public.'

'I am not interested in anything that may be considered unlawful,' Steve replied hesitantly, looking around the square in case someone was eavesdropping on his conversation. He felt uncomfortable with the situation, but for some peculiar reason, he was also intrigued.

'In a few days, I will send you a location and you must decide for yourself.'

Steve could do little to stop the arousal of his curiosity. He was beguiled by his compulsion to know more. He fought an irresistible urge to seek an understanding. He was about to ask for clarification, but his questioning was cut short.

'If I were to say, the time has come again, for the sinners to face their fates and to pray in the face of mercy. Would that pique your interest?'

Steve opened his mouth to answer, and with that, the call was terminated.

14

Tate and Jonathan had walked back along the river's north bank to the MI5 building at Thames House on Millbank, where the Metropolitan Arts and Antiquities Investigation department occupied a tiny corner of the building. They had a small amount of office space on the fifth floor and a single room in the sub-basement, where Jonathan spent most of his working day identifying, restoring and preserving stolen antiques and works of art. They had breakfasted at Ottolenghi in Sloane Square. As usual, the swimmer who touched home first at the end of their early morning swim would choose their breakfast location. Today's restaurant choice had been Tate's. They had both chosen the North African braised egg dish of Shakshuka. A triple shot espresso for Tate and a macchiato for Jonathan. They had discussed the recent developments regarding Lena and the possible return of the Narcissus. Tate would call a full team meeting later in the afternoon to bring everyone in the department up to speed. He knew Harriet would be doing the same at some point during the day with her team in Bethnal Green.

Tate had spent the morning sifting through the mountain of emails that had accumulated in the relatively short time of two weeks away from the office. The resulting number needing a response or further action being very few. The lion's share of his time was apportioned to prioritising the 'out of the office' call messages the MET call centre had collated for him. Again, those requiring an immediate response were sorted according to their relative importance, and he had then started to follow up on those now sitting at the top of his in-tray. Despite the need to respond to these calls, Tate's priority was to contact Inspector Ricardo Moretti, his counterpart and friend with the Italian Carabinieri T.P.C.

Moretti was the officer charged with the recovery of the Caravaggio painting when the Narcissus had stolen the 'St Mary Magdalene in Ecstasy' from a villa on the outskirts of Rome. It had been Moretti who had invited Tate to continue investigations into the missing painting on

UK soil. They had regularly communicated over the past months as the case file of the stolen Caravaggio was still an active investigation running in conjunction with the Narcissus murder case. Tate had called Inspector Moretti to inform him of the situation that had arisen due to the Narcissus' recent email. They had shared their opinions and speculated on the underlying content and timing of the message. Both had also provided the other with the progress and direction of their current investigations into the missing painting. The call ended with Tate reassuring Moretti that he would contact him should any new developments occur in either case. The call had lasted just under an hour.

Tate stood to the rear of his office and looked out across the Thames. The view from the window was of the river between the Vauxhall and Lambeth bridges with the Millbank Millennium pier to the right. The treelined north bank path ran alongside the river below his window. As Tate continued to gaze, occasional glimpses of the sun pierced the glass of the large Georgian window, periodically peeking through the thick, cloudy canopy that had enveloped the entire city since daybreak. Although Tate looked fixedly at the vista below, his thoughts were elsewhere. From the moment the email had arrived, Lena's return had plagued his headspace. Images of the rooftop encounter at Battersea Power Station flashed through his memories, sometimes tormenting or disrupting his sleep in the early hours. He questioned his actions, whether he could have done more or reacted sooner to prevent the pernicious crimes left in the murderous wake of the Narcissus. Why had he not recognised the signs earlier? Had Lena displayed an increase in the animosity and malice she held towards those of the art community prior to her crimes? Had a change in Lena's demeanour gone unnoticed? He had difficulty clearing his mind of the paranoia eating away inside and that he was in some way accountable and responsible for Lena's actions and misdoings. However, he knew deep down that there was only one person truly culpable for the acts of the Narcissus.

And now it seemed that one person had returned.

The reality of the situation was once again knocking at the door.

But this time, he would ensure Lena would be answerable for the crimes of the Narcissus.

Tate returned from the window and retreated from his deliberations and doubting. He knew when the situation presented itself, he would react, and justice would prevail. Along with Harriet, he would ensure Lena would serve the punishment she rightly deserved and that the missing Caravaggio would be recovered and returned to its rightful owner.

His attention returned to the present moment. Looking back through his office and through the glass partitioning into the room beyond, he felt a strong sense of reassurance and fortitude as his fellow officers assembled together. It was encouraging to be reminded that he was not fighting the battle alone. There were others who had his back. It helped to restore his confidence in not only himself but the establishment, too.

His team had gathered in the anterior office. Jonathan slouched straight legged in a swivel chair, DCs Tom Chamberlain and David Morrison perched on the corners of desks, and newly appointed DS Jane Garrett stood with her arms folded, facing the trio of men. Jonathan looked to be talking and the other three intently listening, for they habitually nodded in agreement and visually communicated their understanding with a series of accepting gestures. The occasional chuckle or chortle escaped the room as Jonathan continued his anecdote and the remainder of the team reciprocated due to the hilarity of the situation.

As Tate entered the room, the three detectives burst into a crescendo of laughter and Jonathan, still sitting in the chair, raised his arms towards the ceiling.

'I was just telling the guys about the evening we walked back to the cottage along the coast path in the dark. The three of us slightly worse for wear after an evening in the Old Success Inn and the surprise encounter and stand-off with the badger.'

'And did he mention who jumped out of his skin and screamed like a baby?'

'He did actually,' declared Tom, 'but apparently, it was the biggest, scariest badger you could ever have imagined.' Once again, a merriment of chuckles spread throughout the room.

'If I could hazard a guess, the surf was also a consistent 10 foot, and the fish that got away when he spent the morning beach casting was this big,' Tate challenged, as he over-exaggerated, spreading his arms wide. The jocosity continued.

Tate allowed the witticisms and gaiety to endure until it naturally subsided and an ambience of professionalism returned to the office. He need do no more. His team were relaxed and ready for an update on the current situation.

'If it's ok with everyone, now is as good a time as any to bring you all up to date regarding the Narcissus case,' declared Tate, receiving a nodding of heads in return. 'As you will be aware from the email I sent you, the situation has changed somewhat. After just over a year without any contact whatsoever and no known sightings that we are aware of,

Lena Johnson, aka the Narcissus, has sent an email from my mailbox to my mailbox in the same way as the messages I received throughout her hellish campaign of last summer. The content of the email is in the same style as those I received previously. That being lyrics from a song. I sent a copy of this to each of you as an attachment to the email.'

It was acknowledged as before, with a nodding of heads.

'The words are once again taken from a song by the band Neptune's Finger, the only difference on this occasion being the chosen lyrics are from the second album entitled *After the Flood*.' Tate let the words hang and remained silent. It had the desired effect.

'Both the album title and the latter lines of the message could be taken to signify a return,' stated DC Morrison, filling the silence left by his superior. 'In folklore, the raven is seen as a symbol of change. Their colour and carrion appetites are also frequently associated with bad luck and death. But many mythologists around the world believe they are more significantly associated with opportunity and are often seen as intermediaries between the material and spirit worlds.'

The room was silent once more.

Stunned silence.

The rest of the team looked at David in awe.

'I'm heavily into role-playing games in my spare time. The raven crops up frequently, very often at a crossroads. Together, they can symbolise decision, change and opportunity.'

Still, no one had a need to interrupt.

David continued. 'The album title, *After the Flood*, could also be taken as a sign of change. In the Bible, the flood symbolises God's punishment of the sin amongst men, and after the flood, the world has been cleansed.'

Dumbstruck, the others looked on.

David noticed the vacant stares. 'Sunday school. Every weekend of my childhood.' He shrugged and raised his palms.

Tate spoke once more. 'As the Narcissus, Lena sees herself as an avenger of sinners, believing they must be punished for their wrongdoings. She may well see herself as a cleanser of sin. We would not be mistaken if we interpreted *After the Flood* as the devastating trail of dead bodies she left behind the last time.'

Tate paused briefly and Jonathan took up the mantle. 'Lena has unfinished business here in London. She would not have sent Tate the message if she was going to curl up and disappear for good. The message was sent with intent. There is an objective behind the action. It means one thing and one thing only. The killings are about to start once more.'

15

'So, we may be chasing a ghost. Or, worse still, the shadow of a ghost. In fact, there's nothing substantial to even suggest she is contemplating entering the country, let alone whether she is already here or attempting to enter through one of the European corridors.'

Harriet only had a small window of opportunity to catch up with her team on the first morning of her return to Bethnal Green CID before she was required to cut things short and attend a pre-arranged meeting with her ranking superior officer, DCS Leslie Gibbs. With the formalities and 'nice holiday?' pleasantries swiftly swept aside, they had quickly knuckled down to the bare bones behind the reasoning of the prompt meeting. Harriet had brought DCS Gibbs up to date with the current situation of the Narcissus case. Gibbs listened intently, stroking his large grey moustache down from the philtrum to the corners of his mouth with his index finger and thumb. A habitual mannerism he was utterly unaware of. Harriet sat in the chair opposite in her customary black jeans and tan leather jacket, open to the white blouse beneath. She sat cross-legged, gently tapping the heel of her leather ankle boot against the toe of the other. She spoke with confidence. With the conviction that her team had initiated all the necessary protocols in her absence.

'Border Force has been informed there is a high probability that a person of interest on a 'red notice' may attempt an international border crossing. Possibly from mainland Europe to the UK.' Harriet sipped a black coffee she had brought to the meeting, and Leslie Gibbs continued his grooming. 'Passport control is flagging all persons travelling on first-use passports, especially those returning to the UK and not registered in the system as having exited the country in the previous 30 days. Lena would without doubt travel on stolen or false papers.'

'She will have almost certainly made a significant change to her appearance,' DCS Gibbs declared as he fidgeted with a gold cufflink at his wrist.

'Entry surveillance is being collated of these individuals and others of interest. DS Stevens has a team going through the footage as we speak. However, no luck, as of yet.'

'A peak time channel tunnel crossing is a distinct possibility,' asserted Gibbs. 'High footfall and rattled through passport control at St Pancras like cattle late for the market. That would be the safest bet if you wanted to get in undetected.' Harriet nodded in agreement. But only to appease her superior's prestige. She knew Andy Stevens would have also played that card and would have officers scrutinising every detail, photograph and facial recognition image available. Harriet sipped from her cup once more. The unwashed staining on the cup's walls now evident above the remaining liquid.

'Although we must be cautious, there is no concrete evidence that Lena has entered, attempted, or is considering entering the country. She may well have been here all along. There has been nothing to prove she ever left the UK. The email Tate received just days ago is the only communication in over twelve months. And that in itself is a riddle which can be interpreted in a dozen different ways depending on how and who reads it.'

'But it is highly suggestive,' DCS Gibbs conferred, 'It seems like a 'Hey, remember me? I'm back,' kind of statement.'

'Yes, I agree. So until we get confirmation of a positive sighting or further evidence that Lena is indeed back on British soil, we should cover all bases,' stated Harriet, exhibiting the decisiveness Gibbs had entrusted in her as she firmly took the reins once again and the DCS could be assured that no stone would be left unturned.

'The Narcissus is a cunning and calculated individual. Nothing must be left to chance. We must remember she is nefarious and believes she has the power to instil justice. She has a twisted mind and adjudges herself above the law.'

DCS Gibbs nodded in agreement as he again pulled down his chevron moustache. It was a mannerism he not only did when in agreement but an idiosyncrasy he unconsciously performed when preparing to talk. 'When she does return, and unfortunately, I believe at some point she will, I have every confidence that you will bring her to justice, and she will be charged with the crimes of the Narcissus as she rightly deserves.'

16

It was just beyond his reach. With his right arm extended to its absolute limit and the extensor tendons of his fingers virtually stretched to rupturing point, he fought to achieve the extra inch or so he needed. He moved his head to look down the length of his body to see where the toe of his shoe was placed. If he could swap his feet over, his left foot to where his right was at present, it would allow him to lean ever so slightly further in the direction he sought. Ensuring he had a firm grip with his left hand, he twisted the toe of his right shoe onto the very edge of the tiny blue angular climbing hold. This freed just enough space to move the tip of his left shoe onto precisely the same spot. This small adjustment of his feet allowed him to gain the extra reach he required, and he could now crimp his fingertips across a small orange edge. Now that his right hand was in charge, he extended his left arm behind and down, shaking it through its length to release the lactic acid that had built up in his muscles. He was now in a much more comfortable position and took the opportunity to rest while planning his next moves.

Tate had spent the final hours of his afternoon meeting individually with each member of his team. Each detective had brought Tate up to date with the status of the case they were currently investigating. They discussed any major leads that had arisen during Tate's absence, ascertaining the relevant facts and how they may affect the direction of their inquiries. Other more minor leads were reviewed to establish if they warranted any further scrutiny and how they might be beneficial to moving an investigation forward. By the end of the afternoon, Tate was assured that his team had a firm hold on their current standpoint.

Having rested and visualised his next series of moves, Tate reached behind his back one hand at a time and re-chalked his fingers from the small bag attached at his waist. He reached his right leg out and up onto a sizable red hold and by slightly adjusting the grip of his left hand, he could rock across onto his right foot and stand relatively comfortably on the hold's upper surface. Again, he contemplated his next moves and continued his traverse upwards and to the right.

He had left his office on Thorney Street just after 6 pm and taken the short drive north through Islington to the Castle Climbing Centre in his late grandfather's Series II Land Rover. Tate had owned, driven, and cherished the vehicle since passing his driving test on his 18th birthday. He liked to use the Land Rover whenever possible. However, living and working in London had its difficulties, with parking being one of them. A large vehicle with no power steering was not the easiest thing to negotiate into the tightest of spaces. Luck had been on his side today, as he had found an empty end-of-bay parking space just a few roads from the centre.

Tate had been a member of the Castle Climbing Centre for several years. The grade II listed Victorian building had been erected in the 1850s as a water pumping station, part of a new initiative to improve the quality of drinking water within the city. The redundant building was redeveloped and opened as the Castle Climbing Centre in 1994.

Tate liked to use the facilities as often as possible, but the constraints of the job meant planned sessions were very often cancelled at the last moment. Time spent at the wall was not only about maintaining a level of fitness, but it was so much more about destressing, taking an opportunity to clear his headspace and being free in mind and spirit, if only for a relatively short time. While Tate was working through a series of moves on one of the bouldering walls, he would need to clear his mind to focus solely on the precise sequence of his foot and hand placements. He could cast aside the shackles of the job, leave his stresses and tribulations outside on the city's streets and fixate his entire self on solving what climbers call a boulder problem. A low-level traverse across a specific selection of holds with several crash mats below to break your fall should you not complete the sequence.

Tate chalked his hands once more to absorb any moisture and ensure maximum friction during the next sequence of moves. The sticky rubber soles of his snuggly fitted climbing shoes would provide the traction for his feet. He began to move across the wall once more, using a series of the coloured holds. Each hold requiring a different position for both his hands and feet. Sometimes, the hold would have a hole or a pocket to insert his fingers. Others would need to be held from underneath or by pulling sideways. He also used his feet in a variety of ways. Reaching his leg out to full stretch and pushing his toe against the tiniest of holds to maintain balance or hooking a heel around the side of a hold to pull in that particular direction. All the while, his mind was totally committed to the here and now; everything else would be put on hold and left waiting in the world outside that continued to spin without him.

With his feet now on two good sized edges, Tate looked up at a large hold about eight feet above him. He stretched an arm upwards. It was beyond his reach, but it looked to be what climbers called a super-size jug; a large open hold with a deep lip that is fairly easy to grip. He sized up the movement. It would mean committing to a dynamic leap and catching the hold with one hand, leaving the rest of his body hanging beneath. He bent his knees to gain maximum momentum. With his mind and body in equanimity, he rocked back and forth, focusing completely on the one hold. As his body rocked forward, he sprung from the wall like a leaping lemur. His body's momentum travelling in the desired direction and his hand outstretched in anticipation of regaining contact. His fingers grasped the lip.

The jug stuck.

The leap of faith had held.

17

She thanked the driver and handed him a twenty-pound note through the window.

'Keep the change.'

'Thank you, Sweetheart,' came the reply swathed in a slight cockney accent.

The West End of London was bustling with a cornucopia of crowds. The streets were awash with after work drinkers, early diners, theatregoers and those just happy to wander and take in the city around them.

The sun still peeked above the towering skyline. Its blazing arc reflected in the glass of the city's western facing superstructures. The shadows below slowly elongating along the length of the streets. The luminescent neon heart of London was slowly awakening to colour another night in the city.

Harriet's first afternoon back at Bethnal Green had panned out pretty much like Tate's. She first met with DS Iain Richards and newly promoted DS Andy Stevens to establish the progress of the investigations that had been active before her break. The Detective Sergeants also informed her of two new cases the department had been assigned during her absence. As she expected, everything had run smoothly and without a hitch. She had a deep respect and profound confidence for the senior officers in her charge. In fact, she held all of her team in high regard. She could rely on every one of them. No task was ever too much, and when circumstances required, the long hours were never questioned. Responsibilities and decisions were openly accepted and an air of positivity and trust was the lifeblood of her team.

Knowing that they had organised an evening out to celebrate a colleague's birthday, Harriet had arranged to meet with all personnel towards the tail end of the afternoon to bring them up to speed with the current situation regarding the Narcissus case. It took twenty minutes or so to communicate the information that had come to light recently and to hear further updates from DS Stevens. Harriet then excused the team, insisting they all finished early before tonight's celebrations. She had also intended to finish at a respectable hour.

But as usual, it didn't happen.

Having got caught up in the mountain of paperwork that had accumulated on her desk, she had completely lost track of time and the clock on the wall had been two hours further on than she had anticipated.

So now she found herself scuttling along Lisle Street, a cardboard box precariously balanced in her arms, hoping the team had not noticed her absence and she had not missed the celebratory chorus as she was carrying the cake and the candles. Harriet was mostly cool, calm and collected at work, but always found herself late and rushed when it came to commitments outside of the working day. A situation she always promised herself to address but never found the time. As she climbed the stairs, she caught sight of her dishevelled hair in a Chinese mirror. She tutted at herself. Again, there was no time to do anything about it now.

Harriet's crew had booked a private dining room at Tao Tao Ju. One of Chinatown's most popular dim sum restaurants. She could hear the raucous laughter and merriment before she turned from the corridor into the party room. The whole department had turned out. Nobody would have dared not to, or they would have Sarika to answer to, as it was her party. Sarika Rajamani was the team's senior indexer, charged with inputting and analysing information collated on Home Office databases. She was Harriet's go-to, a chocoholic, and today was her 40th birthday. Noticing Harriet's arrival, Sarika, who never missed a thing, dashed across the room and wrapped her arms around her superior's neck. Harriet tried desperately to keep the box she held upright, as Sarika hugged her with her forearms so to avoid any unnecessary contact between her sticky fingers and Harriet's jacket.

'Happy Birthday, Sar,' announced Harriet, stepping out of the embrace and offering the cake box to her colleague.

'Chocolate?' enquired Sarika. Harriet had no need to respond. She just smiled as Sarika knew only too well that it would be nothing but. 'Come on,' beamed Sarika. 'I've saved you the seat next to me. There is still plenty to eat on the table.' They crossed the room together, Harriet having to stop several times to exchange pleasantries with other members of the team. The table was an abundant banquet of dim sum. Steamed, grilled or fried. Prawn, pork, beef, duck and vegetables. Sauces of black bean, satay, oyster, Hoi Sin. Even sweet egg yolk custard buns. The food was plentiful, the wine and beers as bountiful. The atmosphere was euphoric and joyous.

For the next few hours, Harriet's team would revel in the conviviality of the moment. People snacked on finger foods, and nobody sat. They mingled, chatted, joked, laughed and simply enjoyed each other's company. Sarika blew out the candles while they all sang their birthday wishes. The opening of numerous cards and presents followed. Sarika cut the cake, and to much surprise and the wink of an eye, she gave the first slice to George Quinn, the team member she frequently fought with for the only chocolate doughnut in the box. The fact that a serial killer could have returned to London never entered anyone's mind. Tonight was about being happy-go-lucky and carefree.

Tomorrow would be another day.

Financial District
London, England

18

The headtorch provided sufficient light to see the full length of the air conditioning duct. Its beam illuminated the stainless steel boxed walls, refracting off the silvery mirrored surface to produce further light. He continued his commando crawl towards where a gap in the shaft's floor should be; if he had remembered the schematic plans correctly, it would drop away through the ceiling to the floors below. He passed over the void and then tracked his feet back into the opening. Using the opposing pressures of his back, feet and hands, he began to carefully descend.

William had gained access to the building with relative ease. A change of occupancy two floors above that of the financial company's offices gave him the window of opportunity he needed. Due to noise and other disruptions associated with reconfiguring the floor's layout, the restructuring work was to be executed outside normal working hours. His surveillance of the construction team's comings and goings during the nights of the previous week had given him an insight into how the building could be accessed after dark. A company jacket and hard hat stolen from an unlocked van and a copy of an employee's ID card, photographed while feigning a selfie in the coffee shop across the road, had provided him with the semblance he would require. Once inside, it would simply be getting on with the job, as usual.

The screws released with ease as William manipulated his battery-powered flexible screwdriver through the face of the grill. As the last screw came away, he gently eased the covering and lowered himself to the floor below. With the only live-feed cameras on the lifts and the stairwells, his entry to this floor would go unnoticed. There were no further cameras on this side of the office's entry points.

The painting he sought tonight was hung on the corridor wall, which extended from the main reception area to the CEO's office on the south side. It was in this office that he now wandered. He strode about, hands deep in his pockets, as if he didn't have a care in the world. Nobody would have the faintest idea he was here. And when he left, the only sign of his presence would be the sun-bleached outline where a picture had once hung. William sauntered over to the room's southwest corner and looked out of the floor-to-ceiling glass walling. The labyrinth of the city spread out in all directions below him. Its lights glinting and glimmering in contrast to the vast dark universe of the night sky above. Only its brightest stars signalling back to their counterparts on the Earth below.

William, aka 'Billy the Owl', stood perched above the capital and watched as the streets pulsed and resonated as if they were actually breathing life into the very heart of the city. All the while, not a soul amongst the thousands below was aware of his isolated presence above. As he continued looking out across the rooftops, he pondered where his next acquisition may be hanging at this very moment.

The sound of a siren below broke his speculations, but he remained in the window. It would not be for him. Nobody had the slightest inkling of his whereabouts. He had no reason to feel concerned or dash away. It was not often that a view, such as the one before him now, presented itself as it did at this very moment. It was one of those rare opportunities to ask yourself the 'what's next?' and the 'where do we go from here?' questions.

Immersed in the present moment, William lost track of time while losing himself in his inner being. He returned his thoughts to the task at hand. The 19th century Dutch painting of the 'Girl with a Vase of Flowers' was painted on oak panel and was only a little over 12 inches high. It would easily fit in the satchel at William's side. It took him little time at all to remove and secure the painting, closely followed by the satchel being deposited into the open vent and William pulling himself up and into the shaft. He would have to crawl to the nearest junction to enable him to turn through 180 degrees and then retrack to refix the grill.

Forty minutes later, he walked amongst other construction workers as they descended for a tea break on the ground floor. Each worker was oblivious to him walking straight past the porta cabin and on into the small access road at the rear of the building.

Having retrieved a larger rucksack he had stowed earlier, he consolidated his tools and the picture into the bag. As he fastened the buckles, he heard a voice from behind. Unsure, he remained at a squat, with his back to the source.

'Hello there. Sorry to trouble you. I seem to have lost my way. Am I heading in the right direction for Fenchurch Street?'

It was a woman's voice.

But it could still be the law.

He was still sceptical as he stood and turned.

It was a woman. She was not in uniform, and she was unbelievably attractive.

She drew closer. 'If you could just point me in the right direction,' she continued to move forward, 'I'll be out of your hair and leave you to…' she paused and looked at his rucksack, 'whatever it is you were doing.' She was now standing immediately to his left. The woman raised an arm to point. 'Is it that way by chance?'

He felt a sudden sharp prick to the side of his neck. He instantaneously raised a hand to the pain. He looked at the beautiful woman in disbelief. His mind fought the confusion. A fuzziness perforated his thoughts. His eyes felt unusually strange, as if the pupils were trying to invert themselves. Perhaps he had tried to stand too quickly when he had heard the voice.

The world around him started to close in. He had to fight to remain conscious. In recent years, he had started to find the confined spaces more demanding. Maybe that was it. He was having a funny turn. His field of vision was contracting. He found it increasingly difficult to orientate himself. Where had the woman gone? There was no logic to what was happening. He could hear the woman's voice once more, but the words made little sense.

But then she was holding his arms. It felt as if he was being lowered. He felt something against the backs of his legs. What was it. She had got him a chair. She was sitting him down. He'd been lucky that the woman had come along when she had.

Hang on, he seemed to be moving. More confusion flooded his mind. He fought to understand. Still moving. A moving chair. That was it. The woman had helped him into a wheelchair. The outer edges of his vision faded further as the darkness clawed inwards. The movement changed as he battled with unconsciousness. He felt as if he was rising, but he was unsure why. His brain struggled to rationalise a reason. He laboured to understand. From the depths, he fathomed a possible answer. An ambulance. That's why the woman had appeared. She must be with the emergency services.

'But how? Who could have called them? How had they arrived so promptly?' he thought. His confusion now spiralled out of control.

The questions would remain unanswered.

A blackness finally enshrouded his world.

19

The sun continued along the arc of its rise, the deep blazing red of daybreak mellowing to a citrus orange that washed eastwards along the waters of the Thames. The surrounding city began to ease from its slumber, its arteries slowly filling once again with the life of another day.

There had been no early morning swim for Tate, his day starting with breakfast on the go and a pre-arranged meeting with newly appointed DS Jane Garrett. Tate had bought take-out coffees and Danish pastries. They sat informally in the two chairs to the rear of Tate's office overlooking the Thames. It was not an over-the-desk type of meeting. More of a one-to-one catch up. They discussed the current situation regarding the missing Caravaggio. DS Garrett had been overseeing investigations since joining the department a little over eight months ago. However, the case had hit a brick wall with no further leads or information coming to light since Lena's disappearance, shortly after murdering Harriet's partner and leaving her body posed on their bed in a portrayal of Caravaggio's painting of 'Narcissus'. The only other significant lead was that of the art dealer, Jeremy Grayson. Again, the line of inquiry had stonewalled when he had been crucified to one of Battersea Power Station's iconic chimneys during the rooftop altercation, which had subsequently resulted in Lena's escape and disappearance. Having survived the ordeal, he was currently serving a five year sentence for aiding and abetting the sale of stolen artworks.

Having taken the reins of the investigation, DS Garrett had two possible avenues open to her and the investigation. Firstly, looking into Jeremy Grayson's previous clientele, especially those who had completed deals involving large sums of money. There was a possibility that a deal for the Caravaggio painting had been completed before Grayson's tribulations. She was also following a line of inquiry into recent purchases of works by Emile Moreau, the French artist who had painted the 'Rendezvous a la Mer', the painting thought to have been used to conceal the Caravaggio. The only other plausible theory was that Lena still had the work in her possession. Having so little to go on and no new evidence offering anything feasible, it seemed more and more likely that the Caravaggio had simply been used as an enticer during the Narcissus' murder campaign and the location of the painting would remain unknown for the foreseeable future. But they still had a sworn duty to keep the investigation active.

'How would you feel about Tom following the current lines of inquiry, but still with your guidance as and when needed,' suggested Tate. He had always been a proponent of shared decision making and supportive leadership. Tate was fully fledged to the idea and instilled in those in his charge to take ownership of tasks and be responsible and accountable for their actions. A culture he found beneficial to the continual development of those within his team.

'I do not see any problems in doing so,' Jane reciprocated, 'I imagine Tom is more than capable of further investigating the aspects of the case we are currently exploring.' Even though she was the senior ranking officer, Tom had been with Tate's team far longer and had a respectable understanding of art and antiquities, having previously worked in his father's emporium. 'I will suggest we meet frequently to ensure he and the investigation are on track. If you're happy, I would like to continue to liaise with the Metropolitan CID should any further contact be made or any new evidence in the murder investigation come to light.' Tate nodded in agreement to his recruit's proposals. He was more than happy with how the DS had integrated into his team so quickly. She had most definitely been the correct appointment.

'If that's the case, what would you say to joining me in moving the Palmer forgery investigations a stage further? I believe we now have sufficient evidence and satisfactory need to ask Ms Palmer to informally answer a few questions?' DS Garrett's reply was cut short by a knuckle knocking on glass. Both detectives looked to the door.

'Is this a private party, or is anyone invited?' mused Jonathan, who was already halfway across the floor and still coming. Tate looked to Jane and light-heartedly shook his head in concession.

Jonathan noticed the pastries. 'Are those going free?' he asked as the first bite passed his lips.

'Apparently so,' resigned Tate, still slowly shaking his head at his friend's presumption. 'I was just thinking of asking Jane if she would care to join us on the Palmer case.' DS Garrett nodded her acceptance in the direction of both men.

'An extra set of eyes sometimes sees that which others may miss,' declared Jonathan, wiping crumbs from the corners of his mouth with the back of his hand. He continued without a care, his mouth full with the last of the pastry. 'Good timing. I had just come to ask when you wished to talk about identifying marks on fake ceramics.' He strode back across to the office door, reached around to the top of a filing cabinet on the other side and returned with a vase and a bowl.

'Looks like now is as good a time as any!' conceded Tate. He ceased to be amazed by his best friend's candid nature. Sometimes, his open leadership style when it came to Jonathan was not so much that the door was always open but more that the barn door had come off its hinges.

Woodford Green
London, England

20

Tears welled in the corners of her eyes. She tried to wipe them away with the backs of her hands. But no matter how hard she resisted, they kept coming. It was no use, she could not tolerate it for a moment longer. Harriet put the knife down and reached for the kitchen roll, her nose now sniffling alongside the onion tears. She liked to cook, however, the constraints of the job all too often threw a spanner in the works. Last minute cancellations and 'I'm so sorry' pleas were frequent occurrences for CID officers, along with microwave meals and cold leftovers. Since rekindling their relationship, Harriet and Tate had tried their damnedest to eat together at least once a week. With both of them holding senior positions, there had been frequent apologetic texts and pot noodles for one.

However, tonight's plans were running like clockwork and the trauma of onion chopping was now a thing of the past. Harriet turned her attention to the remaining vegetables, preparing, oiling and seasoning them in readiness for roasting. She had already marinated her lamb in Ras-el-Hanout and honey and steeped the couscous for the tabbouleh. Most importantly, Tate had messaged to say he was on his way.

Harriet had showered, changed into a comfortable, loose-fitting, knee-length dress, and had just finished laying the table when the doorbell rang. A quick glance in the mirror on the way to the door, an unruffling of the dress while on the move and a euphoric feeling filled her with delight for the evening ahead.

Tate lent across the breakfast counter, a glass of Argentinian Malbec in his hand. Harriet chatted over her shoulder as she focused on pan frying the marinated lamb. She sipped intermittently from her glass.

'How was last night at Tao Tao?' enquired Tate.

'Yeah, really nice, thank you. Sarika was her usual self. Life and soul of the party. Well, I suppose we can forgive her, it was her party, after all.' They both laughed. It felt good to laugh. Both were guilty of the pressures and constricting nature of the job. Neither of them was very good at finding the time for those moments together, which they both deserved. Having Tate around and simply cooking a meal for the both of them was just what the doctor ordered.

It had taken Harriet four months before she had felt comfortable returning to her home. The memories of finding her then-partner murdered and posed upon the bed they had once shared would live with her forever. Having made the decision, uncertainties still haunted her mind. She had questioned her judgement. But she had grown to like the surrounding area and its convenience regarding work. A complete bedroom refit had been fundamental before she had set foot inside the property again.

'Could I trouble you to put the flatbreads and the tzatziki on the table, please? I think we are just about ready to go,' declared Harriet as she turned from the oven with a tray of Mediterranean roasted vegetables. As Harriet plated the food, Tate topped up both wine glasses and put one at each place setting upon the table. He sat at the farthest one just as a large serving of Moroccan lamb was placed before him.

'Smells great,' he complimented as Harriet returned with her plate and sat opposite.

'Cheers.'

They chinked glasses across the table.

'Let's hope it tastes good too.'

'If it doesn't, I will just lie,' jested Tate before biting a chunk of lamb from the prongs of his fork. The tender meat broke apart in his mouth and he had little need to chew.

'Wow… that's wonderful,' he declared.

Harriet let a cheeky smile escape her face. She knew all too well that when it came to food, Tate was a connoisseur of fine dining. He found immense pleasure in the art of eating and drinking. He was a gastronome through and through.

The compliment warmed Harriet's heart. She smiled at him once again across the table. 'I'm glad you like it.'

'No word of a lie. It's really good. The tabbouleh is also delicious. Just the right amount of lemon and parsley.' The warmth from her heart was now radiating throughout her entire body. Some would call it a cosy, snuggly kind of feeling. Moments like this were few and far between. There had been no talking shop. No discussing the negativity of today's news headlines. Neither of them allowed the recent developments regarding the Narcissus to flood their minds. Just the two of them enjoying one of the simple pleasures in life. Each other's company.

But if only they knew.

Things were about to take a turn for the worse.

Bring the pages alive...

Explore artworks, locations and more.

Go to gnsbooks.com (Interactive) or scan the QR code to unlock images, maps and facts as you read.

East Ham

London, England

21

He was still unsure whether it was the right thing to do or even if he wanted to go through with it. A gnawing pang was eating at him from the inside out. His subconscious was feeding him a contradiction of choices. He debated numerous dilemmas, many with undesirable outcomes. His internal monologue questioned his values and the morality of the situation that now presented itself.

Decisions. Decisions.

The courage of his convictions could make or break him. One path may catapult his career to the dizzy heights of success. At the same time, a stumble in the wrong direction may scuttle his future straight into the gutter. It may be the answer to his wildest financial dreams or the first step in a downward spiral to ruin.

These questions and more had dominated his thoughts and bedevilled his mind since receiving the phone call from the individual calling themselves the Narcissus. Just as he had been informed, a few days later, he had received a message with directions to premises in East Ham and further instructions on how best to enter the building.

Despite his uncertainties, Steve now hesitantly entered the rear of a property via an unlit alley and a small enclosed yard. It was evident that the business had been closed for some time. The boardings on the doors and windows were cracked and weathered, whilst weeds and detritus were beginning to take over the yard. The handle and lock had been forced and the door stood ajar. As instructed, Steve followed a small flight of stairs down into the building's basement. A single timeworn dust covered bulb offered the only light to the room. A small window on the far side had been covered with folded sheets of newspaper; it provided no further light or view from the exterior of the building.

Steve stood, paralysed, at the foot of the stairs.

A lone figure sat, tied to a chair.

And blood.

More blood than you could ever imagine.

Steve had never been squeamish; he was not the type to be easily shocked. He had watched his fair share of B-rated horror and slasher movies. But nothing could have prepared him for this. His stomach was signalling it was time to leave. The hostilities in his head were still a conflict of interests awaiting judgment.

The camera flash ignited. Instinct took over. Unconsciously, his finger worked the shutter button.

Decisions had been made.

Tate Modern
London, England

22

The woman with the short, spikey, vibrant red hair and the striking scarlet leather boots to match entered the building's turbine hall. She wore figure-hugging black leather trousers and a cropped bolero leather jacket. Her Bvlgari sunglasses were pushed up to sit at her hairline. An oversized tote bag swung from her shoulder. Again, in brilliant red. She was a woman who wanted to be noticed. Everything about her appearance screamed, look at me, right down to her cherry nails and ruby red lips. She walked with purpose but did not rush. It was half an hour before the gallery was due to close.

There was plenty of time.

The Tate Modern sits on London's South Bank, facing St Paul's Cathedral on the opposite side. The brick-clad former power station first generated electricity for the city in 1891 and continued until its closure almost one hundred years later. When the building was earmarked for demolition in the early 1980s, a campaign to save the structure was successful. From that day, the iconic building with its dominating 320-foot central chimney has housed the national collection of modern and contemporary art.

The woman in red turned to the right and entered the stairwell. She nonchalantly took the stairs to the 4th floor. She knew the gallery's surveillance operation would be recording her every move. She displayed no signs of concern and did not try to avoid the camera's ever-present eye. She wanted to be seen.

As she meandered amongst the few remaining visitors on the 4th floor, each desperately scampering for one final glimpse of a particular work before closing time, she took the opportunity to gaze fleetingly at some of the works as she wandered through the Media Networks exhibition area.

But she was not here to view.

She was here to exhibit.

Finding herself in the small room, void of both visitors and gallery attendants, she placed the tote bag on the floor and removed an A3-sized picture frame. The next stage had been meticulously planned. The picture's position had been decided during a previous visit several days ago, and the frame she held in her hands had been primed to stick on contact. With a glance over her shoulder to ensure no one had entered unseen, she pushed the picture to the wall, applying sufficient pressure to ensure a good fixing.

The Narcissus stepped back to admire the picture. It was exactly as she had envisioned it. All had gone to plan. She knowingly looked to the side of the room where the video surveillance was tucked in the corner. She crossed the floor in the camera's direction, once again wanting those behind the lens to see the woman in red. Calm and calculated, she mouthed two words, emphasising each syllable for her intended viewer. She held her gaze towards the lens for a moment longer as a malicious grin materialised across her ruby red lips. Turning her head from the camera with an air of sly and cunning, the Narcissus retrieved the tote bag and slung it over her shoulder. Without looking back, she serenely left the room.

'Billy the Owl' had been her subject.

And the Narcissus' performance had just begun.

23

Students spilled into the corridor, a teenage jailbreak from the doors along its length. No sooner had they escaped the confines of the classroom did they immediately re-arm themselves with their trusty mobiles. Some removed the device from their pockets at such speed that they would have fared well in a duel in years past. As the phones reconnected to the network, a symphony of message alerts reverberated along the hallway. As more students joined the ensuing masses, a crescendo of chatter escalated, each student keen to catch up with happenings they dare not miss.

Tate and DS Garrett weaved their way through the swarming students towards the studio at the far end of the corridor. They were the only two bodies attempting to move in their current direction. It was easier to step to one side and let the herd escape. Eventually, they stood outside the door marked 'Ceramics'. They knocked once and entered. The solitary figure inside was clearing things away from work benches.

'Ms Palmer,' stated Tate. It was not a question, they had been acquainted before. But still, he produced his ID. 'DCI Tate Randall and DS Jane Garrett.' They needed no further introduction. Kate Palmer had been on their radar for some time.

'And to what do I owe the pleasure of your company?' she briefly checked the classroom for any dawdling stragglers. There were none. She knew that, but you can never be too careful.

'We were hoping you could spare us a moment of your time to help us with our inquiries?'

Kate Palmer rested her bottom against a work bench and reached for a towel. 'I'm pretty sure I can do nothing to help you unless you are interested in signing up for evening pottery classes.' She focused on drying her hands and not the detectives.

Tate ignored the mockery and continued. 'A number of ceramics in a recent auction were withdrawn when doubts were raised over their authenticity. Subsequently, we have confirmed that they are indeed fake.'

'And the reason you are telling me?' she did not look up from the towel.

'We have reason to believe they are similar to items we seized from your possession during a previous conviction for which you were acquitted.' DS Garrett stepped forward and handed Ms Palmer a series of photographs.

'I was not guilty then and I am no more guilty now,' spat the teacher, slamming the photos down on the bench without looking at them.

'Then, if you are, as you say in no terms guilty, I presume you would have no objections in volunteering to informally answer a few further questions down at the station?'

'As you can see, I'm quite busy at present.' She looked up for the first time, a smug grin across her face.

'At a time that would be more convenient for you then,' declared Tate, stepping forward and handing Ms Palmer a card. 'My number is on there. It would be much appreciated if you would call us when you have more time.' She took the card and placed it straight into the rear pocket of her jeans.

'One last question, would you have any objections if my partner,' he motioned towards DS Garrett, 'also arranged a time and date to take a look around your home studio? Parson's Green, if I remember correctly? Again, when it best suits you. If you are innocent, then I'm sure it will not be too much of a problem.' Ms Palmer had nothing in reply; she stood and looked at the detectives. Tate needed to say no more. He had sown the seed just as he had wished. They had already organised a tail to follow her every move.

'We look forward to your call and further assistance in these matters. Enjoy the remainder of your morning,' stated DS Garrett. And with that, both detectives turned towards the door.

When she was sure her visitors had departed, Kate Palmer snaked her way through the workbenches and potters wheels towards a door at the rear of the room. She opened it, stepped inside and closed it again behind her. The temperature controlled drying room was lined with shelves. Each containing all manner of ceramics produced by the pupils. Vases, bowls, plaques and sculptures. She passed these and moved to the farthest corner of the cupboard-sized room. Her attention was focused on the highest shelf. She reached up and retrieved a small jug. Its finish was far more precise than the works by the pupils on the lower shelves. Kate Palmer turned it in her hands as words and thoughts filled her head.

Unconsciously, she found herself talking aloud.

'You are most welcome to come to my house, for you will find nothing there.'

Tate Modern
London, England

24

The school parties had started to gather with other early bird visitors as a queue began to materialise outside the Turbine Hall entrance to the gallery. Each was keen to enter when the gallery opened at ten o'clock to avoid the onslaught of the masses later in the day. London had awoken under clear skies; however, the river and its bankside walkways were enshrouded in a downy blanket of mist. The air tasted of a salty brine, and an aura of mystery pervaded those queuing as they could sense the presence of the river but could not easily see its waters through the murky veil.

The queue had filed through the entrance quickly and with relative ease. One group of Year 12 art students, along with two members of teaching staff, had spent a period of time in the Turbine Hall, where they were given an informative insight by a Gallery Attendant. A lengthy discussion about various aspects of modern and contemporary art followed a brief history of the building and the gallery. The students were then given time to explore the various collections and exhibits before gathering again for lunch.

Thomas Jones and Harry Willis breezed through the collections on floors 1 and 2, taking little time to study or view each work they passed. They found more interest in a group of teenage girls from another visiting school. It was one pair of girls in particular that they had followed to the 4th floor. As Thomas and Harry mischievously explored the interlinking rooms, more in search of the girls than to study the exhibits, a particular painting caught Thomas's eye. Harry tugged at his friend's jacket after spotting the girls again, but Thomas shrugged his friend's advances; his interest was no longer for feminine company, his curiosity being diverted to the peculiar painting. It appeared to be a photograph that looked to have been overpainted with oils. However, it was not the technique that had piqued his interest.

It was the subject matter.

He found himself mesmerised as if the painting was consuming his entire self. It was also not the lone figure of the composition that enraptured him.

It was the blood.

He discovered an abnormal fascination with the extent of the gore around the figure. He did not hear his friend's tenacity for the girls or see the schoolmaster enter the room. The sanguineous image transfixed him.

'Something finally got your interest, Jones?'

Thomas answered the familiar voice but did not divert his hypnotic gaze. 'It is so grotesque, and the artist has made it look so realistic.'

The teacher strolled to where the boy stood before the picture. His eyes were immediately drawn to the artwork's subject matter as an air of concern spread slowly across his face.

25

Turner took a bite of the almond croissant before sipping the take-out coffee, both of which he had purchased during his walk to work along the South Bank. He always looked forward to his daily commute on foot. The city's skyline was forever changing. Every day, something different caught his eye. Be it a new construction rising from within the bedrock of neighbouring towers or an advertising shroud hugging the scaffold during a building's rejuvenation. Sometimes, it would be the simplest of things. The changing colour of the leaves on the trees. The jabber of multilingual accents or the smell of the mudbanks during each stage of the tides. Even the river hugging mist of this morning painted a contrasting view.

Turner was calculating the specifics of available space and lighting implications for an impending exhibition of contemporary sculpture when the portable transceiver laid upon his desk crackled to life. He would casually listen to the numerous staff communications, transecting the airwaves throughout each working day. However, this one was directed at him personally. He retrieved the handset.

'This is Turner Randall.'

'Mr Randall. This is Peter Morgan on Floor 4. I have a matter that requires your immediate attention in Room 7, Media Networks.'

'Could you please be a little more specific, Peter?' he enquired, wondering what could possibly be so urgent.' The reply sparked his curiosity further.

'I think you should come and see for yourself.'

Turner's inquisitiveness subsided as an air of prudence pervaded. 'In which case, I will be straight down,' he declared, listening to the gallery attendant's final words as he headed for the stairs. He began to speculate on what could require such urgency. An incident with a member of the public. Maybe damage to an exhibit. It was most unusual for his presence to be summoned to the gallery floor during opening times. His position as a curator was typically concerned with coordinating future collections and exhibitions; it rarely required his involvement in day-to-day occurrences.

He reemerged from the stairwell, crossed the concourse and began to pass through a series of inter-connecting rooms. As he rounded a corner from one exhibit space to another, Turner was surprised to see a sizable group of visitors had crowded together to one side. He could just make out Peter Morgan. He appeared to be ensnarled by the huddle of curious onlookers.

'Excuse me. Excuse me. Could you please take a step back? Thank you. Excuse me,' Turner repeated as he weaved, with his arm extended before him, through the amassed bodies. As he broke through the frontline of onlookers, he was immediately confronted by the morbid work on the wall. Like those who had gathered, he was unconsciously absorbed into the picture. He had difficulty drawing his eyes from the image.

Peter's voice broke the bewitchment. 'I tried to move them back, Mr Randall, but as I asked one to move along, two more would arrive.' Turner was still dealing with his own understanding of the situation. He did not recognise the picture as a work owned by or on loan to the gallery. He had walked through the room only yesterday afternoon but had no recollection of it being there.

Again, Peter's words pulled him back to the present moment. 'As soon as I noticed your name on the picture, I thought it best to radio you immediately.'

'Sorry, my name?' Turner queried, his face frowning in bewilderment.

'If you take a closer look, you will see it in the bottom left-hand corner. It is clearly signed T. Randall.' He followed the attendant's direction, moving his whole body in front of the picture. Turner studied the autograph mark. Indeed, it read T. Randall, but he instantaneously recognised that the 'T' was not for Turner.

'Call security,' he demanded, 'we need to move these people back now and seal off the room. I believe we may have a crime scene.' He sensed more than believe; he was absolutely sure. From seeing the picture to reading the signature, he had realised the full extent of what hung before them. He needed to make an urgent telephone call.

Turner needed to talk with his brother immediately.

26

The frame in which the painting hung was around two metres square. It dominated the main wall of the room. 'The Lady of Shalott' was painted by John William Waterhouse in 1888. Following in the style of the Pre-Raphaelites, the large oil on canvas depicts the lady in a small boat upon the water as she travels to Camelot to face her destiny. She is portrayed sitting upon a large tapestry. It was woven with scenes she had viewed as reflections in a mirror after being forbidden to look at the outside world.

Tate stood at a distance and viewed the exquisite work. He was familiar with the painting. Both his parents had worked in the gallery throughout his childhood. Tate was perusing the gallery walls on his way to the exit, having dropped by to arrange a meeting with an art expert to aid a case his team was investigating. He was thinking he should get back to his office when his phone vibrated in his pocket. He retrieved it and looked at the caller ID.

'Turner. What a coincidence. I'm standing looking at one of Mum's favourite paintings.'

'Tate. We have a situation here at the gallery.' The gravity of the predicament could be heard in his brother's tone.

Tate instinctively knew something was amiss. Turner continued. 'I have just been called to the gallery floor. A grotesque picture has been discovered on an area of wall space. A picture that can only have been hung there by an outsider. It is not the property of the gallery and appears to have been installed in the last 24 hours.' Tate was listening intently. His mind was already racing towards a conclusion for his brother's urgency and concern. He knew what was coming even before he heard his brother's words. 'The artwork is signed T. Randall. I instinctively knew it was meant for you and not me. It's Lena, isn't it? She has hung a picture of the Narcissus' latest victim in the Tate Modern, hasn't she?' Tate could sense the trepidation creeping into Turner's voice.

'Do you know if anyone has touched it?' Tate enquired calmly.

'I can't be sure, but quite a few visitors have seen it.'

'Clear the room. Seal it off. Don't let anybody in whatsoever. And that includes the gallery staff.'

'I've already instigated a course of action to do just that.'

'I'm ten minutes away,' Turner knew precisely where his brother was.

'I'm leaving now. And Turner, get security to upload the camera footage from the last 36 hours.'

Cambridge Heath
London, England

27

Lights flashed. Music pounded. Muscles burned and sweat dripped.

'OK, ladies. Let's step it up a gear. On my count. Three 20-second stand-ups. Let's increase that heart rate. Are we ready? 3-2-1, take it up.' Each cyclist stood up on their pedals and increased their pedal rate. As they did so, their heart rate monitors registered their increased effort. Harriet pushed her legs to the limit, matching the rotation rhythm of the instructor at the front of the class. Her crank rotation reached 90 revolutions per minute. As the instructor eased off after the 20-second bursts, Harriet sat back in the saddle and welcomed the respite of the decreased pedal rate; she could feel the burning ache in her calves and thighs.

Sometimes, like today, she would have a late start and attend the spinning class before the day ahead. It would be an opportunity to clear her mind and be ready to focus her thoughts. At other times, she would use the class at the end of the day to unwind and let off steam and the pressures that sometimes came with the job.

'Are you still with me? Let's pick it up one final time,' encouraged the instructor, looking at the reflections of her class on the mirrored wall. 'One last 20 seconds of maximum acceleration. The finishing line's in sight, ladies. Let's get up on those pedals and take it up to 100%. Heads up, engage that core, 3-2-1, ride those pedals.' Harriet drove with her legs, increasing her rotation rate to 100rpm. She pushed through the pain barrier, giving it every ounce of strength she could muster.

The instructor continued her motivation. 'Ride into it, ladies. Through that burn.' Harriet gave it everything she had. Her thighs feeling the eruption of the torment.

'Well done, girls. Ok. Let's back it off to 60 or 65 but hold that gear. Let those muscles warm down gently.' Harriet slowed her aching legs, leant forward into the handlebars, and rested her head.

After taking a few minutes to recuperate, she gathered her water bottle, towel and phone, thanked the instructor for a great session and headed for the changing rooms. As she wandered down the corridor, she habitually checked her messages. She had a missed call from Tate, and her answerphone icon was in the lineup at the top of her phone. She held the phone to her ear and retrieved the message.

'Hi. Call me as soon as you get this. I will explain more when you get here. Tate Modern, 4th floor. It looks more than likely that the Narcissus has a new victim.'

Bring the pages alive…

Explore artworks, locations and more.

Go to gnsbooks.com (Interactive) or scan the QR code to unlock images, maps and facts as you read.

Tate Modern
London, England

28

Turner was waiting at the concourse when Tate arrived. The usual high number of visitors were still entering through security. Tate was pleased that the gallery staff had already erected two temporary A-Frames with signage clearly stating that Floor 4 was temporarily closed. Turner noticed his brother's arrival and motioned for the entrance staff to allow him immediate access, bypassing security. Tate offered his ID as a matter of course before a quick business-like handshake with his brother. Now was not the time to be fraternal.

'We will have to take the stairs,' proffered Turner, his hand gesturing to the right, 'access via the lifts to Floor 4 has been suspended.' Tate nodded approvingly. It appeared that the appropriate protocols had been implemented promptly. Turner held the door; they crossed to the stairwell and began to ascend. As he followed his brother to the fourth floor, Tate was rerunning a train of thought he had been mulling over since he had taken the call from Turner. If the picture he was about to view was a new victim in the murderous campaign of the Narcissus and, indeed, further evidence of Lena's return, Tate's speculations all converged to one inevitable conclusion. Despite the cases of both the Narcissus murders and the missing Caravaggio having remained active, they would once again become priority one investigations and become the sole focus of all those involved. It would also affect everyone who had become embroiled in the web of turmoil spun in the wake of the Narcissus' crimes.

They climbed the final flight of stairs and were met on the 4th floor landing by a large, bearded security officer who stood legs apart with one hand on his chest-mounted radio.

'Mr Randall,' he affirmed with a nod of the head.

'Younus. This is my brother, Tate. He is with the METs Art Investigation department.' Both men once again formally nodded. 'Younus is one of our longest serving security officers.'

'Pleased to meet you,' said Tate, offering his hand to the other man.

'If you wouldn't mind,' Turner asked, motioning to the security chain. Younus removed the fastening and lowered the access chain. Turner and Tate entered and thanked Younus, who promptly secured the chain behind them before returning to his previous stance.

They proceeded swiftly through the corridor of anterior rooms. The smaller room they sought was discernible from the hazard warning tape stretched across its entry and exit points. A security guard stood at the room's perimeter, and again, brief introductions were made before the tape was lifted to one side to allow entry.

Turner turned to the guard. 'Would I be correct to presume that nobody has been permitted access to the room since the floor was closed to the public?'

'Yes. As requested, we cleared both the room and the floor immediately. Nobody has been in whatsoever. Not even the directors or those higher up the food chain,' smiled the security officer. Turner responded to the jest with a polite chortle before turning back to Tate, who was assessing the room. He had noticed the out of place painting as soon as they had entered but knew better than to approach it immediately. He scrutinised the aspects of the room, the other paintings, the position of the security camera and the attendant's chair. He also studied the sight lines from both entry and exit points.

'Through footfall would have been considerably high. Fibre and trace analysis of the room will probably be futile,' hypothesised Tate as he turned to where the incriminating picture hung. He walked forward. 'There will be a much higher probability of retrieving trace from the frame and the picture itself.' Turner joined his brother in front of the picture. Tate studied the morbid composition for the first time. Like others who had viewed the painting, he was taken aback by the amount of blood. However, Tate instantly noticed two aspects others may not have been aware of. The picture was, in fact, a photograph quite possibly of an actual murder scene. The victim in the chair appeared to have had the skin of his entire naked body overpainted with what looked like oil-based paint.

The subject himself was a physical oil painting.

It brought a whole new meaning to realism.

But it was another component of his observations that concerned him the most. The realisation sent a ball of solicitude tumbling through his head, which provoked unwanted recollections of the events of the Narcissus' previous crimes.

Quite simply, Tate recognised the victim.

It was 'Billy the Owl'.

'I know the man in the picture,' exclaimed Tate. 'He is an individual currently under investigation for a series of burglaries and art thefts in the metropolitan area.' Tate's perception of the situation raised concerns about what the picture portrayed and the subsequent consequences that would no doubt arise.

'The MO is different. However, the transpiring chain of events and the victim all strongly suggest the work of the Narcissus. Like those previously murdered, the victim has once again been a suspect of our recent inquiries. If this is indeed a new murder victim, it is vital that the location of the body is discovered before crucial evidence is disturbed.' Tate's eyes drifted to the security camera in the corner of the room.

Turner followed his brother's gaze. 'Security should have collated the CCTV footage by now,' he surmised, 'shall we head up to the control room and take a look?' Tate nodded, but his curiosity was still drawn to the picture and, furthermore, the reason behind the location of its hanging.

'Ready?'

'Yes. Sorry. Now would be good. I left Harriet an answer phone message. She is probably on her way here right now. I'll try her mobile again if she has not arrived by the time we have viewed the footage.' They turned to leave, Turner reiterating instructions to the security guard to keep the room in lockdown and to radio the entrance staff to pre-empt Harriet's arrival.

Once again, Younus held back the chain, and they entered the stairwell. Tate could not resist a moment of brotherly inquisitiveness in the relative calm of the enclosed space.

'How was your dinner date? If I remember correctly, Mum said her name was Sarah.' Turner started up the stairs, throwing a nonchalant answer over his shoulder as he climbed.

'Unfortunately, she had to cancel. Something came up at the last minute. Had to help a friend with something or other. She is keen to rearrange for another time, though.'

Tate grinned. It sounded very much like his brother had been blown out.

Tate Modern

London, England

29

Tate leant in next to the security officer who sat in the console chair. His arms locked straight and his palms clasped the edge of the desk to support most of his body weight. Turner adopted a similar position to his brother on the opposite side. Three monitors filled the space before them, each showing images from a trio of CCTV cameras. The officer was about to commence a sequence of footage when a knock at the door paused his actions. All three men turned to ascertain the interruption.

A fellow security officer entered. 'I have been asked to bring DI Stone to join you,' he stated, stepping aside to allow Harriet to enter. She thanked the officer, and he departed, closing the door behind him. Brief introductions were made, and Turner stepped to the rear, allowing Harriet to take up his position nearest the monitors.

The security officer clicked, tapped, and double-clicked a series of keys on his console and the frozen image on the central monitor began to play. He provided a running commentary as the footage played.

'These images are from the camera in the exhibit room from first thing this morning before the gallery opened to the public. You can clearly see that the picture was already hung on the wall.' He paused the footage, tapped a key, and the CCTV image on the monitor to the left came to life. 'The same is evident on the camera footage recorded after closing yesterday evening.' The others in the room followed his narration while their focus remained fixed on the monitors. 'We did not need to review the CCTV recordings back too far to discover the point at which the picture was hung on the wall. It was, in fact, only 15 minutes before the gallery's closure yesterday evening.' He tapped a single key. The final image began to play. Turner, Tate and Harriet stood entranced at the screen of the third monitor as the CCTV footage played back. They anxiously anticipated what they were about to witness but could not foresee what the images would reveal.

They continued to watch the footage as the final straggle of visitors passed through the room. After a minute or so, the gallery attendant rose from their chair and left the room.

'At this point, the attendant, Karen Morley, left to check the other interconnecting rooms and to probably inform the remaining visitors to begin making their way to the exits.' As he finished his sentence, a striking woman appeared on the captured CCTV images. She entered the exhibit room from the opposite entrance from where the attendant had just departed. They continued to watch intently as the recording ran through its sequence.

Nobody spoke. Each was captivated by the images before them.

An air of curiosity coupled with the edginess of apprehension absorbed those present. From the moment the woman entered the frame, it left little doubt in the viewers' minds, that the woman, dressed in leather with more than a splash of red, was indeed Lena Johnson. She was most definitely making a statement. They continued to watch as she removed the frame from her shoulder bag and hung the picture. The time sequence in the corner of the screen read 17:42. The frozen image on the centre monitor changed as the security officer cued another sequence of captured CCTV footage.

'The external camera at the riverside picks up the woman's arrival at 17:28. She then passes through security at 17:33.' The images on the screen continually changed from one camera to the next as the CCTV tracked the woman dressed in red through the gallery to the 4th floor. Again, the atmosphere in the control room remained reticent.

Harriet was the first to comment. 'She is definitely making every effort to be noticed from how she is dressed to ensuring every camera captures her movements from her point of entry to the moment she exits the building.'

'I don't believe she has changed her appearance,' interjected Tate, standing to address the others in the room, 'I think her flamboyant attire is a statement of her presumptuousness and nothing more. She wants us to see her. She made sure she stood out from the crowds. It's all an act, part of the performance, done purely to be ostentatious.'

The security officer had cued the CCTV back to the point where Lena had hung the picture. 'I believe this final piece of footage may well be significant.' He played the sequence on the central monitor at half speed. After spending a moment viewing her work, Lena could be seen purposely turning towards the camera in the corner of the room and fixing her gaze. Staring directly at the lens, she slowly mouthed two aphonic words.

'Hello Tate!'

30

'The work from your previous visit looks to be healing well,' declared Sean, running his fingers across the inked area between her shoulder blades. 'There is still some scabbing but nothing of concern. It appears you have followed my instructions and maintained a daily routine of applying coconut oil to the area.'

'It has been a little tricky to reach at times. I am missing long soaks in the bath, though.' Sean chuckled as he tried desperately to prevent an image from forming of the beautiful woman sitting before him, lying naked in a bath of foam and bubbles. The image dissipated as he quickly moved the conversation forward.

'So, correct me if I am wrong, we are working on the figure of the man at the rear left of the picture. The one who appears to be drinking,' Sean affirmed, pointing to the area he had described on a colour printout of the original painting.

'Yes. It is an image of Samson drinking from the jawbone of an ass to quench his thirst after slaying a thousand men with the very same bone,' replied Lena, looking at the picture the tattooist held forward as she started to unbutton her loose-fitting black shirt. The bathtub image began to reanimate within Sean's head. He made an excuse to absolve himself from the situation while his client undressed.

'If you are still happy to sit with your bra on, as you did the last time, that would be fine. However, rather than lying down, it would probably be more comfortable if you could straddle the cradle chair. It would make it far easier to work in the area you have chosen to have tattooed today.' Sean moved away and busied himself, preparing his inks and cartridges.

Several minutes later, he looked across to his work area and was happy to see Lena straddling the chair, chest down. He moved his workstation alongside his client.

'There is a large amount of shadowing in that area, so I'm afraid, once again, I will have to pack a reasonable amount of ink into some sections to get the toning just right.'

'That's fine. As I have said before, I find the pain strangely satisfying.'

'The colouring of the main figure will be within the more sensitive areas of the flanks and rear ribs. Just let me know if you need a break. Remember, it's ok to tap out at any point. Even the toughest sometimes require a moment's respite from the needle.'

Lena looked back over her shoulder and replied with a cheeky wink of her eye. Sean knew there would be no breaks until he instigated one. The client seemed to relish the discomfort associated with the needles as if she welcomed it as some form of punishment.

Firstly, he needed to prepare the area of Lena's back where he would be working during today's session. He would ready the skin by shaving away any downy hair or dead skin cells with a razor. He would then washed the area with a non-alcohol based antiseptic known in the tattooing world as Green Soap. This would sanitise and cleanse the skin. He turned back to the client with the razor in his hand.

'I just need to—'

'That's fine. I am sure it's not the first bra you have needed to undo,' jested Lena, this time without turning her head, her voice laced with cheekiness. Sean unclasped the strap of the crimson bra and continued to shave the area. As he pulled the razor across the skin, Lena suddenly sat up. The blade nicked her skin.

'Oh shit, I'm so sorry,' exclaimed Sean. Lena ignored the remark as she turned to face the tattooist.

'I almost forgot,' professed Lena, cradling the cups of her bra to her breasts as she leant across with her free hand to reach for her handbag. She removed a small glass vile. 'I remembered you mentioning about how people are now getting memorial tattoos. Using ink mixed with a small amount of cremation ashes from the person they are getting inked in memory of. I would like you to do the same for me.' She handed the tattooist the vile. 'I would be grateful if you would mix those with a red ink when you are blending colours today.'

'Would it be rude to ask whose ashes you wish to be bonded with eternally?'

Nonchalantly, she replied.

'Just someone who has died recently.'

Bethnal Green

London, England

31

Harriet had driven directly from her spinning class after receiving Tate's answerphone message, so before returning to the CID room at Bethnal Green, she had put the wheels in motion to commence an investigation while sitting in her car behind the gallery. She had contacted the Scenes of Crime team to retrieve the picture and process the room. A Forensic Unit was most probably already on its way to the scene. Harriet had also contacted DS Iain Richards to rally the team for an immediate meeting on her return. Tate had agreed to gather a series of photos of the scene on his phone before joining Harriet.

On her arrival back at the station, she checked in briefly with DS Richards before knocking on the door of her senior officer, DCS Gibbs and informing him of the recent incident and change in circumstances regarding the Narcissus. It resulted in him giving her the authority to upgrade the Narcissus investigation once more and for Tate to act as a consulting officer. Harriet was in the glass-walled office she called the fishbowl when Tate was shown into the incident room by a uniformed officer.

'In here, Tate,' she called, 'come on through,' before turning her attention to her colleague at the nearest desk. 'Would you also join us, Iain?' All three gathered around Harriet's desk, Tate sharing the pictures he had captured on his phone before DS Richards transferred the images via Bluetooth to his desktop and sent hard copies to the incident room printer.

Ten minutes later, Harriet and Tate stood in front of the investigation board at the far side of the incident room, ready to address her team.

'OK, let's gather round crew,' announced Harriet, using the nautical collective noun she frequently used when referring to her team. Those present paused tasks they were currently undertaking and gave their full attention to their lead investigator. Some spun their chairs, others scooted to more appropriate positions or reparked their backsides on the corners of desks. Armed and ready with pens and notebooks, each was poised to receive details of delegated tasks. Her crew were mustered and ready for the call to arms. 'Firstly, I believe most of you have met DCI Randall,' she professionally used his ranking title, 'of the Arts and Antiquities Investigation Department. DCI Randall will be acting as a consulting officer, liaising between our Narcissus murder inquiries and his own department's case of the missing Caravaggio.'

'Morning,' he declared in conjunction with a simple nod of the head.

'As DS Richards will have informed you, there has been a significant development resulting in a strong possibility of the reappearance of Lena Johnson, aka the Narcissus.' Heads nodded in silence. Each detective was fully aware of the importance attached to the change of circumstances.

'A picture, possibly a new murder scene, was hung in a public exhibit area at the Tate Modern. CCTV recordings confirm the hanging of the picture just before the gallery's closure yesterday. Further footage from this morning shows a number of visitors viewing the said picture before the room was cleared and secured. DCI Randall was contacted by his brother Turner Randall, a curator at the gallery, soon after the discovery of the unexplainable picture. DCI Randall, his brother and I have subsequently viewed further CCTV footage, which clearly shows a woman dressed in red hanging the aforementioned painting. We believe this individual is not attempting to conceal their identity, but quite the opposite, we suspect the radical appearance has been created to ensure the individual is seen and is easily distinguishable from the crowds.' Harriet paused momentarily. Every person in the room waited apprehensively as if what came next would be a bombshell. But there would be no thunderbolt or shocking revelation. There was no need for speculation or assumption. Each was aware of the direction in which this was all pointing.

'Iain, could you run the footage please?' DS Richards pointed a remote device towards a large digital screen to the side of the investigation wall. Footage compiled from the gallery's surveillance cameras began to play. All eyes in the room scrutinised the images, the hum of the air conditioning unit being the only sound. A descriptive interpretation from Harriet occasionally broke the silence. All watched as the woman dressed in red wandered casually through the gallery's interconnecting rooms, looking purposely in the direction of each camera, deliberately holding a fixed gaze for the slightest moment too long.

'Despite the radical change of appearance, I think you will agree that this individual is, without a doubt, Lena Johnson. Her eye-catching attire and the manner in which she plays the cameras are all part of a twisted game. Along with the email recently received by DCI Randall and the next final piece of CCTV footage, it all points to an egotistical statement of vaingloriousness.' Harriet turned to DS Richards once again. He took his cue, and an edited close-up segment of footage began to run on the screen at half speed. Again, those present focussed their attention solely on the video feed. Each watched as the subject mouthed two words, each easily distinguishable and together delivering a message. All eyes then turned to Harriet and Tate.

'I think that pretty much sums up all I have just said. She is goading us to react. She is seeking the attention she needs to satisfy her narcissistic needs. If the subject of the picture she hung at the gallery is what we believe it is, then she has definitely got our attention,' stated Harriet as she gave DS Richards a further nod. A close-up of the picture hung in the gallery filled the screen. She turned to Tate on her opposite side.

'Having seen the picture first-hand, would you care to walk us through the details?' Tate stepped forward to enable him to pick out individual aspects within the image.

'We believe in the first instance that the format of the picture is a photograph. It appears that the skin of the individual who is the focus of the work has been covered with some form of paint before the photograph was taken. The individual is tied to the chair at the points of the wrist and ankles.' Tate pointed at the specifics he was describing. 'Blood pooling is evident in the immediate area around the base of the chair and there appears to be a further volume of blood across the individual's torso. A length of what looks like plastic tubing can be seen running from the left forearm to what looks like a plastic jug at the foot of the chair. From the focal point of the camera, there are no obvious signs of further trauma to the body. We would most probably be right to assume the individual is deceased due to the significant volume of blood loss.' Tate again changed positions, this time stepping back to allow Harriet to address her team.

'Thank you, DCI Randall. What are your first thoughts on the possible application of paint to the victim's skin?' asked Harriet as she moved closer to the enlarged digital image to scrutinise the area in question.

Tate continued. 'During the Narcissus' first murder campaign, the victims' bodies were left purposely posed to replicate various works by Caravaggio, who we subsequently have discovered is an ancestor of Lena's paternal family lineage. Caravaggio worked in oils and used life models to bring realism to his works. It could be possible to conceive that the victim's skin has been painted, possibly with oil paints or acrylics, to create a real-life three-dimensional painting.'

Harriet's nodding head and facial expression relayed her agreement with Tate's hypothesis, but her eyes were drawn back to an area to the rear of the enlarged photographic image. 'What do you suppose those are to the rear right of the picture? Again, they look to have been over painted?'

'Could be plastic curtain walling?' suggested DS Quinn, a bearded, heavy-set detective perched on the corner of a desk. 'It's commonly used in the butchery industry. I believe they are what's called 'Strip Curtains'. The partial surface in the left-hand front of the picture could also be the corner of a butcher's table.'

'Good shout,' declared Harriet. DS George Quinn was the veteran of Harriet's team and a stalwart she could regularly rely on. 'If it is the location of a murder scene, the premises are most likely to be empty and unused, or someone would have reported it by now. George, look into butchery businesses in the Greater London area which have closed in the last twelve months. While you are at it, it would probably be a good idea to check the industrial buildings list for abattoir closures, too.'

'No problem, Ma'am.' DS Quinn responded respectably to his much younger senior officer. George Quinn held Harriet in high regard. Mutual amounts of reverence flowed between them. Harriet had always advocated surrounding herself with those more knowledgeable and experienced than herself. Having the best people within your closest circles would lend a hand to a coordinated and cooperative unit when challenging situations arose. Harriet was confident that her crew were competent and committed to the cause.

'The window to the left of the picture, Ma'am?' enquired DC Jake Evans, pointing with his biro in the direction of the screen, an inquisitive look breaking through a speculative squinting frown. 'Iain, can you zoom in on the window?' Within seconds, the image expanded, filling the screen with the area around the window. DS Richards continued manipulating the image, sharpening the definition and filtering the pixelation to produce a clearer reproduction of the close-up.

Jake continued his conjecture. 'The newspaper covering the glass. If we could read the print, then maybe we could identify the article and which paper printed it.'

'No need,' injected DS Quinn once more, 'I'd recognise it anywhere. I pick up a copy on my way home each Wednesday. It's the Newham Recorder. It has a local distribution around the Newham area, including East and West Ham.'

'The paper looks to be untarnished. It would have probably yellowed if it had been there for a while,' Tate interjected. 'It could well be a purposely directed clue. Lena once again wishes for her work as the Narcissus to be seen.'

'Great work, crew. Let's focus our butchery lead within those areas to start. Sarika? Could you support George with the initial inquiries?' Sarika blew a kiss to DS Quinn. He remained stone-faced, but the gesture did not go unnoticed, and a ripple of chuckles crept around the room.

'Iain. I have a gut feeling about this one. Take DCs Evans and Thompson and get out on the streets. Start with East Ham High Street. In particular, any vacant premises.' Each nodded an affirmation. Harriet turned to DS Stevens, who had been heading the Narcissus investigation since it had been downscaled during Lena's prolonged disappearance.

'I would like you to run point with me on this one, Andy. You've been the one true constant on this from the start. It will be a good opportunity for you.'

'Thank you, Ma'am,' replied the recently promoted Sergeant. Others in the room gestured their endorsement and concurrence with the notion.

'Two gallery attendants and a security team at the Tate Modern are still to be interviewed. Ok, to leave that in your hands, Andy?' This time, there was no further need to acknowledge her edict. The Narcissus case had been reinstated as priority one and would again be the team's primary focus. It was time to set the investigative ball rolling.

'Forensics should have removed the picture by now. It's most probably on its way to the Lab for trace. Do you fancy a trip south of the river?' enquired Harriet, her question directed towards Tate and laced with presupposition.

32

The kaleidoscope of multicoloured panels produced a surreal oneiric atmosphere for all who passed through the tunnel. The external structure of the Adams Plaza bridge, along with its capacious entrance, resembled the launch pad of a futuristic space dock. In contrast, its inner space played with the mind like a hallucinogenic 1960s acid trip.

Steve Brooks had passed through the geometric rainbowed artwork and was awaiting security clearance at the double-bowed reception desk, which was backed by a floor-to-ceiling wall of deep pink marble. Unlike the drones of city workers clad in three-piece suits, Steve felt like an incongruous alien on each occasion he had needed to visit the building. Fortunately, these visits were few and far between. To the security and front desk staff, he was just another tiny fish in a very big glass bowl. His hoody, jeans and high-top canvas boots most probably went unnoticed due to the continual throngs of couriers who passed through the lobby on an hourly basis.

Having been issued a visitor's pass, he had ridden the lift to the 24th floor and was again waiting in an entrance lobby for a secretary to check his credentials. The reception area of The City Chronicle publishing agency had numerous acclaimed front pages dressing its walls. Headlines of war, treachery, murder and deceit hung in juxtaposition to stories of courage, jubilance and success. Steve perused the frames as he waited, wondering if one day he too would capture an iconic shot that would still be talked of many years later.

'Mr Brooks. You can go through now. It's the fourth door on the left.'

'Thanks,' declared Steve as his eyes followed the framed headline stories along the corridor wall to the office he sought.

He knocked twice, his eyes fixed on a front page of John Lennon's assassination.

'Come in.'

As he entered, he was met by a firm handshake and a patting of the opposite shoulder.

'Brooks. Good to see you. Seeing you being a rarity. But those are some great shots you've been getting recently.' The City Chronicle had become a good client for Steve in recent years. However, his visits to the building had become less frequent due to how the digital age was evolving the industry, with captured images now being sent directly from the scene to the papers.

'Thanks,' said Steve once again, 'It's not only the fight to get that all-important picture but a scramble to edit and submit it first.'

'Journalism has always been dog eat dog,' quipped the photo editor.

'And it's becoming increasingly more difficult to ensure the dog doesn't go hungry,' replied Steve more in earnest than jest.

'I guess the doggie wants me to throw him a bone,' the editor continued his witticism for what was probably only his own benefit. 'You mentioned on the phone that you had received the offer of an exclusive.' Steve felt a quiver of apprehension ripple from inside. Goosebumps popped up on his arms and the hairs stood to attention. A shiver fluttered down his spine, and his mouth instantaneously dried up.

Ever since seeing the murder scene in the flesh, Steve had questioned his own conscience and how ethical it would be to publish the images he had captured. Since becoming a paparazzi, he had pushed his morals to one side, and this was the first time he had begun to question his principles. But it was also his first real chance of an iconic front page, and with that came the opportunity to uncover the pot of gold at the end of his rainbow.

'I was contacted by someone, a woman, who claimed to be the Narcissus. Remember the one?' He faltered, hesitant of the next words. 'Responsible for the killings of the art collectors last summer.'

'How could I not remember? It provided worthy front page news for weeks.' At the first mention of the Narcissus, his interest was piqued. Whatever Brooks had been offered, it could only mean that the Narcissus had resurfaced or was planning to do so.

'I have no idea, whatsoever, why she contacted me.'

'It doesn't matter why, only that she did,' replied the photo editor, ravenous for a breaking headline.

'The thing is Ed,' said Steve, who still found it somewhat amusing to have a photo editor called Edward, 'I'm not sure if I even want to be part of this.' Edward frowned. Unsure of what this was and, more importantly, why Brooks would not want an exclusive laid upon a plate for him.

Apprehensively, Steve continued. 'She asked me to record her legacy.

She said she was going to complete the work she had started last summer. She wants it photographed for the public to see the truth and the reasons behind the killings.' Edward could see and feel in his gut an opportunity too good to be missed. He could not understand why Brooks looked so sullen.

'I was in two minds whether to come here today or to take what I have straight to the police.' For the first time, Edward noticed the folder in Brooks' hand.

Steve looked Ed directly in the eye. 'She has already killed again.'

Ed held Steve's soulless stare.

'She offered me exclusive access to photograph the body before the authorities were even aware of a crime scene. And do you know what, Ed? I went. I bloody went. And I photographed the dead man's body. A man who more than likely has been declared missing by his family. Someone's husband or some poor child's father. I took pictures of a murder scene to make money. And do you know what gripes me most? At the time, I didn't think twice about it.'

Edward sensed a foreboding anxiety rising within Brooks, and the photo editor within Edward recognised a set of favourable circumstances that were too good to be missed. He just needed to stall Brooks' trepidation.

'May I?' Edward enquired, motioning to the folder, which he assumed contained a set of photographic prints. Steve handed over the folder, and his photo editor spread the contents across the desk. Both of the men looked fixedly at the cadaverous images. Each man captured in the morbidity of the subject matter. Each lost and reticent in their thoughts.

Steve was the first to break the haunting silence. 'Don't get me wrong, I am completely aware of the possibilities and prospects a scoop like this could generate. However, I am also mindful of the potential fallout if I were to become involved in any way or form. It is conceivably a make-or-break opportunity. But we cannot brush to one side the death of the journalist who got too close the last time and the art dealer who is now serving a sentence for his involvement and is nursing the scars of the stigmata after his attempted crucifixion at the hands of the Narcissus.'

'I completely understand your concerns, but we must weigh up the possible outcomes,' declared Edward, knowing he may need to coerce Brooks in a favourable direction, 'Do the prospects surpass the dilemmas? We can manage the risks to ensure an advantageous outcome for all involved. The paper would take overall responsibility for anything that is published, and I can guarantee we will have your back at all times.' The photo editor continued to justify his reasoning and convince Brooks, thus ensuring his decision was the correct one for the good of the paper. 'Of course, we will protect your anonymity and any subsequent lawful inquiries will be safeguarded with an unidentified source agreement.' The editor could sense that Brooks was considering his options. He knew all too well the clear-cut way to sway a decision in the paper's direction. Everybody could be bought one way or another. He turned one of the pictures over and wrote a figure across the back before casually sliding it across the table in Brooks' direction. Steve reached forward with one hand, knowing that a financial offer had literally just been put on the table. He remained poker-faced and gazed down at the propoundment. He allowed the smallest indication of a smile to form. Enough to suggest he might consider such an offer but leaving room in his expression to warrant a further proposition. Edward wrote a second figure on the reverse of another photograph and again wordlessly manoeuvred it towards Brooks for approval. This time, he nodded modestly. The new offer was much more substantial. He allowed his smile to broaden. The photo editor mirrored the gracious expression, jubilant in getting his man.

Little did he know that the photographs had already been posted on the dark web.

East Ham

London, England

33

The High Street was bustling with a hive of activity as swarms of pedestrians dodged, weaved and sidestepped countless kerb mounted delivery vans, fast food scooters and commercial wheelie bins, each adding to the chaos that spilled out across every square foot of the shop fronted pavement. A clangour of vehicle engines, blaring horns and a jabbering of voices gave rise to inharmonious pandemonium.

The three detectives had separated shortly after exiting the squad car. Each searched a section on either side of the street for the small paper covered window. They remained in contact via their two-way radios, strategically attached to the lapel of their tactical vests.

The majority of the shops did not have street-side basement windows, and it was not long before DC Thompson's voice came through over the radio.

'I think I found it, Sarge! What appears to be a boarded up kosher butchery business at the north end of the street. Next to Blooms Flower shop just past Balthazar Wines.'

'Sit tight, Greg, remain outside until we arrive,' came the reply from DS Richards, 'Can you see anything further through the window?'

'Negative. The newspaper is obscuring the view.'

Five minutes later, the three detectives had gained entry to the property through a rear entrance, having each scaled a high stone wall running the entirety of a narrow back alley.

DC Evans had remained outside the back door in case of unwanted visitors or over curious neighbours. The remaining two officers entered the building before once again separating. With the majority of the property's lighting having been vandalised since the closure of the business, each officer had to illuminate their search pathways with police issue Defender Lumos torches. DS Richards searched the ground and upper floors for further signs of disturbance and the possibility of squatters. DC Thompson drew the shorter straw and the task of descending the stairs to the basement to confirm they were at the correct location and that the crime scene they had borne witness to in the photograph was indeed that of a kill site.

DS Richards had just descended the stairs back to the ground floor when movement to his right broke through his torch beam, and he was momentarily blinded by the 230 lumens of an identical torch. The figure behind the beam rushed forward in DS Richards' direction. It took a moment for his eyes to readjust to the increased light levels as the effulgence flooded the room that would have once been the premise's main butchery preparation area.

The sudden confrontation caused DS Richards to take a backward step, and his hand instantaneously reached for his belt and the bright yellow electrical taser.

'Hold your position. I am an armed police officer. Slowly place your hands on your head,' Iain instructed as his eyes refocused on his surroundings. He extended his arms forward, the taser firmly within his grip, his fingers gently teasing the trigger. He would not think twice about discharging the weapon should the circumstances require him. 'I will not ask you again! On your knees and place your hands upon your head.' The figure before him leant forward, his hands on either side of his hips, a jumble of indistinguishable words fumbling from his mouth. A red target laser appeared in the centre of the intruder's chest. 'For one last time. On your knees, hands on your head, or I will discharge my weapon!' The intruder raised his head just a fraction, and DS Richards caught his first identifiable glimpse of the assailant's face. 'For god's sake, Greg. I was seconds from pulling the trigger. I almost zapped you with 50,000 volts.'

The young Detective Constable stood motionless and abruptly vomited across his polished shoes. He motioned with a pointed finger over his shoulder as he fought to regain his composure, mouthing silent words between each accentuated breath. The senior detective de-activated and holstered his weapon. Both men stood in silence, each taking a moment to decrease their heart rates and regain a hold on the situation. DC Thompson wiped his mouth with the back of his hand. The pungent taste of acrid bile lingered in his mouth and nostrils. Eventually, he spluttered just two audible words.

'He's downstairs.'

DS Richards cautiously descended the steps towards the cellar below. His younger colleague's reaction had been enough to pre-empt the horrific sight he was about to encounter. His stomach tightened in anticipation of the scene he was moments from experiencing. A partially closed, aged wooden door obscured his view further into the room. With an outstretched arm, he tentatively eased the door to one side. The image his mind had somewhat painted was far from the scene that unfolded before him. His eyes again took a moment to adjust to his new surroundings and contemplate the bloodbath spilling across the small, poorly lit cellar.

And there the victim sat.

The painted human figure tied to a chair in the dead centre of the room, a room where no matter in which direction you cast your eyes, the view was one of blood.

Copious amounts of blood.

A substantial quantity had pooled around the victim and the chair, where it emulsified with the oily paint substance that trickled down the victim's limbs. Strangely, no arterial blood patterning was sprayed across the walls, and no blood residue had spattered on adjacent work surfaces. Just puddles and puddles of blood. Rivulets of the red coagulating liquid, mixed with pink foaming bile and dark regurgitated vomit to form a rufous discharge that spewed from the victim's mouth.

DS Richards stood at the doorway. He knew better than to enter the room. He turned and shone his torch in the direction from which he had descended. No blooded footprints on the stairs meant Greg had also ventured no further. He reached into his pocket and retrieved his phone. He wished to speak directly with DI Stone. His call was answered almost immediately.

'What have we got then, Iain?'

'A bloody bloodbath, Ma'am. That's what we've got.'

East Ham
London, England

34

DI Stone had departed the Bethnal Green police station at the soonest possible convenience. She had briefly gathered together the remainder of her team to bring them up to speed with the change in circumstances since the discovery of the body. Members of her team refocused their investigations where necessary, whilst others used the new information to pinpoint their current lines of enquiry. She had also telephoned DS Stevens regarding the recent developments to keep him informed while he continued his inquiries at the Tate Modern gallery. Harriet knew all too well that she would still arrive at the murder site ahead of the Scenes of Crime team and would have to wait for them to conduct a primary walkthrough and perform their preliminary investigations before she would be allowed anywhere near the location of the body. Still, she felt compelled to be present at the scene to be readily accessible if and when further details emerged. A reignited fire in her belly to gain an advantage and move one step closer to finally apprehending the Narcissus fed her appetite to succeed and drove her determination to seek justice.

Harriet had parked the BMW 320d as close to the secure perimeter tape as the busy High Street would allow her. A local PC had checked her credentials and lifted the tape, allowing Harriet to join her fellow detective at the property's street-side entrance. DC Jake Evans explained that the rear entrance to the property had been secured, and SOCO were due to arrive shortly. He then gave his senior officer an overview of the current situation. DS Richards appeared from within the premises as Jake finished his summary.

'Ma'am', he acknowledged, addressing the lead investigator's presence. 'You certainly wasted little time in joining the party.'

'And you look a little pale, Iain!'

' You should see DC Thompson. He saw his breakfast for a second time today and was seconds from doing a 50,000-volt tango with my taser. He's currently repolishing his shoes while S&Ping the access to the cellar.'

'Secure and preserve if you are acronym acrimonious,' came the answer as a new voice joined the conversation. It was followed by the briefest of chuckles as a blonde bespectacled woman, half-dressed in white coveralls and carrying an oversized Gladstone bag, ducked under the crime tape. 'Hi Harry,' she beamed cheerily, 'How was the holiday? Did you remember the Cornish fudge you promised me?' The new arrival shook hands with the trio of detectives.

'Far too short as usual. And yes, it's on the worksurface in my kitchen, next to the wine rack,' replied Harriet, continuing the gaiety of the exchange.

'Sounds like a girlie night in is on the cards. Paired with the latest rom-com on Netflix and we could have ourselves a fabulous evening.'

Senior forensic investigator and close friend of Harriet's, Penelope Carter-Moore, was held in high regard by her peers as a leading authoritative figure in the field of criminalistics. However, her incomparable work ethic meant her dress code was more often 'white PPE' than 'black tie' and her infectious smile was regularly hidden behind a faceless protective mask. Despite Harriet's toils and endeavours in matchmaking and not for the want of trying, Penny's dedication and commitment to the job left little time for the allure and mystique of romance. When time permitted, the furthest she ventured from the job was curling up on the sofa with Mr Tibbs, her shorthaired Siamese, a steaming mug of hot chocolate and a good paperback crime thriller. She was still very much a catch waiting to be hooked.

'Who and what awaits us on this fine autumnal afternoon?' enquired Penny, focussing her questioning in Harriet's direction. Harriet diverted the enquiry and raised her eyes in DS Richards' direction.

'Appears to be a single male, possibly deceased—'

'Possibly? Please don't tell me that those first on the scene didn't think to check?' Penny declared with more than a hint of exasperation.

'When you see the crime scene for yourself,' asserted DS Richards, batting the allegation back in the forensic officer's direction, 'you will understand why we have needed to, shall we say, 'tread' carefully with this one. I think we can safely assume the victim is deceased.'

Penny placed her bag to one side and began to pull her white coveralls up and around the remainder of her torso. 'Best not waste any more time then,' she lifted a leg, stretching an elasticated overshoe over her current footwear. 'How was the victim found?'

DS Richards was about to reply but was beaten to a response by Harriet. 'We responded to a tip-off by way of a picture of the crime scene having been hung in plain sight at the Tate Modern gallery. CCTV footage clearly identifies the individual responsible for doing so, and the same individual is more than likely accountable for our crime scene. It seems that a certain someone wishes to make a grand re-entrance.' The assertion caused Penny to stop midway through covering her second shoe. She looked to her friend and colleague for something further. 'Tate received a new taunting email towards the end of our break. Once again, it was in a lyrical format and from a Neptune's Finger song and signed Narcissus. And she makes no qualms in ensuring she is completely conspicuous to the gallery's surveillance. In fact, she plays to the cameras.' The blitheness could be seen to vanish from Penny's composure. Although not directly impacted by the Narcissus' previous exploits, she had witnessed each crime scene and had seen first-hand the effect it had left on those embroiled in the aftermath. Her concern turned to her friend.

'Are you sure you are OK with this, Harry?' The two men remained silent, for they both could foretell their senior officer's impending answer. They had both worked alongside DI Stone long enough to gauge the situation.

'Absolutely.' Harriet stood fast. 'Lena is not the only one with unfinished business. There is a crime scene in there, and Lena is probably the perpetrator. If she has indeed returned with intentions to once again inflict punishment on others for their crimes, then I hope she is ready to meet her match. She may have had the upper hand the last time our paths crossed, but I will not rest until she is locked up tightly in a padded cell and I have personally thrown away the key. So how about we get this investigation underway?'

Penny eased the coverall hoodie over her ponytail and manipulated the elasticated opening around her face before reaching into her bag and handing Harriet a sealed pair of coveralls.

'Ok. Let's go take a butcher's. Sorry, I couldn't resist.'

35

Further Scenes of Crime personnel had arrived while Harriet donned the anti-contamination overalls and Penny readied herself for a primary walkthrough of the crime site. An evidence tent was deployed within minutes to minimise the field of vision into the building, create a common entry point and also to provide a concealed area for evidence collection and, eventually, the body before it was removed for autopsy. The crowds would, without fail, begin to gather at the perimeter tape as soon as the gossip and rumour mills promulgated. Along with the exclusion zone, it would further disrupt the already busy shopping street.

Harriet appointed DC Evans the primary role of logging all entries and exits. He was also instructed to maintain surveillance of those who had gathered at the tape for any sightings of the suspect. It is not uncommon for the perpetrator of a crime to return to the scene and inconspicuously mingle with the crowd to prolong the thrill of the kill by observing the aftermath. And Lena was most definitely audacious enough to do such a thing. DS Richards was to start door-to-door inquiries and gathering witness statements relating to the comings and goings associated with the premises and the rear access. He was also tasked with ascertaining the property's owner and anyone associated with the current lease agreement.

Penny had agreed to have Harriet join her for the primary walkthrough of the crime scene. However, she insisted that she stay three steps behind and not touch a thing. Having worked on many cases together, Harriet would abide by the request, as she held her friend and colleague in high esteem.

Moving from the common entry point that had once been the entrance to the shop, Penny moved slowly through the adjoining rooms, identifying and recording any signs of potential evidence, disturbance and anything untoward and out of keeping with the remainder of the site. She strategically placed the occasional evidence marker and photographed all within its proximity. Anything and everything could hold evidence vital to the investigation and, ultimately, a conviction for the crime. The evidence along this pathway would be collected and catalogued first to create a free passage for those coming and going to the primary scene. It would be the focus of the first arriving SOCO members.

It became apparent as they moved through the ground floor of the building that access to the cellar was most probably made through the rear of the building. However, no stone could be left unturned and examining each area was as important as another. There was distinct evidence that forced entry at some point had been made through the rear door. Penny captured her primary photographs and recorded specific details for her fellow SOCOs to focus their investigations and evidence collection.

'Are those tyre tracks?' enquired Harriet, who had followed Penny's lead but had also made her own first observations as they had moved through the building. Penny looked across in the direction relating to Harriet's remark. Two parallel impressions could be made out at sporadic intervals within the dust and detritus of the shop's rear yard. Penny listed a final observation of the area around the rear door.

'Let's take a look, shall we?' The two women moved towards the area in question, each paying particular attention to every planted footstep, both aware of the possibility of disturbing important evidence. They stood together and traced the route of the irregular furrows that seemed to define a line from the gate at the rear of the yard before ending at a pair of bulkhead doors. 'These most probably open straight into this end of the cellar. If I were to hazard a guess, it was once the delivery point for carcasses ready for the butchery process.'

Harriet nodded in agreement as she continued to gauge the impressions. 'Maybe the victim was pushed or pulled in with some sort of trolley.'

Penny continued to scrutinise the markings on the ground. She stood between the pair of lines and looked along their line of travel. 'I think a stronger possibility would be a wheelchair. Look at the distance between the tracks. It's quite narrow, and at points, the lines are scuffed out, which could account for the wheels slewing due to a change in direction.'

'Which could conceivably point towards the victim having been murdered or incapacitated elsewhere,' pondered Harriet as she followed Penny alongside the tramlines in the direction of the yard's rear gate.

'Or simply gagged and restrained,' proposed Penny as she knelt to examine the frame of the gateway. She held her camera forward and ran off a burst of close-up shots before reaching into her forensics bag and removing a transparent evidence envelope and a set of tweezers. As

Harriet looked on, she used the tweezers to remove a small sample from the framework before carefully placing it within the sealable envelope. She held it up for Harriet to view. 'Black material, possibly polyester. It may well be from snagged clothing.' She took another sequence of photographs before turning back along the line of travel. 'Shall we?' she invited, sidestepping Harriet as she returned towards the building and the cellar bulkhead. Head down, eyes forward, she surveyed the ground ahead before placing her next step. Slowly and methodically, she worked the trail. Occasionally, she would stop, place an evidence identification marker, capture another series of images and record her initial observations. The smallest detail could be vital later when accumulating the timeline of the crime.

Just before the two investigators reached the rear of the property again, Penny stopped, holding out a hand to prevent Harriet from moving forward. She pointed to an area where the concrete slab gave way to a grassy border. A tyre impression with a good deal of tread ridging was distinguishable in the turf.

'It looks extremely likely that a wheel has slid to the edge of the pathway and left us a perfect imprint,' Penny expressed before placing a further evidence marker and repeating her recording of evidence. 'I will get a forensic technician to create a casting of this ASAP. You can never be sure of the local weather reports. I would hate for a sudden downpour to wash away such a detailed impression.' Harriet nodded in agreement, but something further had caught her eye. Her curiosity got the better of her as she stepped towards the cellar hatchway. Penny reacted instantly, clutching her colleague at the elbow as she made to pass.

'Hold on there, Missy. My lead, remember?' Harriet stopped dead in her tracks, allowing Penny to proceed. The large handles at the centre of the bulkhead doors appeared to have been tied together with what looked like a red ribbon. Penny once again photographed a series of shots, each one tightening the angle of the image until a detailed close-up revealed that it was no ordinary red ribbon. On closer inspection, uniformed writing could be seen to scroll across its length.

Enter if you dare. Happy Halloween   Enter if you dare. Happy Halloween

As the two women moved side by side to further examine the band of writing, it became apparent that someone had penned additional text within the space before the scrolling wording repeated.

Enter if you dare. Happy Halloween TATE Enter if you dare. Happy Halloween

The additional word could easily be seen to have been written by hand with a black marker pen.

'She's got some balls! I'll give her that,' proclaimed Harriet.

'At least that pretty much confirms the perpetrator of our crime scene,' added Penny as she removed another transparent envelope and tweezers. 'She is not hiding the fact either. I would hazard a guess that fingerprint analysis, trace and fibres will all point that way too. She is not going to have covered her tracks. She wants the world to know that the Narcissus is responsible for the killing.' Penny focused on the neatly tied ribbon and cautiously began to unfurl the bow with the tweezers. It came away with little effort, and Harriet held forward the collection bag. Penny assiduously eased the ribbon through its opening. Zipped in, concealed and preserved, the pair observed the bagged evidence.

Penny was the first to speak. 'She has used pinking shears to cut the ends. The serrated crimping pattern is easier to match than standard scissor blades. It looks like the Narcissus is purposely leaving a trail of evidence.'

'Again, she is self-possessed and callous enough to taunt the investigation whilst showing no disregard whatsoever for those ensnared in the horror of her crimes.' Harriet handed the envelope to Penny. 'I have never been so determined to catch a killer. The Narcissus' notoriety will not be remembered for her ghastly murderous acts, but it will be looked back upon for the way Lena was brought to justice before she could complete her vindictive campaign.' Penny could not deny the vehemence Harriet held towards the Narcissus and the trail of devastation and suffering she had left in her awake.

'If that is the case, we must focus on the here and now. Vital clues to put an end to this killing spree are clearly necessary. We need to complete our investigations. At some point, the Narcissus will make a mistake, fail to notice an oversight, or slip up and provide us with that one crucial piece of evidence that will lead us straight to her door. Trust me, all criminals, without fail, make an error at some point. It's our job to spot that discrepancy and use it to greater effect. I say we finish this walk through and get to the body. From what we have discovered so far, we are still to confirm this as a primary crime scene or whether the body has been transported here and we have a secondary scene on our hands.' Harriet nodded in agreement. Inside, she was chomping at the bit, but procedures were there to be followed and follow she did. Taking in every little detail as she walked back towards the property along the evidence-free path Penny was creating. This would allow those present to move freely through the building and continue their investigations with a reduced risk of contaminating the crime scene.

Penny spent several minutes photographing, documenting, and identifying areas for further forensic analysis around the area outside the rear door of the property. From this perspective, she also paid further attention to the area around the broken lock, the door's internal and external handles and the area on either side of the lock stile where hands would be placed to push the door closed. Happy that she had documented her initial findings for the remainder of the SOCOs to complete further detailed analysis, she motioned to Harriet, and they moved to the top of the stairs that led to the cellar below.

On the third step from the top sat DC Thompson, who jumped up on sight of the two investigators. 'Sorry, Ma'am. My legs were killing me. Well, not literally. But to be honest, my stomach still isn't feeling too great.'

'That's fine, Greg. This is Penny Carter-Moore, Senior Forensic Investigator. I am not sure if the two of you have met before.' Both parties exchanged pleasantries and DC Thompson stepped to one side.

'No one has been further than the bottom step. When you get down there, you will understand why. You best take this,' he said, handing his superior officer his torch. Penny took the cue and removed her own torch from her bag.

'There is a wooden chair in the anterior room,' declared Harriet, 'Grab it if you like and position yourself at the top of the stairs.' She could tell the younger officer was still shocked by his earlier discovery. She looked across at Penny, who nodded her consent that it would be acceptable to move the said chair.

'Thank you, Ma'am,' Greg affirmed as the two women shone their torches ahead and descended the remaining stairs into the tenebrosity below. 'And Ma'am, prepare yourself for the worst.' Harriet glanced over her shoulder but could no longer see Greg in the darkness of the unlit stairway.

The first thing illuminated by the beam of the torches was the underside of the bulkhead door, positioned to the left of the lower steps. An iron crowbar had been slid behind a pair of internal pull handles to prevent entry. It could easily have been replaced after an entry had been made. Harriet followed Penny's lead. Their torches traced a path across the opposite wall, the shafts of light illuminating sections of the room as each criss-crossed the other's beam. In the murkiness of the semi-darkness, the appearance of the walls was indiscernible. A look of dampness ran down every surface. As the torches swept further into the room, the two beams passed across a distinctive silhouette in the darkness. Both torches immediately diverted back in the direction they had travelled to re-illuminate the distinct profiled shape. The beams intersected and converged, both lighting the middle of the room.

And there he was.

A lone figure sat tied to a chair in the dead centre of the room.

And around the chair. A soup of dark crimson, viscous liquid that coagulated at its edge.

As their eyes adjusted to the sombre surroundings and the reality of what lay before them, both women stood transfixed, rooted to the final step of the stairs. Each said nothing. Each silently evaluating the situation. Each calculating the next move.

The reality of the horror manifested before them. The barefaced brutality of the crime scene suddenly became more perceptible. For the first time, the extent of the bloodbath became clearly visible to both investigators.

'Surely, that amount of blood cannot have come from the one victim?' declared Harriet as she continued to scrutinise the scene.

'The average adult has around ten pints of blood. Considering the coverage area, I agree that from where we stand, it appears to be a far greater amount. There also appears to be no substantial wounding to the body.' Harriet failed to respond. Her eyes were drawn to the edges of the room and the colouration that had seemingly been added to the walls and the surrounding area. The appearance created the illusion that you were physically walking into a painting. What looked like an oil-based paint had been applied to the surfaces around where the body sat. Brushstrokes added further texture, shadows, tones and highlights to the real-life composition. Streaks of the oily paint ran and dripped, mixing with the pooling blood to form multicoloured puddles around both the legs of the victim and upon the chair in which he was restrained.

'The Narcissus has created her own masterpiece. You could say she has taken realism to a whole new dimension.'

'Completely. I was thinking the same thing. It's as if she wants us to step into the picture itself,' replied Penny, her eyes moving to the floor between the stairs where they currently stood and the victim's chair. 'The first job will be collecting anti-contamination stepping plates from my van. We will need to preserve as much of the floor area as possible. The stepping plates will help to minimise the chance of contamination.'

'If you'd like to begin processing all you can from here, I'll get Greg to collect anything you need,' Harriet proposed, extending an empty hand in Penny's direction. 'I'm going to head back upstairs and check how door-to-door is going. With the property being on a busy high street, hopefully, someone must have seen something or maybe we might get lucky with an image from the multitude of shop security or on-street cams.'

Penny handed a bunch of keys to Harriet and retrieved her camera. She held the viewfinder to her eye to capture the next series of images. 'Can you also get one of the forensic team,' she called over her shoulder as she began to manipulate the camera's shutter, 'to get some Nomad lighting down here as soon as it is practical to do so. I will definitely require more light than a single bulb can offer.'

'Ok, will do,' came a reply from above.

Over the next couple of hours, Penny processed and documented the scene in close proximity to the victim. She worked methodically along paths from both the entrance stairway and the inside of the bulkhead doors. She had to be particularly careful in her approach, as she needed to work from one strategically placed stepping plate to another, not unlike crossing a series of stepping stones.

When Harriet returned, a perimeter of the stepping plates had been placed around the circumference of the victim and the chair, allowing the forensic investigator to process the body more easily. Penny had completed her preliminary assessment of the scene and was currently collecting trace and fibres.

'How are you doing, Pen?' came a familiar voice from behind. She had no reason to turn. She continued placing a strand of hair into a small plastic tube before sealing it in a clear evidence envelope.

'You can come across if you'd like. I don't have to tell you to stick to the stepping plates,' replied Penny as she labelled the sample in the envelope.

'You just did,' Harriet jested as she followed the pathway across the floor of amalgamating blood and paint. As ever, Harriet processed the scene emerging before her. She studied the victim and his surroundings, taking in every little detail. Penny continued to work the body, recording and documenting each stage of her examination on a digital recorder.

'He doesn't appear to have any obvious wounds,' proclaimed Harriet as she studied the dead man's naked torso.

'The overpaint isn't helping things. The lack of defensive wounds and nothing to suggest a struggle may well weigh towards a sedative having been used at a primary location. That would also account for the possible wheelchair tracks. She would have needed to find a way to move the dead weight of the body.'

'So he may well have been alive when he got here,' implied Harriet, as in her mind she began to piece together a chronological sequence of events, 'waking to find himself in an unknown location, naked and tied to a chair. Probably knowing no reason whatsoever for his being here.'

'If we call to mind the Narcissus' previous exploits, her MO was to sedate the victim. The Narcissus would need and also want time for accusations and confessions before his life was taken. I believe he was most probably tortured, too.' Harriet looked slightly perplexed. She could not make out any physical signs of how the pain would have been inflicted. Penny noticed the vacant look on her colleague's face.

'If you come around to his left side,' Penny motioned, moving slightly aft of the body, as far as the stepping plates would comfortably allow. When Harriet joined Penny on the far side, she immediately noticed the anomaly. 'What looks like a 21-gauge venipuncture needle has been inserted into the median cubital vein. The needle has then been attached via a luer lock connector to the length of tubing that you can now see running to the floor.' A two-litre plastic jug lay on its side in the pooling liquid below. It was evident from the staining of its internal surface that it had been used at some stage to collect blood. As Harriet continued to piece together what had happened, Penny continued her supposition.

'A tightening and loosening of the tourniquet on the upper arm would have been sufficient to stop and start the blood flow. She has basically drained every last drop of blood from this poor man's body. However, it doesn't stop there.' Harriet looked up, an inquisitive look etched upon her face. 'There are significant signs of regurgitation. You can see a large amount of dark vomit across the front of the torso. The addition of the pink foaming bile has come from his lungs.' Harriet's expression changed as she preconceived what Penny would announce next.

'By all appearances, he has been forced to drink his own blood.'

Harriet finished the sentence for Penny.

'Resulting in the victim drowning in his blood.'

36

Tate had returned to Thorney Street via the Jubilee line and a short walk through Victoria Tower Gardens. His visit south of the Thames with Harriet to the forensic laboratories had been cut short after Harriet had received the call confirming the discovery of the body's location. Harriet had returned to Bethnal Green to update her team before joining her fellow officers at the crime scene. Tate had remained a while longer with the forensic team as they examined the picture retrieved from the Tate Modern gallery. Fingerprints and trace evidence had been lifted from the frame and the photograph within. Two super detailed prints had been lifted from the surface of the photograph. Tate was not one to speculate, but he'd put money on the prints being Lena's due to the fact that it looked very much like the two near-perfect thumbprints had been purposely rolled into the glossy celluloid surface. Again, the Narcissus was deliberately leaving a trail of evidence. One that would point to her involvement and nothing more. So far, she had played her cards carefully. There had not been one single thing that would lead to her location or that of the missing Caravaggio. She was playing a game but doing it well. It was like chasing a ghost. But this was a ghost from Tate's past that he knew all too well. A ghost that he would one day exorcise.

Tate had entered Victoria Tower Gardens at the north entrance, first passing the statue of Emmeline Pankhurst, the leader of the Suffragettes, before rounding French sculptor Auguste Rodin's famous sculpture. The 'Burghers of Calais' is one of twelve original castings installed worldwide commemorating the Hundred Years War. The statue depicts six high-ranking French officials who heroically surrendered themselves to Edward III in return for him sparing the people of their city. The six figures portray the heroism of self-sacrifice. The pain, anguish and stoicism of their submissions are captured in each statue's face. It had been at this point that the image of the cadaverous body captured in the recent picture had resurfaced in Tate's mind. He reimagined the agony, torment and suffering that had been inflicted by the Narcissus' hand. Even with the victim being a known criminal currently under their investigation, it did not change the fact that he would most probably have been tortured for his misdoings and pleaded for mercy whilst questioning the reasons for his punishments. His sufferings spurned and shown no remorse at the hands of his accuser. These thoughts of maltreatment had caused a feeling of angst to ball in the pit of Tate's stomach. A sense of unease had crept through his bones. He had always known deep down that this day would eventually come and the Narcissus would resurface to haunt his world once again. The Narcissus had unfinished business, meaning Tate would need to face his ghosts. This time though, there would be no abscondment, no vanishing act; the Narcissus would be brought to rites and made answerable for her crimes. Retribution would be served.

After passing the Buxton Memorial, which celebrated the abolition of slavery at the park's southern end, Tate had crossed Millbank and stopped by the Westminster café on John Islip Street to collect coffees and pastries for all of his team. He would normally take the stairs to the 5th floor, but with the two coffee carry trays and a handful of bagged pastries, he thought it would be best to take the lift. The doors parted at the 5th floor to find DC Tom Chamberlain awaiting its arrival. He had a small marble statue in his hands.

'You wouldn't, by chance, be heading toward the basement?' asked Tate as he struggled to maintain a hold on his take-out purchases.

'Yes. I was returning this to the artefact storage cage. Is one of those for Jonathan?'

'Yes. But could you give him a shout, and then both of you join us back up here in the main office? I have some important information I need to share with the whole team.'

'No probs,' declared DC Chamberlain, stepping to one side for his hands-full senior officer to pass.

'Tell Jon, no excuses. I want everyone present,' Tate called out as he headed down the corridor, and the lift doors closed on the Detective Constable.

Ten minutes later, the Arts and Antiquities Investigation team had gathered as one. There was no longer a pastry in sight, but some were still sipping coffees. Tate sat on the corner of a desk as the rest of his team convened around him. He wasted little time and came straight to the point.

'As you are all aware, Lena Johnson, aka the Narcissus, has re-established contact via the email I received, the content of which we discussed and interpreted a possible meaning to when we last met.' Tate turned to DC Morrison and nodded. The remainder of the team also acknowledged David's breakdown of the message with a nod or a wink in the direction of the new guy. 'Earlier this morning, I received a phone call from my brother, Turner, who is a curator at the Tate Modern. A picture of what appeared to be a crime scene had been hung amongst its collection late in the afternoon of the previous day. The picture, or more specifically, a photograph, shows an individual tied to a chair in an empty room.' Tate's team listened intently, occasionally sipping their coffees as their boss continued. 'The picture was removed, but not before several visitors, including a group of teenagers, had witnessed its presence. CCTV footage captured from the previous day clearly shows Lena, dressed to stand out from the crowd, as the individual responsible.' Tate sipped from his coffee and continued. 'The CID team at Bethnal Green have since identified the location of the room within the photograph and have subsequently sealed off the property as an active crime scene.' Tate retrieved a series of photographs from a folder and handed them around. 'The individual has been declared deceased, and a murder case has been opened. DI Harriet Stone will be leading the investigation. Some, if not all of you, will recognise the deceased. William O'Connor, aka 'Billy the Owl'. An individual currently under investigation by this department for crimes relating to items of stolen artwork. Formal identification has yet to be made, but I think you will agree it's undoubtedly him.' The others in the room nodded in unison, conveying a gesture of agreement with their superior officer. Each listened intently to the confirmation of their former colleague's return and the prospect of a new series of killings by the hand of the Narcissus.

Tate continued. 'What we can deduce from the picture is a possible change of MO. With the series of murders last summer, each victim was posed to closely replicate subjects from Caravaggio paintings. This latest victim is naked. Presently, there appear to be no similarities in this case.'

Jonathan raised the photograph in his hand in a gesture to make an observation. 'If I remember correctly, Caravaggio painted numerous naked seated subjects. His paintings of 'John the Baptist' often purvey naked flesh. As do his paintings of 'St Jerome', 'Sleeping Cupid' and 'Amor Victorious'. But as you just said, in no way does the body in the photograph remotely resemble any of his works in any form. I am in no doubt whatsoever, knowing Lena as I do, there will definitely be a link of some kind. She would not have paid so much attention to detail during the first killings, not to link her latest murder and possibly further crime scenes too.' Tate sensed his friend had more to say, so he remained still. Jonathan needed to explain, so he continued. 'I took some time to look further into the life and works of Caravaggio. The further I looked, the further I began to understand. Caravaggio was a disrupted soul. He needed to blow off steam, to release his inner demons. Hence, his frequent episodes of excessive self-indulgence and the excessive use of alcohol to escape reality and numb the pain. In today's world, his extreme mood swings would most probably be diagnosed as bipolar. Lena may well endure similar agonies.' Jonathan paused briefly to collect his thoughts. 'I wanted to understand what drove Lena to become the Narcissus and to carry out those awful crimes. I wanted to come to terms with and understand if there was a connection between Caravaggio's periods of pugnacity and turmoil and the crimes of the Narcissus. I believe if we can begin to understand her reasons, then there is a chance we can stop her before this escalates out of control once again.' The team sat in silence, their involvement in the crimes of the Narcissus was far less involved than the other two men.

Tate broke their stillness. 'The one link we do have is the continued sending of messages. We have received two since the death of the journalist Rebecca Crawford last summer. The first was discovered as before within Rebecca's oesophagus. The second was sent to my mailbox while I was on holiday recently. Lena would have known of my annual surfing break. There have been approximately twelve months between the two messages. I believe the timing of the newest message and the new murder are significant. She would have planned her re-surfacing in precise detail. The messages, however, I still believe are attention seeking. David's interpretation of the most recent probably echoes her underlying intentions. The one found in the journalist's throat being of a similar nature.' Tate blu-tacked enlarged copies of both messages side-by-side on the front of the filing cabinet to his left.

Within the chasm an evilness summons

All those tempted by Lucifer's call

Morality drowns in the depths of devilry

A fiery inferno beckons all those who fall

The day of judgement is now upon us

Come forth the guilty at God's command

Those unforgiven, bow down and relent

Absolution bestowed by an almighty hand

Narcissus

Take forth the quest of flesh and skin

Lay bare the souls of all man's sin

Casting judgements upon the meek

Salvation promised for all who seek

Yet time and tide await no man

As flooding waters rape the land

The Raven's return is a merciless sign

Destiny's message for all mankind

Narcissus

Tate's team sustained another unusual silence as each read, interpreted and construed their rationale of both messages.

DC Morrison was once again the first to speculate his thoughts. 'The message on the left, the final message from last summer's murders, seems heavily weighted toward redemption.'

Jonathan interrupted. 'The song from which the words come is actually called "The Redemption". It is the final song on the album. However, each set of four lines comes from a different section of the song. Needless to say, they have been paired together here for absolute effect. You are definitely the word sleuth when it comes to riddles.'

David replied, smiling. 'Redemption is also a collectable trading card game. Players use Biblical Heroes to rescue Lost Souls from the game's Evil Characters.' He raised his hands in submission. 'It's another of my favourite pastimes.'

It was Tate who, this time, interjected. 'It seems the floor is yours once more,' he motioned, stepping back as he offered the space to his newest recruit.

David tentatively stepped forward half a step, pushing his glasses back up his nose as he did so. 'If I were to hazard a guess, these particular lines were chosen to convey how the victims needed saving from their temptations or wrongdoings. It weighs towards the Narcissus believing it is lawful to take the souls, by way of death, of those who have sinned. They will be redeemed on Judgement day and granted forgiveness and clemency for their sins.'

'That would be in line with the accusations I overheard when Lena was crucifying Jeremy Grayson on the roof of Battersea Power Station last summer,' announced Tate. 'Once again, she has changed the words.

Or, more correctly, word! The original verse reads, "his almighty hand." Here, it has been changed to "an almighty hand".'

'Is there anything further in the second set of words? If I remember correctly, they appear on Neptune's Finger's second album. I believe you said it was called *After the Flood*, DS Garrett questioned, speaking for the first time. 'God unleashed the flood to save mankind from his own sins. If she is comparing her return to the second coming of man, does Lena now see herself as some sort of God with a mission to rid the earth of those who, in her eyes, have transgressed?'

David stepped up and continued the linguistic deconstruct. 'With both messages side by side, it is not only easy to see how they relate to each other, but to the fact that Lena sees the calling of the Narcissus as a cleansing. She seems to see the atonement of those who have committed a crime to be worthy of nothing less than death. But she also seems to believe that through the act of killing, she is absolving those who are guilty, in her eyes, of their criminality.'

DC Chamberlain, who had been contently listening with interest, eased himself from the table upon which he had been leaning to make his presence felt as he proposed a question. 'If she is again targeting individuals currently under investigation by this department, how do we protect them without them becoming aware that they are on our radar? We do not have enough manpower to put every individual under 24-hour surveillance. Even with the help of local forces, it would be a mammoth operation.'

Tate addressed the question. 'If this latest victim is confirmed to be William O'Connor, aka 'Billy the Owl', then we must readdress the Narcissus's MO. The earlier victims were individuals we had previously investigated, but all three had celebrity status and would capture the headlines.' He hesitated and looked across to his friend before continuing. 'Jocelyn Roberts and Rebecca Crawford were both killed to gain our attention. They could be seen as collateral damage.' He paused once again. A nod of affirmation from Jonathan indicated his blessing for Tate to continue after mentioning his deceased girlfriend. 'I believe Jeremy Grayson was always part of the plan. William O'Connor only fits the 'on our radar 'criteria. He is unknown to the general public. We need to question why he was chosen?' His next question was interrupted as his mobile on the table to his side lit up, vibrated and began to ring. The caller's ID captured his attention, and he engaged the call without hesitation.

'Harriet. I have my team with me. Are you happy if I put you on loudspeaker?' Tate instinctively did not need to ask what the call would be about.

'Sure.'

There was the obligatory pause before Harriet continued.

'We've found him. The body is located in the cellar of a vacated butcher's shop in East Ham. The MO appears to be very different from the previous crime scenes. It would not be easy to link the two if the picture had not been found at the Tate Modern and the CCTV footage had not been so conclusive. However, she appears to have over-painted the body, as if she were creating a real work of art. Apparently, the trademark message has been found in the victim's throat. As of yet, I have not seen it.' There was another short silence before Harriet continued, 'But get this…

The victim's tongue is missing.'

East Ham

London, England

37

A gaggle of onlookers had already gathered around the crime tape's perimeter. A pack of baying journalists in pursuit of a front page hustled amongst them. Steve Brooks was part of the hunting pack, but little did his fellow shutterclickers know he already had his headline pictures. He was here out of curiosity and hunger for the thrill of the chase. Or was it more to settle his own moral emotions? The blameworthiness of his wrongdoing still tugged at his conscience. Guilt and shame continued to plague his mind. He still fought to justify his actions. He had discovered a dead man, photographed the corpse and then failed to report the crime.

But here he was again.

Waiting.

Waiting for the chance of that one winning shot.

The winning shot that the big players in the press would pay good money for.

The ubiquity of press photographers engaged into action, rapidly firing their hand-held shooters at the slightest movement emerging from the forensic tent that now concealed the shop's entrance. The reporters amongst them threw questions into the air.

'What can you tell us about the crime scene?'

'Can you give us anything further?'

'Are the rumours of a body true?'

Brooks allowed those around him to jostle for the best possible position to capture that sellable picture. He had very little fight in him today. In fact, the constant push and shove was actually quite annoying. He allowed those around him to wrestle forward and soon found himself ejected from the herd. He surrendered to the fact that he had no need to be here. Other opportunities were waiting to be exploited in other corners of the city. He was about to turn tail and leave when his mobile began to ring. He recognised the number immediately but was not as enthused to answer as he would usually have been.

But he answered anyway.

'Brooks!' bellowed the voice from the other end of the line. 'Where are you? I've heard through the rumour mill that CID has found the body. Great news for us if they have. Means we can go for a front page as early as tomorrow.' Steve attempted to reply but could not get a word in edgeways. 'Of course, we will have to wait for confirmation. We are going to format the layout anyway. We should have a dummy up and ready in a couple of hours. Can you get back here at some point? Where are you anyway?'

'At the crime scene as we speak,' replied Steve as the editor finally paused to breathe.

'Bloody hell. Well, that's as good as confirming it for me. Your photos will be all over the front page tomorrow. This could well be this year's big seller. Make sure you come by later.' The editor was about to hang up, 'Hey, Steve. Find out who the SIO is, will you? DI Stone, no doubt. What with it being the Narcissus and all. Get a shot of her outside the crime scene, will you?

And Steve, well done mate. Bloody well done.'

Central London

London, England

38

A consistent drizzle hung in the morning air. Commuters hunkered into hoods and pulled the neck baffles of their overcoats up around their chins. Some scurried from station exits before leapfrogging from shop to shop in a bid to remain as dry as possible. Others promenaded umbrellas along the pavements, chasséing around and between those heading in opposite directions. Everyone was dampened by the grey start to the day.

Turner meandered amongst the suburbanites as they bustled their way along the South Bank. He would occasionally extend his brolly skywards while a 'late for work' scuttled inattentively past him. Turner had no need to hasten his step. Each morning, he allowed enough time to relish his journey to the gallery. Although the skies this morning were the same shade as HMS Belfast, Turner still found solace in the way the capital's skyline of silver and glass reflected a reversed replication of the sombre skies.

Tate sat behind the wheel as the early morning traffic ahead slowly filtered one by one into the congestion of the roundabout. Radio 4 was currently broadcasting from the radio of Tate's vintage Land Rover. As he sat in the queue, he listened attentively. The news headlines were up next.

Harriet increased the resistance to the wheels of the cycling machine; this resulted in the need to increase the torque of her crank rotation in order to maintain her current rhythm. The intensified vigour increased Harriet's heart rate and breathing, but she could still maintain a constant eye on the ticker tape news as it scrolled across the bottom of the silenced TV monitors that lined the front wall of the gym.

The Narcissus sat at a counter stool in the coffee shop. The high street outside was already a flow with a constant stream of pedestrians. As she turned her head to the left, the tape of the crime scene perimeter was just visible through the foggy rain-smeared window. However, the Narcissus' attention was preoccupied as she scrolled through 'today's front pages' on her mobile phone.

Steve Brooks sat in the tube carriage, currently held on a red light just outside of Blackfriars station. He stared mindlessly through the carriage's Perspex window at the tunnel wall beyond. He should be happy. He had got his front page and, more importantly, a couple of zeros had been added to his bank account. But still, an overwhelming sense of guilt plagued his mind. Across the carriage, a fellow passenger was reading the inner pages of The City Chronicle. The front and rear pages were spread wide open. The headlines cried out from the front page alongside Steve's exclusive pictures.

As Turner continued along the bankside path, his attention was unexpectedly drawn to a riverside newsstand. He was not one to buy a paper, especially a tabloid. He would usually catch up with the latest stories from around the world via an online media outlet. However, his curiosity got the better of him this morning as he found himself drawn towards the headline of the newsstand's sandwich board and the south London accent as the hawker bellowed, 'Narcissus Returns!' Without a thought, Turner hit the speed dial on his phone.

Tate had pulled the Land Rover into the underground car park at Thorney Street but was still sitting behind the wheel. The Radio 4 headlines had come and gone, with the news of a body having been found within a property on East Ham High Street. It was the live talk show that currently piqued his interest. The two presenters discussed the front-page pictures from one of today's tabloids.

Harriet was warming down with a steady pedal rate as she relaxed forward over the handlebars. The image on the multiple wall monitors changed to that of a newspaper front page. The ticker tape headline feed quickly followed suit, announcing a breaking story. Harriet stopped pedalling and reached for her phone.

The Narcissus was more than satisfied with the City Chronicle's front-page story. The first stage of her return had gone to plan. She turned her head once again, looking across the street in the direction of her latest exploit. A furtive and devious smile curled at the corner of her mouth as she reached for her phone.

Tate was engrossed in the radio show's two-way discussion as the presenters continued to debate the front-page pictures. Were they ethical? If they were, in fact, real, was it lawful? His phone burst to life from the passenger seat. He did not need to verify the caller's identity.

'Have you seen the breaking news story? I've just purchased the City Chronicle for the first time in a long while. The main picture is far more detailed than the one we discovered hung in the gallery yesterday.'

Tate listened as his brother questioned the paper's moral obligation before adding his own thoughts. 'How the pictures were obtained would be my first port of call,' he replied as his phone signalled another call was attempting to connect. 'Turner, I have another call connecting. Can I call you back?'

'Yes. Completely understand. Talk to you later.' The call disconnected.

The Narcissus typed the final number into the handset and waited for the recipient to answer the call. After just three rings, the call was answered.

'Steve Brooks. Journalist. How can I help?' The line remained silent long enough for Steve to repeat himself and question the caller's presence. 'This is Steve Brooks. Do you have the correct number?' Still, the line remained soundless. Steve was on the verge of hanging up the call when a voice at the caller's end said just two words.

'Great Pictures.'

Tate accepted the second call. Once again, he did not need to second guess who the caller would be. He did not get a chance to greet the caller as she was already in mid-flow when the call connected.

'Are you seeing what I'm seeing? Those photos have to be from the crime scene. They have been taken from a different perspective to the one hung at the gallery,' ranted Harriet as she rattled off the sentence without pausing for breath. 'She must have sent photos to the press to satisfy her own narcissistic needs.' Tate did not get a chance to reply and declare that he had not seen the front-page pictures, but he could speculate about their graphic nature.

Harriet continued her verbal onslaught. 'She's not getting away with this. We'll get an injunction to stop the papers. The eyes of the public don't need to witness this. Do they not understand the damage they can cause to an investigation by printing such a thing.' Harriet paused briefly, and Tate saw a chance to comment. But he missed his opportune moment as Harriet returned with a new line of thought.

'If Lena didn't send them, then how the hell did the press get the pictures?'

Southwark

London, England

39

The emaciated body was no longer tied to a chair. It lay unrestricted on a table. An autopsy table. DI Stone and DS Stevens looked down from the viewing gallery above. Chief pathologist Happy Jiang stood to one side of a stainless steel trolley with an arsenal of knives, saws, hammers and forceps upon its shelves.

'Looks like this poor fellow has literally had the life sucked out of him,' jested Happy as he rounded the table. 'The vampires of Halloween appear to be feeding earlier than usual this year.' He let out a little chuckle to himself. DS Stevens was trying his best to suppress a grin from materialising across his face. Happy Jiang lived up to every letter of his given name. He was, more often than not, in a joyous mood. His ebullient character brought a radiance to what could sometimes be a cheerless and solemn occupation. He would often find the light in the gloomiest situations, and his sanguine nature would frequently rub off on those around him. He needed to do little to make others smile.

The partitioned section of the room in which the body lay was part of a three-bay laboratory within an ultra-modern autopsy suite, the majority of which was glass curtain walling, not unlike the pyramid at the courtyard of the Louvre Palace. This particular double-sealed section of the laboratory was only used for black bag cases of the highest profile when the prevention of cross-contamination was of the greatest importance. Mainly when death was thought to have occurred at the hands of another or under unusual circumstances. With a strong possibility that the current corpse had been murdered by the hand of the Narcissus, the highest level of protocol was required.

The body lay face up. It's feet nearest the end of the room where the two detectives looked on from the suspended walkway. The oily paint applied to the body at the crime scene had been washed off prior to the preliminary observation stage. A few small coloured blemishes remained in the skin creases around a joint or skin tuck. With the paint layer removed, the extent of the pallidity and sallowness within the skin was eminently evident. The usual bluish-purple colour of post-mortem lividity was lacking due to the suspected blood loss. The body was skeletal and wasted. Areas of tissue were sunken, and the skin looked to be clinging to the bones. The deceased's face was gaunt. The cheeks hollowed, and the eyes excessively sunken. The corpse looked as if it had taken its last breath weeks ago rather than a matter of hours.

'If this is indeed by the hand of the same individual who last summer made the headlines as the killer named Narcissus, then we have some distinct points of difference and quite a significant change of MO,' Happy declared with a more seriously edged tonation. He walked around the table to the far side of the body, where he leant in and stretched the skin of the victim's neck. 'During the preliminary examination of the body, a single needle entry mark was discovered on the right side of the neck.' He pointed to the centre of the stretched area with a finger of his other hand. 'If my memory is correct, this is consistent with the previous victims of last summer. I wouldn't be at all surprised if toxicology results show the presence of some type of sedative.' Happy moved down the torso to the lower arms. He lifted the hand nearest him and gently turned the wrist toward the viewing gallery. 'Both the wrists and the ankles show signs of ligature marks congruous with Penny's report and the securing of the victim to a chair. However, the marks at all four points are anaemically pale. Most probably due to the significant lack of blood volume at the time of death. The markings also show very little sign of struggle. Once again, consistent with the use of a sedative.' The pathologist moved back to the left side of the table.

He continued his elucidation as he did so. 'Now, this is where it gets interesting.' He lifted the corpse's left arm and extended the elbow to straighten the joint. 'You can most probably see from where you are standing that there is a significant puncture wound to the inside of the antecubital fossa. That is the inside of the elbow to the less educated among us.' He took a crafty upward glance towards the gallery. Harriet raised her eyebrows and slowly shook her head. Happy's witticism never failed to catch her attention. DS Stevens was oblivious to the remark as he was still attempting to spell 'antecubital' within the notes he was taking. Still holding the extended arm, Happy resumed his indicatory. 'There are also several smaller needle entry points that have only become visible since the removal of the over paint. These are synonymous with numerous attempts to find an appropriate entry vein. The median cubital, cephalic and basilic veins show signs of complete collapse due to the trauma. The whole area is indicative of Penny's observations of the incision of a cannula with the intent of draining the blood.'

Harriet, who had been remarkably quiet while listening intently, found the need to comment alongside Happy's explanation. 'The cannula and a length of tubing were still attached at the discovery of the crime scene. I am assuming the withered state of the body is due to the pure lack of blood?'

Happy eased the arm back to the side of the shrunken torso and walked to stand below the two detectives. 'The average human body holds around ten pints of blood. This varies due to factors such as an individual's size or age. It accounts for approximately 8% of an adult's body weight. A person can lose about one pint without causing significant harm to the body's main organs. Hence, blood donation is only ever one pint.' Happy paused and looked up. Andy Stevens was still taking notes. Knowing her colleague sufficiently well and his ability to overtalk the detail, Harriet nodded her approval.

'Carry on, Happy. It may be useful as we develop a timeline of events.'

Happy didn't need a second chance and continued his dialogue. 'If the body loses 3 pints of its blood volume, it will enter hypovolaemic shock, resulting in a significant drop in blood pressure and a decrease in the amount of oxygenated blood reaching the vital organs. The heart must work much harder to pump blood around the body. At this point, it can already be life threatening. A further loss of blood would result in multiple organ failure, and eventually, the body would shut down, closely followed by death.'

Happy returned to the autopsy table but remained at the end closest to the viewing gallery. 'Just before your arrival, we placed a blood drain in the popliteal artery just below the knee.' He pointed to the mark. 'This poor chap had less than 2 pints of blood left in his system.'

'On the scale of things, what effect would such detrimental blood loss have on the victim's point of death?' inquired DS Stevens, momentarily looking up from his notes.

'Good question, detective. But we have another factor to consider. The last of the blood we drew from the body seemed to lack clotting properties. It suggests a thinning agent may have been administered at some point. It would have made draining a large amount of fluid much easier. Going back to your question, the deceased would have lost consciousness at a point when his blood volume and pressure had decreased sufficiently enough to become anaerobic and unable to provide enough oxygenated blood to the vital organs. The viscosity of the blood would have played a factor in the process, as the clotting properties would have been diminished. I wouldn't be surprised if toxicology were to find the presence of a fast-acting anticoagulant such as heparin.' Happy paused for a moment, anticipating further questions. When none materialised, he continued.

'Two more points to note, which I believe Penny has previously brought to your attention.' Harriet's ears pricked up, and DS Stevens' attention withdrew from his notes. Happy now stood over the corpse's head. He leant in closer and carefully teased the lips and mouth apart.

'As you are aware, when Penny examined the victim at the scene for the Narcissus' calling card, she found a roll of what we can assume to be pigskin within the same area of the oesophagus as with the previous victims.'

'Penny has already informed me that she will send the evidence to Bethnal Green as soon as she has finished her technical analysis of the item,' declared Harriet.

'Well, the Narcissus not only planted something this time but removed something while doing so.' Both detectives knew all too well where Happy's examination was heading. 'This poor fellow's tongue has been removed.' Neither detective commented. 'A single forced cut has been made at the base of the lingual frenum. Most probably made with something as simple as a pair of gardening secateurs.'

'Or poultry shears,' proffered Harriet. 'At her previous crime sites, we found links to the butchery business, her adoptive father having also worked in the trade and this new body having been found in a disused butchers. I'm sure my suggestion will not be too far removed.' She paused as a thought materialised in her head. 'Do we have the tongue?'

'I am afraid the answer is No. There was no sign of the tongue or a cutting tool found at the crime scene. The possible anticoagulant has made our detailed examination of the removal site far more difficult. However, the victim may well have still been alive when the tongue was removed.'

An air of malaise arose before Andy Stevens asked the question Harriet was poised to offer. 'Did she feed him his own tongue?'

'That is a question we may be able to answer shortly. However, there is one more point to show you before we open this poor fellow up.' Happy moved from the head to the victim's feet. 'When the over paint was washed from the body, we also discovered these.'

Cut into each sole of the victim's feet were the letters **M** and **W**.

40

The Narcissus had followed the woman across the city via the underground network. At all times, she had sat at the far end of the carriage. She kept her head down, reading a book to avoid unnecessary attention. She only raised her eyes as the train entered a station. Only then, just enough, to see if she was disembarking or remaining seated. After travelling from Moorgate on the Hammersmith & City line, they had resurfaced at Aldgate East. The lighter footfall of the mid-morning crowds had allowed her to keep the woman in her sights from a safer distance, albeit when they had transferred trains at a busy terminus. Where possible, the Narcissus used adjacent escalators to enter and exit the platforms and kept at least a carriage length between them while waiting at the platforms. With the woman completely unaware of being followed, it had been easy to travel unnoticed.

The woman had made her way north along Commercial Street, the Narcissus continuing her pursuit from the pavement on the opposite side of the road, always keeping four or five car lengths behind. She had turned left on White's Row, where the Narcissus briefly lost sight of her quarry due to numerous delivery and refuse lorries. She finally caught up with the woman at the top end of Crispin Street just as she turned left onto Brushfield Street. The pursuit ended not long after the woman had entered Bishops Square. Here, she was met by a middle-aged gentleman with receding hair and wire-rimmed glasses. They shook hands before heading off together toward Spitalfields Market.

The Narcissus had relaxed into a patio chair outside the Noxy Bros front window. From here, she had a good view of the woman and gentleman who were now sitting in The Ten Bells pub opposite. She could sit and observe without being too conspicuous. The Narcissus had ordered a chai latte and a salmon and cream cheese bagel before choosing the best available table to continue her observations.

Through the pub window opposite the bagel shop, the woman and the gentleman appeared to have ordered drinks and were currently conversing across a small table for two. A large shopping bag that had travelled with the woman now sat to one side of the table. The dreary skies and persistent mizzle of the early morning were now beginning to clear, and glimpses of the sun occasionally broke through the cloudy skies. The Narcissus kept one eye on her quarries while scrutinising her current surroundings. She was beginning to wonder if her order would arrive before she needed to up and leave when a young barista with sun-kissed Mediterranean features and a taupe-coloured apron approached her table. He held a tray in one hand.

'Chai Latte and a salmon cream cheese bagel?'

'Thank you,' replied the Narcissus, accepting her order. While placing the serving on the table, the waiter held his gaze on the Narcissus a moment too long to not go unnoticed. Lena politely smiled back. She was used to attracting second glances. Her natural beauty rarely went unnoticed and frequently captured the attention of many a man.

'Italian?' the barista enquired with a slight nervousness to his voice.

'Yes, I grew up in the Umbria region. You?'

'Sicilian. I come from Palermo.'

Lena smiled. 'I, too, have been to Palermo. I visited the Oratorio di San Lorenzo to view the replica of the stolen Caravaggio painting.

'It is not far from where my parents still live. They are both,' he paused to find the word. He did not know the translation. They are both 'Parrocchiani'.'

The Narcissus noticed movement in the corner of her eye. 'Nice to meet you,' she offered, her focus wavering to the window opposite. The barista took the cue and withdrew from the exchange.

The woman the Narcissus was watching, slowly and carefully removed what looked to be a small pale blue jug from the bag at her feet. She placed the item on the table before reaching into the bag again. This time, she retrieved a small vase. It was decorated in the same way as the jug but with a yellow finish. Each of the ceramics was decorated with white cameo figures. The man picked up the jug. He turned it through his hands as he carefully examined the object. After a while, he removed a pair of pince-nez glasses from an inside pocket and placed them at the end of his nose in front of the glasses he already wore, before turning the jug to study its base.

All the while, the Narcissus watched from across the street. She sipped at her latte and took an occasional bite from the bagel. Her eyes were engaged and absorbed in the actions of the woman and gentleman, both of whom now appeared to be engrossed in an intense conversation. The Narcissus watched on. The woman looked to have become unsettled. Her actions had become flustered. Something had rattled her cage. As the gentleman and the Narcissus looked on, the woman packed the ceramics back into the bag with far less care than when they were first removed, grabbed her coat from the rear of her chair and promptly left the building. The gentleman remained seated.

The Narcissus was contently smiling to herself when a voice interrupted her reverie.

The barista stood at her shoulder.

'Would Signora care for another latte?'

'I won't thank you. I think we are done for now.'

Bring the pages alive…

Explore artworks, locations and more.

*Go to gnsbooks.com (Interactive) or scan the QR code
to unlock images, maps and facts as you read.*

41

Harriet would usually have made her excuses and departed the autopsy before the opening of the body. It wasn't that she had a fear of blood, she was in no way haemophobic or squeamish. In fact, the sight of copious amounts of blood at the crime scene had not bothered her in the slightest. But the opening of a human body didn't sit well with her. However, her history with this particular case and her grit and determination to see justice served outweighed her justification for leaving. It would also be beneficial for DS Stevens to witness the procedure. His recent promotion would likely make his presence at autopsies more frequent.

The double sealed doors in the room below opened and another man dressed in blue scrubs and a disposable apron joined Happy at the autopsy table.

'David. I think you know DI Stone and DC Stevens,' Happy stated, gesturing towards the viewing gallery.

'DS Stevens, actually,' responded Harriet. 'Andy gained his third chevron recently.'

'Well, it seems congratulations are in order. We'll no doubt be seeing more of you in the future then. Just make sure it's up there and not in a bag down here,' joked Happy as he turned back to the body. 'I believe it's time to have ourselves a look inside.'

David handed a rubber block to Happy, who carefully placed it under the neck of the corpse. This would hyperflex the spine beyond its normal range, arching the back and pushing the chest up and forward into the strongest position to make a Y-incision.

Starting at the top of the torso, Happy drew the blade of the scalpel down from the front of the right shoulder to the centre of the chest. He repeated the procedure on the left side so that both incisions met at the lowest part of the sternum. His third cut traced a straight line down to the pubic bone with a small deviation around the naval. Each cut was made with purpose and precision so to cut cleanly through the abdominal wall.

Very little blood escaped from the wounds due to the lack of blood pressure, the absence of cardiac function and the volume of blood loss during the Narcissus' torture. Having put the scalpel to one side, Happy began to manipulate the torso's skin, flesh and fat to either side of the body and abdominal retractors were used to hold the body wall open. Lastly, the upper flap of the Y-incision was folded up and over the corpse's face. With the abdomen open and the ribs now exposed, the technician handed Happy a pair of stainless-steel bone shears. While applying sufficient pressure to the tool, Happy made his way along the right side of the ribs, cutting through each at the joint between the costal cartilage and the sternum. A distinctive crunch echoed with each separation. He replicated each cut on the left side before separating the ribs and removing the breastbone.

Harriet and DS Stevens looked on. They watched as Happy cut away any remaining soft tissues. Periodically, he would record his findings on a digital headset, sometimes taking a tissue or fluid sample, which would then be handed to David, who would label and record the necessary details. Of the two detectives watching, Andy Stevens paid far more attention to the proceedings. He watched attentively. At each stage of the dissection, he made notes for his own future reference. Having experienced a full autopsy only once, his watchfulness had him totally absorbed. In comparison, for Harriet, it was just a matter of fact; she waited for the details, significant findings and anything of real importance. Such was her role in an investigation of this calibre, her time would be better spent elsewhere. Happy would present a full report within 48 hours anyway.

'Apart from the distinct lack of blood volume, so far, there appears to be no trauma to the exterior frame of the torso,' Happy declared, turning his attention once more to his two observers. 'We may well learn more with the removal of the organs. In the interest of DS Stevens, we will use the Virchow technique and remove each separately, rather than the more frequently used Rokitansky method where the organs are removed as one.' Happy noticed Andy Stevens' constant scribble and could not help but offer further mockery. 'I shouldn't worry about the spelling too much, DS Stevens. The test at the end will be multiple choice.' He chortled to himself as he returned to the focus of his attention.

With the chest cavity exposed, Happy began the operation to first remove the heart. He made incisions to the aorta, pulmonary artery and the super and inferior vena cava to detach the organ from the major vessels. After placing his scalpel on the instrument trolley, he reached in, and with both hands, he diligently lifted out the heart. It was placed on a surgical tray for weighing and Happy recorded his initial findings.

'The pericardium and myocardium both show preliminary signs of cardiac dysfunction, most probably due to the heart overworking to maintain blood circulation. Again, don't worry about the spelling, Andy!' He couldn't help himself.

'I used 'muscle and 'heart failure',' fired back the detective.

'Looks like we have an A-grade student, hey Harry?'

'Exactly why he is now a Detective Sergeant,' Harriet stated light-heartedly.

With the heart removed, the left lung was now exposed. Harry began work to remove the lung and its counterpart. Much like the heart, it was a case of separating each organ from its major vessels. This time, the primary bronchus, pulmonary arteries and veins were removed at the hilum. Both lungs were once again weighed, sampled and labelled.

Happy gathered the right lung in a surgical tray and approached the viewing platform. 'The thick pink frothy foam associated with drowning is evident around the inside of the bronchus and the trachea. It is slightly richer in colour than one would normally expect. There is also evidence of a significant amount of blood in the lobar bronchi.'

'Could it be that blood has been digested?' Harriet questioned rhetorically.

'Let's take a look at the stomach and, more specifically, the contents. It may well confirm your suspicions.'

With the organs of the upper chest removed, access to the stomach, intestines and bowels was relatively straight forward and it took very little time before Happy and his technician had all three laid out on trays. Happy's primary focus was to empty and identify the stomach contents while also looking for the presence of abnormal constituents. While David held the stomach, Happy washed the contents into a secondary bowl. Again, he proffered the evidence to the onlooking detectives.

'I think it is fairly obvious from the colour as to what this poor fellow has consumed in the final stages of his life.' Despite preconceiving the result, all four in the room struggled with the reality of what they were witnessing. Each built a picture within their mind of the ramifications connected to the answers the evidence was presenting. Looking quizzically back at the body, Happy handed the bowl and its contents back to David before retreating to the autopsy table. En route, he collected an endoscope from the rear of the room. Happy leant in over the open cavity of the chest and inserted a long, thin fibre optic into the dissected tube of the oesophagus. He held the other end to his eye and adjusted a focussing ring. He moved the apparatus within the area he was examining, his head following the eyepiece's every movement. After a minute or so, he turned his attention back to the others in the room.

'There is notable damage to the inside of the oesophagus and the top of the epiglottis. Both conducive with the insertion of an external vessel.'

Harriet had pre-empted Happy's discovery and was piecing together the evidence from the crime scene and the confirming factors from the autopsy. 'Could the injuries have been caused by the insertion of a plastic pipe? Possibly a hose pipe with a funnel attached to the other end?'

Happy nodded. 'Yes. The continual insertion and extraction of a nylon pipe could have quite easily caused sustained damage.'

Harriet needed no further proof.

The victim had most definitely been forced to drink his own blood.

42

Tate and DS Jane Garrett had taken the tube to Hyde Park Corner and entered the park at the Queen Elizabeth gate. The early afternoon sun had been warming as they meandered along the park's south perimeter. However, a cold easterly breeze had nipped at their collars when they passed through areas shaded by the park's trees. As they walked and talked, they had chatted about aspects of each other's personal lives. There had been no talking shop. Tate had been particularly inquisitive about Jane's background. With her recent appointment to his team, Tate had been keen to learn more about Jane's passions and what made her tick. She had been only too happy to make known her love of horses. She divulged stories of her childhood years and gymkhanas. The teenage years on her uncle's cattle station in Queensland and her recent membership to the Wimbledon Village Stables. While they conversed, they strolled through the rose gardens, passing the fountains of the 'Boy & Dolphin' by British sculptor Alexander Munro and the 'Huntress' by Feodora Gleichen before stopping for a light lunch at the Serpentine Bar & Kitchen. It had only then been a short walk through Knightsbridge, passing Harrods with its kerbside collection of supercars and its numerous world renowned 5-star hotels that lined Brompton Road.

They had arranged an appointment at Bonhams on Montpelier Street with Mr Robert Jones, an 18th & 19th centuries ceramics and glassware expert. The Art and Antiquities Department often used external sources to identify, authenticate and sometimes evaluate items recovered during an investigation. They also sought further information to support active inquiries when the extent of knowledge amongst the team had been exhausted.

Tate and DS Garrett had been met at the reception desk by a middle-aged man dressed in leather trousers, a 'London Calling' T-shirt, silver-tipped Chelsea boots, short liberty spiked hair and numerous piercings to his ears, eyebrow, nose and lips.

'Good afternoon and welcome to Bonhams. I'm Robert Jones,' announced the gent as he offered his hand to both detectives. If you would like to follow me, I have a readily prepared room.' He walked through a door to his left, his hand trailing behind, holding the sash ajar until the first in his wake took the door. He did not look back but talked over his shoulder. Both Tate and Jane looked at each other in bemusement. Robert Jones continued his discourse as if he were using a sixth sense. 'Please don't worry yourselves. It's a reaction I frequently encounter. People so often expect a snuffy nosed, corduroy clad, eccentric old codger. And as if by magic, I appear. A snotty nosed, body pierced anarchist.' They were led deeper into the building through a warren of corridors to a room frequently used for in-person evaluations. Again, Robert opened the door and continued without so much as a glance to his rear. The room simply had two tables and four chairs. The space of two walls was broken by a pair of framed 20th century artworks. Both were cityscapes of what was most probably central London.

'Please, take a seat. Can I get either of you a tea or maybe coffee?' Both declined, having just had lunch. 'So, I believe you wish to gain further knowledge about Wedgwood or, more specifically, Jasperware. Is that correct?' Robert enquired, leaning on the back of one of the remaining two chairs.

Tate looked to Jane, who motioned for him to continue. His reply was far from the question he was posed. 'Before we continue.' He paused and again glanced at DS Garrett. 'We first have to ask. How on earth did you get into antiques? I mean, you are openly aware that you don't tick the usual boxes of an antiquarian.'

Robert smiled. 'It is indeed a question I am frequently asked. The antiques came first and the punk in me did not emerge until my late teens. However, both have remained and play two distinctive roles in my life. The allure of ceramics, porcelain and glass dates back to spending weekends at my grandmother's while my parents partied in the West End. As a child, I was fascinated by my Granny's cameos, oriental vases decorated with dragons, and especially the detailed scenes of her Chinese Blue Willow tea set. The punk was my rebellion against my parent's abandonment.' He sniggered and the two detectives joined his laughter. 'This is a nod to those past times and a gesture to my gran,' continued Robert as he uncurled the helix at the rear of his ear to reveal a small cameo stud earring. 'It's a coral relief on ebony.' The detectives could tell he was incredibly proud of his concealment from the look etched upon his face. 'Enough about me. How about you bring me up to speed with the reasons behind today's visit? I had a brief outline from my boss and I have put together some examples, which I hope will aid your inquiry.' He pointed to a table in the corner. 'Shall we move the chairs a little closer?' He picked up the chair he was leaning on, Tate and Jane following suit.

Tate sat and explained the situation. 'We are currently investigating an individual whom we suspect to be producing Jasperware forgeries. The individual in question has previously escaped conviction on similar charges. We believe the individual has produced reproductions of 19th century tableware, which has recently entered the market. We hoped to gain further knowledge from your expertise of the subject.'

'It would be good to gain a greater understanding of how to spot a fake,' added Jane, her attention already drawn to the ceramic wares.' Robert turned to the table and Tate accompanied him.

'Now, where shall we begin?'

'With the basics would be good for me,' stated Jane, 'my knowledge is far from Tate's. I have only recently joined the department and any insights would be invaluable.' Tate nodded his agreement and Robert rubbed his hands together before moving what looked like two identical jugs to the front of the table.

'We can tell much about objects by merely picking them up. Often, a reproduction can be lighter, but more often than not, it can be weightier. Two factors can determine the outcome of an item's weight. Firstly, the type of clay used. Clays will have different compositions and mineral impurities and be dug from distinct parent rocks. Each is a component relating to the base material weight. Different clays require firing at different temperatures, resulting in varying porosity and solidity. Simply, each will bake and dry differently. The other factor to affect an item's weight is the thickness of the throw. There is an art to gaining a consistent thickness. Often, a reproduction can be ever so slightly thicker because the potter has underworked the piece or overworked it to a thinner finish. These discrepancies can be minute and it can take a trained eye to spot them.' Robert handed the first of the jugs to Jane. She carefully turned it over in her hands. She especially examined the thickness of the ceramic's wall. Robert offered the second identical jug in Jane's direction. She handed the first to Tate. She could feel an obvious difference as soon as she held the second example. She once again looked at the thickness of the finished throw. It appeared to be no different than the first. She looked to Robert, who had foreseen her question.

'Yes. They appear to be the same thickness but are made from two very different clay compounds.' Tate handed back the first jug, and Jane appraised the weight differences in each hand. 'We now need to ask the question, is the jug in your left hand lighter than the one in your other hand? Or is the jug in your right hand heavier than the first? Which jug is of the correct weight and most probably the original? There is little difference, even to those with many years of experience.' Robert held out his hands and Jane handed back the pair of jugs. 'So we need to consider other accompanying factors. Again, we can look at the thickness of the throw. Reproductions can often vary in thickness through the body of the piece. Originals are more than often more uniformed.' He picked up two small tapered flute vases and handed one to each detective. Both looked their vase over, each studying the item for evidence of the imperfections they had just been made aware of. They swapped vases and repeated their observations.

'The one Jane is now holding appears to thicken towards the bottom,' declared Tate.

'I agree,' confirmed DS Garrett, 'but it's very subtle.'

'Correct. It is quite evident in this pair, but it is not always as simple.' Once again, Jane returned the items, and Robert handed her a large bowl. She scrutinised the surfaces while turning it over and over in her hands.

'The glaze is another aspect to consider. Often, it can be applied more densely than on an original, or the finish of the surface may be duller. Take note of the lines and the paint strokes around the inside of the rim,' Robert encouraged. Jane tipped one side of the bowl and raised it to the light. 'Here, they are too precise. The painter has paid too much attention and been too meticulous. The artist's hand on an original will be far freer and loose in its application.'

As DS Garrett continued to scrutinise the bowl, Tate posed a question. 'With regards to Jasperware. Are there any of the designs or colours that are more frequently copied?'

'Good question, Inspector. The raised accents of neoclassical themes borrowed from the Romans, Greeks, and Egyptians are popular with collectors, so they tend to be often copied. Classical pieces from the 18th & 19th centuries hold much higher financial value, so they are also frequently faked.' Robert reached for a large red Portland vase with white accents and handed it to Tate. 'About your question of colours, as you are probably aware, the more common colours are the paler shades of blue and green. Yellow and even black are not seen as often, so once again, they fetch higher returns and can regularly be found to have been reproduced.' He offered his empty hands in Tate's direction. 'Red is the rarest and most daring and was only produced for a very short period. We are quite often wary if one is submitted for sale. They are always examined in further detail by those most knowledgeable.' Tate handed the vase back. Robert smiled. 'It's ok, Inspector. It's a fake!' Jane giggled and Tate exhaled a thankful sigh.

'As with most antique wares, the identifying markers can be the determining factor to the authenticity of a piece.' Robert handed across two highly decorated teacups. Both Tate and Jane spontaneously turned their cups over. 'From time to time, the markings or the position of the maker's stamp are not quite right. They can simply be in the wrong place or aligned in an incorrect position. The use of lower-case letters in place of upper-case letters, and vice versa, is an inaccuracy we find from time to time. Sometimes, they are also found to have been stamped in an incorrect font. Occasionally, the misuse can be a small difference, for example, in the written form of 'a' instead of 'a'.' He drew each form in the air with a finger. Both detectives nodded their understanding. 'A classic mistake when reproducing a fake maker's mark for "WEDGWOOD" is the adding of an 'E'. Countless cheap reproductions, especially those imported from the Asian continent, frequently encounter this error. However, it can be easily missed by those without a keen eye.'

Jane was still studying the bottom of her cup when a question sprang to mind. 'What about the date stamps and date codes?'

'Another good question. A common mistake we often find is that the date code letter does not match the period of the piece it refers to. A particular item may not have been produced, shall we say, before the start of the 20th century, but its date mark represents 1870.' Robert had also picked up a teacup and repeatedly turned it in his hands as he spoke.

'It's a complicated field and like many things, it takes work and many years to gain the knowledge needed to spot the discrepancies. And worst of all. Those who produce these reproductions are getting better and better at what they do and it is becoming harder and harder to spot the fakes from the originals!'

43

DS Richards and DS Stevens were spellbound in the mesmeric glow of their computer monitors. Neither was aware of the presence of the other. Both were so absorbed in the task at hand that neither had noticed the lifelessness of the incident room, with the remainder of the investigation team having departed long ago. Neither one nor the other was mindful of the stillness and solitude that the usually bustling room pervaded as it snoozed, cloaked in the semi-darkness of eventide.

In the shadows of the far corner, a third light glimmered. It was not unusual for the senior investigating officer's room to be lit when all else was dark. Harriet was known to work through the night when an investigation consumed her. Many a gallon of midnight oil had been burnt in the quest for justice.

Harriet was sitting in the ray of the desk lamp, working her way down a pile of case and custody paperwork, all needing her signature, when a rhythmic knocking broke her engrossment. She withdrew her attention from the paper pile and gingerly looked up for the source of her distraction.

'Deliveroo for an overworked, underfed Detective Inspector,' the short oriental man announced. A smile of contentment began to radiate across Harriet's face as she recognised the familiar voice. Happy stepped across the threshold. A brown paper bag hung from his extended arm. 'I brought noodles,' he exclaimed. 'I stopped by the 'Wok & Go' on the Bethnal Green Road. I'm afraid they are not a patch on Mrs Jiang's. But they're still lip-lickingly good.' Happy noticed the three-day-old curled cheese sandwich on one side of the desk. 'And it looks like I turned up just in time!' Harriet noticed his observation and immediately tipped the remains into the bin.

'I have Hoi Sin Seafood or Chicken Teriyaki. The choice is yours?'

'The Chicken Teriyaki would be wonderful if you don't mind?' Happy removed the first box from the bag and passed it over the desk to Harriet before drawing two pairs of chopsticks from a rear pocket.

The next few minutes hung silently in the air as both tucked into the rapturous delights of takeaway stir fry. Harriet welcomed and savoured every morsel.

'How's the family?' she finally asked through a mouthful of escaping noodles. The chopsticks fighting to control the food.

'Mrs Jiang has a little more time on her hands, with both girls now at University. She is thinking of taking driving lessons, god help us.' They both laughed. Each doing their best to retain their mouthfuls. 'Joy is now in her third year of Modern Medicine and Lucky is an undergraduate at Brunel University London studying anthropology.'

'And you, Happy? How is the world outside of forensic pathology?'

Happy twisted his chopsticks around a knot of noodles dangling before his chin. He guided them safely back to his mouth before responding. 'For once, I have listened to the advice of Mrs Jiang. Like yourself, I was guilty of 'all work and no play.' She has repeatedly suggested I find myself a hobby. At least one that doesn't involve sticking stamps in an album.'

Harriet was slightly taken aback. 'I had no idea you were a philatelist.'

'I inherited my late grandfather's collection, having shown some interest as a young child. I found I still possessed that interest many years later. Although, I now focus on collecting stamps from the Asian continent.'

'So what's the new hobby?'

'David from the lab offered to take me to a driving range. Who would have thought that hitting a little white ball would be such a good way to let out the frustrations of a busy day? We have now started to play 18 holes on a Sunday. I'm quite enjoying it, really. Although, at present, I seem to lose more balls in the longer grass than I putt into the holes.'

They both chuckled. Both doing their best to contain mouthfuls of noodles.

Happy reached for the takeout bag on the floor. 'I almost forgot these,' he declared, placing two cans of cola on the desk. Harriet's eyes lit up and she reached for the desk's bottom drawer, returning with a bottle of Grey Goose in her hand.

'I wouldn't want the cola to feel lonely in a glass on its own.'

'You have glasses?' replied Happy in disbelief.

Harriet glanced briefly around the room. 'Sorry. You will probably have to make do with a coffee-stained mug as per usual.'

Happy popped the ring pull on one of the cans and drank a couple of mouthfuls.

'Maybe just a small amount in the can then, please.' Harriet obliged before finishing the remains of a cold black coffee, pouring a sizeable measure of the vodka into the mug and adding an equal amount of cola.

Armed with a stiff drink and her belly comfortably satisfied from the takeaway, Harriet was keen to hear the results that Happy, without doubt, had come to deliver. The pathologist sensed the swing in his colleague's state of mind. It was time to report the results.

'The lab reports confirmed our initial speculations.' He handed the written report to Harriet. 'High levels of both a sedative and an anti-coagulant were present in the blood. The tranquiliser was, once again, Etorphine. The Narcissus used the same drug on previous occasions. The anti-coagulant was found to be Heparin. It is a glycosaminoglycan which decreases the clotting ability of blood. It is normally only dispensed within a hospital or medical facility. It needs to be administered intravenously. Together, they account for the two needle entry points found during the PM.'

Harriet scanned down through the remainder of the report. She noticed just two other abnormalities. 'Apparently, his HbA1c was unusually high.'

'Not really of concern. It just means he had a high blood sugar level. He may well have been borderline diabetic without knowing. Or the Narcissus force fed him Jelly Babies.'

Harriet ignored the witticism. 'Fe^{2+} levels in the stomach samples are also high.'

'That's an irregular level of iron. If you force someone to drink their own blood, it most probably has a counter effect to the chemical balance within their gut.'

Harriet placed the report aside and took a large mouthful of her vodka and coke. She savoured the alcoholic hit as she swallowed. 'How long do you think it took? I mean, how long do you think the poor chap lasted before he passed out?'

'It will have depended on how quickly a sufficient amount of blood took to enter his lungs in order to enforce drowning. If I were to hazard a guess, the Narcissus most probably prolonged the torturous act to inflict the maximum amount of suffering. He would have only lost consciousness when his blood volume was such that the heart could not maintain blood pressure and circulation.' Happy sipped from the can and Harriet took another sizable swig from her coffee cup. 'Either way, the mental torment would have been horrific.' They both sat for a moment in silence. Each considering the pain and anguish such an act would inflict on any man. Each envisioned the final moments of the deceased's suffering and the taking of the final breath.

Happy shifted uncomfortably in his chair. Harriet sensed a bombshell was about to drop. The pathologist did not disappoint.

'We found no evidence of material relating to the tongue when we analysed the stomach contents. He wasn't fed it.' What should have been a positive outcome suddenly became a whole new can of worms.

'If there are no signs of him having been fed the tongue and no evidence of it has been found at the scene, it can mean only one thing…'

'She took it with her!'

Once again, they sat for a moment without speaking as they both interpreted the implications of such an act.

Harriet offered up the Grey Goose bottle. Happy placed a hand upon his cola can and silently shook his head. Harriet added another good measure to her mug and a small amount of cola. Again, she took a good glug to appreciate the vodka's stronger concentration. Eventually, Happy stood and rounded the chair. Prior to sharing the noodle supper, he had hung his jacket on the backrest. He reached into an inside pocket and retrieved a sealed evidence envelope, which he handed across the desk. Harriet knew immediately what it contained. There was no mistaking the pigskin.

'When I mentioned that I planned to pop by on my way home this evening, Penny asked if I would mind delivering you the envelope.' Harriet held it under the desk light to get a clearer look at the words tattooed upon it. 'Handwriting analysis shows that the tattoo is of the same hand as that used in previous messages.' Harriet continued to hold the enclosed skin within the light's beam as she leant in and read the words tattooed in red.

Can man not see what he has become
A solitary tear for all of God's sons.
I pray a great sadness shadows the land
Guilt is the shame on all man's hands.

Narcissus

Parson's Green
London, England

44

Although it is generally considered to be on the fringes of Central London, Parson's Green feels and looks like a small English countryside village. Nestled in the borough of Hammersmith and Fulham, its boutique shops, independent cafés and many a pub with outdoor green spaces lend itself to brunch on a weekend morning, where eggs Benedict or smashed avocado on toast are savoured as opposed to a greasy all-day breakfast. Centred around its triangular green where the Fulham rectors once resided, residents can still buy a pound of handmade sausages at the local butchers, be enticed to the bakers by the smell of freshly baked bread and handpick the freshest of vegetables at the village grocers.

Kate Palmer relished the affluent neighbourhood that Parson's Green had to offer. Her three-bedroom Edwardian terraced house sat on a tree-lined street, and the District line station allowed her easy access to the city and the school in Kensington. She also reaped the benefits of the larger than average back garden the period properties afforded their residents. Kate's rear garden extended to the south via a small patio and a long expanse of lawn. Her pottery studio occupied the full width at the far end of the garden.

After a long day of teaching, Kate was keen to spend her evenings in the studio. It was her escape from the humdrum of the 9 to 5. It was also where the majority of her yearly income was produced. The pieces she turned out in the studio more than tripled her teaching salary. With the taxman being unaware of her little sideline it would also be tax free. With the evenings beginning to draw shorter, Kate would frequently light the log burner in one corner of the studio. Sat in the other corner would be her tri-coloured cat, Picasso, who would eventually venture to the floor and stretch out before the log burner.

Kate kneaded the clay in her hands to remove any air bubbles or break down firmer lumps. It also allowed her to gain a good consistency by mixing the wetter and drier parts of the clay. Satisfied that she had a good mix, she slammed the clay ball down onto the central bat of the potter's wheel, sealing it with her finger. With the wheel spinning, she coned the ball up and down to centralise the clay. Bracing her elbows into her thighs, Kate formed a divot in the centre with her two thumbs before pushing one hand down to create an opening. All the while, she continually added small amounts of water to keep the mixture malleable. She slowed the wheel down and opened the clay to a thickness she was happy with. After wetting her work once more, she began claying up the walls of the pot by applying pressure to the outside edge and pulling upwards. She repeatedly moved the clay until the pot's shape began to appear. As she began to shape the piece to the correct height and thickness, her phone buzzed and broke her concentration. She slowed the wheel and carefully removed her hands.

Kate recognised the notification alert as the property's front doorbell. She leant across to where her phone sat on a work surface and touched the screen with the tip of her little finger, it being the only clayless part of her hand. The on-screen camera image displayed a cardboard box and a person's waist and legs.

'Hello,' called Kate, trying her best to keep the dripping clay off her touchscreen.

'I have a delivery for Ms Palmer.' It was a female voice.

'I am in my studio in the rear garden. Would you be able to bring it around to the back? You can come through the side gate. It's not locked.' Kate heard a tut of disapproval before the box person moved from the camera's field of vision.

Kate was back at the wheel, pushing and pulling the clay in and out to shape the final look of the piece, when there was a polite knock on the window. Kate did not look up.

'Could you please bring it in and pop it on the side? My hands are a little messy at present.' She continued manipulating the clay, concentrating on the finer details. She heard the click of the door and felt the presence of someone entering. Picasso jumped down to investigate the new arrival. 'On the table will be fine.' Still, Kate focused on the work in her hands as the pot neared the desired finish.

'I'm afraid I am going to need a signature,' said the voice, now audibly closer to where Kate sat.

'You are going to have to wait. I can't stop for a minute.'

'I've got all the time in the world.' were the last words Kate heard before she felt a sharp prick in her neck, followed by the spinning of the pot, becoming hypnotically nauseous as the world around her closed in and her head slumped forward into the rotating clay.

Camden

London, England

45

'I'll tear out your heart. And that's just the start. I'll eat you alive. Let's see you survive,' screamed the voice. 'I've got the devil in me.' The song broke into a melodic guitar solo. The bass and drums resonated around the room. The speakers in the bar pulsated as they pounded out the '81 classic by Barracuda Bite. The music was so loud that many of the drinkers found it difficult to hold a conversation. You could feel the thump of the bass through your chest. Many stood alone with a pint in their hand. They tapped their foot to the music and sang along with the familiar chorus. Those in groups of three or four attempted to shout the occasional remark above the sound of the music.

Tate and Jonathan sat at a small table upon short stools on either side. They occasionally came to the Black Heart when work commitments allowed. They enjoyed the atmosphere with both of them being progressive rock fans. After finishing work at a reasonable time, they took the tube north to Camden Town. It was not long before they had both demolished a bowl of Smoked Mac 'N' Cheese from the vegan kitchen. At this present moment, both men were nearing the bottom of their second pint. They had begun to play a game that often provided them with a little entertainment as they enjoyed a drink together. They called it the 'Guess the Intro' game. It was simply the first to identify the song title and the artist as soon as the bar's music system started a new track. They would also need to stipulate the album on which the song first appeared and the year of its release. Currently, Tate was 4-2 up, having correctly guessed intros to tracks by AC/DC, Led Zeppelin, Black Sabbath and Bad Company. He failed to guess the release year of the latter.

Jonathan took two large gulps to finish his Guinness. 'Another pint for the music maestro?' he asked rhetorically as he proffered Tate's glass at him to finish his beer.

'Go on then, twist my arm,' Tate jested, downing the dregs of his pint. 'Can you make it a London Pride this time? I can't drink that heavy stuff all night.' Jonathan took the empty glass and headed in the direction of the bar. The next song track began. Tate sat back and played the 'Intro game' in his head. While trying to fathom the possible release year, his mobile signalled a message delivery. He retrieved the phone from the table.

'Where are you?'
'The Black Heart, Camden. With Jon.'
'Can I join you?'
'Of course.'
'Be there in 20 mins. I have something I'd like to run by you. x'
'OK. See you soon. x'

A pint arrived upon the table just as Tate put his phone down.

Jonathan stood above him and sipped the head from his new pint of Guinness.

'Blackfoot. 'Highway Song'. From the album *Strikes*, but I can't decide on the year.' Jonathan took up the stool opposite his friend once again. 'I'm thinking '79.'

'Not sure,' Tate replied, 'It's either '78 or '79. So I'll punt for '78.'

'If it were '79, then *Tomcattin* would have been released in 1980. Shall I ask Google? I noticed you on your phone while I was at the bar. You wouldn't happen to have had a sneaky peak?'

Tate mused at his friend's mocking. 'Why would I? For your information, it was Harriet. She is on her way. She said there was something she wanted to talk about.'

'It must be bloody important. She hates this place. She always complains about the music and the volume. If I remember correctly, she once threatened to issue the owner a breach of the peace order.' Tate and Jonathan broke into laughter and chinked their glasses.

The two men continued their joviality. They discussed what could be so important for Harriet to venture out to a rock pub in Camden. Many of the suggested reasons were foolish and senseless, but it maintained their convivial spirit. Jonathan was quick off the mark and brought the 'Guess the Intro' game to 4-4 with Iron Maiden. 'Aces High'. *Powerslave* '84.'

'Sorry, the train was held at Liverpool Street.' Harriet hollered over the music as she removed her coat and pulled up a stool beside Tate.

'Not a problem. We have been keeping ourselves amused,' yelled Jonathan, causing both the men to burst out laughing momentarily until Jonathan noticed the scowl in Harriet's expression. 'Wine? White? Large? I'll get it. Back in a mo.' As Jonathan headed in the direction of the bar,

Harriet complained about the noise level, asked if Tate had eaten and told of Happy's visit to Bethnal Green. She had to practically shout her narrative.

'Wine! White! Large!' apprised Jonathan above the music as he handed Harriet the glass and threw two bags of crisps into the centre of the table. 'So, what's so important for you to risk stepping over the threshold of this fine establishment?' Harriet repeated what she had divulged to Tate for Jonathan's benefit. She spoke of the blood reports, the sedative and the anti-coagulant, the condition of the lungs and the stomach contents. She described the letters cut into the feet and the removal of the tongue.

'Please don't tell me she's now collecting tongues,' proposed Jonathan, unconsciously pinching his own between his teeth. 'I don't recall any of Caravaggio's works with the subjects having their tongues removed.' He paused and looked thoughtfully into space for a moment. 'However, there is a painting attributed to him called 'The Tooth Puller.' Maybe she has changed her MO. She has had a year to think about it.'

'Serial killers have been known to develop their killing style over a period of time,' interjected Tate. 'However, there are usually particular characteristics that remain throughout.' Harriet reached into her jacket pocket and removed a folded sheet of paper.

'Well, we have one unequivocal sign that she hasn't completely changed that MO.' She handed it to Tate, who read the verse before handing it to Jonathan.

'It is tattooed on pigskin as before, and once again, it was found placed inside the oesophagus. I colour copied the real thing. It's the same approximate size as the previous ones.' Jonathan put the paper on the table, leant across and split open the bags of crisps. They all took a moment to scrutinise the four lines.

Can man not see what he has become
A solitary tear for all of God's sons.
I pray a great sadness shadows the land
Guilt is the shame on all man's hands.

Narcissus

Harriet was the first to speak. As she did so, she motioned with a crisp.

'Neptune's Finger. "Naamah's Tear". From the Album *After the Flood* '77.' She smugly put the whole crisp in her mouth and rubbed her hands. The two men looked dumbfoundedly at each other. Harriet raised her hands. 'Ok. I had to look it up. Bet you're impressed, though.' Both men said nothing at first, each supping their drinks. Tate spoke as Jonathan reached for more crisps.

'They are from different verses of the song.'

'Yes. I think the first two lines are from verse four,' spluttered Jonathan through a mouthful of chomps and crunches. 'The last two are definitely from the first verse.'

'Lena is interchanging the words to produce the efficacy she wishes for. I believe once again the desired effect is to taunt those investigating, but her most recent messages now seem to hold other underlying meanings.'

Harriet followed Tate's notion. 'With this message she seems to be implying that men have done wrong.' She continued her rationale, accentuating each point with another oversized crisp in her hand. 'In the last three messages, she equates the actions of the Narcissus with those of God. Since her return, it seems Lena can no longer see past her own beliefs. She sees it as her duty to judge those who have transgressed the law. I seriously think she now sees herself in the guise of a God. She is intent on punishing those who she believes have committed mortal sin and fallen from grace.' Both men again sat with little to say.

'Wow. You have certainly been thinking rationally about all of this,' were all the words Tate could find.

'I spent some time in the office after Happy departed, analogising the three messages. I wanted to express my ideas to you while they were still fresh in my mind.'

'How far do you think she may take this God complex?' enquired Jonathan while pouring the final crumbs of the crisp packet into his mouth. 'With each kill, her mania is escalating and feeding her narcissistic personality disorder. And what's with the new behaviour of removing the tongue?'

'Many serial killers take specific body parts as a trophy. It feeds their NPD and often makes them feel powerful, but more than often, it allows them to relive their crimes.' Tate looked briefly in Harriet's direction, hoping Jonathan had not noticed his glance. They had still not located the remainder of Jonathan's ex-girlfriend's body after she had been decapitated and the head sent to Jonathan towards the end of the Narcissus' murder campaign last summer. He certainly didn't need reminding of it. Tate threw a peek in his friend's direction. He was suspicious that the thought was crossing and permeating his friend's mind. Tate thought it best to quickly change the subject.

'Who fancies one more drink to round off the evening? We could grab one at The World's End on the way to the tube station?' All three downed the last dregs of their drinks. Tate playing to his distraction. Harriet more than happy to escape the pounding music and Jonathan following suit, knowing all too well, why his friend had played the card. Jocelyn's severed head still frequently troubled his mind.

They had just stood to leave when Jonathan motioned to have remembered something. He typed into his mobile. There was a short silence as he scrolled through the screen.

'Blackfoot. *Strikes* was released in '79. I believe that's 5-4.' He bowed.

As he rose, Tate offered his hand. 'Well done, my friend.'

46

She'd woken. Or had she? Her mind was a ball of confusion. She had a headache beyond all headaches. As the surroundings began to materialise before her, they did not seem to be familiar at all. A wave of shivers uncontrollably quivered through her body. She was naked but could not make sense of why she would be unclothed. But she was definitely cold. The log burner must have gone out. That's what it was. Her face felt peculiar, almost stiff. A terrifying thought struck her. Oh god, not a stroke. Panic swept through her. Surely not. She was in the prime of her life.

A voice spoke. Was it a neighbour. Maybe something had happened to her. She tried to move towards the source of the sound but found her limbs would not respond. A soreness began to emanate from her arm, and a similar discomfort manifested in an area on her leg. As her senses continued to awaken, she thought she could smell burnt bacon. But there would be no rational reason for such a thing.

'Are you hungry?'

There was the voice again. Kate found she could move her eyes, but her face remained rigid as if wearing some kind of mask. A figure stepped into view. It was a woman. But she did not recognise her as a friend or neighbour. The woman approached with something in her hand.

'Here. You must eat.'

The woman offered Kate the very thing that smelt of burnt bacon. Kate tried to raise her hands to accept the offering, but her arms would still not budge. It felt as if something was restricting her movement.

'May I have something to drink?' Kate asked. 'Maybe some water?'

'You must eat first,' came the reply, in a tone that Kate was not sure she liked. The woman held what looked like meat to Kate's mouth. She tentatively took a small bite. It tasted weird, not a taste she could recollect having had before. It smelt as if it had been barbecued, especially the small amount of crispy skin on its surface. She was given another bite. As she chewed a second time, Kate could not decide if the texture or even the flavour was something she liked.

'May I have a drink now?'

'Not until you have finished your food.' A third piece of the meat-like food was pushed into her mouth. She tried her best to chew, but the meat was proving difficult to consume. Kate eventually managed to swallow the meaty morsel. But no sooner had it reached her stomach than her body regurgitated it. Her mouth now tasted of the sickly bile that had risen with the disgorgement.

'Please, can I have some water now?'

'Only when you have eaten the offering,' replied the Narcissus as she forced the ejected vomit-covered food back into Kate's mouth and callously closed it with her hand.

'Eat it.'

Kate suddenly became fearsome of the situation. Why was this woman acting in such a way that it seemed to be menacing and threatening? And for what reason? A chain of scenarios flashed through her mind. Each envisagement casting more fear into what was now becoming a surreal ordeal. It was quickly becoming freakishly frightening.

Once again, the figure of the woman appeared in front of Kate. She seemed to be squatting to look directly into her eyes. For the first time, Kate could focus on the woman's appearance. There was something quite familiar about her face. She racked her brain to match the face to that of a friend or acquaintance.

The woman spoke again. 'Are you not hungry? You are certainly greedy enough.'

Kate was unsure what the woman meant but perceived her words as threatening.

'Your greed has tainted your soul. You are happy to mislead others in your cheating ways. You display no consideration for those you fleece. Now is the time to confess your transgressions. Your fate will depend on the affirmation of your mercies.'

A perilous dread washed over Kate. She could make no sense of what was happening. The horrific ordeal was inexplicable. In fact, it was way beyond belief. Her questioning could no longer perceive rational answers.

Kate looked up as she heard movement. The woman was no longer standing before her. A sound stirred from behind. She tried to turn, but her shackles held firm. The realisation that she was secured to a chair ensued.

She felt the woman's presence once more. This time close to her left ear.

'Declare your transgressions,' announced the Narcissus.

Kate found enough strength to wrestle with her bindings and spit a reply.

'This is craziness. What the hell do you want?' She had barely ended her question when a searing pain emanated below her right shoulder. Kate cried out and hunched forward, pulling at her restraints.

'Accept your punishments!'

Once again, an excruciating agony erupted from her upper back.

'Stop this, please. It's complete madness.' She tried to turn towards her tormentor. She twisted and turned, fighting to free her bindings.

'Admit to your sins.'

Kate could no longer contain her suffering. A deep fear and loathing spewed from her mouth. 'You're deluded. This is insane. You're out of your mind. You bloody evil bitch.' The torrent of abuse was rewarded with two further incisions and followed by pain way beyond Kate's threshold. So agonising that she lost consciousness.

As the pain of her maltreatment subsided, Kate's eyes opened slowly. It took a moment to find herself again. The memories came flooding back. It had not all been a horrid dream. She winced as the pain in her back returned, reminding her of her situation. She tried hopelessly to comfort the affliction, but her hands were still tied. As she grappled with her bindings once more, the woman reappeared in front of her. Kate watched as the woman retrieved something from a table to her left before squatting at her captive's eye level as she had previously done.

Suddenly, the reality of what was happening hit Kate and made her blood run cold. She had been fairly certain that she had known the face or at least seen it before. Now, it finally dawned on her. The face had been all over the news last summer. The panic within began to spiral to a level she struggled to contain. A single word rose above all else. A single word that may well be her last.

'Narcissus.'

On hearing her name, the woman reciprocated with a simple smile as she moved ever closer to Kate's face. They were virtually nose to nose when the Narcissus thrust a hand into Kate's mouth and grasped her tongue. As she pulled the tongue forward, her other hand came into view.

The hand held a pair of stainless-steel poultry shears.

47

Harriet looked up from her position at the front of the room.

'Who's not here?'

'Me!'

'Thank you, Jake. Not helpful. Where's Greg?'

'Just coming, Ma'am,' came the reply and the raising of a hand.

'Has anyone seen Andy?' Harriet asked as she scanned the room. The remainder of the crew were perched with their ears pricked and ready to hang on their senior officer's every word.

'He was just finishing up assembling some CCTV footage onto a USB stick ahead of the meeting,' declared Sarika as she placed her hot chocolate to one side. Harriet caught sight of the words printed on the outside of the mug.

'New mug?'

'Yep. It was a birthday present from George.' He smiled from across the room.

'What does it say on the side? I can't quite make it out from here?'

'Touch my hot chocolate mug and CSI will have a new case to investigate!' A peal of laughter encircled the investigation room. As the hilarity subsided, there was a tapping on the door glass, and Tate appeared. Harriet beckoned him to come in.

'I hope you weren't waiting for me. The traffic in the city is terrible.'

'No, not at all. We were just giving DS Stevens a few—'

'Sorry, Ma'am. Took a bit longer than expected,' justified Andy Stevens, holding the USB stick up before sitting on the nearest empty table edge.

'Ok. Let's not waste any more time. I think we can be fairly certain that the Narcissus has begun a second killing spree. I know we only have one crime scene, but with everything else included, I am pretty sure it won't be the last. So, we need to get onto this fast and stop this blowing completely out of control.' There was a nodding of agreement from around the room. Each person was prepared and ready to fulfil their role in bringing the Narcissus to justice once and for all.

'Perhaps you could provide the team with a run-through of the victim's background to start,' Harriet asked, emphasising the question in Tate's direction.

'Be only too happy.' He handed a profile picture to Harriet before continuing. 'The victim is William O'Connor. He was also known within certain criminal circles as 'Billy the Owl'. He was a career criminal. He worked alone and always after dark, hence the moniker. He was one of the few old-school cat burglars still active in the city. He has had numerous run-ins with the law on and off for the last forty years or so. He has served three stretches inside for domestic and non-domestic burglary, handling stolen goods and trading stolen wares. My department has recently been investigating Mr O'Connor for a series of breaking and entering crimes, coupled with the stealing and trading of several stolen artworks. As far as we can attest, he has no known associates and no known family or next of kin. Hence, there has been no formal identification of the deceased at present. Although, fingerprints match those we have on file.' Tate leant across once again, this time handing Harriet a file.

'Thank you, DCI Randall.' Harriet pinned the victim's picture to a blank section of the investigation board and turned back to eye DS Richards. 'Iain. Could you update us on how things are at the crime scene?'

DS Richards took a quick sip of his coffee and proceeded with his report. 'The crime scene at the 'East Meats West' butchery shop is still active. Scenes of Crime investigators are still processing the final details. The chair and bindings have been removed from the scene and taken to their lab for further analysis.' Pausing momentarily, he retrieved three evidence bags from the desk to his rear. 'These have already been processed. Fingerprints on all three are a positive match to those held in the police database for former police investigator, Detective Inspector Lena Johnson.' He placed the two larger evidence bags containing a funnel and a short length of piping to one side. He held forward the third clear windowed bag. 'The plastic Halloween banner tape used to secure the outside of the cellar doors has again been analysed, and the suspect's fingerprints were found.'

Tate looked curiously across at the bag in the Detective Sergeant's hand. His attention was aroused by the item within. 'May I take a look, please?' Iain handed the evidence across to Tate. As he did so, a sudden realisation struck Harriet.

'Oh gosh. It completely slipped my mind,' she declared, briefly covering her face with her hands. 'I meant to tell you when we first discovered the body. Bugger.'

Tate turned the bag over in his hands so he could read the wording scrolling around the folded banner. A moment of disbelief manifested upon his face. He returned the evidence to DS Richards without so much as a word. A moment of awkwardness hung in the air.

Tate broke the unease. 'It's not your fault at all, Harriet. You have an awful lot to think about. We are all prone to forgetting the odd thing now and then. We cannot be expected to remember every little detail.' He paused and returned with a smile. 'It seems someone does not want me to forget who they are.' The air of discomfiture lifted. 'It would seem they are keen for me not to let Halloween go unnoticed this year. Looks like I had better get myself a costume. I'm not so sure I could carry off the Buffy the Vampire Slayer look.' A ripple of amusement refilled the meeting's tone. 'Although, I could see myself more as George the Dragon Slayer.' More laughter ensued, and Harriet pushed her unease to one side.

'Has anything interesting come from the door-to-door inquiries?'

DS Richards motioned for DC Thompson to respond.

'Not much, really, Ma'am. Mostly, nothing of interest or those not wishing to get involved. One gentleman remembered seeing a light on in the cellar when he passed on his way home from the Red Lion a couple of days ago, but he can't be too sure of the day as he goes to the pub most nights. Apart from that, very little else to report.'

'Thank you, Greg. How are we getting along with CCTV, Iain? Anything from the cameras on East Ham High Street?'

'Again, nothing of interest really. The usual comings and goings to the neighbouring properties. Deliveries, waste collections, road sweepers. Unfortunately, all the cameras we can access are street cams along the north and south ends of the High Street or shop cameras that point to the same aspect. So far, we have no cameras at the rear of the properties or the adjacent back alleyway.'

'You don't just push someone into a crime scene in a wheelchair without being seen,' propounded Harriet quizzically.'

'We are going with the assumption that she must have used a vehicle. Her previous exploits were meticulously planned. So, we are second-guessing that she parked a vehicle in a pre-reconnaissance blind spot. Our current avenue of interest, regarding the camera footage we have, is attempting to track larger vehicles seen passing through cameras positioned to both the north and the south ends of the High Street. Especially those with an unusually longer time frame between the two. The problem is the high number of interconnecting roads. It's a bit of a tough call, really.'

'Thanks, Iain. Has anyone else have anything relating to the current crime scene?'

Sarika raised her hot chocolate mug to indicate she had information to contribute. 'DS Richards ask me to look into The 'East Meats West' Butchery business. It has been leased to a Mr Adir Yehuda since 2009. The property has been empty for several months since Mr Yehuda closed the doors in April this year. The property is owned by a financial conglomerate registered at Companies House as the Crown Corporations Group.'

'To be fair, the Narcissus probably only chose the property because it was empty and for no other reason,' added DS George Quinn.

Sarika continued. 'The plastic piping can be purchased at a multitude of stores. The same goes for the Halloween banner tape. It can be purchased at supermarkets and discount stores at this time of the year. The funnel, however, has traceable possibilities. It is marked as a branded product from B&Q. There are 17 stores in the Greater London area. We have asked them to provide CCTV footage and payment transactions corresponding to the product barcode. We can then cross reference them, therefore reducing the hours of footage both George and I have to sit through. Although with a packet of biscuits between us, it's a bit like a movie night in.' She blew a kiss across the room in George's direction. 'It's a long shot. If we find footage of Lena purchasing the funnel, it may lead to tracking her on the street cams to a residential address.

'Let me know if you need civies to help trawl through the footage. I'll see who I can muster up,' declared Harriet before turning her attention and shuffling through some papers in her hand. 'Results from the post-mortem findings,' she said, referring to one of the pages. 'The cause of death is cerebral anoxia due to submersion in liquid. The liquid being his own blood. Toxicology reports show a large amount of Etorphine in the victim's blood, along with an anticoagulant known as Heparin. Heparin is an intravenous drug used in the treatment of heart attacks and angina. It decreases the clotting ability of blood. The Etorphine was most probably used as per the Narcissus's previous crimes to incapacitate the victims.'

Harriet removed two sheets of paper from those in her hand and pinned both to the investigation wall. 'The victim had the letters M and W carved into the souls of his feet. Any suggestions?'

'The only thing that springs to mind is the old-fashioned symbols on the toilet doors down the pub,' proclaimed George, half-jokingly.

'If I remember correctly, M&W is a silver hallmark used by a cutlery manufacturer in Sheffield. Probably not significant,' added Tate.

DC Evans was next to comment. 'I have just done a quick internet search. Results include Maison & White homewares, M&W clothing and M&W custom trombones.' Again, sniggers boomeranged across the room. 'There are also numerous other companies using their partner's initials.'

'Can I leave that one with you, Jake? Maybe dig a little deeper.' He acknowledged his superior officer and Harriet moved on. 'Last, but by far not the least, the Narcissus' calling card was once again found within the victim's oesophagus.' She held up an evidence bag before handing it across to Tate, and again, she added a photograph to the wall. This time, it was a colour copy of the message that Tate was looking over. When a new piece of evidence was added to the 'Crazy Wall', it was like adding a piece to an unexplainable jigsaw. The outcome only revealed itself when all the pieces were in place. They were still a long way from collating all the pieces of this investigation, but eventually, everything would fit into place. Only then would justice be served.

'Can I hand this over to you, Sarika? Along with the previous two messages, could you start a web search and see what comes up? There may well be something looking us straight in the face that we can't see. It's a bit of a long shot, but it has worked before.' Harriet glanced at her watch. She was keen to move things along. Although 'crew' meetings were vitally important to any investigation, Harriet was also conscious that time could be better spent being more productive.

'Ok, Andy. Bring us up to speed with what you have uncovered concerning the Tate Modern incident.'

DS Stevens cued up the footage he had collated on a USB. He hit play and gave a running commentary as the CCTV clips played. 'After putting on quite a show for the gallery's security footage, the Narcissus can be seen leaving the building by the riverside exit. The camera, covering the outside of the building towards the Bankside path, follows her to the river's edge. She could have just as easily exited via the Balavatnik exit and disappeared quietly towards Southwark tube station and beyond. But I believe she was intent on being ostentatious and making a show for the cameras.' The footage continued and a different camera angle cut in. The Narcissus flaunted her red outfit, and just as she would have wanted, she was clearly visible amongst the crowds. 'Here, the riverside camera picks her up on the approach to the Millennium Bridge. We can follow her across the bridge before cameras on the north bank pick up her approach.' A new camera feed continued to capture the Narcissus's movements. 'This camera tracks her on Peter's Hill, and we can see clearly that she turns left into Castle Baynard Street. Unfortunately, there are no cameras from here. The next cameras are on White Lion Hill and Queen Victoria Street. Neither of which captures our suspect.' The footage froze on the final image of the Narcissus and DS Stevens handed Harriet an identical still shot. Again, the image was added to the evidence board.

'Look into all possibilities of what may have happened in that blind spot. Blackfriars, Mansion House and Cannon Street tube stations are all in close proximity. Did she go underground? Did she make a change of clothing or appearance? Did she get into a taxi or get on a bus? Hell, someone may have even picked her up.'

DS Quinn raised a hand and cut in, interrupting his superior officer. 'Sorry, Ma'am. I just wanted to add that the Baynard House car park is directly across White Lion Hill from Castle Baynard Street. It was on my patch, back when I pounded the beat.'

'Thanks, George. Did you ever take the cabbie's Knowledge of London?'

'No. Ma'am. Just spent way too many years as a Bobbie.'

'So, she could have left a vehicle waiting. Whichever way, she would have had it planned down to the smallest detail. We know that from the way she planned her escape from the roof of Battersea Power Station last summer. Get down there, Andy. See if there is anything stashed or discarded. Look at the bus routes. If she got onto a bus, she will be on camera. Obtain the footage from all buses whose routes pass through that area. Tell the TFL I will get a warrant if need be. Also, check the black cabs, taxis, Ubers and alike, for fares with a woman in red. If she had taken a cab, the driver is bound to have remembered her. A woman dressed in red would have been so distinctive that nobody will forget her in a hurry.' Andy Stevens jotted down an arsenal of bullet points, each relating to his required actions, and Harriet took a short break to sip from her Relentless drink before running her hands back through her hair.

'Ok. Where were we?' She looked at the investigation board. The photograph of the victim sitting in the chair caught her eye. 'Jake. Where are we with the papers and the source of the photographs?'

'The usual brick walling and red tape. The City Chronicle would not comment directly on whether the source was the Narcissus or not.'

'Get straight on the phone when we finish here. In fact, no. Get down to their offices. Find out what's really going on. Hound them until you get an answer. I want to know how, where and when the Narcissus is sending the photos. Don't take no for an answer. If they put up a wall of client confidentiality, threaten them with a subpoena. Any contact with the Narcissus could provide us with vital evidence of her whereabouts, where she is currently living and possibly where the stolen Caravaggio might be.'

48

The Botanist, Sloane Square, is a popular haunt for young city workers who wish to socialise and network while sipping hand-crafted cocktails or sharing a bottle of sparkling Cuvée. Its chic Chelsea location lends itself to all day fine dining and prolonged weekend brunches.

Turner had sat at the bar cradling a Gin & Tonic as he looked through the street side windows. A slight sense of apprehension had begun to flutter within his stomach as each minute had passed. His edginess became more apparent when their pre-arranged meeting time had crept past the hour, and there had yet to be any sign of his lunch date.

He had repeatedly turned his wrist to see if time had moved forward from when he had last checked two minutes earlier. He continuously checked his phone for a message of excuse or an apology for running late, despite a lack of pings and buzzes to alert his attention. Occasionally, Turner would catch sight of his reflection in the mirror to the rear of the bar's optic selection. This did nothing to ease his angst of being stood up for a second time. In fact, they had only messaged each other until now. He had no idea what his date would look like and questioned his own appeal to women. Even though they had messaged frequently over the previous weeks, it was still a blind date. A thought struck him. Maybe she had stalked him online, and upon seeing a profile picture, she had become less interested. This thought did nothing for his current state of unease.

Feeling slightly dejected and with the prospect of informing the front of house staff that he would no longer be needing the table, Turner turned to stare into the optics rear view mirror once again. His reflected self was distracted by the attractive woman approaching the stool to his left, or was it his right? He did not immediately turn but remained eyeballing the reflected image as a new wave of optimism began to pulse through his body. A brief moment of emotional excitement made his heart palpitate and his palms sweat before the trepidation of the blind date gripped him once more.

'Turner?' asked a voice in a hushed tone. With his pulse rapid firing and the butterflies flailing, he tentatively turned. His eyes were immediately drawn to the innocence of the woman's face.

'Sarah?' replied Turner, trying his best to remain calm.

'It's lovely to finally put a face to the messenger,' she smiled. 'Although I do have a little confession to make. I could not stop myself from looking up your profile online. I hope you don't mind. It's a bit silly of me, really. It spoilt some of the fun of a blind date.'

Turner was somewhat pleased he had not done the very same, for the nervous tension may have been too much.

'It's lovely to meet you too,' he replied, offering his hand in a timorous first date gesture. 'What can I get you to drink?'

Sarah reached for a drinks menu. She took a short while to peruse the selection. 'A glass of rosé would be wonderful, thank you.'

'Anything in particular?'

Sarah handed the menu across. 'You choose,' she replied with a slight impish undertone.

Turner ordered the wine and a staff member showed them across to their table. He politely gestured for Sarah to follow first. As they were guided between the tables, Turner could not help but notice the petite frame beneath the summery floral dress and the dark curly ringlets that tumbled across his date's shoulders.

They chatted, enquired, questioned, and quizzed each other about the other's background and current situation. They divulged, revealed and uncovered each other's likes and dislikes as they mused over the menu's offerings. The conversation continued as their orders were taken and their discussions swung from one subject to another. Soon, they found the common interest was inevitably art, which wasn't surprising, having first met on an online art forum and both working in the art world. Turner was only too happy to discover that Sarah was currently working on an art restoration project in the heart of the city.

The waiter returned with their orders. Peterhead cod, baked oyster and crushed new potatoes for Sarah and Turner's choice of slow-cooked Welsh lamb shoulder and garlic mash. They both ordered another drink. As they ate, the topic of conversation more than often returned to art. Each talked about their jobs, interests in particular fields, favourite artists, artworks, and galleries.

The desserts, each simply choosing a sorbet, came and went. Coffees followed and the conversation continued to flow. A joint admiration for the portraiture of Rembrandt and Giovanni Boldini was discovered and

Turner's unparalleled passion for the works of Picasso was dissected and became their first differing of opinion.

When the bill arrived, Turner offered to pay, but Sarah suggested they go 'Dutch' as it was their first date. This fostered a sense of gratification within Turner. If today was referred to as a 'first date', was it suggesting the possibility of engendering a second meeting? They were both apprehensive and cautious as they embraced on the pavement outside the front of the restaurant. Neither was in a hurry to leave, and the conversation continued before Sarah insisted she needed to go as she had a project to deliver and a deadline to meet. They said their goodbyes, and Turner stood and watched as Sarah headed towards the tube station.

The butterflies within his stomach were now flittering in a dance of merriment.

49

The journey back from Bethnal Green had been just as exasperating as his earlier trip through the city. The traffic was still heavy. Roadworks and traffic lights had seemingly risen out of the earth during the short time he had spent meeting with Harriet and her team.

Tate had spent the remainder of the morning within the confines of his office. Armed with a large take-out Columbian black coffee sweetened with an amount of sugar that would put most people on the verge of hyperglycaemia, he had worked through the appropriate channels and procedures to reinstate the missing Caravaggio as a priority one case. The reappearance of the prime suspect and the recent unlawful activity matching the incidents by the very same hand last summer, increased the likelihood of the 'St Mary Magdalene in Ecstasy' resurfacing and the increased chance of the painting making an appearance on the black market once again.

Since that day in August the previous summer, when Lena had narrowly escaped his clutches, Tate had continued investigating the stolen Caravaggio. His team unceasingly followed up on lines of enquiry and information pertaining to the eventual recovery of the painting. However, he was reasonably sure that the trail of the Caravaggio had gone cold because Lena had most probably stored the painting in a secure location before going to ground herself. He had continued to investigate the possibility that she may still be attempting to sell the work on the black market. However, the idea did not sit comfortably due to her family's connections to Caravaggio and her reasons for stealing the painting in the first instance.

Now that the likelihood of Lena being back on British soil was irrefutable, Tate knew deep down that, at some point, their paths would cross once more. It would be what Lena wanted, and an encounter would have undeniably been part of her plan when she had decided to return.

With that being the case, Tate would refocus his team's ensuing inquiries on high-security storage facilities. If Lena had stored the Caravaggio before her prolonged disappearance, she may now decide to retrieve the artwork or visit a facility to view the painting. This would mean viewing hours of footage from CCTV cameras in the streets around significant banks and security vaults. Client confidentiality within such establishments would prevent any investigation of their client lists. He would hand the scrutiny of the surveillance cameras to DC Morrison. However, Tate was also aware that the 'St Mary Magdalene in Ecstasy' could quite simply be hanging in plain sight on a wall in a residential property that they knew nothing about. It may also have been transported back overseas; a viable option made less challenging with Lena's knowledge of customs and border patrol. It was also not beyond the realms of possibility that the Caravaggio had already changed hands and was now hanging in a private collection of a wealthy individual. Whatever the circumstances, Tate and his Italian counterpart Ricardo Moretti would leave no stone unturned until the 'St Mary Magdalene in Ecstasy' was returned to its rightful owner.

Tate and Moretti had spoken regularly since the stealing of the Caravaggio. They had kept each other updated with developments on their respective sides of the investigation. The Italian inquiries had long gone cold, and they firmly believed that the Narcissus had worked alone on the night the painting had been stolen and subsequently hidden within the carrier painting. From this point onwards, Tate would continue to keep his opposite number updated with any further developments occurring from the reappearance of the Narcissus. He would do everything in his control to ensure every necessary measure would be implemented to intercept the Caravaggio were it sold or trafficked abroad.

Tate wandered about his office as he pondered his next move. After considering all the facts and information, he concluded that now would be as good a time as any to visit a certain friend. Someone who constantly had his eyes and ears to the ground when it came to the corruptive black-market underworld of the capital's art scene.

If a major work were rumoured to be creating interest behind closed doors, Tommy would have heard.

50

Brooks had received the text message just as he was about to shower. It was an address and nothing more. He had then drunk three cans of Guinness before deciding on whether or not to photograph what he was fairly sure, or if he were truthfully honest with himself, would most definitely be a second body. He took the fourth can with him, and the shower didn't happen. He now found himself standing outside the door of the cold storage unit. He was one step away from another sizeable paycheck. But still, his conscience fought to justify all the reasons why he should walk away.

He found himself with one hand on the door's handle.

A voice saying, 'Walk away now,' tugged at his other arm.

But the money had the final say, and he stepped across the threshold.

Brooks looked at the naked woman's body. The kill site was in no way the same as the primary scene. On first appearance, there appeared to be little comparison to the blood lust of the initial killing. In fact, there appeared to be very little blood at all. However, as with the previous crime scene, the hands and feet of the victim had been bound to a chair. The naked woman's breasts had been streaked with red paint. The hair of her pubic mound had also been coloured a deep crimson. Steve moved around the body, his camera capturing images from each different perspective. The woman's face appeared to have been covered by some kind of mask. The edges of which blended into her hairline. It reminded him of the beauty face masks his sister had applied as a teenager before going to bed. However, the woman's mask was not the colour of the rejuvenating clay mud of the Dead Sea, it was far from it. He could not draw his aperture from the brilliant ruby red mask. It somewhat reminded him of a picture he once saw of Dante's death mask. The red of the victim's mask was the same deep tone as the cloth lining of the display case in which the great poet's mask is now displayed. Splashes of the vibrant colour were easily visible on other parts of the woman's body.

Small diamond shapes, again overlaid with the same clay and painted, gave the impression of a harlequin's coat. A patchwork of the four-sided shapes, each a shade of red, embellished the dead woman's body.

Brooks zoomed his lens to frame a closer perspective and through the viewfinder, he could make out the remnants of vomit splashed across the front of her torso. Had the woman retched in fear? Or had she been fed some form of poison? His head started to fill with the suffering the woman would have encountered before succumbing to the Narcissus' torments. Pushing the thoughts that troubled his mind to one side, he reached into a pocket and retrieved a pair of gloves. With his hands covered to prevent the transfer of fingerprints, Brooks reached to touch one of the areas daubed in the clay-like substance, the surface still wet from its overpainting. As he pressed lightly against the clay covered shape on the woman's thigh, the surface cracked, separated and fell in two pieces to the floor, where it immediately shattered in an explosion of fragments. However, the breakage was of little concern to Brooks.

His attention was absorbed by the bare, mucilaginous, blood encrusted area upon the woman's thigh where her flesh had been taken.

Bring the pages alive...

Explore artworks, locations and more.

Go to gnsbooks.com (Interactive) or scan the QR code to unlock images, maps and facts as you read.

Parsons Green
London, England

51

They had departed Thorney Street in the latter half of the afternoon. Their chosen route hugged the northern banks of the river towards Chelsea. The traffic was easy-going, with the school run having finished and the evening commuter traffic yet to clog the city's main arteries. DS Garrett had recapped the Palmer case notes from the file in her lap. She had also updated Tate on her observations from a recent surveillance outing. DS Garrett and DC Morrison had followed the movements of their suspect, Kate Palmer, for the previous four days. During the operation, they had followed the suspect to the Spitalfields market area. They witnessed Ms Palmer meeting with a gentleman, who was later identified as a known dealer of 19th century ceramics. During the meeting, DC Morrison had captured photographic evidence of their suspect producing two items of stoneware for the gentleman's inspection. Kate Palmer had also failed to attend a pre-arranged formal meeting. Her failure to attend the meeting and an accumulation of sufficient evidence instigated the reason for today's unannounced visit to the suspect's property.

As they left the riverside road, taking the A308 towards Parsons Green, the low autumnal sun to the west shot sporadic beams of radiant orange directly into Tate's view, making it difficult to see the road ahead clearly. He flipped down the sun visor and asked Jane to do the same on the passenger side. Being a vintage vehicle of 60 years, the narrow sun visors had little effect on shading Tate's line of vision.

'It may not be the height of luxury, but the Land Rover sure has some credibility,' declared Jane, adjusting the sun visor to find its optimum position.

'I had to get the visors fitted. The old girl didn't have any when I first inherited her from my Grandfather. Driving into the rising or setting sun used to be a hazardous pastime. I'm not sure these early visors are that much help at all.' Tate had to slow the Land Rover to enable him to squint his vision and safely pass an occasional parked car.

As they passed Eel Brook Common, Jane began to feed Tate directions to the street they were looking for. She followed the navigation arrow on her phone due to the lack of technology in the 1963 Land Rover Series 2. As they neared the property they sought, Jane noticed a cassette case balanced precariously in the vehicle's ashtray. She reached over and removed the case. Her eyes lit up.

'Wow. *Red Octopus* by Jefferson Starship. I haven't heard this since borrowing my brother's record collection when he first went away to university.'

'It's in the stereo—'

'Left before the crossing,' Jane interrupted, noticing the street they wanted was fast approaching. 'If we have time, perhaps we can listen to it on the way back?'

Tate signalled and turned the Land Rover into the side street. 'For sure. What number are we looking for?'

'Number 2. It should be at this end of the street on the right.'

Tate parked the Land Rover in what was probably the only space available along the tree lined street; it resulted in the need to retrace their steps, having passed No. 2 a couple of hundred metres back.

'What's with all the lions along the rooftops?' enquired Jane.

'Apparently, local folklore implies that in the late 1890s, when this part of the Peterborough Estate was built, the builder, whose trade mark was a lion, placed an order for the sandstone statues but mistakenly added an extra zero to the quantity required. The original sculptures were only to be used on the grander houses, but the larger number they received meant a lion would adorn every brick fronted property. Since that day, they have been referred to as the lion houses.'

'Your mind really is filled with useless information,' chuckled Jane.

'It's never useless if you use it. And it provided an answer to your question,' Tate advocated as they approached the door of No.2.

They rang the bell and waited. No one answered.

They knocked on the door. Still, no one appeared.

Tate looked through the partially closed curtains. Nobody could be seen.

'Maybe she got twitchy and has done a runner!' exclaimed DS Garrett.

'You may not be too far from the truth,' Tate suggested, stepping back to the roadside to look up at the second-floor windows. 'Let's see if that side gate is unlocked and maybe take a look around the rear of the property.'

Tate checked for signs of life through the patio and kitchen doors. The house appeared to be empty. 'You don't live in a property like this on just a teacher's salary.'

DS Garrett walked towards the far end of the garden; she did not hear Tate's assertion. As she approached what looked like a summer house-come shed, a cat appeared and bunted up against her leg.

'Hello. Where have you come from?' She bent down and stroked the cat, who continued to encircle her legs, all the while arching its back and rubbing its head. DS Garrett looked in the direction from which the cat had approached and noticed the door to the shed was ajar. With the cat in tow, she proceeded towards a long window running the length of the front façade of the wooden building. As she neared ever closer, she could hear a rhythmic whirling. The sound was somewhat relaxing, almost hypnotic. It drew her to the window.

Like the house, the inside of the shed appeared to be empty. The alluring sound came from a potter's wheel as it turned repeatedly. What had probably once been the beginnings of a clay pot was collapsed at the centre of the wheel.

'Anything?' asked Tate as he, too, approached the window.

'Looks very much like someone left in a hurry.'

Tate peered through the glass. 'That's if she left of her own accord.'

Being fairly certain that nobody was lurking within the potter's studio, the two detectives entered through the unlocked wooden door. Their suspicions were right; the building was empty. Tate continued into the room, putting on gloves. As he did so, he turned off the potter's wheel. He looked around for any signs of a struggle but found nothing. The only thing that looked out of place was a brightly coloured box on a table to the rear. He curiously approached the box and cautiously removed its lid.

Inside was a cake decorated with orange and black icing.

Words encircled its circumference.

Happy Halloween Tate

Duke of York Square
London, England

52

London had once again awoken enshrouded in a gloomy murk. The dawning sun did little in its feeble attempt to burn through the bleakness. The fog crawled along the serpentine coils of the Thames, meandering under the bellies of its bridges, engulfing the river's banks and neighbouring streets under a haunting cloak laden in grey.

Philip Henry Woodrow would typically have cycled the remainder of his journey from the platform at Waterloo. However, this morning's soupy murkiness meant that cycling would have been foolish and walking had been the far safer option. However, the fifteen or so minutes longer that walking had taken, meant he had to hasten his morning walk-through of the gallery's floors.

The Saatchi Gallery opened in 1985, exhibiting works from Charles Saatchi's private collection in numerous premises across the capital before settling in its current location in 2008. From its early days exhibiting works by American artists such as Judd, Twombly, Ryman and, of course, Warhol, it soon gained a solid following and became home for a new generation of young British artists, namely Damien Hirst. Today, it is recognised globally as an authority in contemporary art.

There were still twenty minutes until the gallery's doors opened to the general public. It still left Philip Henry with enough time to complete his daily inspection of the gallery's fifteen exhibition rooms over three floors. He would have preferred to have more time. Each morning, he savoured his private tour of the current collection within the walls of the Grade II listed 19th century building known as the Duke of York's HQ.

He had held the title of Gallery Director for a little over six years. Before this, he had been Consultant Curator, a role that commissioned artists and bespoke works for future exhibits.

His route through the gallery would always start at the public entrance and he would systematically work his way through the exhibit rooms, floor by floor, to end on the second floor where his office was situated. Philip

Henry had covered the rooms on the ground floor a little quicker than he would have liked, making a mental note of anything he felt needed attention and to whom the responsibility fell should action have to be instigated. On the first floor, he worked his way through galleries 6-8 and checked that the door to the gallery store room was securely locked.

Philip Henry stood at the entrance to Gallery 10. From where he stood, he could see the entire length of the room. Numerous pedestals were positioned throughout the gallery to encircle a large floor sculpture of the human brain. Each pedestal held further sculptures depicting various forms of the human head. The exhibit by students of UAL was entitled 'The Minds of Tomorrow.' As Philip Henry surveyed the room, his attention was immediately drawn to something on the wall at the far end. For this exhibit, the composition specified pure white uninterrupted walls on all four sides.

With a sense of incertitude and concern, Philip Henry made his way between the pedestals. As he neared the far wall, the relevance of the anomaly became clear. It had not been there the previous day; he was sure about that. But when could it have been installed? He had seen the headlines relating to a similar occurrence at the Tate Modern some days ago. Standing before the picture, Philip Henry found himself engrossed in its composition. It was not the image but the subject matter. If indeed this was a similar occurrence to the one at the Tate Modern, he was looking at the victim of a murder. A murder at the hands of the headline capturing killer known as the Narcissus. A sudden impulse of realisation hit him and a chain of events unfolded in his head. He addressed the likelihood of several possibilities and the outcomes of each dilemma.

Postpone the opening of the gallery.

Close the first floor to the general public.

Seal off Gallery 10 only.

Or remove the picture.

It did not take Philip Henry long to make a decision. He had yet to collect his staff radio set from the security room, so he headed in that direction. As he walked briskly, he thought about the other protocols the gallery would need to initiate to remain open. The door to the security room was ajar and Philip Henry walked straight in.

'We need to secure Room 10. Seal it off so that the public can't go in. Get a sign up there saying 'Exhibit Temporarily Closed.' And get another down to the entrance to explain the closure. Once you have done so, please have yesterday's security footage ready to be viewed. Any questions? Thank you chaps.' He left and headed for his office.

Philip Henry knew precisely who to call, for this time tomorrow, the Saatchi Gallery would be on the front pages.

But for all the wrong reasons.

Hyde Park Corner
London, England

53

They sat in the queue of traffic. Every junction of the oversized roundabout that encircled the Wellington Arch was nose-to-tail with vehicles. All were hurrying to get somewhere, but all were going nowhere.

After their early morning swim in the Serpentine, Tate and Jonathan chose to have breakfast at the So French café in Seymour Place. Each had ordered espresso, pain perdu and croissant. The only thing detracting from the total French experience was the weather, resulting in them having to sit inside rather than al fresco.

Both tapped away to the rhythm of the drum pattern. Tate's fingers rapped along on the steering wheel and Jonathan's upon his thighs, with the occasional drum fill across the dashboard.

'What a great instrumental. Released in '73, I believe.'

'It was on their debut album. *They only come out at night.*'

'Wasn't it released as a single?'

Tate's phone interrupted the deliberation. Jonathan turned off the music.

'Can you get it for me? And remember, it may be work related,' stated Tate, knowing that Jonathan often answered his own phone with the occasional wisecrack.

'Tate Randall's phone. Jonathan speaking.'

'Good Morning to you, Jonathan. My name is Philip Henry Woodrow. I am the Gallery Director over at the Saatchi. I was hoping to talk with Tate.'

'He is driving at present.' Tate motioned to Jonathan, who understood the gesture.

'I am putting you on speakerphone. Just hold on one moment, please. Ok. Fire away.'

There was a slight hesitation from the other end of the call. 'I believe we may have another picture similar to the one that was unexpectedly hung at the Tate Modern the other day,'

Tate glanced across at Jonathan. The look in his eyes said it all. He spoke, the microphone capturing his voice. 'Who else might have seen it?'

'I can't be sure at present. We have yet to identify when it was hung.'

'You have done the right thing in calling me,' stressed Tate. He had worked alongside Philip Henry several times and knew he was a man set in his ways. 'Seal off the room. No one, including staff, should enter, please. Traffic permitting, we are only five minutes away. It may be a good idea to hold off allowing the public to enter the gallery for now.'

The Gallery Director was about to question the necessity of the complete closure of the Saatchi when Tate continued.

'I need to hang up now. I have another call I need to make! We will be with you as soon as we can.' Jonathan ended the call and began scrolling through the phone's directory, pre-empting his friend's next move. The dialling tone sounded through the hands-free speaker.

'Tate. Hang on a second, will you? I'm on a treadmill.' Music filled the background.

'Sorry. Ok. Fire away.'

'You are on speaker phone; Jon is sitting in the Landy with me.' The serious edge to Tate's voice warranted no reply from the other end of the call. 'I have just received a call from the Director at the Saatchi Gallery. There is a strong possibility that we may well have a second picture, which would strongly suggest a second crime scene. If this is indeed the fact, then I have a pretty good idea who the victim may be.'

'I take it they have sealed the room?' affirmed Harriet rhetorically.

'Yep. No one in or out. Jon and I are stuck in traffic about five minutes away.'

'Ok. I will meet you there as soon as I possibly can. I will call Andy Stevens now. He will hopefully be able to get there before me. Could you get the gallery security to sort the CCTV recordings for when I arrive?'

'Will do.'

Harriet ended the call just as the traffic began to move. Tate nosed the Land Rover forward. They would now be exiting the roundabout at a different exit to the one they had planned to take prior to the two phone calls.

Duke of York Square
London, England

54

The stereo remained silent for the duration of their short but slow journey into the heart of Chelsea. The traffic congestion added minutes to what should have been a comparatively easy drive. Tate had parked within the Cavalry Square gated community after showing his ID and a short explanation to the security guard at the entrance. The Land Rover looked particularly incongruous alongside the affluent resident's vehicles. But the Saatchi's main entrance was only a short walk from the Landy's abandonment.

A small number of visitors were gathered outside the gallery's door and a member of the security team was trying her best to convey the current situation to those eager to view the gallery's display. Tate and Jonathan swept past, each presenting their ID to a second security guard. They were immediately greeted by Philip Henry, whose composure exhibited a man who was both concerned and unnerved by his earlier discovery. He led them to the second floor and Gallery 10 via the main stairway. Hazard tape had been strung in an 'X' across the entrance.

The picture hung in the centre of the bare white wall beyond the gallery's current exhibit. It was of a similar size to the previous one and was once again signed 'T Turner'. Tate and Jonathan examined the picture. They both looked at the subject of the painting. Despite the mask covering the face, Tate instantly recognised the victim.

Kate Palmer had not absconded.

Something far worse had bestowed her.

Unlike his friend, a look of puzzlement had begun to materialise across Jonathan's face. Tate sensed an air of discombobulation.

'You seem confused. Have you noticed something disconcerting?'

'Aside from a second victim who once again is under our investigation, I see no connection between these two recent killings and those of the Narcissus last summer. In fact, looking at this latest photograph, I am struggling to find anything to associate this crime scene with the last.'

'I completely agree. There appears to be a significant change to the MO of each killing. It's like the pattern is unravelling. Maybe the relevance now lies in the way she is overpainting the scene.' proposed Tate as he moved closer to get a better look at the detail.

'Well, one thing is for sure. I don't remember Caravaggio painting a woman in a clay mask.'

'I believe the mask may well be indicative of the victim.'

If so, what was the connective thread with the first body?' questioned Jonathan.

Tate offered a few suggestions. 'Blood. Owl. Bird of Prey. Carnivorous. Bloodsport?'

His thoughts were cut short as a fourth man joined them before the picture. They had not heard his approach. 'DCI Randall. Harriet informed me that you may already be here.' He extended a hand in Tate's direction. The pair shook hands.

'Jonathan Harvey, AAID and Philip Henry Woodrow, Gallery Director. This is Harriet's newly promoted Detective Sergeant, Andy Stevens.'

With the introductions done, DS Stevens examined the picture while Tate expressed his and Jonathan's previous thoughts. Philip Henry pressed Jonathan to indicate when it might be possible to re-open the gallery. Jonathan cleverly diverted the question by asking the Gallery Director if he would take them to view the CCTV footage.

As they made their way to the security room, Philip Henry provided the three detectives with information he had acquired before their arrival.

'The security team have run the CCTV footage back from the point of the gallery's closure at 6 pm yesterday evening. The picture in question was hung just after the last entries to the gallery at 5.20 pm. Apparently, it is evident that a woman hung the picture.'

'Reception desk requesting Philip Henry,' announced a voice through the two-way radio.' The Gallery Director addressed the call and reception continued. 'I have DI Stone of the MET CID with me. Would you like me to walk her through the building?'

'Yes. That would be best. Could you bring her straight up to the security room? I have her colleagues with me. We can all convene there. Thank you.'

The four men had entered the security room moments before Harriet's arrival. There was little room to spare with the two security staff at the console, Philip Henry and the four visitors. Although he had yet to see the footage for himself, the Gallery Director removed himself to the rear of the room. The senior of the two security officers explained the CCTV sequence he was about to run and the time frame it related to. He started the camera feed and remained quiet as the loop played. He then rewound the footage and replayed the sequence once more. This time providing a few details to clarify the images.

Again, they all watched as the CCTV time clock showed 17:22 and a woman dressed in a figure hugging, black body con dress and a full length trench coat passed through the gallery's entrance. She paid for her entry on arrival. The first cameras followed her approach to the main stairs. Her black attire was accentuated by a large buckled yoke belt, 4-inch platform super heels, a mini crossbody bag and a pair of 1950s Cat Eye glasses. Each accessory was finished in striking red. In contrast to her vibrant red embellishments, her pin-straight hair was cut in a shoulder length platinum blonde bob. As the Narcissus proceeded from the ground floor to Gallery 10, she ensured that every camera captured her approach. She did not stop and hesitate at any point. Her walk was audacious and decisive. Without hesitation, she stepped across the threshold of Gallery 10 and walked straight to the rear wall. Here, she removed the picture frame from the inside of her coat, and without a care for who may be watching, the Narcissus pushed the pre-adhesive coated frame to the wall.

She took a step back and admired the picture. The Narcissus was not only appreciating the photograph, but she also savoured the harrowing torture that had led up to the very moment when the image was captured. She remained self-absorbed in her egotistical world as a presumptuous smugness emerged upon her face. As the smile morphed into a villainous grin, the Narcissus turned and walked purposefully towards the corner of the gallery, where she stood directly in the security camera's field of vision. She eased the Cat Eye glasses to sit on her forehead and stared directly into the lens. The smile morphed once more and a smirk appeared. She took one step back and raised her hands. While staring straight into the camera, the Narcissus began to string together a series of signs and hand shapes. Her fingers extended, curled and pointed. All the while, her face emphasised and accentuated her movements as she communicated her unspoken words.

The four investigators watched, each fully aware of the Narcissus' actions.

Once again, she was leaving another message.

Bethnal Green
London, England

55

Harriet knew all too well that every passing minute was crucial to a victim's recovery. Vital lost minutes could mean the difference between life and death. The clock was already ticking, but if she were completely honest with herself, she knew deep down that this victim was most probably already deceased. However, until a body was recovered, there was always a glimmer of optimism.

Harriet wasted no time. She walked into the incident room with a sense of imperativeness. Each passing second was time they could not afford to waste.

'Round everyone up, will you, George? Meeting in ten.' Without waiting for an answer, she continued through to the SIO room, where she busied herself in readiness to address her team. The minutes vanished before her eyes, and before she knew it, she was pinning another victim's picture to the investigation wall.

'We have a second picture. This time, it was hung at the Saatchi Gallery. CCTV footage captures a female entering the room and hanging the frame. She later reveals herself to a camera as the Narcissus, aka Lena Johnson,' stated Harriet before adding a second picture to the wall. This time, a close-up camera still of the suspect's face. 'Andy is still accessing further footage at the gallery and is waiting for forensics to process the picture and frame.' Harriet moved before the picture she had just pinned to the wall and referenced the previous picture of the second crime scene.

'Once again, it shows a person secured to a chair. However, the MO appears to be different. The victim looks to be wearing some type of mask. Quite possibly clay. DCI Randall believes the victim is again a person of interest in a case currently being investigated by his department. He believes the photograph's subject is Kate Palmer, a known pottery forger.' She retrieved her phone from a back pocket and sent a document from her draft file. A chorus of phone alerts pinged around the room.

'All of you should have received a duplicated image of the second crime scene taken from the photograph discovered earlier at the Saatchi Gallery.' Each detective retrieved their phone and opened the photo file. Each turned their phones to landscape to enlarge the picture. Each zoomed in and out to study the detail of the image.

'We need to locate this crime scene as quickly as we did the first. Ok, crew. Tell me what you see,' Harriet requested as she, too, manipulated her phone. A silence fell upon the room as each team member looked for that one detail, which, in turn, may lead to the discovery of the crime scene's location.

George was the first to comment. 'If you look past the overpainting, it could well be a cold store. The shelving on the right of the picture looks similar to the type commonly used in the catering business.' George's observation set the ball rolling.

'Which may well point to the butchery business again,' added Sarika.

'Could that be some sort of tracking running along the ceiling.' suggested DC Evans. George continued the elucidation, 'commonly used to hang carcasses via a meat hook.'

'They are also found in abattoirs and meat processing factories,' DS Richards expressed as he pinched out the image on his phone. 'Is that the corner of a crate stack in the bottom left corner?'

'I've just been looking at the same thing,' declared DC Thompson. 'I've been playing around with the brightness and the contrast, and I think I can just make out the letters 'P E R' under the overpainting.' He handed his phone to Harriet. The rest of the team zoomed in on their phones to the particular area of the image.

'Per what?' Harriet pondered, leaving the question hanging for her crew to bat around.

'Per kilo or pound.'

'Percentage weight, personnel only.'

'Permit.'

'Perishable' were all answers thrown into the pot.

'If the crate is in a cold store, then the prefix may well be the beginning of a company name,' announced DC Evans as he started a search on his phone.

'Sarika. Start a search—'

'Already on it, boss.' asserted the team's senior profiler as her fingers scurried across the keyboard. 'Butchery businesses with registered premises within London, prefixed P E R. Good gosh, there are rather a lot.'

'Perkins of Peckham, Pernell's in Hackney.'

'Perryman's in Tottenham, Perzinski's in Ealing.'

DC Evans looked up from his phone and interrupted Sarika.

'Perkins Abattoirs,' he suggested, 'they might be delivery boxes from a meat supplier rather than a butchery business.'

George Quinn backed his younger colleague. 'Perkins Abattoirs had two premises. Both were shut down some time ago. One was in Park Royal, the other in Brixton. I'd say they were our best bet, Ma'am.'

'Ok. Let's start with the abattoirs. Iain and Greg, you take a look at the Brixton site and George, you take Jake and check out Park Royal.' A consensus of nodding heads confirmed Harriet's command. 'Sarika. Compile a list. Cross-check the details. Look for anything that relates to what we have so far. Rank the possibilities accordingly. We may well need to change direction quickly. Keep me posted. The clock doesn't stop. I want the location of the body before anyone sleeps tonight!'

56

Things were happening fast. A second body was inevitable. A further picture, once again hung in a recognisable gallery, pretty much confirmed the fact. There would undoubtedly be another front page headline. The Narcissus' second coming was most definitely attracting the attention that Lena hungered.

Tate had set in operation a forensic team to document the crime scene at the home of Kate Palmer in Parson's Green. He had photographed the personalised Halloween cake and sent copies of the pictures to Harriet soon after calling her about the developments he and DS Garrett had discovered. Back at Thorney Street, Jonathan and the remainder of Tate's team explored the possibility and logistics of implementing a large scale surveillance operation to provide a vigilance blanket to those currently subject to their investigations. Persons who could conceivably be the Narcissus' third victim. Such an operation could easily jeopardise their inquiries should the suspect become suspicious of any abnormal activity. They may well find themselves in need of compromising an investigation in order to save a life. A decision they would not make without serious thought.

Tate had re-surfaced at Embankment and crossed the Thames via one of the two Golden Jubilee footbridges that flank the older Hungerford rail bridge. The earlier fog had hugged the riverside well into the latter half of the morning before lifting to unveil a glorious autumnal afternoon. The Bankside paths were already astir with those who needed to be somewhere and, in juxtaposition, those who had the pleasure of exploring the city at a more leisurely pace. Tate hoped Tommy would be at one of his preferred afternoon locations. As he descended the steps at the south end of the bridge, the scene did not disappoint. A small gathering of onlookers encircled a street artist sitting on the riverside path. Tate instantly recognised his friend.

A London College of Art graduate, Tommy's passion for graffiti art had fed his hunger and soon after graduating, he found himself immersed in the symbolic world of street art. He would capture the curiosity and wallets of tourists with his stencilled aerosol paintings of London's famous skyline. He had built a reputation within the street scene to become one of the city's most recognisable artists. He was also Tate's go-to when he needed information on current events in London's art world. Tommy was always engaged with 'the word on the street' and was more than happy to share this information should a twenty-pound note find its way into his pocket.

Tommy was adding his moniker to the bottom of a picture. The encompassing crowd had been captivated as he interchanged numerous stencil shapes and aerosol shadings to build an image of the Houses of Parliament and Big Ben. Appreciation for the finished picture was rewarded with plaudits from the crowd. He stood and accepted the gratitude of those around him. Most of his audience moved swiftly on to the next in a line of street entertainers. Some stayed to chat and offer further recognition of his work and a few purchased pictures he had created earlier in the day. As the tail-end of his spectators drifted away, Tommy turned to find Tate standing on the grass verge directly behind him.

'Whoa, Tate, you scared the bejesus out of me, man,' exclaimed Tommy, holding his heart in mock.

'Sorry. I didn't want to interrupt a last minute purchase. Looks like you're still pulling in the punters and the pennies.'

'To be honest, it's not been the most lucrative of times, what with the seasonal visitor numbers dwindling, coupled with the changeable weather of late. Nobody wants to stand around Bankside in the gloom and the drizzle. The rain doesn't help my colour blending much either,' chuckled Tommy. 'I was wondering if you would be paying a visit sometime soon. What with the Narcissus making the front pages once again. Have you seen this morning's Chronicle?' Tate's blank response was sufficient. Tommy reached into his trolley cart and handed Tate a copy of the paper. Tate opened the half-fold to reveal the headline story. Although he knew all too well what to expect, he'd seen the picture in the gallery, but seeing the yet to be discovered crime scene in print still brought a sense of realism to the situation.

'This Narcissus seems to be having a bit of fun with you all, this time around. What with displaying the pictures in public view, alongside feeding the newspapers with a pictorial record of her crime scenes.' Tate heard Tommy's voicing, but his attention was absorbed in the front page pictures. Were the killings no longer just about retribution? Was this now becoming about the Narcissus creating a legacy? Was Lena, in some sick and twisted way, intent on creating a lasting personification of her own, in much the same way that her ancestor had done many years before? Were her narcissistic needs craving much more than attention? Was she becoming lost within the idealism of a grandiose image of herself?

'…becoming unsettled with the change,' continued Tommy, with Tate still not hearing.

'Forgive me, Tom, I was lost in a train of thought there for a second. Carry on.'

'I was just saying that there are those within the capital's art circles who are getting spooked and becoming unsettled by the recent actions of this Narcissus. It's not just the rich and famous who are having to watch their backs. Just about anyone who has dirtied their hands in the past should be worried that they could well be the next.' Tate nodded to concur but could not reveal their intelligence that the first two targets of the Narcissus' second campaign had both been subjects of their current investigations. They did not want word of the fact becoming general knowledge at present. It was a detail that the press was unaware of, and it would be beneficial to the investigations if it stayed that way.

Tate removed his wallet and a twenty-pound note, which he folded was handed to Tommy. It was their usual agreement for information for which Tommy was always good for.

'Have you heard any developments concerning the Van Henal brothers? Anything further to the rumours concerning the arrival of a shipment?'

Tate's team had been investigating two Dutch archaeological artefact importers for nearly two years. They were gathering evidence relating to the possibility of artefacts having been stolen from war-torn countries before entering the market via the Dutch brothers lucrative cultural treasures business.

Since the beginning of the 20th century, it has been commonplace in the homes of the western world to collect historical artefacts from past human societies. The discovery of the undisturbed Tomb of Tutankhamun by Howard Carter in 1922 attracted a global audience, resulting in a media frenzy and the import of such cultural treasures to decorate the homes of the wealthy and those happy to pay for the privilege. Buyers who were quite happy to ignore the fact that the artefacts were most probably obtained without the permission of the relative cultural officials and their governments.

'There is an escalating rumour that a number of crates within a recent consignment from the Middle East includes archaeological relics from both Syria and Iraq. Apparently, interested parties are already speculating about the fact and postulating what the artefacts may be. Where would we be without all the hearsay and the tittle-tattle,' jested Tommy, kissing his newly acquired twenty-pound note and placing it in a rear pocket.

'Have you heard if anything has come to market yet?' enquired Tate.

'Nothing as such. If I were to hazard a guess, it's most probably still being sorted at one of their warehouses. In the past, they have been known to hold similar stashes at a warehouse east of Victoria Dock.'

Tate was taking note of everything. It was rare for the information he acquired from Tommy to be futile. More often than not, it was invaluable to gaining a conviction.

'Any talk of the whereabouts of the Caravaggio or anything associated with the movements of the Narcissus?'

'Not a whisper. As quiet as a grave. Excuse the pun. It's completely gone to ground. My guess is, you catch this Narcissus and the painting will re-appear, somewhere, somehow.'

'If only it were that simple,' commented Tate.

'She appears to be a devious dark horse with a major vexation with the art world.'

'It does appear to be that way. Anything else circulating on the rumour mill?'

Tommy looked about, up and down the pathway, before speaking again. 'Only news that CUTZ has defaced yet another artwork. This time, it is an Otto Schade piece over in Shoreditch. Bloody criminal if you ask me. He needs locking up.'

Tate was just about to respond when his phone began to ring. He reached into his jacket pocket and retrieved it. He looked at the caller ID on the screen. 'I need to take this,' he said, waggling the phone in the air to back his statement. He hit the incoming call icon but was not the first to speak.

'Have you seen today's City Chronicle?'

'As a matter of fact,' replied Tate, 'Tommy has just shown me a copy.'

'They've certainly not complied with what we have asked. Andy spoke directly with the editor. In one ear and out the other, as per usual. And this time, they have gone to print before we have even located the body.'

'Where do we stand at present with a location?' Tate moved slightly away to avoid Tommy overhearing.

'We identified two possible locations from the Saatchi picture. Both pertain to an abattoir company. As we speak, there are two separate teams, each searching one of the company's two disused warehouses. If she is there, we should have a location in the next hour or so.'

Park Royal & Brixton
London, England

57

The two squad cars had left Bethnal Green, each heading to a possible crime scene. Only one would result in the discovery of a body. Or, if neither located the kill site in the photograph, it would mean a pair of dead-ends and it would be back to square one.

DS Richards and DC Thompson had exited the city via Blackfriars Bridge toward Elephant & Castle before following the A2 south into Brixton. With a high volume of traffic within the first part of the city, the journey took around 50 minutes.

Although the distance to Park Royal was almost twice that of their fellow officers, DS Quinn and DC Evans took approximately the same amount of time to reach their location. The A501, followed by the 2.5 mile elevated dual carriageway section of the A40, known as the Westway, were less congested, and the traffic became significantly lighter as they approached North Acton.

DS Iain Richards and DC Greg Thompson parked on the roadside of what had once been a sizeable industrial site. Most of which had now been demolished and was most probably earmarked for brownfield development. Along with two smaller units, the building that once housed the Perkins Abattoirs' slaughterhouse looked unusable and run down. The remainder of the site around the buildings was a barren concrete wasteland that looked to be a common ground for fly-tipping. Amongst the weeds and arching thickets of brambles, an abandonment of supermarket trolleys, discarded fast food boxes and a mosaic of broken bottles littered every corner of the neglected site.

In contrast, DS George Quinn and DC Jake Evans pulled into a vacant visitor parking space of a newly built commercial retail building. The empty Perkins Abattoirs' building sat in the adjacent plot. The Park Royal site was the newer of the company's previously occupied properties. A high-security steel palisade fence enclosed the site on three sides. At the foremost part of the building, there were four loading bays, each facing a pair of double boom barrier gates and a security control point. The remainder of the yard surrounding the building was empty and devoid of discarded matter. The only sign of any sort of presence were two homemade wedge skateboard ramps in the yard to the side.

Temporary wire meshed fencing encircled the ramshackled Brixton site. Many sections of the fence lay twisted, some disconnected from the next, and it did not take DS Richards and DC Thompson long to find a suitable place to access the yard surrounding the property. As the two officers checked the perimeter of the graffiti covered building, they found further evidence of vandalism, plundering and depredation. Most of the building's doors and windows were smashed, pried open or were simply missing.

They entered the building where a door had once been. The first thing that hit them was the smell. A mixture of urine, rotting matter and cheap cider. A lingering smokiness also hung in the air. As they proceeded into a larger central area, it was evident that the building was being used as a squat and a refuge for countless homeless individuals. Several of whom were currently sleeping in makeshift cardboard beds. Drug paraphernalia and budget alcohol containers were discarded about the floor. Iain and Greg continued their sweep of the building, discovering further inhabitants as they did so. Each of them paid little attention to the arrival of the detectives.

'There is nothing more here than we have already seen,' declared Iain, 'It's an established squat. There is way too much foot traffic. There's very little chance of being undisturbed. Call it in, Greg. She's not here.'

Each of the four loading bays was secured with heavy locks, as were several further doors about the building. Every window was fitted with external wire mesh grills. As they looked for a possible entry point, George and Jake wondered if they may have to contact the current owners to gain entry. As they rounded the corner to the rear of the building, Jake stopped at a pair of doors with a window to the side. A gently sloping ramp ran up to the door's sill. From a distance, nothing appeared to be any different from what they had already encountered around the building. It was locked up and secure.

The detectives approached the doors together. As they drew nearer, it became clear that the padlock securing the door's hasp and staple was closed but not locked. They shared a look of curiosity. George was about to don latex gloves when Jake beckoned him to the window.

A large plastic Halloween bat had been fixed to the window's grill. Both men examined the spookish adornment. Each becoming increasingly curious. Jake cupped his hands to his face and looked in through the window. At the far end of a long, unfurnished room, he could just make out the silhouette of a person sitting in a chair. Jake stepped away from the window and indicated for his senior officer to take a look.

George took no time at all to confirm Jake's discovery. 'Call it in Jake. I'll let Iain and Greg know.'

Jake already had his phone at hand. He hit the pre-stored number. It rang just twice before being answered.

'Jake?'

'We have her, Ma'am. Park Royal is the kill site.'

58

Harriet had not rushed to the crime scene as soon as she had received confirmation from Jake Evans that they had discovered a body matching that of the one captured in the Saatchi photograph. Penny and the forensic team would need to preserve the crime scene and the surrounding area before an increased footfall could safely view the kill site without fear of further contamination. Harriet had spent time with DS Andy Stevens on his return from the Saatchi Gallery. They had again sat through the CCTV footage alongside additional footage from local street cameras. Andy had apprised Harriet of having requested camera images from TFL and that he would also inquire about the possibility of obtaining further footage from shop cameras in the immediate area. He had also located another carpark close to the gallery, which the Narcissus may have used in a similar way to the one suspectedly used after the Tate Modern incident. Like the previous car park, it lent itself to being less visible and unobserved, with both sites being underground facilities. They would, however, be viewing entry and exit footage to account for every vehicle coming and going on the day in question. Once again, Andy had informed Harriet that a request for the footage from the second carpark was already in motion. Before Harriet departed, they had agreed for Andy to collate all current lines of investigation ready for a meeting on her return.

The business park was bathed in a blue hue by the time Harriet arrived. The awash of colour intensified as more police vehicles arrived at the scene. Each added depth to the cerulean glow and to the physical number of personnel now present at the crime scene. Cordons were in place and manned by uniformed officers. The usual disturbance of rubberneckers were huddled at the crime tape, undoubtedly theorising and postulating worst case scenarios.

A local officer had pulled the outer cordon to one side, allowing Harriet to park the BMW 320d beyond the sea of blue. She exited the car to be met by DC Evans, who provided his senior officer with the current situation. They were then met at the inner cordon by George Quinn, who recorded all those entering and exiting in the crime scene security log.

'Evening George. We have a busy little scene on our hands already. Would you mind asking one of the local boys to take over the security log? You would be of more use elsewhere.'

'No problem, Ma'am. I will see to it right away.'

'Let's look at the surrounding businesses. Collect camera footage from those working through this evening. Come back first thing tomorrow for the remainder.' DS Quinn once again acknowledged his instruction and excused himself.

'Looks like a local crew is using the vacant lot as a skate park,' declared Harriet, motioning to the two skate ramps she had noticed on her arrival. 'Have yourself a wander around the local estates, will you, Jake? Talk to local teenagers, especially those with bikes, scooters or boards. One of them may well have seen something. Can you also organise for the local uniforms to come by over the next few nights and do the same?'

'I thought I might get uniform to chat with the kids at the Acton and Harlesden youth centres over the next few nights, too. It might prove fruitful,' declared DC Evans as he and Harriet began to go their separate ways.

'I totally agree. I'll leave it with you. And don't forget to go home. We wouldn't want that new baby to forget who his daddy is.'

As soon as Harriet entered the disused buildings, her ears pricked, her sense of smell heightened, and her eyes began to capture all that presented before her. Her raptor-like perceptions began to systematically scrutinise every part of the scene she was encountering. Her senses worked in conjunction and she had a gifted ability to process the smallest of details in a way that may not be evident to the average mind. She would look beyond the physical presence of the objects she encountered and question whether something was out of place or even missing. Does it belong and should it be there at all? What was producing a particular sound, or why could she not hear something that should be there? She would leave no stone unturned.

It was a smell that first caught her attention as she neared the far end of the area that would have once held butchered carcasses. But it was not the smell of prepared cuts of meat or the ripe smell of decomposing matter. It was a smell that, once encountered, would never be forgotten. Often, it was associated with arson attacks and other fire related incidents.

You never forget the smell of burning flesh.

Harriet remained at a distance but circled the chair containing the body. Outbursts of flashes from Penny's camera momentarily illuminated the scene. The overpainting of the corpse was far more elaborate than that of the first victim. A patchwork of multicoloured squares covered the majority of the body's nakedness. It was akin to the chequered costume of the harlequin. Once again, the victim had been tied to the chair at the wrists and ankles. Small amounts of blood pooled on the floor, but nothing comparable to the volume encountered at the first scene.

Penny lowered her camera and acknowledged Harriet's presence for the first time.

'The evident similarities in MO appear to be torture and aggressive forcible behaviour. The scene and overpainting also have strong correlations with the previous site. Once again, the location of the crime scene has connections to the butchery business,' Penny stated as they both continued to closely study the body while encircling the chair. Harriet moved in closer to specifically examine one of the coloured areas of the skin. It was painted red. As she carefully inspected the coloured area, the realisation of the situation hit home.

A square of flesh had been removed from the victim's limb.

Penny had just referred to forcible behaviour.

The recognisable smell in the air.

'The Narcissus made her eat her own flesh?'

Penny continued her circle until she stood side by side with her colleague. 'I have found pieces of masticated meat, most probably her own flesh, in the upper oesophagus, and there are also traces within the tooth cavities.' She held up an evidence bag containing the chewed remnants. Harriet took a brief glance before diverting her eyes. She had no further need to look.

'This was pushed into the rear of the chair when I arrived,' declared Penny, holding forward a larger evidence bag. 'You most probably would not have been able to see it in the picture. The body would have obscured it.'

Harriet accepted and examined the bag and its contents. 'So this accounts for the pungent burnt odour. The Narcissus barbecued slices of the victim's flesh before force feeding them to her.' Harriet studied the barbecue fork within the bag before her eyes diverted to the surrounding area.

Penny noticed her colleagues drift. 'There are spits of cooled fat and tiny flecks of burnt skin extending in a circular pattern across the floor to your left. My best guess is some kind of camping stove or gas torch. At present, I haven't found any further evidence of either.' Penny paused for a second as she perceived Harriet was contemplating something further.

'The drinking of blood, followed by the eating of flesh. I am sure I remember Tate's friend Jonathan mentioning a horror film he had watched that centred around flesh-eating vampires. That coupled with the succession of Halloween references that the Narcissus has left to provoke Tate.' She explained the cake and the spider that the forensic investigator had probably not heard about.

'What do you suppose is the meaning behind the mask?' enquired Penny.

'My first thoughts are some kind of death mask. Any further than that is beyond me at present. I am beginning to realise that each new killing is becoming increasingly more repugnant and incomprehensible. Each crime scene is noticeably becoming more aggressive. This escalation of violence suggests a further increase in anger and the need to feed the thrill. Satisfaction of the kill becomes less, so with each new crime, the intensity of the murder has to increase to satisfy the need. It is also the reason why the time between the killings is becoming shorter. The need to hunt becomes uncontrollable and must be satisfied.'

'Hence the step up and the removal of the tongue,' added Penny. 'I believe the keeping of an item or part of the victim as a trophy is also part of the escalation. A kill trophy provides memories between the crimes and can enhance the reliving of the killing, again a necessity of a serial killer.' She handed Harriet a further evidence bag. The square of pig skin lay flat in the window of the see-through bag. The words were clearly visible. 'The leaving of the messages is another driver of narcissistic behaviour commonly found in serial killers. The need to have control and the compulsion to challenge those they see as adversaries of equal intelligence are actions they seek to satisfy their pretentious nature.

Harriet continued to study the pigskin and read the newly discovered verse tattooed upon its surface. As she did so, she began to ponder what Penny had just said.

The lyrics were beginning to make more sense now. They were a direct link to Tate and a significant part of who he was. The chosen verses were not only meant to challenge but were also intended to draw Tate into the bosom of the Narcissus so as to feed her craving. The words were being used to express the Narcissus' frustrations and impart the blame for who Lena had become. All the while bolstering her inner desires and the want for notoriety.

Each kill was a step towards symbolic immortality and the legacy of the Narcissus.

59

The needle entered the skin, immediately followed by a second and rapidly followed by dozens more. The head of the tattoo machine hummed and oscillated as the needles penetrated the skin a little over 200 times per second. The tattooist worked in a series of closely repeated circles to pack the colour into a thick line within the area he was colouring. After every 10th cycle of the process, the tattooist wiped the area of his work to remove the excess ink upon the surface. The process was repeated until the area in question was filled with the appropriate shading of ink. Working methodically to pack the colour with precision allowed the tattooist to fill the area in one pass, therefore causing less trauma to the skin.

Lena once again sat straddling the tattooist's cradle stool, which was similar in design to an orthopaedic massage chair. This position provided the client with far greater comfort when sitting for an extended period, warranted by a more prominent back piece or one of significant detail. With the client leaning forward into the chair, it also afforded the tattooist a far better work angle than if the person getting inked were lying flat.

Sean Ripley, proprietor and senior tattooist at Ripper Tattoos, had shown an artistic flair from a very early age. His mother noticed his creative side and his want to make marks with crayons well before he took his first steps. She would often say he could draw before he could walk. Her encouragement continued, and soon, he started sketching cartoon characters rather than watching them on TV. It was not long before he began to create his own caricatures of his friends and family. School satchels soon became his canvas, and friends were more than happy for him to adorn the cotton, denim, and leather surfaces with motifs, football badges, and pop artists' logos. Art college beckoned until an opportunity of an apprenticeship at a local tattoo parlour drew him away from the mainstream. A successful career emerged, and he never had a need to look back. His work spoke for itself. Over time, his client list grew, and fellow artists held him in high regard. He frequently produced tattooed works for celebrities from the worlds of film, TV, and music.

Sean scuttled his 360-degree swivel stool back over to his previous position to continue colouring the area he was currently working on. He had mixed a new colour at his workstation, once again adding a small amount of the ash supplied by his client, before changing the machine's cartridge to a smaller needle alignment to enable him to work more freely in a tighter area of the tattoo.

'Happy for me to continue?' he asked.

'Absolutely,' came the reply from the tumble of black hair draping over his client's neck. Sean started the machine's motor again and continued adding colour to the skin. He worked in an area on the right-hand lumber region, a fleshy part of the back, which usually does not create a great deal of discomfort for the sitter. Following the outline from an earlier sitting, he continued to shadow the folds of a dress worn by a woman of ample proportions who appeared to be feeding an elderly gent with milk from her breast.

'I am interested to know and understand why you chose to add the red tones to the image rather than sticking with the original picture's colour scheme,' Sean enquired as he stretched and worked the skin to create the fall of the woman's dress.

Lena spoke through the entanglement of her hair. 'The emphasis of the red I have asked you to add to the detail of each area is representative and symbolic of the distant relative whose life the tattoo is to honour. He, like yourself, was an artist. He was noted for his contrasting use of light and shade. He frequently used a distinctively striking, rich red cloth to accentuate an aspect of his subjects. Be it a dress, a shawl, a cloak or a simple throw. It is an expression of seduction, violence and danger, but could also be seen to emphasise power, passion and love.'

Lena pulled the flow of her dark hair to one side so the tattooist could see the sincerity in her eyes.

'The red is my forever bond to him.'

Southwark

London, England

60

Tate had arranged to meet Harriet and DS Andy Stevens on the South Bank for lunch before all three would attend Kate Palmer's autopsy. He had walked from his office at Thorney Street. The route had taken him through Parliament Square and across Westminster Bridge before heading east along the Queen's Walk, the riverside path that follows the south bank of the Thames. He had passed the London Eye and spotted Tommy surrounded by a curiosity of tourists. A sky of broken clouds with frequent breaks of sunshine was no doubt the reason for the animated crowds along the river edge. Tate did not stop to chat but waved as he caught Tommy's eye. The three detectives had agreed to convene in front of Shakespeare's Globe Theatre before getting a bite to eat in the Swan Bankside pub. Having arrived ahead of time, Tate had checked availability for lunch to find the popular pub awash with visitors. By the time Harriet and Andy had arrived, Tate had scouted an alternative eatery.

The second option had been the Real Greek Bankside, just a few hundred yards further along the path. They had found a quiet spot at the rear of the restaurant, away from the crowds. A hot and cold mezze platter to share was ordered and the three detectives discussed the current aspects of the Narcissus' return and the two resulting crime scenes. They talked as they picked, dipped, scooped and nibbled their way through the selection of savoury dishes.

Suitably fed, they had then taken the short walk down Southwark Bridge Road to the cast concrete eyesore that housed Greater London's ultra-modern forensic laboratories and autopsy suites. Tate had not seen the interior refit of wall-to-wall glass panelling since its facelift some five years previously. Having checked in their credentials at reception, the automated lift system delivered them to the second floor, where they stepped out onto the glass bridge of the autopsy suite viewing platform. The ammonia like smell of methyl alcohol and formaldehyde captured their breath after the sterile cleanliness of the anterior reception area.

Below them were the two interconnecting autopsy rooms and a body receiving area with its stainless steel trolleys. Each trolley supported a deceased body awaiting autopsy or transport back to the mortuary. There was also a refrigeration unit for body parts, evidence samples and other items that required storage below 4.5°c.

The first autopsy suite was in the central room. Two autopsy technicians dressed in medic scrubs, disposable aprons, latex gloves and rubber overshoes were replacing the vital organs into the open cavity of a body. The organs were being placed in viscera bags to prevent leakage after the Y-section was resewn.

The majority of bodies requiring examination are processed through this room. The farthest room of the three was only used for suspicious deaths, homicides and bodies in a state of decomposition. It had double access decontamination doors and was where cases of the utmost importance were autopsied to prevent cross contamination of materials and ensure the confinement of evidence adhered to the highest of standards. It was known amongst employees as the 'Frankenstein Suite'. Due to the fact that a high number of bodies that enter this room are extensively dissected and require extensive stitching before the corpse is prepared for embalming. Hence, they can end up looking a little like Frankenstein's monster.

The three detectives continued along the suspended glass walkway to overlook this third room. Below was the body of Kate Palmer and senior pathologist Happy Jiang, who noticed the casting of shadows and the presence of people in the viewing gallery. He paused the procedure he was currently performing and diverted his attention to his new arrivals.

'Ooh… a trio of detectives. Now, there's a thing. Is there such a word for a trio of detectives,' he pondered, scratching his chin in a comically suggestive manner. 'You could say it's more a "gendarme à trois" than a "ménage à trois".' As usual, Happy chuckled to himself and the smallest of grins escaped each of the detectives.

'And is that DCI Randall I spy with my beady eye? It's been a long while since you have graced us with your presence. How long has it been?' Happy took a moment to retrieve a memory, playing with the motions of the thought process like only Happy could. 'I should hazard a guess… about five years?'

Tate smiled as only one could do in Happy's company. 'Correct. There are not so many cases in the field of Arts & Antiquities that require an autopsy.'

Happy continued his reminiscent performance. 'If my memory serves me right, it was an art thief practically cut in two when a security lockdown panel came down upon him while the poor fellow was making his escape.' Tate nodded, confirming the recollection.

'Open and shut case, really,' chuckled Happy for his own amusement.

'Anyway, you've just missed the best bit. I have just this minute 'run the bowels',' he stated, holding part of the intestine. The term was used amongst technicians for one of the less desirable jobs during an autopsy. The opening of the intestines wasn't the most pleasant of procedures. It required the entire length of both the small and large intestines to be slit along its length and the contents to be extracted and examined before the faecal remains were washed down into the medical sink and the effluent tanks below. The combined length of the two organs in the average human adult is about 7.5 metres, making the process no easy feat. The entire process takes practice not only due to the precision required but also having a strong stomach to do so.

'The intestinal contents reveal nothing one wouldn't normally see. There appear to be no abnormal constituents. Food can take up to four hours to pass through the stomach and small bowel before reaching the small intestine. Anything digested in the final hours before death would normally still be in the stomach. Shall we take a look?'

The removed stomach sat in a large stainless steel tray at the far end of the surgical table. Happy took a scalpel and made an incision along the length of the stomach's wall. He then emptied the stomach contents into a fine mesh sieve, the liquefied matter flowing through into the medical sink. Happy removed the larger undigested food parts with a pair of medical forceps, placing each piece back onto the stainless steel tray. He took a moment to organise the sections into size order.

'There are numerous intact pieces of a meat substance. The gastric rate of digestion suggests they were consumed right up to the point of death.' Happy used a small endoscope camera to send pictures of the sample to a monitor screen above the walkway, where the three detectives looked on. 'Signs of charring to the edges of the sample suggest the meat was cooked at close range with a naked flame.' He placed the meat back alongside pieces of a similar size. 'We will morphologically identify the taxonomy of the meat source, but I think it would be a fairly safe bet to assume the source is her own flesh. That being if we take Penny's report conjointly with other confirmations discovered in the earlier part of the autopsy.' Happy moved to a computer monitor at the rear of the room, and with the tips of his gloved hands, he tapped a series of keys on the keyboard and hit 'Enter'. A close-up picture of an upper leg materialised on the screen before the detectives. 'Six more identical squares of flesh were removed from the victim. Clotting patterns to the edges of each area confirm the flesh removals were antemortem. The heart was still active at the time each cut was made.' Happy tapped the 'Pg Up' key and the image on the screen changed to show the same area before the overpainting was washed off. Happy continued his analysis report.

'Each of the seven squares was of a similar size, and each area of flesh removal had been refilled with some form of modelling clay before it was over-painted in red.'

'I can confirm now, having seen the deceased's face, the body is that of Kate Palmer,' declared Tate. 'Ms Palmer has been subject to our inquiries for some while. She is a recognised forger of 19th century ceramics. The use of clay, especially in creating what we can assume is a 'death mask', is the Narcissus forming a link to a rationale in which she believes the victim has sinned and must, therefore, pay for her misdoings. I believe the overpainting is a psychotic behaviour in which she believes she is continuing her family legacy. She will see the significant use of red as a paternal homage to Caravaggio's repeated use of the red cloth throughout his paintings. We need to remember that Lena has lost touch with reality and her delusional mind will see and believe things in a very different way. Her behaviours will become more and more erratic and unpredictable with each murder. Her narcissistic behaviour will warrant her need to be in control, part of which will be the need to provoke and beguile the investigation like a game. She is leaving a trail to follow because she wants and needs to control that game. She has no emotional connection, and the deeper she falls into her psychosis, the more extreme her behaviours will become. This is only the start of the next phase, which she envisions as a 'second coming'. The second chapter of her story has just begun. The only way we have of stopping the Narcissus' murderous campaign is to think like her. We must predetermine her thoughts and actions. We need to be one step ahead.' The others in the room could only agree. Each knew that Tate's words would no doubt become a reality. Each had a role in preventing further crimes at the hands of the Narcissus. Each was immersed in the investigation in one way or another.

Having listened intently to Tate's reasoning and agreeing with all he had said, Happy returned to the gurney on which Kate Palmer's dissected body lay. Taking the end of the trolley nearest her feet, he spun the table 180 degrees so that the three detectives on the viewing platform could see the soles of the victim's feet. He did not need to explain.

The numbers '2' and '5' could easily be seen carved into the soles.

Beckton

London, England

61

The lorry backed into the loading bay. The driver and the driver's mate jumped down from the cab and rounded to the rear of the vehicle. While the driver opened the roller door, the mate collected a hydraulic pallet trolley. One by one, they unloaded the sealed wooden crates. Each crate transferred into the warehouse was stamped on two sides in large black lettering.

COUNTRY OF ORIGIN: TURKEY

As the two lorry drivers unloaded the delivery, two other men watched from the rear of the goods-in area. One stood tall and athletic. The second man of a smaller build sat in a wheelchair to his side. Other than their physical differences, the two men's appearances were identical. Each had blond hair cut in a medium crop. Their eyes were azure blue, their faces broad but long, each having a small upturned nose. Despite his withered appearance from a lifetime in a wheelchair, the thinner man matched every inch of the six-foot stature of the other.

The Van Henal twins were quintessentially Dutch in all respects. Eduard and Aleksander were raised in a small town on the River Lek on the outskirts of Rotterdam. Born to parents who were both accomplished painters, each of whom worked in the desirable style of 20th century Dutch realism. Their father produced works representative of earlier Dutch artists such as De Hooch and Vermeer, whilst their mother preferred the still-life style of Ruysch and Bosschaert. The precise depictions of Dutch realism with compositions and intricacy of the finest detail, whether in a scene of domestic life or the complexity of the foliage in a vase of flowers, were popular with art lovers across Europe. Both husband and wife had frequently exhibited and profited from their chosen style.

Eduard and Aleksander were inseparable throughout their childhood, despite Aleksander being confined to a wheelchair from an early age. A complication during their births resulted in both babies entering the birth canal at once and Aleksander's neck becoming lodged and contorted. A subsequent intervention to free the twins resulted in an injury to the low cervical nerves at the C5 & C6 vertebra, leaving one twin with paraplegic disabilities. Aleksander was the one to draw the shorter straw.

The drivers palleted the final boxes from the rear of the lorry and sealed the roller door in readiness to leave.

Aleksander toggled the joystick on the arm of his motorised wheelchair and headed across the warehouse floor towards the loading bay. 'Usual arrangement, I assume?' he questioned, removing a bulging envelope from his lap and handing it to the driver's mate.

'Yes. You are most kind,' replied the man, his accent noticeably Eastern European.

'We will contact you when another shipment is ready for transportation.'

'Yes, do please. We would be most happy for you. Thank you,' said the man placing the envelope into an inside pocket while hastening the driver back in the direction of the cab.

The money that had just changed hands was for delivery only. The crates had travelled from Turkey via Romania, Hungary, Slovakia, Poland, Germany and the Netherlands. The items within would be worth far more than an envelope of cash as and when they appeared on the open market.

Eduard appeared by his brother's side again, each man watching as the lorry pulled away. They waited in silence as if anticipating something imminent was about to happen. Nothing did. The world outside remained still. They stood a while longer. Happy that they were now alone, Aleksander manoeuvred his chair to the loading bay door, pushed the red automated button and the door began to come down from above. He toggled the chair and spun through 180 degrees to confront his brother, who stood before him armed with a power screwdriver.

'Shall we take a look,' Eduard gestured, moving towards the nearest crate. Aleksander followed, stopping his chair once more at his brother's side. Eduard inserted the cross-headed bit into a screw and reversed the driver. He repeated this at the other three corners before the wooden top came away, revealing a bed of straw. Aleksander sat and watched as his brother removed layers of straw and numerous items of hand-painted Turkish earthenware. He placed each piece to one side. Each was discarded as unimportant. All had been produced in abundance. Each piece worth but a few pounds. The items of greater interest to the Van Henal brothers were in the mid layers of the crates. Eduard removed another layer of straw before turning to his brother. A suggestively smug grin appeared across his face.

He reached into the crate and removed a beautifully ornate ceramic mask. He held it in his hand, admiring its alluring charm before handing the item to his brother. Aleksander cautiously took the mask, turning it over several times as he appraised its quality. He studied the intricate detailing.

'Quite possibly Byzantine, early 5th century,' Aleksander stated as he looked up to his brother, who now held two small statues, one in each hand.

'And if I am correct, these look to be 8th century Assyrian figurines.' He stood them on the top of a nearby crate and once more reached into the box, already smiling. He looked back at his brother mischievously before retrieving another item. He removed a greenish-brown pottery jar with a geometric crosshatched pattern around its circumference. A smile appeared on his brother's face, too. Both were smiles of delight and contentedness.

'Do you remember how much the last one like this sold for?' said Eduard as he tentatively turned the jar for his brother to see.

'It's Sumerian and around four thousand years old and worth every penny we will make from it. Here, let me take a closer look.'

The removal, stealing and looting of ancient sites has a long, corrupted history. The tombs of the pharaohs were stripped bare by grave robbers. The pyramids of Giza and the ruined buildings of the Forum in Rome were each dismantled in the distant past and the plundered stone was used to build elsewhere. The market for archaeological artefacts has increased exponentially in recent years, with an estimated 500,000 items stolen from war-torn countries to a value of 10 billion dollars a year. Items are being looted from the remains of museums, galleries and sites of historical interest and the profit gained is being used to fund further unrest and corruption. Other sites of cultural heritage, left vulnerable after conflicts and uprisings, are being destroyed and plundered. Monuments and buildings are dismantled to procure further artefacts, memorial stones, statues and obelisks.

Eduard had opened a second crate and removed the concealing layer of ten-a-penny tourist ceramics. Again, he threw an oblique glance in his brother's direction. He removed his hands from within the box of treasures. Laid across the palms of his hands were two jewel-encrusted Ottoman daggers, each within a silver hilt inlaid with further precious stones. Eduard turned and presented the daggers to his brother as if he were presenting an offering at a religious ceremony.

Aleksander's eyes blazed at the sight of the jewelled weapons. '15th century ceremonial pieces. Possibly from the earlier period under the rule of Sultan Murad II and most probably from Constantinople,' declared Aleksander to his brother. But Eduard was no longer listening. He had already removed another pair of items from the crate. Unlike the resplendence of the previous artefacts, the newer finds were plain and utilitarian. Each had a tarnished viridescent patina with earthen encrustations. The deltoid tips had a pronounced central midrib.

'Forgive me if I am wrong. Your knowledge is far beyond my own,' proclaimed Eduard, 'But I believe these are Persian spearheads from around the 6th century BCE.'

Aleksander carefully put the Ottoman daggers to one side and held out his hands in readiness. His brother once again offered forward the archaeological finds. They shared a sense of calm as Aleksander examined the simplicity of the time-worn pieces. He turned them over and over, held them to the light, felt along their ragged edges and thought about the brutality of their existence. He looked to his brother and spoke.

'If the remainder of the crates hold such treasures as these, then we may well be sitting on the deal of a lifetime!'

Bring the pages alive…

Explore artworks, locations and more.

Go to gnsbooks.com (Interactive) or scan the QR code to unlock images, maps and facts as you read.

Bethnal Green

London, England

62

Tate entered the incident room at Bethnal Green, where several of Harriet's crew looked up and acknowledged his presence before returning to their current task. Tate now only needed to show his MET Identification card on arrival. His newly designated role meant he was no longer required to be issued a visitor's pass.

He stood and took a moment to absorb the energy in the room. Each detective was engaged in some form of activity. The ambient murmur of voices, some one-sided with a telephone caller, others two-way between colleagues, each attesting to a purposeful resolve. Some sat alone at desks, CCTV recordings running on their monitors as they trawled through hour upon hour of footage. One or two sat engrossed in the pages of a file, additional folders awaiting their attention were amassed on desks in stacks of stratified cardboard. The continual whirling of printers resonated as further pages were ejected and added to the precipice of paper. The investigation was escalating and each detective's focus was piqued as they sought to uncover the one vital detail that may well lead them to the Narcissus.

An arm appeared from behind. A take-out black coffee held firmly in its grip.

'Penny for your thoughts?' enquired Harriet, handing the cup to Tate.

'I was just admiring the diligence of every member of your team. You know their commitment and work ethic is out of their respect and high regard for their leader.'

'I have a good crew. Mind you, they are also afraid of the old dragon breathing down their necks if they step out of line,' declared Harriet, blowing the steam from her coffee.

'They've heard about your better side then?'

'Oh yeah, they have witnessed it on more than one occasion. It's not always easy to control the beast within. If you rattle its cage, then you'd better be ready to sample its bite.'

Harriet's crew assembled as usual as the minutes ticked towards the hour. The DI and Tate used the remainder of their time assimilating evidence on the incident board as they discussed several aspects of the investigation.

'I would like to start by welcoming DCI Randall. Having spoken with DCS Gibbs, it has been decided that DCI Randall will officially assume the role of second SIO for the duration of the Narcissus investigation. The sharing of his knowledge and the fact of having previously worked alongside the suspect for several years can only be beneficial to a successful outcome of this case.' An agreement of nodding heads confirmed an approval of the decision. 'We have a second pair of crime scenes. Another picture hung in a gallery and a further victim,' Harriet stated, tapping pictures on the 'crazy wall' as she spoke. 'The second body has now been formally identified as Ms Kate Palmer. As with the first victim, Ms Palmer has recently been subject to investigations by the Arts and Antiquities department regarding the reproduction and fraudulent sale of fake ceramics. We are led to believe that this is the reason for her being a target of the Narcissus. Tate?' She offered the floor to him.

'Kate Palmer is known to be a producer of reproduction pottery and has previously been convicted and sentenced for crimes of this nature. She has been on our radar for a number of years, including recent investigations led by former DI Lena Johnson before her departure. My team is currently exploring the feasibility of a surveillance operation to protect those currently under our investigations, especially those who were again subject to inquiries involving former DI Johnson. If such an operation were to be workable, we would have to ensure it had no detrimental effect on our current investigations. The pattern of the victims during the Narcissus' first campaign and its continuation with the more recent victims warrant a reason to consider such an operation.' Tate handed four profile photographs to Harriet, who pinned each to the board. 'We believe these four individuals present the highest risk should a third murder occur. The first pair are Dutch twins known for importing illegal items of archaeological importance. The young man in the third picture is a graffiti artist suspected of defacing the works of other high profile street artists. The final photograph is a well-known art forger. All four were known to former DI Johnson.'

DS Quinn raised a folder as a gesture to interject. Tate opened the palm of his hand in acceptance. 'With the case now being a joint investigation, could the extra manpower you require not come from this end?'

'It's an area that DI Stone and I are currently discussing,' exclaimed Tate, 'we would welcome your input though.'

'Yes, thank you, George. Perhaps the three of us can catch up straight after this meeting,' suggested Harriet. The two men nodded their agreement. 'Is there anything further to add at this stage?'

'Of the four individuals, the forger is out of the country at present, the street artist known as CUTZ has gone to ground, and my DI and I have cause to pay the Van Henal twins a visit as part of our ongoing investigations.' He paused, 'I think that's all for now.'

'Ok then. Let's rewind for a moment and revisit the first crime scenes. Andy. Anything further from the Tate Modern?'

'Nothing more from the gallery attendant who was present the afternoon of the picture hanging. She did not remember seeing the woman dressed in red when shown the CCTV footage. She said she was focused on clearing the rooms for closing and was eager to finish as she was going out later that evening with friends. She said she re-checked the room for visitors but did not notice the picture. Forensics on the frame were positive for fingerprints of the subject many times over. She seems to have no concerns about leaving traceable evidence.'

'Thanks, Andy. Anything more from the gallery's CCTV or cameras in the surrounding area?'

'Yes,' he handed a pair of photographs forward and continued, 'These two shots of the suspect are freeze-frames from the cameras at the Baynard House car park entrance. She can be seen to enter, but from that point onwards, we have no further sightings. There is nothing on the buses or the tube so far and the taxis are drawing a blank, too. No one remembers taking the fare of a woman dressed in red. There were no signs of discarded clothing around the premises, but that's not to say she didn't stash a bag in order to make a change of clothing. She could have left in a vehicle parked beforehand, but eliminating vehicles captured by the exit cameras is time consuming. Number plates will need to be run through the DVLA database, and the owners must then be contacted to confirm their movements on the day in question. And who is to say we have not already talked with her under a pseudonym.'

'She was and most probably still is a bike enthusiast, so it may be an idea to prioritise the plates of any motorbikes you come across,' suggested Tate. 'At previous crime scenes, CCTV footage has shown that she changes her appearance, so also pay close attention to individuals exiting on foot.' Andy nodded, welcoming the new SIO's direction.

'Is there anything from the car park in close proximity to the Saatchi or the gallery itself?' enquired Harriet.

'Much the same, really. We can follow the suspect from when she departs the gallery to where she enters the car park. You can tell that she knows where the cameras are. She is seen when she wants to be and hides in the blind spots when she doesn't. We'll keep at it. I have CIOs coming in to help with the hours of recorded footage.' Harriet was about to move on, but DS Stevens motioned with the remote in his hand. 'One last thing, Ma'am.' He aimed the remote at the flat screen in the corner and a small section of film from the Saatchi gallery's security footage began to play. It captured the Narcissus departing just after the hanging of the picture.

'A translator from the RNID has interpreted the finger-spelt message. It reads as,'

Have you missed me?

Andy Stevens looked across at the new SIO. 'I believe this is once again directed at DCI Randall.'

The room was silent, each person awaiting the response.

'I think you are probably right. However, at this stage, I do not feel it is necessary to read too much into the meaning. As with the previous message, I think it has no further significance than to feed her narcissistic ego. It is no more than shouting, 'Hey, look at me!' An agreement to the fact was silently assented about the room. Each detective was aware of the attention and recognition a narcissistic disposition demands.

Alongside the evidence from other lines of inquiry, Harriet pinned a photograph of a further set of song lyrics discovered within the latest victim's throat.

Rule the lesser of two evils
No easy choice for God to make.
Destiny of man, lay at his command
Misjudgement plays a hand in fate.

Narcissus

Tate no longer needed to wait to be invited to comment. The CID team's acceptance of Tate's position was clearly evident.

'The verse has now become commonplace with each new killing. They are all part of the Narcissus' rationale. She has reason and a compulsive need to justify her actions. But only for her own benefit. They may well play no further part than that. Yes, they may taunt our investigations and could be taken to insinuate those she has murdered, but without the verses being glamorised and glorified within the press, they do little more than feed her own self-importance, and it has little or no effect on the notoriety she seeks. A fact that I am sure does not bode well with her narcissistic needs.'

Tate read aloud the recent four line verse.

'As we have come to expect, they are lyrics from an album by Neptune's Finger. Like the other sections used during this second spate of murders, they are taken from the band's second album, *After the Flood*. However, these differ slightly. They are taken from a song entitled "The lesser of two evils". However, unlike before, the lines do not read consecutively. Each line is taken from a different verse of the song. If this has a purpose, it does not stand out immediately. There is most probably an underlying meaning to the unsound mind who chose them. We must remember that everything is planned down to the smallest detail.'

Harriet agreed with Tate's thinking and reasoning. There had to be more to this than meets the eye. 'I'm guessing nothing of value has come from the web search?' she asked, addressing her question in Sarika's direction.

'So far, the searches I have run relating to the lyrics have given nothing further than the story behind the album's concept and a couple of threads relating to the possibility of developing the story and the music into a stage production.'

'I am still not 100 percent convinced it stops there,' declared Harriet. She turned to study the messages together as one on the board. 'Yes, they are provoking, but the Narcissus has taken time to choose specific sections and realign them to have an ulterior meaning. She's playing a game with us, that I agree.' She paused once again to speculate on an idea. 'Ok. Let's roll with this. Re-run a web search, but this time for the album's entire lyrical content. There may well be some prog nerd who has already uploaded a hypothesis or transposed the meaning of the lyrics. It may give us something to work with or indicate what is still to come.' She now turned to Tate. 'Looks like I might have to listen to the whole album,' she declared in jest before finishing on a more serious note. 'The important thing is that the press do not get hold of the messages and blow the whole thing out of proportion,' she declared. 'We do not need to feed the newshounds with further headline material. They get a hold of this and we will have every crazy in the country finding underlying hidden messages from God to the Devil.' Harriet knew that a leak could be detrimental to the case, but she was confident it would not come from her team.

'Ok… let's take a look at the kill sites. Iain, what more have we learnt from the first?' DS Richards opened the file in his hand and began his update.

'Again, forensics found fingerprints matching those of the suspect throughout the crime scene with absolutely no attempt to hide the fact. The clear tape used to fix the newspaper to the window had a perfect set, blatantly done with intent. The most noteworthy discovery is footage we retrieved from a shop on the far side of the road junction. It's a little grainy. However, you can just about see what appears to be a female pushing an individual in a wheelchair in the direction of the rear alleyway. If they arrived by vehicle, it was craftily parked in a camera blind spot. We are still currently piecing together arrivals and departures of vehicles in the vicinity during the same time frame.' He handed Harriet a grainy still of the wheelchair duo and she added it to the relative section of the evidence board.

'Do we have anything further from the second scene, Jake?'

'Couple of things, Ma'am. A local dog walker who works at one of the businesses that George visited the following morning has come forward.'

'Bit of a nosey parker, really,' interrupted George, 'the type who likes to know the ins and outs of everything. Which, for us, has proved fruitful this time.'

DC Evans continued. 'He was walking his dog as he did every night straight after the News at Ten. As he put it, he liked to discourage the kids from playing around the industrial units. He noticed a light at the rear of the building. He reported it to the local boys the next day. Being a low priority incident, it was not followed up before we arrived at the scene. However, our inquiries at the youth centres have paid off. A local skateboarder came forward, claiming he had seen a van parked at the rear of the building earlier the same evening. Unfortunately, he could only verify it was a black transit style van. The two sightings have enabled us to establish a time frame for investigating further vehicle movements within the local area. Both statements are on the electronic file.'

'Thank you, Jake.' Harriet looked at the assemblage of evidence beginning to accumulate on the board. Her eyes were drawn to the two crime scene stills.

'Two bodies. One forced to drink their own blood, the other to eat their own flesh. Both had their tongues removed,' her thoughts monologued more for her own good than those in the room. 'Each sedated with Etorphine. Both were transported by wheelchair. Two crime scenes. Each is related to butchery. Hidden notes on pigskin. Both bodies with further marks cut into their feet.' She turned back to address her team. 'Jake, have you found anything noteworthy relating to MW 25?'

DC Evans' body language said it all. 'Sorry, Ma'am, but I've hit a bit of a wall with that one. MW is a prefix to a whole world of things. Adding 25 does not really change a great deal.'

Harriet once again took a moment to collect her thoughts. 'Run a series of further searches, would you, Jake? Maybe it relates to someone's initials or a significant date.' Harriet was still pondering when Tate added a suggestion.

'It could also relate to a place or location. Maybe they are some form of coordinate or grid reference. They may well relate to aeronautic or celestial navigation rather than land based forms. There are also various new navigational aids like what3words and Lena was always one to be up to date with all the latest gadgets.'

Harriet turned back to DC Evans. 'Run them all. Let me know if anything of interest comes to light.' She turned to Sarika again and smiled. 'How are you and George doing with the funnel inquiries?'

'The purchase history for the two weeks prior to the first murder has thrown up 152 occasions when an identical funnel was purchased in the Greater London area. Of those purchases, 37 were cash payments. We are still accounting for the other transactions and running the CCTV footage for each cash purchase. The one good thing to come from all of it means George and I will be spending a little more time together.' She gave him a wink. Harriet could not help but smile. Sarika could always find the light in the shade. It also applied to the rest of her team. There was always a sense of positivity and propitiousness through both the thick and thin.

Harriet had complete confidence in every member of her team. She was secure in knowing that each branch of inquiry would be thoroughly investigated to a satisfactory conclusion. Without the need to ask, every detective would knuckle down to ensure the investigation's momentum would escalate to a point where there could only be one possible outcome.

The Narcissus would be brought to justice.

63

Directly after the team briefing, they met with DS Quinn as planned. The conclusion of their discussion resulted in George agreeing to organise extra staff should a surveillance operation be needed. Whilst not knowing the whereabouts of two of the possible targets at present and Tate due to pay the Van Henal brothers an unannounced visit in the next day or two, it had been decided to defer any immediate action. The remainder of Harriet's morning had vanished with a succession of meetings and follow ups. Tate had returned to Thorney Street to bring his team up to date with the progression of the now joint investigation. He had agreed to be back at Bethnal Green before mid-afternoon after DCS Gibbs had suggested that it may be a good idea for Tate to attend the planned press conference later that afternoon.

On his way back to Bethnal Green, Tate had swung by the South Bank on the off chance of seeing Tommy again. He had drawn a blank at both the locations Tommy frequently used to paint the view across the river to Westminster, so he had continued along the riverside path to another spot that had been a lucrative view for Tommy in the past. He had passed the south bank mooring of HMS Belfast and continued along the Queen's Walk towards Tower Bridge when he noticed a crowd congregating in a circle to the riverside of The Scoop amphitheatre. A familiar face sat at its centre, armed with stencils and aerosols. Tate had found his man. As usual, he patiently waited to one side until Tommy had completed his artwork, and those not shy about parting with their cash purchased a painting. Tate had not wanted to take up too much of both his and Tommy's time, so a very brief conversation had resulted in Tate walking away in the knowledge that the street artist known as CUTZ's last known place of residence had been in a large townhouse being used as a communal squat in Notting Hill. Tommy was satisfied with the crispy new twenty-pound note lining his pocket and the appearance of new punters already converging on his pitch.

On his arrival back at Bethnal Green, Tate attended a short meeting for those who would be present at the press conference. Shortly after, Press Officer Claire Wilson, closely followed by DCS Gibbs and the two Senior Investigating Officers, filed into the room where they were immediately met by a synchronised blaze of photo flashes as a horde of press photographers and media correspondents recorded their arrival. The bursts of light followed the assemblage of officers as they shuffled in, one by one, along the conference table. DCS Gibbs adjusted and straightened his jacket before he gave his moustache its obligatory groom. Claire Wilson gently tapped the microphone before her. A static tone confirmed its connection. Both Harriet and Tate sat to one end, their hands clasped forward upon the table.

'Good afternoon and thank you for your patience. DCS Leslie Gibbs will make a brief statement and then any further questions will be welcomed by our two Senior Investigating Officers.' She sat back in her chair and DCS Gibbs simultaneously rose from his. Another flare of flashes illuminated the forefront of the room. The Chief Superintendent took his time and waited for the clicking of apertures to abate.

'The recent discovery of two bodies, each located in two very different areas of the city, is now the subject of a major murder investigation. At this point, we have cause to believe the two crime scenes could conceivably be related to the reappearance of an individual known to us as the Narcissus, who is understood to be former Metropolitan detective inspector Lena Johnson. Recent discoveries have led us to believe these new cases may well be linked to a series of murders that Ms Johnson is thought to have committed last summer. She is currently subject to an active international arrest warrant concerning these matters. The suspect is targeting a very specific group of individuals, poses no further cause for concern, and does not present any foreseeable threat to the wider public. We ask the citizens of London to be vigilant and not to approach the individual in question. Any possible sightings should be immediately reported to the Metropolitan CID.'

No sooner had DCS Gibbs appeared to have finished his statement when a crossfire of questions cannonaded from the frontline of journalists. Claire Wilson had grown accustomed to the media vultures' cannibalistic nature and predatory behaviours. After years of sufferance, she no longer saw herself and her fellow officers as the prey but more as the carrion. Ready to pick up the pieces after the predators have had their feed. She had also learnt to become forbearing and stoical to their clamouring demands.

As the outcry of questions receded, Claire again eased herself from her chair.

'We will now happily take any questions you may have. We ask that you do so in an orderly manner. Please refrain from shouting out. Please raise a hand and wait to be offered your opportunity.'

A ubiquity of smartphones was launched into the air, and a bombardment of surnames and media titles erupted in a hollering crescendo.

'Stubbs, The Mirror!'

'Lawrence, Sky News!'

'Glover, The City Tonight!'

'Kirkpatrick, Global News!'

Claire Wilson once again waited for the vocal onslaught to subside, using the moment to gauge the journalists and determine who she would ask to pose the first question. She noticed the crime correspondent from the Independent sat towards the end of a row with a dictating machine held slightly above her head.

'Helen,' she gestured, 'go ahead, please. DI Stone and DCI Randall will take your question.'

'Can you tell us why you are so certain that these recent killings are once again the work of Lena Johnson, aka the Narcissus? The MO appears to be very different than that of last summer's killings?'

Harriet had anticipated a comparable question and was ready with an answer. She remained seated and spoke with confidence. 'Evidence that has been gathered from both crime scenes is conclusive in the fact that former DI Lena Johnson is our prime suspect and is the focus of our ongoing investigations.' That was all she would give them. The gallery CCTV and written verses would remain confidential for now.

Claire beat the braying pack to it and offered Brian Brown of Channel 5 News the next question.

'DCI Randall. Is there any truth to the rumour that the Narcissus is continuing this killing spree by selecting criminals you have been unable to bring to justice in the past?'

'As you are already aware, the victims of the Narcissus' crimes of last summer were all individuals attempting to procure a stolen Caravaggio artwork. At present, we have no evidence pertaining to that fact.' Tate had little time to finish before another question was fired.

'What are you doing to protect those who may be possible future targets?'

'We are currently exploring all avenues to ensure the investigation is brought to a swift conclusion while doing our utmost to safeguard further victims.'

Claire Wilson stood as she tried to get a hold of the situation. She was about to offer the correspondent from Reuters the next question but was beaten to the punch by an anonymous voice from the middle of the room.

'How is the City Chronicle getting their headline pictures? Are you concerned you may well have a leak within your department?'

Steve Brooks sat reservedly in the back row. His camera in his lap. Its lens cap firmly in place. He had not come to capture pictures of the press conference. That style of picture did not warrant the time and effort for the small financial return the newspapers would offer. Brooks had his reasons to be there. He was covering his own back. He wanted to be sure that those investigating the recent murders had yet to discover the fact that someone other than the Narcissus had been at each of the crime scenes.

64

She had left work at a reasonable hour for the first time in as long as she could remember. A kind young man had offered her his seat on the over-crowded underground service to High Barnet. She had been on her feet all day and it felt good to sit down for the thirty minutes or so that her journey home would take. It also gave her mind the time to contemplate the feelings that had been swimming around in her head all day. She felt nauseous with both expectancy and trepidation but found herself hopelessly smiling as she wondered how her evening ahead would play out. She had spent the afternoon checking the clock on the wall every 15 minutes. Time that afternoon had not exactly flown by, but the butterflies in her stomach had been having a party. She had juggled with her conscience throughout as to whether they had been fluttering in nervous anticipation or dancing with excitement. She had got little work done before deciding to pack up for the day.

As soon as she arrived home, she showered, dried, and styled her hair, and the foot of her bed was now piled high with every dress she owned. Having tried on each and every one before discarding it for the next, she was still no closer to deciding which would be the most appropriate and, more importantly, which would give the correct impression on a first date. Was it a first date? Or just friends meeting for drinks? The pit of anxiousness continued to ball in her stomach as she pulled the very first dress from under the pile and slipped back into it. She looked at her willowy frame in the mirror and nodded to herself. A girl should always go with her first instinct. As she reached behind and pulled up the zip, she jigged on the spot to the chorus of Abba's 'The Winner Takes It All'. The music filling the room in an attempt to distract her collywobbles. Why was she so nervous about tonight? The conversation would not be awkward; there would be others there. It had been over three years since she had last stepped out from hiding within her all-in-one forensic coveralls and gone on a dinner date. Although, the last one had been a complete disaster. Her date had been a fireman and he had received a call out to a major incident halfway through dinner and insisted he had to go, leaving her to share the rest of the main course and the dessert with only the company of half a bottle of Sauvignon Blanc and a bill for two to pay. Every now and then, while lost in a daydream, that evening would rear its ugly head, and she would question if she really had been that bad a date.

Penny continued to wiggle and dance to the tune of 'Money, Money, Money' as she slipped in and out of half a dozen pairs of shoes. Each time, she tipped a heel or pointed a toe as she eyed up her selection in the mirror's reflection. In the end, she tip-toed back across to the first pair, nodding to her reflection that they were indeed the correct pair and sat down upon the dresses still piled at the end of the bed and fastened the straps across her heels. Penny started to hum along to the melody of 'Fernando' before realising that two other tracks had played and finished during her shoe selection. She tipped her wrist and checked her watch. Good god, was that the time? She sashayed across to the dresser and opened the middle drawer containing her cardigans. She removed the first one at the top of the pile, a short-sleeved knit in olive green and slipped it over her shoulders. Penny then recrossed the room to her dressing table and pointed a finger in tempo with the song's rhythm at each of the perfumes lined up before her. She chose the third one from the left and sprayed a small amount into the air. She inhaled its vapour. It was a Jo Malone. Lime Basil and Mandarin. Perfect. Nodding to herself one final time, she sprayed a small amount onto the pulse points on both sides of her neck before spritzing the insides of her wrists. With one last look in the full-length mirror, a teasing of the wave in her hair and the transformation was complete.

Losing herself in the music subconsciously dissolved her uncertainties, and with her mood lifted, she asked Alexa to stop the music midway through 'Voulez-Vous'. Penny flicked off the light switch and headed down the stairs, tossing her hair from side to side with the song still playing in her head.

Tonight was now feeling ever more promising.

Beckton

London, England

65

The black motorcycle turned from the access road into the darkness of the passageway between the two warehouse properties. A small amount of light penetrated the farthest reaches of the alley. The rider engaged the kickstand and dismounted. Dressed in full motorcycle leathers, a full face helmet and wearing a hardshell biker's backpack, the rider walked towards the source of the light, leaving the bike out of sight in the semidarkness.

Inside the warehouse, Aleksander manoeuvred his powered chair closer to his brother's side to enable him to get a better view of the Iranian bovine figurine.

'What do you think?' enquired his brother as he turned the small ceramic depiction of a cow over in his hand.

'Possibly 13th century. Simplistic in its form. The glaze has crackled in places but is easily justifiable due to its age.' Eduard typed on the laptop that lay across his legs. Images of similar cattle-like statuettes appeared across the screen. He enlarged one of the images and turned the screen for his brother to see.

'Yes. Definitely from the same period. What is the list price?'

'Twenty-four thousand! I think we could easily get eighteen in the right market.' He re-opened a previous document and recorded the figure.

Eduard had just picked up a 15th century Cypriot terracotta figurine of a female with a bird-like face and numerous body piercings when the smaller of two entrance doors opened and a courier dressed in leathers walked in with a cardboard package.

'Did you not see the sign, "Disabled person. If delivering, please ring and wait".' The courier replied silently with a nod of the head. 'Well, next time, bloody wait.' Aleksander looked across at his brother in puzzlement. 'Were you expecting something?'

'Not that I can remember. You?'

'Nothing springs to mind. What is the return address on the parcel?' Aleksander requested bluntly. The courier just shrugged their shoulders.

'Have you lost your tongue or something?' continued Aleksander.

The courier placed the package to one side and using both hands, slowly eased the full visor helmet from their head. 'No. But shortly, you might lose yours.' replied the courier.

Eduard stepped back, and a look of concern suddenly materialised on Aleksander's face. Each of the brothers was surprised to see that the courier was not a man but a woman who they instantly recognised. Although unsettled by the woman's unveiling and the revelation of just who she was, Aleksander quickly reanimated his brash, audacious nature.

'What do you want? Turning up here unannounced. Thinking you can just walk straight on in. Come to see if we want to buy your painting, have you? That is if you still have it.' Aleksander did not allow himself time to pause and think about the real reason behind the visit. Eduard had already processed that information and was gingerly attempting to edge his way unnoticed towards the collection of archaeological weapons in an effort to arm himself. The Narcissus remained where she stood and allowed Aleksander to continue his rant.

'I, myself, am not a fan of Caravaggio. In my opinion, he was not good at painting hands.

Hands being the only thing I have that's any bloody use. So I am afraid, my dear, your little trip has been a complete waste of time and effort.'

Suddenly, Eduard lunged toward the Narcissus, a 16th century Turkish 'Mizrak' spear thrust forward of his strike. However, while the Narcissus had been listening to the other brother's verbal onslaught, she had still been paying close attention to Eduard's unsuccessful endeavour to shuffle quietly towards the recently acquired armaments. Without hesitation, she took two steps backwards, reached for the cardboard package she had arrived with and drew a police issue taser from within. Eduard had committed to his attack, and the red dot's appearance on his chest went unnoticed. The Narcissus discharged the taser and two probes with trailing copper wires launched towards their intended target. Eduard was hit with several short pulses of 1,500 volts and was instantaneously incapacitated.

When Eduard regained consciousness, he was tethered to a chair beside his brother. Aleksander was also secured within his electric mobility chair, and a gag was placed around his mouth.

'Sorry,' came a voice from behind, 'I couldn't listen to him jabbering on a moment longer.' The source of the voice appeared to his side and the reality of the situation came flooding back as he fought against his restraints. It was as he twisted and turned that he suddenly became aware of his brother's lifelessness.

66

The three men sat at the speakeasy bar on the second floor of Plumes on Wellington Street. Each sipped a Peroni as they prattled and chattered about nothing in particular, each topic batted to one side and quickly forgotten as they leapfrogged from one subject to another. Two men wore dark chinos with fitted waistcoats over stylish dress shirts. The other man was dressed in a casual two-piece tailored suit. All three wore Chelsea ankle boots, each a slightly different style to the other.

All three were high-spirited; the man sat in the centre was the more gregarious of the trio. His laughter was slightly less restrained than that of his companions. The two men to either side had to lean in slightly to enable them to converse and be heard above the vibrant background of the bar room.

Earlier that afternoon, Tate and Harriet had discussed whether or not to cancel their plans for the evening in light of the current situation. Knowing too well what lay ahead and that things could get a whole lot worse before they got somewhat better, they had decided it wouldn't hurt to spend some time with friends. They had planned to do so since returning from their Cornish break but could never find a time to suit everyone.

'...so the badger just stood there and stared,' roared Jonathan as he took another large gulp from his bottle. Tate smiled affably, he had heard it all before. Turner gave a courteous chortle as he had no understanding of the tale Jonathan was recounting. Not that it mattered, the topic of conversation went off on a tangent at least twice in the following few minutes. Each typically ended in a merriment of laughter followed by simultaneous beer drinking.

'So remind me,' enquired Jonathan. 'How did you meet your new lady?'

'It was through an online forum for Friends of the Tate Modern. We discovered we both have a similar taste for surrealism. We found we have a shared fondness for the surreal works of René Magritte and the earlier 16th century works of Hieronymus Bosch.'

'I'm more of a H.R. Giger man myself,' replied Jonathan. 'I love his airbrushed images of biomechanical beings.'

Tate couldn't help but laugh and didn't think twice about butting in, what with his best friend's nickname being the 'tin man'.

'Don't tell me that you see yourself in one of his pictures?'

'Well, now that you mention it.' All three burst out laughing, Turner struggling to contain his last mouthful of beer.

They continued to jest and jibe at each other's expense, and three more beers came and went. Unwittingly, the conversation moved as it usually did at some point onto the subject of food. They were discussing the likelihood of eating in a nearby pizza restaurant called Wildwood when Tate noticed his brother checking his watch for the third time in a matter of minutes.

'What's up, Turn? You're not worried that she has stood you up again?'

Turner was about to retort when his phone buzzed in his pocket.

'How's about that for timing?' beamed Tate.

Turner retrieved his phone and as quickly as he had done so, he returned it to his pocket. 'It wasn't from Sarah. And for your information, we had a lovely lunch the other day, and she is keen to meet you and Harriet.'

'What about me?' pined Jonathan.

'I don't think she'd be ready for that just yet, do you?'

As the three men chinked their bottles, each became distracted by the reflection in the bar's rear mirror as two women appeared at the top of the stairs. In unison, Turner, Jonathan and Tate spun around on their stools.

Harriet and Penny approached the three men.

Each woman barely recognisable without their usual daily attire.

Jonathan sat strangely silenced, doing his best to contain the smallest of smiles. A smile that Tate had not seen his best friend freely expose for over a year.

Beckton

London, England

67

'Don't you bloody touch me,' came the muffled words from the stifled voice behind the gag. 'Believe me, we have associates who could seriously do you some harm,' squirmed Aleksander, trying his best to wriggle the restraint from his mouth.

His brother was far more discreet and tried a different tact altogether. 'There must be some misunderstanding. What say you let us go and we can pretend this little altercation never happened.'

The Narcissus did not reply to either postulation as she paced before the two chairs, tossing a short curved 'shamshir' sword up and down in her hand. 'The question is where to begin.' She tapped the blade of the sword upon her open palm. 'Eduard has spent most of his life watching your pain. Perhaps now is the time for you to watch his.'

She walked around the chairs and approached Eduard from the front. He fought at his restraints but to no avail. Pulling and twisting as a blind panic arose from within. The Narcissus held the tip of the sword's blade to the underside of Eduard's chin. She then slowly ran it down the entire length of his torso, only stopping when the blade reached his thigh. She looked across to Aleksander with a sly smile as she applied further pressure and pulled the blade in an arc around the top of the thigh muscle. Eduard let out a piercing scream and Aleksander shouted a jumble of obscenities from behind his gag. Blood began to ooze from the semicircular wound. With his limbs tied, Eduard was unable to do anything to stem the flow. The Narcissus returned her attention to Aleksander, pushing the sword's tip into the puffy, soft flesh under his eye. He instinctively made to turn his head but thought better of it as he stared down the curvature of the blade.

The Narcissus stared fixedly into Aleksander's eye and began her accusations.

'Are you, or are you not, guilty of importing items of archaeological importance from war-torn countries with no concern for the damage to historic sites of national importance?' Aleksander spewed further profanities despite his constricted mouth. The words were frivolous to the Narcissus' actions and she traced the sword's tip down from his eye and around Aleksander's cheek in the direction of his right ear. She pushed the curved tip beneath the material of the gag, and with a purposeful jerk, she cut through the binding. It dropped to the floor, and a second wave of vulgarities was hurled in the Narcissus' direction.

Nonchalantly, she repeated the accusation. 'Are you, or are you not, guilty of importing items of archaeological importance from war-torn countries with no concern for the damage to historic sites of national importance?'

'Damn you, bitch. If I wasn't tied to this chair, I'd kill you myself!' Disregarding the remarks, the Narcissus returned her attention to the other brother. Eduard had not uttered a single word. He sat head bowed, looking at the sword wound. Despite the cut being superficial, the exuded blood now covered the majority of his leg. The Narcissus stepped into Eduard's field of vision, and without hesitation, she made an identical cut to the other leg. Once again, Eduard shrieked at the torturous pain, the reactive thrashing of his constricted legs almost causing the chair to topple.

This time, Aleksander's response to the second cutting was directed at his brother, its context antithetical to the last. 'Eduard, I am so sorry. I do not wish to cause you this pain. You have carried the weight of my afflictions on your shoulders throughout our lives. I do not wish to see you suffer.'

Eduard turned his neck to look at Aleksander; the pain being too much to lift his head. 'It is not your fault. All we have done, we have done together.'

'Brothers together to the end. How sweet.' The Narcissus turned her attention back to Aleksander. 'While you have both been lining your pockets with the rewards from your criminal exploits, have you at any point in time stopped to think about the effect the plundering of ancient relics has on the cultural heritage of a country and its people?'

He could not help himself, and without thinking, he let fire with further insinuations.

'What gives you the bloody right to come in here and accuse us of crimes when you have committed far greater atrocities yourself? You contradict your own reasoning. Your judgements of others are misled. You're completely deluded.'

The Narcissus was growing tired of the counterattacks; the words meant nothing to her. She was well aware of who held the strongest hand, and the outcome would not change in any way. Tired of Aleksander's shortcomings in response to her assertions, she walked across to the other brother and without a word, she inflicted further torment on Eduard's ailing body.

Two crescentic cuts, one to each arm just above the bicep.

'Stop this. It's complete madness. Here, cut me. If pain and torture is your plan, then I deserve it far more than my brother,' implored Aleksander.

The Narcissus smirked. 'There will be plenty of time for you to pay for your crimes, too. But first, you must admit to them.' The Narcissus once again stood directly in front of Aleksander. 'Does your greed have no conscience? Are you not concerned that your business is funding further conflict and uprisings in countries devastated by war? Your financial dealings are supplementing the purchase of weapons and armaments.'

The reality of the situation began to dawn on Aleksander. 'Please do not punish my brother. I will pay for our wrongdoings. Punish me. I am the one who makes the business deals and transactions. I am the one who deserves your retributions.' He looked across at his brother, who was on the precipice of his pain threshold. He had also lost a substantial amount of blood. His hold on life was fading before his brother's eyes as he began to slip closer to the abyss of perpetual darkness.

The Narcissus stood before the languishing body of Eduard Van Henal.

'Your pain is your punishment. Your crimes have afflicted suffering to many. Many who have no reason to suffer further for your ill-gotten gains. Blood money has fed your greed and bolstered your wealth. The spilling of your blood is your atonement.' With that, the Narcissus took hold of Eduard's hair and yanked back his head, exposing the taut skin of the neck. She raised the curved blade of the sword with her other hand, bringing the tip forward and down to sit at the jugular notch. Then, in one swift movement, she drew the blade down, opening the skin of the torso from the neck to the navel. Eduard let out a guttural cry. His body flopped forward lifelessly, his strength exhausted. Aleksander could feel his brother's pain. His own pain was felt, bearing witness to his brother's torture. He knew Eduard could take no more.

With his twin in the throes of death, he whispered, 'Without you, I am nothing.'

Eduard opened an eye as he strained to lift his head enough to espy his brother one final time.

'And I too…' The words waned and a death rattle escaped his body.

Aleksander's head fell forward as if life had also departed his body. He, too, was defeated. The Narcissus could now do as she pleased. He would accept his damnation. There was no further reason to go on. He and his brother had lived their entire lives in each other's arms. With his kindred spirit gone, life had no meaning.

The Narcissus moved to stand directly above Aleksander's vanquished body.

'Do as you please. I have no desire to live a moment longer.'

'Your time will come. But first, I will grant you the wish you have forever longed. Have you or have you not, always wished you had been born in your brother's skin?'

Beckton

London, England

68

The last bars of 'Man in the Wilderness' faded as Tate pulled the Land Rover to the kerbside of the industrial area. He leant across and turned the volume button of the cassette radio to the off position.

'It's not linked to the ignition like new vehicles. Manual operation only.'

'That's all part of the listening experience. A vintage stereo playing classic rock. It is evocative and nostalgic,' proclaimed DS Jane Garrett as she unbuckled the lap belt. 'What was the title of the album?'

'*The Grand Illusion* by Styx. It was released in the late seventies. I believe '77 or '78.'

'I remember hearing them at parties in the early '80s.'

'Yeah. They became popular back then. They had a number one single with 'Babe'.'

'Yes. That's the one I remember.'

They exited the vehicle and headed towards the warehouse, where Aleksander and Eduard Van Henal were the registered owners.

'We need to be cautious how we approach this,' declared Tate. 'We can't have them becoming suspicious of the reason for our visit or to the fact that their business affairs are already on our radar. I say we play the 'stolen artefacts' card. Inquire if they have seen or heard anything.'

'Sounds good to me. I will follow your lead.'

Tate and Jane walked along the northern side of the building, discussing the implications of their visit. They were about to turn the corner to the front of the building when a black motorcycle appeared from the opposite direction. Both Tate and Jane instinctively stepped back against the building's wall. They had not heard the bike's approach due to the quietness of the electric motor compared to the growl of a petrol engine.

The rider swerved the bike at the last minute, narrowly missing the two detectives. Having also not expected the encounter, the rider fully applied the motorcycle's brakes, causing the rear wheel to fishtail before the rider regained control, and the bike slid to a sideways stop.

All the while, Tate and Jane were spread eagled against the brickwork.

The rider finally steadied the motorcycle to a stance and the two detectives stepped away from the wall. As if nothing had happened, the rider casually looked back over a shoulder and raised the visor of the full face helmet. Although the amount of visible face behind the visor was no more than that of a letterbox, Tate immediately recognised the eyes. Eyes he had once encountered on a daily basis. Eyes that he would never forget for as long as he lived.

The eyes of Lena Johnson, aka the Narcissus.

69

The Narcissus mischievously winked at Tate, lowered the visor and sped off as fast as she had appeared. Tate did not need to think twice as he sprinted toward the Land Rover. Without looking back, he shouted instructions for DS Garrett to secure the area and immediately call DI Stone at Bethnal Green.

'...and tell her I am in pursuit of the suspect, who is on a high-performance e-bike.' Tate made good time in getting back to the Land Rover, all the while keeping an eye on the direction in which the Narcissus had departed. He jumped into the vehicle, fumbled the keys into the ignition and turned the engine over.

Nothing.

'Now is not a good time to be temperamental, old girl!' He turned the key once more.

Still, the Land Rover did not turn over. However, on the third attempt, the engine spluttered to life.

Tate crunched the lever across and forward into first gear and the 1960s Land Rover Series II pulled away in the direction of where Tate had last seen the Narcissus heading. He headed out of the industrial area and caught a glimpse of the motorbike crossing a roundabout on Armada Way. Foot down on the accelerator, he squeezed every ounce of power out of the engine that the vintage Land Rover would give.

The Narcissus stood on the footpegs of the Solar E-Clipse electric bike, and as she accelerated out of the roundabout, she looked back over her shoulder. As expected, she saw the familiar outline of Tate's 4x4. She sat back into the seat, tucked her head down and accelerated towards the dockside.

Tate continued to follow the road south, overtaking several vehicles at points in the road that would normally be deemed hazardous. But his focus and intent was keeping the Narcissus firmly within his sight. The road turned sharply to the west as Tate saw the bike's tail end take the second left ahead. He dropped the Land Rover down through the gears and made the turn. The bike accelerated ahead and took a right at the bottom of Basin Approach. Tate could see the dockside and the water ahead. Just as he thought he was making ground on the bike and its rider, the road abruptly ended. There was only water to his left. Tate looked to the right. He could no longer see the bike. He edged the Land Rover forward between a couple of wheelie bins and onto the paving of the riverside path. He again looked to his right and caught a further glimpse of the bike as it sped along the path and under the Sir Steve Redgrave Bridge.

The Narcissus emerged from under the bridge arch and continued along the dockside towards Royal Albert Quay. Passing the University of East London, the pathway straightened along the side of the Gallions Point Marina for approximately two miles. The Narcissus opened the throttle of the e-bike, pushing it to its 60mph limit. She looked over her shoulder and spotted the Land Rover as it rounded the corner and approached the straighter section of the path.

He had not lost sight of her. In fact, he may well have gained a small amount of ground. Once again, Tate pushed the accelerator to the floor, the 1960s engine fighting to thrust the bulky one-tonne vehicle forward. With the pathway being straight for some considerable distance, little by little, Tate began to wear down the distance between the Land Rover and the e-bike. Occasionally, he would swerve around students strolling along the path rather than slow his speed, the Narcissus now firmly within his sights.

She passed under the Connaught Bridge, aware that, for the first time, she could hear the following vehicle. She needed a way to stall Tate's pursuit, and she needed it quickly. She tucked into the most aerodynamic position possible, kept the throttle wide open and screamed the bike towards the smaller Royal Victoria Dock and the bridge to the south side of the Marina. Suddenly, the solution became apparent.

The Royal Victoria Dock footbridge.

The Narcissus approached the north entrance of the bridge just as a family of four exited the small lift used by those who wished to avoid the stairs. The father figure noticed the advancing bike and quickly ushered his kin to one side. She had to slow the bike to negotiate the bridge's entrance, but there would be no way for the chasing vehicle to follow. The Narcissus slowed the bike further as she approached the open doors to the lift. Just as she was about to enter, she shifted her weight to the rear and wheelied the e-bike into the cramped space. The doors closed behind her.

Tate could not quite believe what he had just seen. The Narcissus had vanished right before his eyes. This was the second time he had been within a whisker of apprehending the Narcissus and he was in no mind to lose out again. He looked around for a solution. At first, he looked for an alternative way to cross the water, so when no resolution materialised, he looked to the land. Just as he began to lose hope, he noticed a man walking out of a quayside property. In his hand, the man held a helmet. Tate exited the Land Rover and sprinted up the approach path.

The man had just reached his bike when he was intercepted by Tate sprinting in his direction.

'Metropolitan CID. I need to borrow your bike. It's an urgent police matter. These are the keys to the Land Rover over there and this is my ID card.' With everything happening so quickly, the flummoxed man handed over his helmet and accepted the keys and card.

'Call 999. Give them my name. Please inform them I am on the London City Airport side of the marina. I'll return the bike later.' Tate put on the helmet, mounted the bike and took off back towards the water.

The Narcissus backed the e-bike out of the lift, span it through 180 degrees with a rear wheel doughnut, and accelerated across the expanse of the bridge. At the far side, she ignored the lift and rode the bike down the alternating flights of stairs. She could not quite believe what she was seeing as she pulled out onto the quayside. Perhaps her escape plan was not as infallible as she had first thought. It looked as if Tate was determined not to let her escape for a second time.

Tate had gotten lucky. The courier's ride was also a lightweight e-bike, so he did just as the Narcissus had done. He used the lift in a similar manner to ascend to the bridge's deck and then descended onto the far bank via the steps. The course of action had taken longer than he would have wished, which meant he had lost sight of the Narcissus. However, he had seen the direction in which she had sped off as he was crossing the bridge's walkway. He accelerated off on a similar heading.

The crossing of the marina via the footbridge had impeded Tate's pursuit, but the Narcissus was soon to realise that it was by no means the end of the chase. She had been astounded when Tate had reappeared on the motorbike. It also aroused her 'catch me if you can' instinct and gave rise to her audacious side. This may have accounted for the reason she had not immediately cut and run. She had waited to ensure Tate was still coming. The thrill of the chase adrenalised in her veins. She did not wish for the pursuit to end just yet.

Traversing the southern rim of the marina, it was not long before Tate caught sight of the bike and rider he still pursued. Both bikes sped eastwards across the concrete wastelands of the dockland's previous existence. They passed beneath the Connaught Bridge once more and headed in the direction of London City Airport. The prospect of the Narcissus' capture fed Tate's compulsion, along with the realisation that the pursuit's new direction would result in one thing for certain. At some point, the chase would run out of ground. Ahead, there was nothing but the River Thames.

An A-road had become the only option due to the perimeter fence running the circumference of the London City Airport. However, a fortuitous circumstance occurred at the southwestern end of the airport. As the Narcissus passed a commercial freight entrance, she noticed a Swiss Port lorry was passing through the security gates. The arm barrier was raised and the automatic bollards were retracted. Without a thought, she encircled the roundabout and headed for the airport entrance. Exiting the main road, she noticed Tate bearing down on the roundabout. Ahead, the lorry moved slowly forward through the security entrance. The Narcissus calculated the available space and accelerated through the checkpoint alongside the lorry. Exiting on the airfield side, she was not surprised to see the pursuing bike repeat the manoeuvre.

'London City tower. BA8453. Ready for take-off.'

'BA8453. Cleared for take-off.'

'Cleared for take-off BA8453.'

The rumble of the thrusters pulsated through the air as BA8453 powered up its engines in readiness for take-off. The plane began to move forward, increasing its speed as it began to eat up the tarmac beneath its wheels. Halfway down the runway at approximately 120mph, the pilot began to pull back on the controls so that the plane became airborne. As the wheels began to rise above the ground, the pilot could not believe what his eyes were seeing. Two motorcycles appeared to be racing towards the runway he had just cleared.

Tate had the Narcissus firmly within his sights. But he also had one eye on the Embraer E-Jet nearing the runway on an eastwards approach. Both bikes and riders straight-lined down the centre of the airstrip, Tate constantly gaining on the other bike as they raced down the 1.5 miles of tarmac.

The crew of the KLM Royal Dutch Airlines had lowered their landing gear, decreased the thrust and adjusted their wing flaps to increase the drag and slow their final approach. Without warning, an announcement came through on the pilot's headset.

'KL992 Abort landing. I repeat. KL992 Abort. Unknown entities on the runway.'

With the pursuing bike now only metres behind and a large passenger aircraft bearing down on the runway, the Narcissus began to snake her bike from one side of the tarmac to the other. A game of cat and mouse ensued. The Narcissus zigzagged her bike to evade contact with Tate's as he deliberately tried to nudge her bike into a spill.

The KLM pilot pulled back on the yoke and powered the thrusters. The landing gear was metres from the tarmac. The two entities were weaving to-and-fro directly across his line of travel.

The down draft and engine noise caused both riders to slow in order to maintain a hold on their bikes. Both Tate and the Narcissus hunkered low to their frameworks as the jet's wheels swept over their heads. As the plane passed, an upsurge of air endeavoured to suck the riders from their bikes. With Tate hugging her rear wheel, the Narcissus sped towards the runway's end.

As he continued to jolt the rear wheel from under the other bike, Tate occasionally looked up to gauge how much runway remained before the land gave way to the entrance waters of the King George V Dock. He sensed that the Narcissus was running out of options. What Tate could not see from his current position was the low-sitting dredging barge currently navigating through the dock's opening.

With the entrance water to the dock being narrow, the dredging barge had little room to manoeuvre between the dock walls. The Narcissus used the confluence to her advantage and launched the e-bike from the airport dockside onto the rear bed of the barge. Without slowing her momentum, she rode the bike up the barge's load of rock spoil and again leapt the bike through the air to the far dockside.

Tate had no time to think and little time to change his mind. He also made the double leap of faith, landing safely on the far side as the barge cleared the entrance water. Without looking back on his close encounter, which would have resulted in a watery grave only moments later, he scrambled the e-bike over the rough terrain of the opposite bank to catch up with the Narcissus' bike once more.

As she pulled out of the small access road, an opportunity to finally outrun her pursuer emerged before her. The warning signals of the Bascule Bridge began to flash and sound. She slid the bike to a stop, looked at the road before her and back at the length of road behind. The bridge began its pivot and the roadways began to lift.

The Narcissus weighed up the factors. There appeared to be only one solution.

Tate straddled his bike in the centre of the road behind. They sat looking at each other like two combatants at a joust. The Narcissus glanced at the bridge, the roadways had so far risen by about 30 degrees. For her plan to work, timing would be crucial. She revved the bike, holding it on the front brake and allowing the rear wheel to spin, before releasing the brake and gunning the bike towards Tate's position. Tate reacted and sped his bike towards the oncoming target. Each was on a collision course with the other. The e-bikes ate up the ground, and within seconds, they were practically wheel to wheel. Tate did not yield and the Narcissus swerved at the final moment.

But that had been the plan all along.

Tate anchored up and brought his bike to a stop. However, the Narcissus held the swerve, accelerated out of a 180 degree turn and was now heading back towards the rising roadway of the Bascule Bridge. The timing had been dead on, and the roadways were now at a perfect angle from each other. The Narcissus gunned the e-bike up the 45 degree incline. As she reached the summit, she stood upon the pegs and launched the bike through the air. Time froze for a fleeting second until the front wheel touched down on the opposite road surface, closely followed by the rear. The forward momentum was enough to allow the bike to continue down the ramp and come to a stop on the fixed roadway. The bridge's cantilevers continued rising until they were at a full 90 degrees, completely blocking Tate's field of vision.

On the far side, the Narcissus had no need to look back. The plan had been executed nigh on perfectly. She closed the visor on the helmet and rode back towards the city, knowing all too well that she had eluded Tate for the second time.

Beckton

London, England

70

After having watched the Narcissus narrowly escape his grasp for a second time, Tate had first returned to the Royal Victoria Dock to collect the Land Rover. He had taken the more accessible and more direct route via the A112 and the Connaught Bridge crossing. As he rounded the nine-foot high bronze Docker's Statue by Les Johnson, he immediately saw the bike's owner talking with officers from the two squad cars parked adjacent to the dockside cranes of Stothert and Pitt.

He explained the situation to the officers and thanked the bike owner. He had also left his details for the owner to claim any expenses and retrieved his keys and ID card before collecting the Land Rover and driving the short distance back to the warehouse.

Once again, he pulled into the industrial area only to be met by the familiar blue hue of the first responders. A restricted cordon had already been set up. He could see DS Garrett perched on the bonnet of one of the squad cars. He parked the Land Rover outside of the police tape and made his way over to DS Garrett. As he neared his colleague, he could see the colour had drained from her face and she appeared to have a cigarette in her hand.

'I didn't realise you smoked,' declared Tate as he leant against the body of the car.

'I don't. This is the first in about three years. After what I have just witnessed, twenty a day may not be beyond the realms of possibility. What's inside that warehouse you would not wish to see in your wildest nightmares, let alone see it in the flesh.' The use of the word 'flesh' triggered a regressive response and Jane Garrett found herself doubled over by the wheel of the squad car, wishing she hadn't had muesli and beetroot juice for breakfast.

As Tate waited for his Detective Sergeant to convalesce, he politely excused himself and crossed the cordoned area to a BMW he recognised as Harriet's. Assuming she was already inside, he located a set of coveralls in the car's boot. He was just about to step into them when he noticed Harriet exit the building. He tucked the disposable clothing under an arm and walked across the yard to meet her. As she approached, he could see that she did not look her usual perky self. Harriet stopped short of Tate's advance and rested one hand on a hip. The other she held up in a gesture to give her a minute. She took a series of deep breaths as she regained her composure.

'I've seen some pretty disturbing crime scenes in my time on the force, but nothing prepares you for what I have just seen in there.' Tate had no idea what to expect aside from the reactions of the only two people to have been inside. 'Her crimes are definitely escalating, but there seems to be no pattern to the killings. In the wake of this, heaven knows what is coming next.' She paused and looked up at Tate. 'I assume she got away, or you wouldn't be here?'

'It wasn't for a lack of trying. I haven't ridden a motorbike quite like that in years.' Harriet looked at Tate inquisitively. 'Trust me, you wouldn't believe it.'

Tate and Harriet joined DS Garrett over beside the squad car and Tate recounted the details of the chase and how the Narcissus had again avoided capture.

Having heard the particulars of the area where the pursuit had taken place, Harriet motioned to the other pair with her mobile phone. 'I am going to get a hold of DS Richards ASAP,' she began to move away as she talked, 'I want to get him on the ANPR cameras immediately. There may well be a chance to pick up on the bike's trail if she is still on the road.' She began to unlock her phone but turned to Tate one final time. 'It may well be an idea to wait for Penny,' she said, gesturing towards the building. 'If you do suit up to go in, remember, it's not a pretty sight in there!'

Paddington

London, England

71

The usual faces had gathered at the bottom of the steps. Each checking and preparing their equipment in anticipation of the opening of the doors above. Some changed or cleaned the lenses on cameras, while others checked their recording devices to ensure they were cued and ready.

Brooks stood within the freelance fraternity, his camera poised to capture the picture that would earn him another front page or, better still, a series of shots for a colour spread within a celebrity magazine such as Hello! or OK! Over the last few days, he had felt more optimistic than of late. The sizeable paycheck which had inflated his bank balance was possibly as good a reason as any for his rediscovered optimism and good cheer. His usual ebullient and carefree attitude had returned as he jostled and engaged with his fellow photojournalists. The fire in his belly was reignited, and he had even contemplated the possibility of a third invitation to photograph a headline making crime scene.

The opening of a door resulted in a frenzy of camera flash bombs. The appearance of a nurse caused the outburst to wane as quickly as it had begun. The assemblage of paparazzi outside the doors of the Lindo Wing of St Mary's Hospital was lingering in anticipation of a front page shot of pop icon Zach Berryman and women's premier league footballer Kelly Morgan, who had just given birth to the couple's first child.

Further activity from the doors at the top of the steps caused another fusillade of flashes. This time, the exiting party was the anticipated couple, who stood as proud parents on the top step with Kelly holding the swaddled baby in her arms. A bombardment of questions ensued as the reporters within the pack attempted to scoop a statement or quote to run alongside the front page pictures.

'Is it a boy or a girl?'

'Have you named the baby yet?'

'Does he or she have footballer's legs?'

The couple took it all in their stride as they continued to smile for the cameras.

Having taken a good series of shots, Brooks pulled away from the herd just as his phone buzzed in his trouser pocket. Upon recognising the sender's ID, he opened the attached message. He read it through.

I was disturbed upon leaving.
I bumped into DCI Tate Randall.
It's probably not a good idea to go to the scene.
The location was Beckton Industrial warehouses.
You will have to make do with snapshots from my phone's camera.
Trust me. It won't be long before the next one.

Bring the pages alive…

Explore artworks, locations and more.

*Go to gnsbooks.com (Interactive) or scan the QR code
to unlock images, maps and facts as you read.*

Beckton

London, England

72

The uniforms ushered the small audience of onlookers to one side. Most were employees of nearby businesses drawn to the scene by the police tape and thirty minutes to spare for their lunch break. The barrier tape was pulled to one side to allow the vehicle to enter.

Penny stepped out of the forensics van and immediately slid open the side door. Her established regime started with unbagging a set of forensic coveralls and removing her shoes. She would then sit on the edge of the opening to pull the coveralls over her trousers. She would then ensure her hair was in a tight bun before proceeding any further. That was as far as she had got when Harriet appeared from the van's far side.

'Have you had your lunch yet?' enquired the Detective Inspector.

'If half a Twix in the van warrants lunch, then yes?'

'Good thing. The Narcissus has surpassed the morbidity of the previous scenes. My stomach is still fighting to recover.'

'Thanks for the heads up. I will pop a couple of gin gins before I head over,' declared Penny convivially.

'You seem to be in a jovial mood. You're not still enchanted from the other evening?'

'He was so sweet,' she replied. A euphoric smile etched upon her face.

'I have known Jon for a long time and have never heard him described as 'sweet'. It's not a word I would associate with him. But he is a great guy.'

'Anyway, back to the real world. I am told we have two bodies this time,' Penny stated, quickly changing the subject as she continued to suit up.

'We do. Twin brothers, but they are no longer what you would call identical.'

'How on earth did she manage to overpower two men?' asked Penny as she pulled the hoodie over her hair bun and began to pull on her nitrile gloves.

'One has been paraplegic since birth and uses an electric mobility chair.' Penny grabbed her kit bag and slid the van door shut.

As they approached the building, Harriet continued to explain the circumstances behind the discovery of the bodies, how Tate and DS Garrett had almost walked in on the Narcissus and the ensuing e-bike chase across the docklands. They entered the building through the open door leading directly into the main area of the warehouse.

Tate stood to one side against the wall. 'Nobody has been any closer,' exclaimed Tate. 'My DS was first on the scene, and she could clearly see from the state of the bodies that both victims were most probably deceased, so she did not check for any vital signs. Harriet and I are the only others who have entered the building and have been no further than where we are currently standing.' Penny acknowledged Tate and began to appraise the situation. She needed to perform her initial assessment of the entrance and surrounding areas, but her eyes were constantly drawn back to the two bodies seated side by side.

The Van Henal brothers were each sitting in a chair. However, it appeared that Eduard, the able-bodied of the two, was sitting in the mobility chair, and his brother's remains were perched on the wooden chair to his side.

But that was not the case.

The brother in the wooden chair had been flayed. The entirety of the body's skin had been meticulously removed from head to toe. The corpse had been degloved and undressed to its underlying musculoskeletal structure.

He had been skinned alive.

The bloodied surface of the body glistened as the capillaries wept further blood and the fatty tissues secreted plasma fluids. With the skin removed, the outline of each muscle was clearly defined, and the whiteness of the tendons emerged amongst the ruddiness.

As had been the case his entire life, Aleksander remained in his mobility chair. However, it appeared at first glance to be Eduard. But on closer inspection…

Aleksander had been dressed in his brother's skin.

His brother's pelt had been hung across his shoulders and had been dressed to enshroud the majority of the body. It had been over-painted in a vibrant red to match its double. His neck looked to have been slashed from ear to ear through both skins.

The twins were together as one until the absolute end.

'Her killings are exacerbating and she will want that fact to be known,' declared Tate, 'Somehow, we will need to watch the galleries. She will place a picture. Her egotistical, conceited self will need to brag and self-congratulate. She still needs to feed her narcissistic ways by extending the thrill of the chase.'

'The question is, which gallery?'

New Bond Street
London, England

73

The Halcyon Gallery occupies the former Arts Society building of New Bond Street. Originally built in the late 19th century by celebrated architect Edward William Godwin, the art nouveau designed building now regularly showcases exhibitions by emerging contemporary artists and continues to present collections of Neo-Impressionism, surrealism, cubism and other modern abstract arts. The gallery has previously held collections by the likes of Warhol, Picasso and Hockney.

The current collection adorning the abstract spaces within the gallery was entitled 'Jai-pure'. A refreshing collection by contemporary Rajasthani artists whose works of striking, vibrant colour and intricate detail often depict Indian mythology, fables and culture. Live performance arts of Kalbelia and Bhavai folk dances also formed part of the exhibition.

Four London black cabs pulled up alongside the kerb directly outside the entrance to the gallery. A bevy of high-spirited ladies exited the vehicles. A babbling chatter ensued as each lady seemed to be talking at the same time as another. No one appeared not to be talking. And no one noticed as an additional lady joined the soirée.

The Narcissus wore a brilliant red saree and a ruby-encrusted ghoonghat veil. She was instantly absorbed into the animated coterie of brightly dressed women. They, too, were each wearing a saree. Each in vivid shades of orange, yellow and red. Traditional Hindi veils covered their heads and faces, and their bodies were decorated with henna art, precious stones and golden jewellery.

The rainbow of ladies continued to confabulate as they were ushered through the gallery entrance, each so engrossed in the tales of recent events that the first six or so paintings went unnoticed. However, the taller lady in the red saree, appeared to be paying particular attention not only to the artworks but to the gallery's surroundings too. The Narcissus was taking stock of the security guard's movements and the surveillance camera coverage within each room that the huddle of ladies passed through.

Towards the rear of the ground floor, the conversation began to sway away from family affairs as the eloquence and beauty of the artworks emerged as a new topic of discussion. While a modern interpretation of Radha Krishna was discussed and opinions were cast upon the Picasso-styled faces, the Narcissus used the situation to her advantage and removed the first of two pictures from within her flowing saree. Turning to her left, she pushed the pre-bonded frame to the wall. As the huddle moved on to critique the next picture, the Narcissus removed the second frame and repeated the hanging. The two photographs hung to either side of a cubistic depiction of Rakshasa, the Hindu flesh-eating demigod.

'Excuse me, Madam. May I ask what you think you are doing?' The Narcissus turned from the wall to face a security guard she had not previously noticed.

'Yes, of course. Silly me. I must remember not to touch. I do hope nothing has been disturbed.' The security guard stood dumbfounded by the woman's reply. He was in the process of further questioning the woman on what he had just witnessed when, without warning, she thrust an object into his hands.

'Could you make sure he gets this,' she declared as she pulled her ghoonghat back over her head and smiled at the nearest camera.

And with that, the Narcissus walked unflustered towards the exit.

Bethnal Green
London, England

74

Harriet listened intently as Tate recounted the e-bike chase through the Royal Docks area. He provided enough information to allow the CID team to gather a good understanding of the encounter but did not waste time on unnecessary details. The consequential development was that they had a starting point. It would enable them to pick up the Narcissus' trail to begin tracking her route back into the city.

'Cameras please Iain. Start with the traffic and ANPRs around the dock area. As soon as you get something, please let me know.' DS Richards acknowledged the request and Harriet turned to DC Evans.

'Jake. The bike is yours. As soon as DS Richards has an image, get a make and model. Tate mentioned that it looked new. Check with dealerships and rental companies for recent sales and rental contracts. With E-motorbikes being a relatively recent concept, there may not be many of them currently on the road.'

'How about the cameras at the City airport?' enquired DC Evans, 'I could request their security footage. It might be a quicker solution to identifying the make and model of the bike?'

'Good shout, Jake. Get onto it.' The aviation authority would comply without hesitation. However, there would no doubt be further questions that Tate would be accountable for, relating to entering aviation airspace and the subsequent consequences.

Harriet poised herself before continuing. What she had witnessed only hours before was beyond anything the job had previously thrown at her. There was no denying it, the sight she had witnessed at the crime scene had rattled her. She was only human, after all. Before giving an account of the scene to the rest of her crew, she needed to feel level-headed and composed.

'The nature of the Narcissus' crimes is escalating. We have not one, but two bodies on this occasion. However, it is the ferocity and brutality of the killing that is of the most concern.' She paused for the briefest of moments before delivering the gruesome details. 'Of the two bodies, one appears to have been flayed. The entirety of the skin has been removed from the victim's body. Until we get the autopsy results, we cannot say whether this happened pre-mortem or not.' Those in the room reflected a sense of unease as unsettling looks of consternation were cast upon people's faces. Harriet continued. 'The second body has been draped in the flaying, giving the appearance of being dressed in a suit of the other man's skin. This skin has been overpainted in a deep red. Quite possibly to resemble the exposed muscle and tissues of the other man.' She paused a second time for the reality of the situation to sink in. 'First indications suggest this has been done intentionally so that the two bodies would look identical when discovered. We believe the two victims to be twin brothers, both of which are known to DCI Randall and his team. Tate. Could you provide some context?' She offered him the room to divulge further.

'Before formal identification, we can be fairly sure that the two bodies are those of Aleksander and Eduard Van Henal. Twin brothers of Dutch nationality who have been residents of the UK for a period exceeding 20 years. They are known to be dealers of historical artefacts. In previous years, their business and, more importantly, the methods behind obtaining and acquiring these antiquities have been questionable. As with the previous victims, they have both been subject to investigation by former DI Lena Johnson.' Tate's elucidation was interrupted by the ringing of a telephone.

DS George Quinn reached across the nearest desk and lifted the receiver. He knew from the flashing line indicator that the call was being internally redirected from the main call centre. 'Incident room. DS Quinn speaking.'

The remainder of the room remained silent, listening to the one-sided conversation and George's acknowledgements. He gestured in Harriet and Tate's direction that what was being said was important. 'Yes. I am with her now. No problem. I will pass on the information immediately. Thank you.' He replaced the receiver and looked across towards his senior officers.

'Central has just received a call from the Halcyon Gallery. A pair of pictures have just been added to their current exhibition.'

75

They had been met at the entrance to the Halcyon Gallery by an ostentatious sea of silk in a floridity of colours. The curious, predominantly Indian crowd was reluctant to leave. Most probably clinging to the hope of being permitted re-entry or looking for an opportunity to claim a refund. With the gallery having cleared its rooms as soon as they realised what had possibly just happened, no explanation had been given to their visitors. A habitual curiosity captivated the crowd with the off chance of another tale to share.

'She thrust it in my hand and said, "Could you make sure he gets this".'

'Those were her exact words?' Tate enquired, looking inquisitively at the object he now held.

'As far as I can remember. I'd caught her red-handed. She apologised for touching and disturbing the exhibit, but then she pushed that into my hands and walked off all blasé and pompous-like.' Tate turned the mask over in his hand. Unmistakably, written in bold letters across the inner surface were the words,

TATE x x

'It's a Bhairab mask,' declared the security guard, 'I only know that because there is a collection of them upstairs as part of the exhibition. Reading the exhibit labels helps to pass the time. What you can learn is quite amazing. Apparently, the Bhairab is said to represent the evil side of Lord Shiva, the Hindu deity. He is said to be associated with destruction and to be a punisher of wrongdoers. Well, that's what the description says.' Tate looked to Harriet, who removed a folded evidence bag and held it open as Tate carefully placed the mask inside. 'I almost forgot. There is one more thing. Right before she turned and left, she pulled back her veil and looked straight into that camera. Like, on purpose.'

'Can you describe her?' Harriet asked, keen to keep the security guard's train of thought running. 'What was she wearing? Was there anything in particular that stood out?'

'She was wearing a saree and one of those face coverings, the veil thing. To be honest, she looked like the majority of the females who have visited the current exhibition, it being Indian art and all. I did notice that she was much taller than the other women.'

Tate made a mental note before turning his attention back to the guard. 'Thank you. Your recollections are invaluable. Can you talk us through exactly what happened as clearly as you can remember? Please try to be as accurate as possible and try to recall every detail.'

The security guard led Tate and Harriet through the ground floor to the rear of the gallery. As they approached a contemporary picture of two Indian ladies, you could not fail to notice the two new additions. Although much smaller than the other works on the wall, the two photographs stood out due to their generous bright red frames. Both detectives had no need to scrutinise the detail of the images, having seen the subjects of the work in the flesh at the crime scene. The security guard began to question and scrutinise the picture's subject. Tate quickly re-steered the direction of the topic.

'Could you start from when you first suspected something was amiss.'

'Yes, sorry. It's… it's those images. Are they photographs of the murders, just like the ones that have been in the City Chronicle?'

Neither detective answered and Tate once again refocused the guard's attention.

'Did you notice the woman who hung the pictures when she entered the building?'

'No. I'm afraid not. As I said, she looked like she was part of the large party of women who had recently entered the gallery. All very colourful and all very much the same.'

'When did you suspect something was amiss?' asked Harriet.

'I saw her lift her saree. I thought it seemed strange. My first thoughts were a knife or an aerosol. You know, what with all these activists and protesters these days. I thought she was going to deface the painting in some way. Anyway, when she pulled out a picture, at first, I was relieved. But it didn't make sense. You could say I was thunderstruck. I stood and watched her hang the first picture. Like I said, I didn't intervene until I saw her hanging the second frame and remembered the front-page story. You get to read a lot of front-page headlines and back-page sports on the tube.'

Tate once again reeled in the digression. 'Thank you. We are going to need to see any security footage you may have. Are there any street-side cameras?

'Yes. We have three covering the entrance. One is over the doors and the other two point in either direction along the street. There are also extensive enforcement cameras along the entirety of New Bond Street.'

'We can access those directly, but if we could see the gallery's footage from earlier and if possible, make a copy, it would be most helpful.'

76

He felt his client wince. Her muscle contracting a little in reaction to the bite of the needle.

'Sorry. I am just working some finer detailing into an area I have already coloured during this session. The area in question is becoming slightly reddened and a little inflamed. It's been a long sitting with the two areas you wished to be coloured today. Shall we take a short break?'

'I'm fine. But if you feel it would be the right thing to do, then I'm fine with that too.'

'Let's take ten, then when we continue, I will add a little more shading to the rear rib area on your right side. It will give the left side a little respite.' Sean wiped across the area he had been working to remove the excess ink and placed the tattoo machine back on its stand. Lena went to sit up. 'Just hold on a second. I will rub in a little aloe vera to ease the tenderness.' Lena remained face down on the bed as the tattooist massaged a small amount of gel into the lower left of her back.

When the tattooist returned, Lena had reclasped her bra and was sitting at the edge of the bed. He handed across a glass of water, which his client gladly accepted. He stood to the side and sipped a steaming herbal tea.

'Have you ever hurt someone?'

The question took Sean by surprise. 'It's in the job description, I'm afraid. I hurt people on a daily basis, some more than others. It depends on the individual's pain threshold and the placement of the tattoo. I have also left behind several relationships where the other person may claim to have been a victim and been hurt in the process.'

'No, I mean, really hurt someone.'

'I have been known to have a few street brawls in my time, back when I was much younger and rather more naïve. I might have been responsible for a black eye and the odd bloody nose. But that's about it, really.' He was no more ready for the next question than he had been with the first.

'Do you believe in chance?'

He wasn't sure where this was going but was happy to reply. 'I believe everybody should be given a chance in life, regardless of their background.'

'Sorry, I didn't make myself clear,' interposed Lena. 'I meant chance as in fortuitous.' Sean frequently had in depth conversations with his clients. The tattoo process offered the opportunity to step off the ever spinning wheel of life and stop, if only for a short while. Frequently, it afforded the sitter time to think and reflect. There had been times when he had felt more like a councillor than an artist.

'I believe that things happen for a reason. I don't advocate luck. If you are prepared, you can meet any challenge life throws at you.'

'I had a chance encounter with an old friend this week. We just happened to be in the same place at the same time. We used to be very close. But things change and we now don't see eye to eye. He looks at the world from a very different perspective than I do. He believes in justice being served. Fair treatment and accountability without prejudice. Ensuring those who break the law face the appropriate consequences.' Lena paused and looked the tattooist straight in the eye. 'Do you believe in punishment, Sean?'

The tattooist began to feel slightly uneasy with the direction of the conversation but was also intrigued to find out where it was leading.

'I read once that punishment is not for revenge but for reform. If someone is to be punished, should they not be allowed the opportunity to rectify their mistakes?'

Lena offered a devious smile before returning to her previous position, face down on the bed. She spoke without turning her head.

'So, if I told you I had hurt someone. Punished them for doing wrong. Should I then be punished for my own misconduct?'

77

An open box of bitesize chocolate croissants, pain au chocolat and chocolate cronuts sat within easy reach upon the desk. A steaming sizeable black coffee to one side and a hot chocolate with all the trimmings to the other. Each woman picnicking as they talked, each having missed breakfast for significantly different reasons.

Harriet had started her morning with a sixty minute track session at the Lee Valley indoor velodrome. Repetitive circuits interspersed with sprint laps to build both her strength and stamina. Sarika's morning could not have started more differently. Firstly, a visit to the headmaster's office with a reprimanded child, followed by her weekly weigh-in at Slimming World. Both required all the strength and stamina she could muster and these two earlier appointments were the reason for her missing breakfast.

Sarika reached for another cronut, it didn't matter for now, the next weigh-in was a week away. Harriet blew across the surface of her coffee.

'Ghoonghat wearing and facial veiling is slowly becoming a thing of the past across the Indian continent,' declared Sarika, wiping cronut crumbs from the corners of her mouth. 'It is now limited to deeply religious Hindu-speaking areas to restrict the ease with which older men can form relations with younger women. Well. That's the reason I no longer wear one myself,' she sniggered.

'Tell me about the Bhairab mask.'

'It depicts a fierce incarnation of the Hindu God Shiva. The mask usually features angry eyes, sharp teeth and wears a crown of five skulls. He is said to be an annihilator who associates with extinction. He is the executioner of sinners.'

Harriet's ears pricked at the last sentence. 'Maybe the mask holds more significance than we were first led to believe. The Narcissus sees herself as an 'Angel of Death'. Delve a little deeper, would you, Sarika? See if you can find any further comparisons.'

Sarika ran her tongue in an arc over her top lip, removing the skim of whipped cream. 'Will do.'

Her reply was short-lived as Harriet's mobile began to ring and vibrate. She glimpsed at the caller's ID and left the phone on the desk after pushing the hands-free button.

'Morning, Happy. I have you on speakerphone. Sarika, one of my profilers, is with me. Is that OK?'

'Only if she had breakfast more than four hours ago,' Happy jested. Sarika looked at the mini croissant in her hand and swiftly returned it to the bag.

'OK, Happy. What have you got for us?'

'Firstly. I have been a pathologist for over twenty years, and in that time, I have never seen anything quite like this before. The manner of the torture is as bad as it gets.' Harriet looked across to Sarika, who nodded, implying she was okay with continuing to listen.

'Let's start with the easier of the two causes of death. The brother with the disability died due to the severing of the jugular and both the carotid arteries. He would have bled out quite quickly. His torture would no doubt have been watching his twin suffer before his own eyes.' Harriet could see the colour slowly draining from Sarika's face. She guessed Sarika may soon be seeing the chocolate pastries she had devoured once again.

'The other twin's cause of death was exsanguination. To those of you who are not sesquipedalians, it refers to the loss of bodily fluids.' Sarika looked baffled.

'It takes a while to get used to Happy's little quips,' explained Harriet.

'Full exsanguination is reached when the body loses 40% of its blood and bodily fluids. In this case, as the skin was removed, he bled to death very slowly due to haemorrhaging. There is little to no damage to the major blood vessels. The skin was removed, and the dermis had very little tissue damage. The skin removal was mainly within the layers of the epidermis. He would have been alive when the removal started.'

Without a word, Sarika stood and made for the door, one hand firmly held across her mouth.

'Elvis has just left the building,' Harriet stated, knowing Happy would understand the meaning.

'However, his major organs would have begun to fail due to a decrease in blood pressure. His pulse would have weakened, and his heart rate would have increased temporarily as it fought to supply the organs with oxygenated blood. Shock would have occurred, and eventually, he would have lost consciousness. But not before experiencing an awful amount of pain and suffering. The other twin would most probably have witnessed the entire event before he experienced the mental torture of being stripped naked and dressed in his brother's skin.'

Cullum Street
London, England

78

It had been two hours since the sun had dipped below the western horizon. The sky was cloudless and its vastness was a deep shade of raven black. Venus had appeared to the west, and even with the city's light pollution, an opalescent zodiac of stars began to emerge.

He dropped the board off the kerb and pumped his back foot along the roadway. His back foot stepped up as his speed increased to join the other foot on the board. The skater then began to snake the board from side to side to maintain his forward motion.

Born Timothy Cuttifords to parents who were both British overseas diplomats, he spent his childhood boarding at a public school in Somerset. His school holidays were spent in a country where one of his parents was assigned at the time. During his early years of boarding school, he acquired the nickname CUTZ and a talent for drawing emerged. During his late teens, his artistic talents metamorphosed as a rebellious side began to take hold. Sketchbooks and easels were abandoned, concrete and steel were his new canvas. Tagging and stencilling of local parks and bridges became his addiction. The nonconformist in him flourished as he soon appeared as a familiar face on the frontline of rallies and protests across the country. As his dissidence escalated, he found a new direction for his artistic flair and began to create antipolitical posters. As time passed, he moved to more significant works of demonstration upon the sides of buildings. These works led him into the world of Dadaism. An anti-art movement reacting to the discontent and rejection of modern capitalism, which in turn challenged the definition of art itself. Over time, CUTZ found himself frustrated with other statement artists and it was not long before he began intentionally defacing the work of others. He would become known for art vandalism rather than its creation.

He tail-scraped the skateboard to a stop before tail-popping the board into his hand. It looked cool, but nobody was watching. Just the way he would want it. He leant the skateboard against the wall and removed his rucksack. He looked left and right along the road to be sure he was definitely alone. With the coast clear, he removed a number of aerosols and a stencil.

Upon the wall rising before him was a controversial statement piece by a recognisable street artist. CUTZ laid the stencil across the wall in several positions, each time spraying a black outline across the work below. He then alternated between three aerosol cans as he added further shading and detail to each stencilled area. Once he had completed his overpainting, the original work could still be seen. His defacement gave the appearance that the street art had been sliced through several times with a knife.

CUTZ checked the street once more before crossing to the far side and turning to admire his handiwork. He crossed his arms in satisfaction as he mulled over the extent of his reworking. He gave himself a self-approving nod and recrossed the road.

Lastly, he added his moniker to the corner opposite the original artist's.

inc.CUTZ

79

She smiled at him across the table. The kind of smile someone gives when they are content and appeased. Some would call it a smile of serenity. It was a smile that lit a fire inside and left the recipient with a cosy feeling.

They had arranged to meet late in the morning at one of London's most beautiful and unusual coffee locations. The Wren is tucked away within the St Nicholas Cole Abbey. The café takes its name from the building's architect, Sir Christopher Wren. The 12th century church was destroyed in the 1666 Great Fire of London but rebuilt by Wren a few years later. It required reconstruction for a second time after damage during the Second World War. In addition to its daily coffee service, it still operates as a fully functional place of worship.

'Firstly, I must apologise. I am so sorry for letting you down at the last minute the other day,' declared Sarah, 'I had a couple of clients who took up more of my time than I had previously anticipated. There wasn't an opportunity for me to call. They required my full attention.' She looked across the top of the coffee in her hand with adorable dog-sad eyes. How could he not forgive her?

'It's not a problem. I won't lie that I wasn't a little disappointed at the time. But I knew there had to be a perfectly reasonable explanation. My brother, however, took the opportunity to poke a little fun at my expense. As big brothers do.'

'I hope he didn't poke too deep. I wouldn't want him to paint the wrong picture of me. Let's hope we can find an opportunity to get together soon.' Turner held her gaze across the table. Her mesmerising eyes entrapped him. The kind of eyes that lure you in and you can't help but keep looking.

'Tate and Harriet are busy with a difficult case, but hopefully, we can all find an opportunity in the not too distant future.'

'That would be great. I'll look forward to it. Talking of opportunities, how would you feel about going to the Tate Britain gallery together? They have an exhibition of the Pre-Raphaelites that has just opened. "Mariana" by Sir John Everett Millais is one of my favourite paintings.'

'What a coincidence. My mother is also an admirer of the Pre-Raphaelite era. The three pictures based on Tennyson's poem "The Curse of the Lady of Shalott" are some of her favourites, too.'

'Then we should go. It would also be good to visit the gallery where your parents worked, don't you think?'

'Yes. Of course,' replied Turner, slightly perturbed by the suggestion. He could not remember telling Sarah that his parents had both been curators at Tate Britain.

80

She looked at the person in the mirror while applying a deeper tone across the top line of her cheekbone. As she applied further make-up to the prosthetic sculpting around the eyes and the bridge line of the nose, she continually referred to the photograph on the visitor's access pass that hung on a lanyard to the side of the mirror. She continued to reference the picture as she worked the finer details of the face in the mirror. A pair of blue-tinted contact lenses were added to the eyes, and a dental prosthesis was inserted to create a frontal diastema. A short bobbed ginger wig completed the change of appearance. A new face gazed back at the woman she had once been. The woman in the access pass now stared back at her from the mirror.

Forty minutes later, she pulled the Fiat 500 into a vacant visitor's space and checked her appearance in the rearview mirror one final time before crossing the car park to the security entrance. Just two other people were waiting to be checked through security, so she waited patiently in line. She rubbed her thumb across the nails of her other fingers while she bided her time. The woman wished to be as inconspicuous as possible to draw minimal attention to herself. The guard welcomed her forward for her first security check. She placed her phone, keys, and shoes into the scanner tray and put her bag of art materials onto the conveyor. As the items moved towards the x-ray machine, the woman stepped forward, spread her arms and the guard swept a security wand around her limbs and torso. Satisfied that the woman was not concealing any metallic objects, the guard continued with a pat down search. All the while, the woman looked forward at a spot on the wall ahead. The guard extended a hand in a gesture to proceed and the woman stepped forward onto the foot alignments of the full body x-ray portal. The machine's cubicle rotated 180 degrees and returned to its starting position. No alarms sounded and another guard invited the woman to proceed into the waiting area on the far side, where she collected her other belongings. As she was putting her shoes back on, the guard smiled at her in a way that suggested he recognised having seen her before. He had no need to check her security pass.

'You are free to proceed, Ms Stewart.'

Bring the pages alive…

Explore artworks, locations and more.

Go to gnsbooks.com (Interactive) or scan the QR code to unlock images, maps and facts as you read.

81

She pinned two photographs, two print-outs and a report to an investigation board that was growing exponentially with each new crime. There were many pieces of the puzzle that, at present, did not interlock as much as they should at this stage of an investigation. Especially when you have known the perpetrator's identity from the beginning and have a reasonable idea of those who may fall victim in the near future. Each crime had been planned in the finest detail. Planned by someone who knew the investigative process. Someone who was leaving a trail on purpose. Trails of evidence and footage that would eventually lead to a series of frustrating dead ends. Each leading as far as she would have wanted and no further. Just far enough to stimulate the chase. Enough to ensure the perpetrator gains the notoriety that she needs to feed upon.

Harriet turned away from the wall and addressed her crew.

'Three crime scenes and now four victims. The brutality of each crime scene is intensifying and the period between each kill is becoming sequentially shorter. The progression of the timeline intervals gives a strong indication that we can expect another victim relatively soon. With that in mind, we need to cover the galleries. We might not be able to pre-empt the kill site, but her personality disorder will mean she will not be able to resist the placing of a picture after the kill. It is all part and parcel of the crime. If we are going to apprehend the Narcissus, then this is our best chance.' Harriet looked around and focussed her next words in the direction of her new DS.

'Andy. Can I leave this with you? Contact all the galleries in Central London. Get them to heighten their security. Make certain their surveillance teams are aware of the importance of the situation. If they are suspicious of any activity, ensure them they have our backing to not think twice about apprehending anybody they may suspect. The Narcissus may have predicted our actions, but she is devious enough to change her approach. For the first time, she may involve a third party, so apprehend anybody they suspect, male or female, young or old.'

Tate interjected a thought. 'Regardless of the level of risk, I believe she will plant the picture herself. She will wish to continue the high she experiences from the thrill of the chase. She will also be reluctant to trust another person. Remember, it's all part of her narcissistic game. But I also agree with DI Stone, the gallery security teams need to be extra vigilant and be prepared for anything whatsoever.'

Harriet thanked Tate and turned to her other Detective Sergeant. 'Where are we with the camera footage, Iain?'

'We finally have something fundamental to work with. We have been able to track the e-bike back from the Royal Docks to an underground car park in the Knightsbridge area. It took a substantial amount of man hours, as she was extremely enterprising with the route she took back into the city. She clearly expected us to track her on the cameras and there were several sections of the route without CCTV where we lost her completely. But we managed to piece together the footage as the cameras picked her up again. DC Thompson is out there as we speak with a forensic team. It has also enabled us to track an unmarked van back from the Baynard House car park on the day of the Tate Modern picture hanging. DC Thompson and the team are looking for both vehicles and collecting any further camera footage available from the Knightsbridge car park.'

'Excellent, Iain. Thank you. If DC Thompson needs more bodies, please make sure he gets them.' DS Richards nodded in acknowledgement of the fact. 'Jake. Where have you got with the bike?'

DC Evans opened his notes. 'The bike is a Solar E-Clipse. It is one of a few road legal electric motorbikes on the market in the UK today. The company is UK-registered at an address in West Drayton. Fourteen bikes purchased directly from the company have been registered and insured in the London area in the past twelve months. One other bike has yet to be registered as road legal. This is the bike on which we are focusing our investigations. It was paid for from an online account. We are awaiting the details of the account holder.'

'Good work, Jake. Again, keep DCI Randall and myself informed of any updates.'

'Just one more thing, Ma'am. There are currently no rental companies stocking this particular model of bike.'

Harriet thanked DC Evans once more and turned her attention toward Sarika.

'Ok, Sar, you're up.'

Sarika placed a chocolate hobnob she had just removed from the packet on one side.

'Good news and bad news. Which would you like first?'

'Let's get the bad out of the way, shall we.'

'Inquiries into the purchase of the funnel from the first crime scene have hit a brick wall. Of those bought with cash payments, none were seen on CCTV footage to be female. Again, purchases made by bank card were all registered to male account holders. So, a dead end, I'm afraid. However, inquiries into the meaning of the lyrical concept behind the Neptune's Finger album are moving in a better direction.' Sarika handed Harriet a CD case. 'I ordered you a copy from Amazon. I had a listen and nothing obvious jumped out. But I found a mega fan who runs an online fanbase. He is transposing the meaning of the verses as we speak. He is in Sheffield and will email them as soon as he has finished. I am also meeting with one of the creators behind the stage play based around the storyline of the album in the Theatre Café on Shaftesbury Avenue at 11 am tomorrow. I'll let you know as soon as I have something.'

'Thanks, Sar,' declared Harriet, handing back two sheets of paper in Sarika's direction. 'Happy sent these over directly after finishing the autopsies. As on previous occasions, both had been concealed in the oesophagus. Tate, would you care to clarify?'

'The two verses have, this time, been taken from different songs on the album. One is entitled "The Storming of the Seas", and the second is "The Dissolution of Man." They both tell of God's anger towards mankind and the punishing of all who have become sinners. It may be a good idea to let your transposer know the specific sections we are interested in but without our reasons for doing so. He might see a link or something else we may have overlooked.' Sarika noted Tate's remarks, and Harriet handed the CD in his direction.

'That's fine. You listen to it. I have an original vinyl release.'

'I should have guessed, really.' The crew saw the funny side and tittered. Harriet smiled and moved on. 'Happy has also sent across these shots taken during the autopsy.' She pointed at the recently added picture on the investigation board. 'The victims once again have markings to the underside of the feet. One body has a pair of numbers as per our previous victims. This time, a '3' and a '5'. However, the other appears to have just a dot upon each foot.' She took a marker pen and wrote out the numbers, letters and symbols from each of the four victims.

25 35 MW ..

'Does anything spring to mind as to their meaning?' The crew remained silent as they spun the figures around in their heads. Eventually, one spoke.

'It's a Bible verse, Ma'am,' declared DS George Quinn. 'Mathew 25:35'. However, I don't have a clue what the passage is about.' Harriet looked quizzically at her stalwart officer. 'My mother is a devout Christian. Attends church every Sunday without fail.'

'DC Evans,' instructed Harriet. Jake being the closest officer to a computer.

'Already on it, Ma'am,' he replied, pushing the enter key. As the screen filled with search results, he clicked the link to open the site at the top of the list. The site was entitled 'Pathways of the Bible.'

> 35 For I was an hungred, and ye gave me meat:
> I was thirsty, and ye gave me drink:
> I was a stranger, and ye took me in:
> 36 Naked, and ye clothed me:
> I was sick, and ye visited me:
> I was in prison, and ye came unto me.

The officers gathered around the desk; each was silent as they read the verse.

Tate was the first to speak, noticing a sub-title at the top of the screen. 'They are the Works of Mercy. The basic needs of humanity and a model of how we should treat others around us.' Tate stopped and allowed his thoughts to spiral, linking the words on the screen to the recent crimes of the Narcissus. His mind brought forward images from the three crime scenes as he fought to connect each to the list of mercies. Suddenly, the reality of the situation hit him like a ton of bricks. He did not speak immediately. He had to be sure that the associations he had made were conceivable. He ran the thought processes one more time. Again, they all seemed to correlate and conform.

'She is creating her own depictions of man's mercies,' Tate announced, the remainder of the team stepping back from the desk to listen to the senior officer's assertions. 'I believe she has twisted their meaning to suit her distorted mind. The first victim was made to drink his own blood: I was thirsty, and ye gave me drink. Kate Palmer was made to eat her own flesh: For I was an hungred, and ye gave me meat.'

Harriet began seeing the connections and jumped onto Tate's thought train. 'Of the twins at the last crime scene, one had been crippled his entire life and when his body was discovered, he was naked and had been dressed in his brother's skin: I was sick, and ye visited me. And secondly:

Naked, and ye clothed me.'

'That still leaves us with two mercies,' announced Tate, taking a printout DC Evans had just handed him, 'and the likelihood of two further murders.' He mused over the prose and read aloud, 'I was a stranger, and ye took me in; I was in prison, and ye came unto me.' As he read the words, the revelation of what was about to happen became apparent.

'She's going after Grayson!'

82

Jeremy Grayson lay on his bunk, a copy of yesterday's Times newspaper spread across his chest. Unlike his time on the outside, when he would scan the front pages online, he would now read every article, every column, every page and have a damn good go at the crossword. He now had the time to do just that. He especially enjoyed the occasions when his cellmate would be away for the biggest part of the day. Away, somewhere unimportant, flipping burgers, retraining to be a chef on a rehabilitation program. To Jeremy Grayson, it mattered not. The simple difference was the peace, calm and space it afforded him to enjoy his newspaper without having to stop every few minutes to discuss last night's football scores or to be asked his opinion on the latest celebrity to have been eliminated from a reality TV programme.

Jeremy Grayson was the owner of a gallery just off New Bond Street. Over the years, he had become one of London's most renowned dealers of fine art. He was held in high regard within the City's cash rich circles when a collector was looking to add a Cezanne, Matisse or Toulouse Lautrec to their collection. His reputation for locating a work by any means, especially for those who were more than happy to turn a blind eye to a work's recent provenance, had become the most lucrative side of his business. This darker side of backroom dealing would lead to his eventual downfall. His greed and rapacity led to one temptation too many. A request to abet the sale of a stolen Caravaggio had led him to become entrapped in the murderous campaign of the Narcissus. His third-party introductions would consequently lead to the brutal slayings of a succession of zealous collectors. Grayson himself came close to death as a victim of the Narcissus' crimes when he was crucified to one of Battersea Power Station's infamous chimneys. His involvement resulted in a two-year detainment at Her Majesty's pleasure for aiding and abetting the sale of stolen property.

Grayson looked at his watch. It would soon be time for his own vocational programme. Shortly after his sending down, he began an art history degree via a remote learning programme. He had also been actively involved in a series of workshops the system provided for inmates to learn new skills. Art, literature and photography were all part of his weekly resettlement schedule.

His attendance at a one-to-one art workshop beckoned. He neatly folded his Times newspaper and placed it beneath his pillow before swinging his legs off the bunk and straight into a waiting pair of Crocs. He welcomed their roomy comfort. His feet and hands still bearing the scars of stigmata from his crucifixion. Jeremy brushed down his sweatshirt and jog bottoms and headed out onto the landing concourse. Being a category D wing, there were few locked doors and minimal security. Prisoners had the freedom to socialise and interact. He passed several inmates chatting in pairs and small groups as he proceeded towards the stairway. All classes and workshops were on the ground floor in a series of rooms adjacent to the visitor's area.

Jeremy had been sitting in Room 4C for several minutes when a gentle tapping of the open door announced his tutor's arrival.

'Afternoon, Mr Grayson,' said the tutor, entering the room and closing the door behind her. Jeremy looked up inquisitively. His tutors did not usually address him formally with his surname. Things were normally kept informal by using each other's Christian names. Still, he recognised Amy; she had been his art tutor for quite some time. Although he had to look twice, there was something different about her appearance today that he just could not put his finger on. Had she changed her hair? Was she dressed differently? Was it simply the addition of the red nail varnish? No, that was not it. He pondered further until the realisation materialised. She appeared to be taller. Considerably taller. He looked down, expecting to see her wearing heels, but she wore flats. Her voice interrupted his curiosity.

'It's so good to see you again.' The voice was different too.

'It must be a year or so since we last met.' He knew the voice but could not place it.

'I believe we have some unfinished business.'

Suddenly, the realisation struck.

He took a step back, unable to comprehend quite what was happening.

The Narcissus took three steps forward and raised a hand.

Jeremy Grayson took another retreating half step and also raised a hand. He clasped at the implement that had just been plunged into the side of his neck. He withdrew the object and held it forward. It appeared to be an artist's paintbrush with some kind of needle at its end.

'Fair Warning, Mr Grayson,' were the final words he heard as the world around him began to fade to black.

Bethnal Green
London, England

83

The afternoon skies were cast in grey with an ominous feel for further showers in the next few hours. The trees were now beginning to lose their leaves, their bare branches reaching out like bony fingers grasping at the stillness of another approaching winter.

Harriet and Tate exited from the main doors of the station. Security at the HM Prison Thameside had been contacted and the governor had been made aware of the possible situation concerning the inmate, Jeremy Grayson. With the inmate not partaking in an offsite rehabilitation initiative and there being no way of a member of the public breaching the entrance security protocol, the governor had practically dismissed their concerns. Considering the circumstances, he had assured them that Jeremy Grayson was probably in the safest place.

Having missed lunch, they were heading out in search of a quick bite. It would also afford them the opportunity to give their respective headspace a short reprieve. They were in the throes of discussing where best to seek the nourishment they craved when a flash ignited the gloomy atmosphere. A man stepped out of the gateway to Museum Gardens and a further fulgent of flashes exploded in their pathway. Tate held his arm up to defend his eyes, but Harriet made a grab for the man's shoulder. As she did so, the man turned to go, but Harriet's grasp was sufficient enough to turn the photographer back in their direction.

He allowed his camera to drop back on its strap and raised both hands. 'Just getting a couple of shots of the senior investigators on the Narcissus case. The paper wants to run a parallel story. You know, seeing the investigation from both sides and all.'

Tate released Harriet's grip from the man's shoulder. 'He's just doing his job.'

Harriet apologised immediately. 'It's just you caught me by surprise, that's all. You can't be too careful these days.'

The photographer smiled at the investigators. 'If you catch this

Narcissus, you might even make the front pages yourselves.'

'Just as long as you are not responsible for the morbid headline pictures of the crime scenes,' asserted Harriet.

The photographer shied away, happy he had captured just what the editor would have wanted. As he began to make his way back towards the tube station, Brooks' mobile signalled the arrival of an email. He retrieved his phone and opened the app. There were no sender's details. But that meant Brooks knew precisely who it was from.

The subject line read…

Hot off the press.

84

The guard was doing his hourly floor walk when he passed the door to Jeremy Grayson's cell. He turned his wrist and checked the time. By now, Jeremy would have generally returned to his cell after his tutorial. He made a mental note to check the education room when he returned to the ground floor. He did not give it a second thought as he continued his inspection of the second-level landing. It was not unusual for cells to be empty during the day, with inmates attending classes and the permitted freedom to intermingle within the communal areas.

Forty minutes later, the guard sat at the control station console.

'Bugger,' he exclaimed.

'What's up, Brian?'

'Nothing, really. I just forgot to check something.' He took the last mouthful of his tea, carefully avoiding the sunken teabag at the bottom of the cup and headed off in the direction of the visitor's corridor.

Room 4C was at the far end of the hallway, and its door appeared to be closed. That in itself was strange, as all rehabilitation sessions took place in the relative safety of the prison's open-door policy. As an unrestricted access area, there were no cameras in operation.

Brian eased the door and stepped into the room. He immediately froze upon seeing the sight before him. He could not comprehend what his eyes were seeing. In all the years he had worked for the HM prison service, he had never witnessed anything like the scene he had stumbled upon in Room 4C.

85

The prison had gone into immediate lockdown after the discovery of the body. External investigators and forensic personnel had been contacted, and within the first hour, Amy Stewart's home had been raided, and she had been found relatively unharmed, chained to a radiator. Her description of her assailant and Jeremy Grayson's history with the Narcissus quickly led to the conclusion that there was a strong possibility that the two incidents were both linked to the current case.

Tate and Harriet had been sharing a quiet lunch at the Padella Italian restaurant in Shoreditch when they received the news of a further potential murder by the hands of the Narcissus. As they travelled across the city to the Category D prison, neither could quite comprehend the details of the information they had been provided.

Thirty minutes later, they had passed through the prison's security procedure and were now being led the short distance through the locked down area to the crime scene.

The door to 4C was closed and a huddle of authoritative personnel stood to one side, each engaged in deep conversation. Tate and Harriet were introduced by the guard escorting them. Harriet recognised a senior officer from the Greenwich CID team, who explained the protocol for a murder within the HM prison jurisdiction, the discovery at the tutor's house and the current status regarding the crime scene. Knowing that Penny would arrive shortly, Harriet asked to view the security footage.

They had been escorted to the prison's main surveillance room, where the footage from the earlier visitor's security protocol was cued and ready for viewing. Harriet and Tate watched as the figure who had been thought to be Amy Stewart approached the security detail and advanced through the entrance procedure as she would have done many times before. She remained calm and composed throughout. As the footage played, a close-up of the suspect's face appeared as she passed close to one of the cameras. Tate asked for the sequence to be paused. The guard rewound the images until the clearest close-up frame filled the screen.

The face that looked back was that of a middle-aged woman he did not recognise, but some aspects of her appearance seemed familiar. Tate knew the eyes. Although they were a different colour, he had seen them so many times that he would never forget the look of the eyes hiding behind the contact lenses. The shape of the lips and the mouth were also giveaway features of the face behind the make-up. The prosthetics and make-up had created the image of another person, but certain features were harder to disguise. While the footage ran, Tate had also noticed that Lena could do little to hide her habituation. While waiting for security clearance, she had continually and unconsciously rubbed her thumb across the tips of her fingers to polish her nails. A practice Tate had witnessed many times while working alongside one another.

'The make-up is quite remarkable,' declared Tate. 'Equally, her portraiture works that I have seen are also very impressive. But there is no denying the fact that the woman beneath the clever disguise is Lena Johnson, aka the Narcissus.'

'The three guards on entrance security can't quite believe it was not the genuine Ms Stewart,' stated the surveillance operator. 'They have processed her through numerous times, chatted with her and even got to know her a little. They have said that, in hindsight, she was not her usual chatty self this morning. But they thought no more about it as we all have those days.'

'Would it be possible to see the exit footage?' Harriet enquired, glancing at her watch, knowing that Penny would probably have arrived by now, which meant they would be able to view the body. It did not take the guard long to forward the footage to the point where the mimicked tutor departed the building. Harriet made a mental note of the time signature at the bottom of the screen. The CCTV images ran through the sequence as the security detail processed the visitor's exit.

Harriet questioned the observation she had made. 'Did no one think to question why the tutor was departing only twenty-two minutes after her arrival? Surely that's an unusually short length of time for someone to provide a skills-based tutorial?'

The guard sat in silence as he pondered a suitable reply. 'Being a D category open prison, with so many people coming and going throughout the day, I'd imagine no one gave it a second thought. Some tutors can deliver multiple lessons per day, whereas others are here to see a single inmate.' Harriet understood the reasoning, especially since no one had suspected anything and the disguise being so convincible. It was always easier to see and question things in retrospect.

'Could you play the footage one more time, please?' asked Tate.

Almost as soon as the footage began to replay, Tate asked the guard to freeze the image on the screen.

'Is it possible to enlarge a close-up of the suspect, please.' The guard manipulated the control stick on the desk, and the screenshot moved in more tightly. 'Hold it, just there.' The camera angle captured an image of the suspect from behind. It detailed her back and the bag slung over her shoulder.

'Take a look at the writing across the bag,' Tate said, pointing a finger at the image. The words could easily be read:

Best Witches and Happy Haunting. Narcissus X

After Tate's discovery of yet another taunting message, they were escorted back to Room 4C, where the door now stood open and the previous gathering of personnel had dispersed, leaving a solitary guard to secure the room. An unmistakable silhouette dressed in white coveralls stood just beyond the threshold. Harriet and Tate stood before the entrance, each with a clear view into the room, completely aware that they would get a much closer look once Penny had completed her preliminary observations.

'How bad is it?'

'It's not a pretty sight.' Penny stepped to one side, having recognised the voice.

'Been here —'

Harriet's sentence curtailed as she saw the extent of the crime scene for the first time. It took her a moment to process the entirety of the mutilated body. Tate, too, required a short time to make his own perceptions of the killing.

'She appears to be spiralling out of control,' remarked Penny as she took the first of her initial shots of the crime scene's locale. 'The inhumanity and violence is stepping up with each murder and she is becoming more and more unsparing.'

'She is also taking far greater risks. Which will inevitably lead to her believing she is unstoppable. The risk will heighten the thrill she experiences with each kill,' stated Tate.

'I can't quite get my head around the fact that she walked into a high-security prison, murdered an inmate and callously just walked away,' declared Harriet. 'Not only does that take some guts, but it's completely irrational behaviour.'

'I agree with what you are saying. However, there still appears to be a lot of forethought and planning put into each murder. There is no overpainting of the body in this instance,' indicated Tate. 'It would have taken too much time and increased the likelihood of being interrupted. It appears she has instead dressed the body in a distinctly different way.'

Jeremy Grayson had been crucified for a second time. His body was spread across an inverted, wooden, artist's easel, which had been leant against a wall for support. His hands had once again been impaled. However, on this occasion, the scarred wounds of his previous stigmata had not been nailed; they had been lanced with the metal ferruled handles of a pair of artist's paint brushes. His throat had been slashed from ear to ear. However, his torso had been afflicted with far greater injuries. His abdomen had also been sliced from one side to the other. A large gaping wound lay open across his stomach. His intestines had been pulled from the cavity within. Jeremy's arms were spread wide, each wrist tied to a leg of the easel with a length of intestine, and his feet were bound together in a similar manner. The remainder of the entrails had been looped up, down and around his body in garlands as if they were intended as some sort of offering. His head, although lowered, was turned slightly to one side. His face angled forward, locked in a vacant stare. His mouth hung open and a set of novelty vampire fangs had been inserted onto his bite.

Euston Station
London, England

86

CUTZ exited the tunnel and continued along the tracks beneath the bridge. His rucksack of aerosols swung from his hand. Word was out about a new Network Rail installation erected on the track side of a major train route into the capital. More importantly, it was currently graffiti-free, and CUTZ wanted to be the first to tag it. The newly erected electrical cabinet shone with a white brilliance in contrast to the other diesel-sooted, graffiti-riddled trackside units.

Although the night had settled into a dusky darkness and the sun had long before dipped below the western horizon, the trains arriving and departing from the West Coast Main Line terminus would still be running. CUTZ would need to have his wits about him to ensure he was out of sight every time a train approached. He may miss his chance of a blank canvas if he left the tagging until the early hours when the trains were no longer running.

He dropped his rucksack onto the floor, turned his baseball cap so that the visor was to the rear and removed the first aerosol can. He checked up and down the tracks before beginning to spray a basic outline of his tag. Each time he applied his moniker, he would need to quickly visualise the size of the four letters to be able to fill as much of the available space as he could. CUTZ finished the outlining and removed a second aerosol, this time choosing a silver colour. Keeping the applicator nozzle compressed, he began to fill in the body of the letters using a series of short, compact sweeping movements. Halfway through colouring the third letter, he heard a train approaching, and the tracks behind him began to hum. He grabbed the rucksack and tucked himself behind the unit.

Further along the track, someone else also hid themselves from the train driver's view. They squatted behind a large oil drum until the train had passed on its approach to the platform. The watcher stood in the bridge's shadow and continued to observe CUTZ's actions.

He finished filling the letters with the silver colour before reverting to the first aerosol once again. The second layer of black would form a more distinctive outline that would emphasise his unique handstyle. His tag writing font was very angular to accentuate his name's abbreviation. It also held an underlying meaning relating to the etymology of the word 'Graffiti', which stems from the Italian word 'Graffiato', translating to 'scratch or carve.' His finished tags looked as if they had been cut into the surface upon which they were painted.

The watcher continued to stake out CUTZ's work. Both individuals having to disappear from view once again as a train began to pull away from the station. As the watcher looked on, CUTZ added some green accents and highlights to his tag. Each small mark further italicising the letters. He stood back to briefly scrutinise his work before throwing the three aerosol cans back in his rucksack. He returned the visor of his cap to the front, pulled it down over his eyes, raised his hoodie over the cap and headed off towards the station. The watcher stepped from the shadows and began to follow at a distance.

CUTZ followed the trackside to the perimeter of the station before scaling a wall via the top of a wheelie bin. He dropped down on the far side and continued in the direction of Euston Road. A short distance behind and a couple of minutes later, the watcher made the same manoeuvre and caught up with CUTZ once more as he descended the steps into Euston Square underground station.

The watcher kept her distance as she followed CUTZ through the station to the Circle line platform. With fewer bodies along the length of the tunnel due to the time of night, the watcher chose to sit so as not to look suspicious. The train pulled in and CUTZ stepped into the carriage and immediately sat down. The watcher entered the next carriage and took a position which enabled a clear field of vision through the interconnecting window to the seat where CUTZ sat. He paid little to no attention to those around him as he scrolled through his mobile phone. The watcher continued to observe from her covert position.

The underground train pulled into Notting Hill Gate station and CUTZ disembarked and headed for the exit. He slouched against the rail of the escalator as it rose towards the surface. Still, he did not notice the woman behind as she stepped onto the rising escalator. CUTZ exited the station and headed down the Kensington Park Road. The watcher followed at a distance. As he turned into Ladbroke Square, he turned to look back in the direction in which he had just come. A weird feeling came over him. Why had he felt the need to suddenly check to see if he was being followed? He looked back one more time. There was no one there; he had just spooked himself. He shook his head in disbelief and turned into the gardens at the centre of the square.

The Narcissus watched the graffiti artist enter the Ladbroke Square gardens before entering the central green space herself from the Kensington Park Road entrance. She followed the path along the garden's perimeter in the direction of where she had last seen the graffiti artist.

CUTZ had sat on the park bench, having decided to roll himself a joint before returning to the squat. He was running his tongue along the edge of the Rizla paper when an attractive woman stepped out of the darkness. His general angst for society put him on edge, whilst the spliff in his hand added to his trepidation. The woman crossed in his direction.

'I'm sorry to trouble you. Would you have a mobile phone I could use?' The woman seemed flustered and slightly unnerved. 'Two boys on a moped have just snatched my handbag and I would very much like to call a cab.' CUTZ relaxed a little and exhaled a small sigh of relief. He held the spliff forward for the woman to see.

'Thank the Lord above. For a moment there, I thought you were a copper.' The woman stepped forward in reach of the graffiti artist. She smiled as he raised his mobile phone. The Narcissus accepted it with one hand as she thrust the needle into his neck with the other.

'I used to be.' she whispered into his ear before he fell to the floor.

Ganton Street
London, England

87

He stood huddled in the restaurant doorway and pulled the collars of his overcoat up around his ears. The rain had started about an hour or so ago, but it had become far more persistent in the past few minutes. Ganton Street was empty due to the early hour. The occasional couple would wander aimlessly by his makeshift refuge, having just left a nightclub or a similar late night establishment. From his furtive position, he had a direct line of view across the street to the front doors of the Cirque Le Soir nightclub. It had become one of London's places to be seen and was regularly frequented by famous faces from the music and film industries. An opportunity to capture a departing celebrity, hopefully, the worst for wear, was the reason why Brooks was sheltering in a doorway at nearly 3 am.

Brooks peeked out along the street and noticed another paparazzo, who he recognised but could not recall his name, doing the very same thing in his own damp, cramped doorway.

The doors to the nightclub opened, and two security guards stepped out. They were closely followed by a smartly dressed man and his female acquaintance, neither of whom Brooks recognised. He allowed his camera to remain hanging at the end of its neck strap, the other photographer doing the same as no flashes ignited the darkened street. The couple passed Brooks, oblivious to his presence, as they made their way down the street. He, too, paid no attention to their departure as he went back to scrolling through news stories on his phone. The photographs of the murdered twins that he had forwarded to the City Chronicle had once again made the front page. Another sizeable payment would soon reach his bank account, but not for a moment would he consider revealing that he had not taken the shots himself. In fact, looking at the pictures again, he was happy not to have seen the crime scene with his own eyes.

He was about to call it a night and head home when his phone started ringing. The number had been withheld, but he had no reason to second guess who it might be. He answered the call.

'I hope I haven't woken you?' questioned the voice at the other end. Brooks had been correct in who the caller would be.

'Not at all. I'm still in the city waiting to capture the moment when a celebrity stumbles drunkenly out of a club in the early hours, hoping nobody sees them escorting a date they shouldn't be seen with. But the camera has long gone cold and I was thinking of heading off home just as you called.'

'Well, I suggest you don't head off too quickly.' Brooks' ears pricked. 'I recently visited an old friend in prison. We had unfinished business. Once again, I took a few pictures myself, as you would probably not have been granted access. I will forward them to you shortly. I think this one will make a wonderful front-page story.' As Brooks listened, he sensed a higher degree of ostentatiousness in the Narcissus' voice. With each new killing, she appeared to be growing increasingly more conceited and egotistical. She continued talking and Brooks was happy to listen, as she seemed to have done his work for him once again.

'The pictures of the most recent victim, I will leave you to take for yourself this time. I will message you a location in due course. It's high time you started working for your money again.' The Narcissus sniggered just loud enough to be heard. Brooks was taken aback and slightly confused. Was the Narcissus suggesting there was already another victim? He was about to enquire to the fact when he was beaten to it.

'I suggest you take a brolly, you might need it.'

Brooks found he still needed to ask just to be sure of himself. 'Are you implying there is already another body after the victim at the prison?'

'Yes,' replied the Narcissus in a confident yet cocky tone.

'The kill is still fresh. In fact, I am looking at him as we speak.'

Manchester Square
London, England

88

He closed the door behind him with the heel of his shoe and placed the two mugs of tea on the desk. The other guard spun his swivel chair around to face his colleague.

'Yours is the one on the left, no sugar,' said the first guard.

'Cheers, Michael. Have you seen the headlines in this morning's paper? Apparently, some guy got murdered in prison and the suspected killer was a visitor. It must take some bloody nerve to do something like that, don't you think?'

'Yeah, I read it earlier, before we did the crossword. They think it's a strong possibility that it was the Narcissus. She tried to kill him once before, last summer,' declared Anthony as he stirred his mug before dunking a Rich Tea biscuit.

'The Narcissus is a woman? Bloody hell, who'd have thought it.'

'Do you not watch the news or take onboard what you read in here every night?' replied Anthony, doing his best to talk through a mouthful of mushy biscuit.

'Never thought about it, really. Just assumed after all those killings it would be a man, you know, not the usual thing your missus does on a night out.'

Anthony could not tolerate another one-sided intellectual conversation and decided to excuse himself. 'I think I'll take a quick once around, just to check the cavalier is still laughing.'

'What about your tea?'

'I'll drink it when I get back.'

'But it will get cold.'

'You just keep an eye on those monitors and your hands off the biscuits. I'll be back in twenty minutes or so.'

The Wallace Collection occupies 25 galleries within Hertford House, the former home of the Marquesses of Hertford. The entire collection was bequeathed to the nation by the widow of Sir Richard Wallace. The collection of fine arts and old masters from the 15th through to the 19th century opened to the general public in the early 1900s and has remained until this day in the former townhouse on the conditions stipulated by Sir Richard's widow that no work may ever be sold or even loaned to another exhibition.

Nightshift security had its good points but numerous downsides. Boredom was the killer with the overnight stretch. You can only read the newspaper once, and when the crossword and sudoku are finished, a good book becomes your forever companion. After the public has departed and the cleaners have washed, polished and dusted, 99.9% of the time, the CCTV footage at an art gallery remains still. Nothing moves and all remains quiet. If something stirs, it is probably a mouse or a large moth flitting too close to a security sensor. For Anthony, the repose of the gallery at night compared to the bustle of the day shift was his beau idéal. Over the years, he came to appreciate the pictures and desired to learn more about the artists and their different painting styles. His nightly patrols allowed him to view the gallery's magnificent works in the quietude and solitude of his own company. No crowds, no mischievous schoolchildren and no tourists viewing grandiose paintings through the eye of their cameras.

Anthony had checked the majority of the galleries over the three floors and was heading back to the surveillance room when he heard a loud thud from the floor above. He stopped and remained still, waiting and listening for further sounds. He heard nothing more. The gallery was still and silent once again. However, he had definitely heard something.

'Michael, it's Anthony. Are you there?' he said in a whisper into his radio.

'Yeah, what's up? Please don't tell me the Laughing Cavalier has stopped laughing.'

'Did you hear that?'

'Why are we whispering? Hear what?'

'There was a noise like someone dropping something. It sounded as if it was directly above my present position. It came from the second floor, most probably one of the east galleries. Can you see anything on the cameras?' He waited apprehensively for a reply.

'Negative. No movement on the second floor that I can see.'

'Meet me on the second-floor landing. I'm going to take a look. And before you leave, bring up the lighting levels on floor two.'

The two guards converged at the head of the stairs.

'We'll go through the Small Drawing Room and into the east galleries.

I haven't heard another sound since the initial noise, but we had better be alert just in case.' The two guards entered the first room to find nothing out of the ordinary, so they moved on to the East Drawing Room. Again, they found nothing suspicious. As they moved to the far end of the room, they could see through the three interconnecting galleries that formed the remaining length of the east wing.

'I'll go first,' declared Anthony. 'You stay half a room's length behind in case I get jumped.'

'Jumped. By who?'

'Just stay behind and keep your eyes and ears peeled.' They began to make their way through the east galleries, checking the corner spaces of each room. There appeared to be nothing out of place in the first two galleries. Anthony held up a hand as they approached the entrance to the third and final room.

'What is it?' enquired Michael.

'There is a picture frame on the floor,' replied Anthony, trying to make sense of the scenario he had just discovered in East Gallery 3. 'It looks to have fallen off the wall.'

'How can a picture just fall off the wall? Have you seen how they hang those things?' Anthony moved further into the room, checking the corners behind him as he went.

He had become suspicious as soon as he noticed the size of the fallen frame, but now, as he stood over the picture, the realisation of what it may be perturbed him. He bent down and cautiously turned the frame over so it was picture side up. As soon as he saw the image, he immediately knew what it was and what it would mean. The photograph captured the prisoner crucified and disembowelled. The image was harrowing, but he could not pull himself away from scrutinising its every detail.

'What is it?' enquired Michael, curiously edging step by step ever closer.

'Best you get on the phone. We are going to be front page news for the next day or two.'

Manchester Square
London, England

89

Harriet had received the call from the desk sergeant at Bethnal Green while she was in the final fifteen minutes of her spinning class, right at the point when the class instructor had upped the peddle rate and velocity for one final explosion of power to increase the heart rate and push the endurance of the leg muscles. She had called DS Stevens immediately after the workout had come to a close and arranged for him to collect her from the gym in twenty minutes. That would give her time to shower and give Tate a heads up.

Tate and Jonathan had finished their swim, with Jonathan touching home first, so he had chosen to have breakfast at Gail's Bakery on Seymour Place. Tate suggested that he meet Harriet at Hertford House as he was within walking distance.

There had been a small number of people mingling outside the Wallace Collection when Tate, Harriet and Andy Stevens had arrived. The small crowd indicated that the gallery had been sensible and delayed opening to the public. As they waited inside the entrance for the director, a gallery attendant carrying an A-Frame board clarified the temporary closure. The director escorted all three to the second floor, where they were met by two security guards. The director made brief introductions before the two guards gave a detailed account of the events that led to the discovery of the pictures. Both guards had been more than happy to continue their shift to provide a hands-on account of their nocturnal incident. They followed the two guards into the adjacent room and immediately noticed the frame on the floor.

'Apart from turning the painting, no one has touched the frame?' Harriet clarified.

'Correct,' replied the more senior of the two guards. 'I realised the picture could possibly be the work of the Narcissus, similarly to those previously planted at other galleries across the city.'

'God knows how she got in though,' exclaimed the other guard, emphasising the 'she', having recently discovered the fact himself, 'and especially with two frames.'

'Excuse me? Are you saying there is another picture?' enquired Tate. The younger guard, now unable to control his keenness, moved fervently towards the far corner of the room.

'It's over here. We noticed it, although I should confess that Anthony noticed it, while waiting for you folks to turn up.' He continued enthusiastically towards the corner and the picture.

Tate anticipated what was about to happen in the guard's eagerness. 'Please, could I ask you to stop there? We need to contain the crime scene. The less footfall in the proximity of the picture, the better.' The guard moved gingerly back towards the others in the room.

'So nobody noticed anything out of the ordinary on the surveillance footage yesterday?'

The senior of the two guards resumed responsibility for the questions. 'We did not start our shift until after the gallery had closed for the day.'

The director interrupted. 'If the day shift had noticed any unusual behaviour or an individual being disruptive, it would have been immediately reported to me. No such incident took place.'

'Has anyone actually checked the security footage from yesterday?' asked Harriet, addressing her question in the direction of the senior security guard.

'I am afraid we haven't had time to do so yet. We thought it best to stay with the pictures.'

'Perhaps we can take a look in due course?'

'That shouldn't be a problem,' declared the director. 'Anthony. Please make sure the footage is available for the officers whenever they wish to see it.' The guard acknowledged his senior staff member before the three investigators returned their attention to the picture on the floor.

'I guess the adhesive failed,' declared DS Stevens. 'Quite possibly not adhered sufficiently to the wall's particular surface.'

'Or the Narcissus intended for this picture to fall. I wouldn't put it past her,' stated Tate. 'She may well have planned it to draw attention away from the other picture.' Keeping their distance, the three investigators scrutinised the content within the frame.

'There is no disputing that it is the Grayson crime scene. However, she probably had no intention of revealing a kill site, as she would have known that the crime scene would be discovered relatively quickly,' Harriet declared as she turned towards the other picture. 'At present, we are unaware of a sixth murder. However, I believe we may be about to change that scenario.' Harriet asked the gallery staff to remain where they were as the three investigators moved towards the far end of the room. However, unlike the security guard, they remained a safe distance back from where the second picture hung. Tate removed his phone and took a series of shots of the frame. Harriet and DS Stevens looked on as Tate enlarged one of the photographs on the screen of his phone. He was the first to speak.

'It appears our sixth victim is another individual who the former DI Lena Johnson has investigated in the past. His name is Timothy Cuttifords, but he is known on the street as CUTZ. He is currently under investigation for the vandalism of street art. He has previously been convicted for the defacing and criminal damage to artworks as a protestor of the anti-fossil-fuels campaigns. He is thought to be currently living with other campaigners at a large squat in Notting Hill.' They continued to look at the image on Tate's phone, zooming in and out on different aspects of the picture.

'Previously, the Narcissus has purposely included something in the photograph to lead us to the crime scene and the body,' Harriet proclaimed. 'But I am not seeing it here at the moment.' Tate continued to manipulate the picture. They looked at each part methodically.

'There. Top left-hand corner. You can only just make it out due to the over-painting. It's a London bus route number.'

'Well spotted, Andy,' said Harriet, knowing all too well that the picture placement in the gallery would only lead to another dead body. It wasn't something to be jubilant about.

'It also fits with the 6th Work of Mercy,' Tate interjected. 'I was a stranger, and ye took me in. I spent yesterday evening looking at the scriptures relating to the Mercies. In newer revised versions of the Bible, the works are often written in a more present day form. I was a stranger, and ye took me in, can now often be found written as; I needed shelter and you welcomed me into your home or simply to give shelter to the homeless. CUTZ is a regular squatter, and from the looks of the picture, his body has been laid within cardboard boxes.'

'Andy. Get hold of TFL London Buses. Get the route plan for that route number. As soon as you know, get George and whoever is available out there,' demanded Harriet, taking stock of the situation, before adding, 'the service will begin to get busy. We need that body found before the crime scene is disturbed.'

'The appearance of the crime scene might just be to our advantage,' declared Tate, 'most people will ignore or avoid it, thinking it's just another homeless street person asleep in their cardboard shelter. But I agree, the quicker we can secure the area, the better.'

After DS Stevens departed, Tate and Harriet rejoined the gallery staff, asking if now was a good time to look at yesterday's security footage. With everyone agreeing to the suggestion, Tate and Harriet were escorted to the surveillance room. On the way through the building, Tate asked if the guards had found anything else that the Narcissus may have left. Neither had discovered a thing but were puzzled as to the reason why. Tate had to explain the reason for not divulging anything further. Harriet had discussed the possibility of opening the gallery to the public with the director, coming to the joint decision to do so but to close off the entire east wing before re-opening. He excused himself and disappeared to implement the plan.

It did not take Michael long to cue up the CCTV footage from yesterday. Anthony took a back seat to allow his younger colleague his shining moment. Harriet had suggested they start by viewing the footage of the last two hours of the day, as that held the highest probability for the Narcissus' entry. They had been running the images at x3 speed when Tate asked the security guard to stop and rewind the footage a short way back. As the screen began to play back the CCTV at normal speed, an elderly woman exiting the lift had been captured on a camera covering the 2nd floor landing. The woman wore a red beret and oversized red spectacles. A folded red blanket lay across the top of a red tartan-covered shopping trolley, which she shuffled through the open lift doors.

They followed her movements through the second floor. She occasionally stopped to admire a painting before moving on to the next room. She seemed in no rush whatsoever. Just another admirer of the old masters. When she reached East Gallery 3, she took her time to observe each painting in turn as she navigated her trolley around the room in a counterclockwise direction. She even stopped to talk with the gallery attendant, who shortly afterwards wandered into Gallery 2. No sooner had the attendant departed than the elderly woman steered her trolley in a direct line to one of the room's corners. Without delay, she removed a frame from within the blanket and promptly pushed it to the wall before continuing her previous orbit of the room. Without hesitation, she repeated the procedure when she reached the wall on the opposite diagonal. The only difference was that when she removed the second frame, she rested it on the blanket for the briefest moment. Tate asked for the footage to be paused and for the image to be pulled in tighter around the picture frame. As the image enlarged, a drawing appeared to have been

stencilled Banksy style onto the back of the picture.
The silhouetted depiction was that of a witch's cat.

Bring the pages alive…

Explore artworks, locations and more.

*Go to gnsbooks.com (Interactive) or scan the QR code
to unlock images, maps and facts as you read.*

Brixton

London, England

90

The streets had already become congested with late-to-start commuters and sightseers eager to avoid the queues at popular tourist attractions. London buses had been busy since 5 am, with more and more buses joining routes as London awoke to another bustling day around the nation's capital.

DS Stevens had learnt from TFL that the bus route number they had observed in the picture of the latest crime scene was associated with a route between Elephant & Castle and Atkins Road in Clapham Park. It was run by Transport UK for the TFL and ran seven days a week between the hours of 0500 and 0100. It was route number 45.

He had passed the information on to DS Iain Richards, who had gathered together George, Greg, and a uniformed officer. They had decided to split into pairs and scout out the stops along Route 45, each pair starting from one of the route's terminating points. Iain and the uniformed officer were to start in the north at Elephant & Castle and the other pair would commence their search from the opposite end. A total of thirty bus stops in all.

DS Richards and the uniformed officer had begun their search before the other pairing as their location was closer to Bethnal Street. They had ticked off five stops before George and Greg reached their starting location. As they had approached their seventh bus stop on Medlar Street, they thought they had located the crime scene. But on closer examination, there was no overpainting, and the body in the box had turned out to be a very much alive homeless person who awoke at their arrival and insisted they keep their 'dirty little hands' off his shopping trolley of worldly possessions.

DS George Quinn and DC Greg Thompson had also encountered the possibility of the crime scene on a bus stop bench at their second location on Holmewood Road. Even though the scene did not look entirely like the image Tate had forwarded them, they thought it best to check anyway.

Their suspicions were correct when they found the cardboard sanctuary empty of its overnight resident.

Both teams continued to scrutinise bus shelters as they leapfrogged ever closer to each other from the alternate ends of the bus route. Each ever closer to the shelter where they would inevitably discover the sixth victim of the Narcissus' murder campaign.

George and Greg had only passed four further empty bus stops when they approached the shelter at Rush Common. As soon as they pulled the squad car alongside the bus shelter, they immediately knew that they had located the crime scene; it was clearly evident from the overpainting of the shelter. This time, however, the painting was much more extravagant. Tones of red covered virtually every surface. The paint strokes and marks differed from the previous scenes. These had much more of a street art style. Six empty aerosol cans stood in a line below the shelter's bench. A clutter of boxes lay above.

The two officers exited their vehicle and judiciously approached the suspected crime scene. As they neared the cardboard form, its shape began to configure before their eyes. What looked to be a jumble of boxes was, in fact, a coffin constructed from cardboard. Although the entire area had been over-sprayed in red, blood had visibly soaked through the cardboard walls.

'Best get the crime scene tape from the car,' suggested George. 'I'll get on the blower and let the others know we have located the crime scene. Then I'll give the boss a call with the good and bad news.'

DC Thompson collected the tape as his senior officer had suggested and returned to the bus stop to cordon off the crime scene. As he tied the tape to a nearby lamp post and turned to encircle the shelter, an elderly gentleman crossed his path and sat upon the shelter's second and empty bench. 'I'm awfully sorry, sir, this is an active crime scene. I am going to have to ask you to move along.'

The elderly gentleman hesitantly looked up at DC Thompson, holding his roll of blue and white tape. He eased himself back up from the bench, mumbling a discord of words as he began to shuffle off.

'If it isn't the vandals, it's the bloody vagrants.'

Wardour Street

London, England

91

She approached the studio entrance just as a young, tattoo-clad man opened the door to leave. As he held the door back for her to enter, she could not help but notice his fully sleeved arms. Tattoos covered his arms from his shoulders to his wrists, where they stopped in a precision ringing just above what would be the cuff line.

'Nice ink,' proclaimed Lena as she edged between the man and the door frame.

'Thanks. Just sat for the first inking of a backpiece,' declared the man.

'My last sitting for the same.'

'If you don't mind me saying, you don't seem the type for a mural.'

'Remember, beauty is only skin deep,' replied Lena. 'It's a tribute piece for a long lost family member.' She ducked under the man's extended arm.

'Maybe we can compare sometime?'

'I've got a bit of a busy schedule at present, but if we ever cross paths in another doorway, then perhaps we might.' Lena shot the man one final glance and continued into the parlour. The man's eye followed her across the room before he gave himself a self-gratifying smile and stepped out onto the street.

Lena had sat in the waiting area for a good twenty minutes when Sean approached.

'Sorry,' he said before reasoning his tardiness. 'I've just been outlining another backpiece, and I needed a little break and a smoke before continuing with yours.' Sean motioned for his client to come over to his workstation. 'I wasn't planning to see you again quite so soon until I saw your name in the appointment book this morning. It's not long at all since your last sitting.'

Lena took a seat on the edge of the tattooist's bed. 'I needed to rearrange it since I last saw you. I will be travelling abroad again, much sooner than I had anticipated and would very much like to have some further work completed before I do so. At present, I don't know when I shall be returning. Therefore, I thought it best to fit in an extra sitting before I depart.' She twisted around, removed two small vials from her handbag and handed them to the tattooist.

'Two?' asked Sean in a curiously quizzical tone. 'More ancestors?'

'Sort of. Two individuals who I shall never have the displeasure of seeing again.'

Sean accepted the ashes and thought it best not to probe any further. 'I'll mix a small amount of each with the skin tones I will be using today. I can then work them within the last two areas of the tattooing. Assuming you wish to use them in the same way as those of your two brothers whose ashes we used at your last sitting?'

'Yes. That will be fine.' She did not correct his misconception of the brothers.

'Well, if you would like to get yourself ready, I'll mix these into the inks. Are you happy to sit in the straddle stool again today?'

'Whatever best suits you,' replied Lena as she began unbuttoning her blouse.

Five minutes later, the tattooist had run a razor across Lena's back to remove any dead skin and was currently sterilising the area with Green Soap.

'How's it looking back there? Excuse the pun.'

'The area we worked on during your last visit looks to be healing well but still needs daily care as it has not been that long since the tattooing. I wouldn't normally advise sittings in such close proximity. However, due to the circumstances and if you are happy to do so, I will continue with the two areas you wish to finish today, as it will not interfere with the healing process of the previous work.'

'I'm happy to go with whatever you suggest. I can't be sure if I will have time for any further sittings at present,' Lena declared, pulling her hair to one side of her face as she looked back at the tattooist.

'There will still be one area left to be inked. Do you want me to see if there is time to complete that for you?'

'No. That won't be necessary. I'm not yet ready for that final piece to be completed. There is still one more person's ashes I would like to include to fully complete the work.'

Brixton

London, England

92

The traffic was slow as they drove down the A23, Brixton Hill, towards Rush Common. There was no reason for the crawling speed of the cars. There had not been an accident, and there were no road works to disrupt the flow. The volume of traffic was relatively light in terms of London's usual congestion. The cause of the bumper-to-bumper gridlock was the impertinent drivers in either direction, each rubber necking the reason for the crime tape cordon. Each hoping to catch a glimpse of something to fuel their reasons for being late.

Harriet pulled the BMW alongside the kerb about fifty metres shy of the bus stop and turned on the car's blue lights before exiting the vehicle. She and Tate held their ID cards aloft as they excused themselves through the sizeable crowd that had gathered along the line of the barrier tape. George was doing his utmost to encourage the ogling onlookers to move along. Greg was doing a similar job at the other end of the cordon.

'George. Can you organise some uniforms to control this traffic and extend that outer tape beyond the bus lane? If you get any hassle from TFL, then point them my way. Oh, and while you're at it, get a tent down here ASAP,' instructed Harriet as she tore open a sealed bag of white forensic coveralls.

'I have already sorted the tent,' hollered a second voice, 'it should be here in ten minutes or so.' Penny looked up from her preoccupation with the body. 'As soon as you have both suited and booted, it's fine to come on over.'

Penny knelt to the side of a long, narrow cardboard assembly made from several boxes taped together as one. Along with the surrounding bus shelter, it had been overpainted as per the other crime scenes. The face of the victim peered out at one end.

Harriet and Tate ducked under the inner barrier and approached the fabricated coffin. Penny was leaning in close to the victim's head as she fired off a series of pictures that would capture the evident facial injuries.

The face was still recognisable as that of the street artist known as CUTZ. However, the entire surface of his skin had been criss-crossed with a multitude of razor-thin lacerations. It was almost impossible to tell how much of the reddening that could be seen running and matting into the victim's hair was due to blood loss or as a result of the over-painting.

'He has been defaced,' exclaimed Tate. 'Much in the same way as the damage he inflicts to other street artist's works. By the looks of it, he would have suffered an intolerable amount of pain and suffering.' Both Harriet and Penny nodded in agreement. Despite the horrifying disfigurement, all three found themselves gauging the extent of the injuries. Each speculating the torture the victim would have endured.

Penny moved around to the far side of the body to stand directly opposite the other two investigators. She laid a length of plastic sheeting out onto the floor.

'I am going to remove the length of cardboard functioning as a lid,' explained Penny before taking a series of pictures with the lid in situ. She then placed her camera to one side, cautiously lifting the blood-saturated cardboard away from the other boxing and down onto the previously placed polythene covering. The sight that awaited them within the remaining boxing was one that would linger in the depths of the mind for a long time to come.

Every inch of the body's nakedness was covered in an interlacing patchwork of incisions. It screamed of disturbing torture. Lacerations traversed the entire body, again criss-crossing and intersecting each other from every possible direction. The inside surfaces of the cardboard coffin were stained in red. Not from overpainting but from the significant blood loss that would have resulted from a prolonged period of intense suffering.

'The consequential amount of blood we are witnessing indicates that the wounds were made pre-mortem while the heart was still beating. Although they are only skin deep, this number of superficial incisions would cause the body to bleed out relatively quickly. But only after an extraordinary amount of pain had been experienced. The victim may well have passed out from the shock long before the heart finally stopped beating.'

'She is torturing each victim to prolong the kill,' declared Harriet. 'She wants each of the victims to suffer for their misdoings. Each would have undoubtedly pleaded for mercy and in the Narcissus' eyes, she would be silencing those woeful cries by granting them the opportunity to end their suffering by the taking of their lives.' Tate agreed with Harriet's analogy of the crime scene; however, this sixth kill site was not about the method of the murder.

'It's not about the kill this time. It's about the location,' Tate stated, looking at the bus shelter. 'The act of Mercy is, "I was a stranger, and ye took me in." In other words, you sheltered the homeless, hence the bus stop and the cardboard boxes. The bus route number is also of importance this time.' The two women listened intently as Tate continued his rationale. 'Route 45. The Narcissus did not pick this particular route at random. There is always a reason for her actions. Remember, to her, it's all part of a bigger picture. She has planned each murder in meticulous detail and each kill is in some way related to the Acts of Mercy as described in the book of Matthew. It is the bus route number that completes the chapter and verse sequence.'

MW25:35-45

Tate continued.

'The book of Matthew. Chapter 25. Verses 35 to 45. There were no markings found on Jeremy Grayson's feet like the other victims. However, he has a pronounced elongated stigmata wound on his left foot from when the Narcissus crucified him to the Battersea chimney last summer. I believe this may signify the 'hyphen' between the verse numbers. I will also hazard a guess that when the autopsy is performed on our current victim, there will be no further marks on the feet. The bus route number is the significant factor here.' Both Harriet and Penny concurred with Tate's reasoning and his conclusions. However, Harriet knew Tate better and could tell by the look on his face that there was a 'but' still to come.

And Tate did have one more thing to add.

'The King James version of the book of Matthew does not have 45 verses. It has 46.

There is still one verse the Narcissus has yet to play.'

93

He held the surrounding skin with his other hand as he added further detail to the area he was inking. He ran an RL3 needle configuration with a steeply angled taper to make the marks as precise as possible. At present, his work was focused on inking the highlighted face of a pilgrim who is approaching an innkeeper on the far left. As the details of the feature began to emerge, Sean needed to constantly remove the excess ink to ensure the needlepoint continued along the finer points of the image.

'So, where are you thinking of travelling to?' enquired Sean.

'Europe to start. I am planning to meet a priest in Naples. I wish to give his confraternity a sizeable donation. The original altar piece of the tattoo you have been creating is hung in the chapel of his church.'

'The Pio Monte della Misericordia,' Sean replied with a slight hesitancy to his voice.

Lena grinned to herself but did not turn to face Sean's moment of irresolution. 'I see you have been doing your homework,' retorted Lena, still holding the grin across her face and with a mocking tone to her words.

'I hope you don't mind. I looked it up after your initial consultation. I was curious about the reasoning behind your choice of artwork. It being such a large composition for a first tattoo. There had to be a fundamental reason for your commitment to such a statement piece. One that you would wear with dignity and honour for the remainder of your life.' Once again, Sean waited apprehensively for his client's reply, hoping he had not overstepped the mark.

Lena sensed the tattooist's unease at the prospect of his admission, so she waited a little longer than usual before offering a reply. 'I, too, seek absolution. Hands up. I confess to looking you up too, Sean!'

'Really?'

'Well, I needed to know that the reputation that precedes you was correct. What with me entrusting you with such a life changing beautification.' Lena could not help but chuckle to herself as she rounded off her sentence. 'You think I would commit to having someone sticking needles in me without first checking who was holding the gun?'

Sean removed his tattoo machine from Lena's back and paused the needle's rotation as he, too, saw the funny side of his client's witticisms. He used the brief interlude to give the current workable area of the tattooed skin a more thorough clean. He also took the opportunity to change the needle configuration before recommencing his work.

As the needles began to pierce her skin once more, Lena was first to resume the conversation.

'My first stop when I leave will be Milan. I have a family heirloom to sell to an interested party before I visit the priest.'

'So, I take it this is happening sooner rather than later. What with you moving your sitting forward to finish the work.' He wiped the excess ink to one side before changing the direction of the line he was inking.

'Quite possibly within the next few days or so, depending on how long it takes to clear up some unfinished business and tie up some loose ends.'

'Do you plan on returning at some point?'

Lena was quick to reply. 'Of course, I will have an unfinished tattoo that will require completing.' They both laughed silently to themselves. Each finding amusement in their light-hearted banter.

'That's good to hear. I would hate to see it going unfinished.'

'And I wouldn't contemplate the thought of anyone else completing it.'

The complimenting sentence meant a great deal to Sean. He always valued the gratification his customers afforded him. 'I appreciate that, Lena, it means a lot—'

He stopped mid-sentence. Lena turned her head and gaped at the tattooist. Sean froze aghast, transfixed like a rabbit in the headlights, dumbfounded by the one defining word that had mistakenly escaped his mouth. One word for which he could never turn back the clock. They remained locked in each other's enquiring gaze. He had not once, during the numerous sittings, referred to her by her given name. She had used one of her aliases when providing her personal details during her initial consultation.

Each remained locked in an uncomfortable silence. Neither knew how to proceed, and each was unsure what would happen next. The realisation of the situation stalled their humorous raillery.

What happened next came as a complete and utter surprise to Lena.

Sean's name-drop bombshell had been an absolute bolt out of the blue.

'I have known who you are, Lena, right from our first sitting.'

Kennington
London, England

94

It looked as if London would be blessed with another fine day of autumnal weather as the sun continued to rise towards its midday zenith. The streets and roadside pavements were now abounding with pedestrians. Many dashed and dodged, unaware of those around them, as they hurried to make their engagements on time. Others, with no fixed agenda, were happy to wander casually without a care as they rejoiced in the warmth and eudaimonia the smallest amount of sunshine can bring.

The traffic flow was noticeably heavier on their return journey into the city. A far greater number of buses were stop-starting along their routes, delivery scooters and cyclists bobbed and weaved the queuing traffic, and heavy goods drivers sat motionless, praying to make their drop before their driving hours ran dry, each adding to the daily congestion that clogged London's roads.

Harriet eased the BMW to a stop behind the queuing traffic that waited for the next change at the lights. She looked across at Tate, who was scrolling through search engine results on his phone.

'What are you looking for?'

Tate stopped and looked up. 'I am no expert in the late Italian Renaissance, that now seems to be Jonathan's forte. But I seem to remember from my childhood trips to Italy with my parents that we visited a church somewhere and if I remember correctly, there was a large painting by Caravaggio.'

'And…?'

'It seems my memory has not failed me.' Tate angled the phone's screen towards Harriet, who quickly glanced at the image before returning her attention to the traffic ahead. 'Caravaggio painted 'The Seven Acts of Mercy' for The Pio Monte della Misericordia in Naples. It still hangs within the chapel to this day. The large altarpiece depicts all seven acts in one scene. Figures in the streetside representation portray each of the mercies. Caravaggio was known to frequently integrate themes of a religious nature into the reality of the world outside his door. He frequently used individuals from the lower social classes to model for him and heighten the realism of his works. Hence the establishment of the term 'realism'.'

'Correct me if I am wrong, but twice you have said 'seven'.' Tate noticed the lights ahead as they changed to amber and motioned for Harriet to return her attention to the traffic as he continued his explanation.

'Apparently, in early versions of the biblical texts, Matthew Chapter 25 speaks of the behaviours for which we shall be judged. Verses 35 to 45 detail how the fate of each person will be decided and whether or not they will be granted eternal life or be banished to hell and the devil. The Acts of Mercy are the six deeds that Jesus considers when judging those who stood before him.' With the traffic moving, Harriet kept her eyes on the road ahead. The focus of her attention still absorbed with Tate's elucidation of the facts concerning the links he was discovering between the Bible verse, the Caravaggio painting and the recently associated crime scenes of the Narcissus' second killing spree.

Tate continued to open internet sites. He would skim-read relative sections of a page, extracting any relevant details before giving Harriet a summary of any critical points relating to their current situation. She listened intently, occasionally asking questions to clarify or seek further information on a particular detail.

'The Narcissus is twisting the deeds of each merciful judgement on their heads and using them to determine the fate of those she sees as having done wrong. Put simply:

you were thirsty; I gave you blood to drink.

you were hungry; I gave you flesh to eat.

In her own delusional mind, she is probably alluding to a false belief that she is herself being adjudged and by performing the Acts of Mercy, she will be atoned with immortality.' Harriet had been so absorbed in Tate's explication that she had failed to notice that the traffic had once again moved forward. A gentle reminder from the horn of the vehicle behind averted her attention back to the road ahead. However, one thing still plagued her mind and she could not help but repeat her previous query.

'So am I correct in my understanding that there are not six, but seven acts of mercy?'

'Yes. Correct. I have just read that in more recent versions of The Gospel of Matthew, a seventh mercy is often added to the verse. The brotherhood who commissioned the artwork to Caravaggio were proponents of the additional act. This seventh mercy is difficult to see in Caravaggio's work as it is depicted in one of the much darker areas. On the right of the picture, the soles of a pair of feet can just be seen. The two men in close proximity are said to be carrying the body of a dead man.'

'The Seventh Act of Mercy is 'to bury the dead'.'

Lewisham

London, England

95

She indicated right and inched the car forward, waiting for a lull in the traffic so she could make the turn. She took the opportunity to take a quick glance in the rearview mirror, ensuring that the make-up she had spent a great deal of time and effort over was still as meticulous as the moment she had applied it. She gave her other self a cheeky wink in the mirror before noticing a car approaching from the opposite direction, flashing its lights in a gesture for her to cross.

She made the turn into Upwood Road. She was in a buoyant and optimistic frame of mind about the evening ahead. However, there was still that gnawing feeling of trepidation that goes with a newly found relationship. They had met on previous occasions, but this time was a far more significant affair. She was driving to pick him up. She would see his house. He would invite her in. They would be alone as two for the very first time.

She counted the odd numbers as she passed the manicured shrub-lined gardens, each with a large SUV parked in front of the garage. Most of the affluent detached properties also had a smaller family-sized car occupying the remainder of the driveway. The residence she sought was the next on the left, and she slowed the vehicle to a stop, opposite the property's front garden before noticing that the drive was unoccupied. She decided it would be better to park on the driveway and joked with herself that it would make for a quick getaway should she need to.

Having exited her car, she gave a quick glance up and down the street. All was quiet in suburbia. She gave herself one final appraisal, adjusted her jeans, stepped up to the porch and rang the bell. She could not wait to see the look on her date's face when he opened his front door to find her standing outside.

She did not have to wait long as the door was answered almost immediately. She threw one of her best smiles. However, her date's face was a mixture of surprise and confusion. He managed to execute just one single word. Her name.

'Sarah!'

'Hi. I thought I'd surprise you and pick you up.' Turner stood in the doorway as he tried to comprehend what was happening. He managed just five more words before his sentence ended unfinished.

'But how did you know—'

His mind continued to fathom a logical answer.

'It's not hard to find out someone's address these days. I thought it would be nice to swing by and pick you up.' Turner's eyes moved to the parked car. Not in his wildest dreams could he have imagined a bright red sportscar parked on his drive. Still lost in his thoughts, his bewilderment was broken by his next unstrung five word sentence.

'I'm not even showered yet.' He was clueless about what he had just said.

'It's fine. There is no hurry. I am happy to wait.' Turner remained transfixed, still unsure of how or what to do. 'You're not going to leave a girl standing on the doorstep now, are you?'

Turner blinked as if coming out of a deep, mesmerising dream. 'Sorry. Excuse my bad manners. Please. Come in.'

Sarah took a step forward. 'I hope you haven't forgotten how to greet a girl too.' Turner, still in a haze of perplexity, leant forward to greet his date in a more polite and respectful manner.

As he held one of Sarah's hands and pressed his lips to her cheek, he felt a sharp and unsuspecting scratch upon his neck. Sarah cupped a hand around Turner's neck and pulled him closer as she whispered in his ear.

'Posso sentire il tuo cuore.'

'I can hear your heart.'

96

There was a turbulent air of disquietude throughout the office. Those present were on edge and apprehensive of how the next twenty-four hours would unfold. Jonathan, DS Garrett and DS Andy Stevens had gathered together with Tate and Harriet at Thorney Street. All five were currently gathered around Tate's desk, each knowing the inevitable would almost certainly happen. Six killings had taken place, each escalating in ferocity and the intervening period between each incident diminishing considerably. If the frequency of the killings continued along its current timeline, then they could expect to uncover a seventh crime scene in the next forty-eight hours. Although the Narcissus was always one step ahead and they were constantly running against the clock, there was still a strong possibility that they could intervene and put a stop to the Narcissus' second wave of killings once and for all.

'It's the final act. The Narcissus will want to stage a momentous epochal show for her grand finale,' declared Tate. 'She will have planned it to the finest detail.'

Harriet cut in. 'Today is Halloween. The items she has been leaving for Tate, including the plastic spider that Happy found during the autopsy of the latest victim, I believe were all leading us to this point and play no further part than that. As Tate has just said, she will have planned the escalation of the killings to coincide with her envisioning of the final act.'

'I, too, believe the killing will take place at some point today,' intervened Jonathan, motioning with a printout in his hand. 'I looked into the traditions and folklore of Halloween. Originally known as "All Hallows' Eve", it was a holy evening of celebration preceding "All Saints' Day", a day dedicated to venerating the saints who are not honoured with their own recognisable feast day.' He looked down at the information within the printout before continuing. 'Christian beliefs are that "All Hallows' Eve" marks one final opportunity for the dead to avenge their enemies before the last judgement.'

It was Tate who, this time, took the baton and continued the reasoning. 'Both of the Narcissus' killing sprees have been about retribution. She believes that all of the victims must pay for their previous transgressions. In her eyes, she may see a final killing on "All Hallow's Eve" as a homage to her maternal bloodline and a commemoration of the Caravaggio painting we have yet to recover. The likeness that Caravaggio used when painting the 'St Mary Magdalene in Ecstasy' was that of her maternal grandmother, Maddalena Antognetti. She could be intent on honouring the Magdalene and Caravaggio himself before she plans to disappear again.'

'That reinforces the omission of the 46th verse from Matthew 25. It has not been included with the other inscription verse numbers cut into the victim's feet.' Harriet moved towards one of four whiteboards, standing in an arc towards the end of Tate's office. The others in the room followed. She read the final scripture at the bottom of the board.

> And these shall go away into everlasting punishment: but the righteous into eternal life.

'She has left the final verse for her last judgement. I'd hazard a guess that she plans to mark a final victim's feet with the verse number. Then, having delivered those she believes should be sent to purgatory, she is free to start a new life.' There was a nodding of heads, each agreeing with the interlinking theories. Jonathan had another factor to be taken into account. He crossed past Harriet and stood to the side of the furthest whiteboard. It contained the Neptune's Finger song lyrics found within the oesophagus of each victim.

'The lyrics found with Jeremy Grayson's body are from a song entitled 'The Lesser of Two Evils'. It relates to God's choices when faced with mankind destroying his world, thus his need to destroy humanity to save his creation. I feel this is the Narcissus justifying her actions. She is taking the lives of those she sees as corrupting the art world and, in doing so, believes her crimes are forgivable.' Jonathan's attention turned to the most recently discovered verse. He read the lines aloud.

> Now we approach the Day of the Reckoning
> Hope and fear await the Quick and the Dead.
> All men bow down to receive holy judgement
> Redemption bestowed albeit blood has been bled.
> Eternity beckons those who gave mercy
> And the damned will be cast into unending hell.

Jonathan paused to allow those who were not as familiar as Tate and himself with the lyrics a moment to hypothesise their perception of the words. 'The verse is from a song called 'The Last Judgement'. Again, I am sure you can see how it also fits alongside Matthew 25 and the Acts of Mercy. The Narcissus is entrenched in the notion that her endeavours are for the good. She attributes this to the fact that she will be granted salvation. She can no longer see beyond the confines of her mind.' Jonathan was about to step back when he remembered one final thing. 'The last song on the album is a closing instrumental entitled 'Rebirth'.'

After they had all digested Jonathan's presumptions on the lyrical content of the Narcissus' messages, they turned their attention to the adjacent board where the Seven Acts of Mercy were listed alongside the victim's names, a profile picture and their cause of death.

Tate took up the elucidation once again. 'So far, we have six victims over five crime scenes, there having been two victims at the third scene. There appear to be no links of any real significance to the locations. Apart from the first two being premises associated with butchery and the known fact that Lena's adoptive family ran a small chain of butcher shops during her teenage years. The location of crime scene number three and the double killing of the twin brothers was their own warehouse. The locations of the fifth and sixth murders were predetermined by the act of mercy itself. Jeremy Grayson was murdered by a prison visitor and Timothy Cuttifords' body was discovered within a bus shelter on TFL Route 45.' Tate referred to each merciful act and its accompanying details as he clarified their accumulated information. 'The acts associated with these two final murders are "to visit the imprisoned" and "to provide them shelter".' He moved his hand down the list and stopped at the seventh and final listing.

'Bury the Dead.'

'The statement suggests that the Narcissus' final act will involve burying the seventh victim. However, as we have learnt from the previous six killings, it will most probably not be quite as simple as the words suggest. As we mentioned earlier, she will wish for her concluding crime scene to have a pivotal impact.' Once more, Tate pointed to the seventh Act of Mercy. This time, he phrased the three words as a question. 'Bury the Dead? The obvious location would be cemeteries or churches. Where else would be befitting of a final crime?'

DS Stevens was the first to throw a proposition forward. 'Mortuary or funeral parlours,' he offered before adding, 'crematoriums or crypts.'

'Maybe one of the large cathedrals if she is looking for a visual impact,' was a suggestion from DS Garrett.

'War Memorials. The Cenotaph on Whitehall. Again, it would attract maximum attention,' declared Jonathan. 'Cenotaph comes from the Greek for 'Empty Tomb' and the words upon its face read, 'THE GLORIOUS DEAD'.'

The others in the room nodded, agreeing it could be a strong possibility.

Tate deliberated each suggestion before commenting further. 'Cemeteries and churches would possibly be the obvious choice. But there are hundreds across the capital. How and where would we start?'

'Unless there is a clue hidden somewhere in all the messages and photographs she has been taunting us with,' propounded Harriet. 'Although saying that, we never found any underlying significance to the messages she sent during her first murder campaign.'

'Mortuaries and crematoriums would be far more difficult to enter, along with going unnoticed for some time. Having said that, she has managed to get in and out of a prison and murdered an inmate while doing so. The same goes for a major tourist attraction like a cathedral or the Cenotaph.' Tate looked across the room and made eye contact with DS Stevens. 'Your suggestion of crypts, along with churches and cemeteries, is our best chance for now. Or at least a starting point.'

Harriet was keen to add something further and chipped in. 'The location will need to be significant and link to all we have discussed. It may have historical importance or be recognisable for some factual reason. Andy. Could you get everyone together at Bethnal Green and start the ball rolling? I would guess that we don't have much time. Start looking at churches and cemeteries. Look for links to the seven acts, the Last Judgement—'

This time it was Harriet who was cut short. 'Churches of St Matthew may well be a good starting point.'

'Good shout, Jon. Get onto it, Andy. Let me know as soon as you have anything.' DS Stevens was about to leave when his superior officer held out a hand to stall his exit.

'I don't think we can rule out the major religious buildings either,' declared Harriet, acknowledging DS Garrett's suggestion. 'St Pauls, Westminster Abbey and Southwark Cathedral among others. Start with Christian places of worship as it ties in with everything we have so far. But don't limit your search parameters. Include all faiths and religions if need be. Also, the central London galleries are on alert for anything out of the ordinary. Get DC Evans to heighten their security and make it clear that we are expecting another picture hanging.'

'No problem, Ma'am. I'll get the team straight onto it. I'll phone DS Richards from the car.'

'Jane. Could you start in the same way with our team?' asked Tate. 'The more heads, the better at this stage.' DS Garrett acknowledged the suggestion and followed DS Stevens out of the room.

The three remaining officers reverted their attention to the fourth of the evidence boards. This final board bore just three names. Each was the subject of a current investigation by the Arts & Antiquities department and had been investigated in the past by former Detective Inspector Lena Johnson. Alongside DS Garrett, Jonathan had been compiling a list of those who met the criteria to be a subsequent victim of the Narcissus. It was their duty to protect those under investigation, who were presumed innocent until proven guilty. However, they did not wish to jeopardise an ongoing investigation unless it was absolutely essential. Giving a suspect the slightest inclination that they were currently the subject of an active investigation may result in months of investigative and surveillance work becoming worthless and a guilty party avoiding prosecution.

Jonathan began to explain the reasoning behind the three names on the board. 'Andrew Hamilton, the forger. Border patrol systems still show that he has not returned to the country as of yet. The second possibility is Tomas De Adman. He is currently a subject of the department's investigations for importing and selling 19th century Dutch works of still life. He was subject to a similar case about three years ago, but a false paper trail is thought to have quashed his conviction. He is currently residing in a rented apartment in Richmond. Our last sighting of him was just two days ago when OIFR, Operator Initiated Facial Recognition, picked him up as he disembarked an east coast train at London Kings Cross.' Jonathan underlined the suspect's name before doing the same with the final name. 'Art Dealer Cynthia Townsend. She has been on and off our radar for several years now. An investigation Lena was part of, had her convicted for selling several stolen Chinese GongBi sketches, and she was given a two-year non-custodial sentence. She is presently—'

Their discussion was interrupted by a polite tapping on the door. Tate turned to address who it was and motioned for DC Morrison to enter the room.

'Sorry to disturb you, Sir. But—'

He did not finish the sentence but remained stock-still in the doorway, a perplexed bewilderment upon his face as if he had just seen an apparition.

Tate noticed the puzzlement on his officer's face. 'David. What's wrong? You look like you have seen a ghost.'

'It's not a ghost, Sir. But it is a Matryoshka. I don't know why I hadn't noticed it before. But seeing it written as it is on the whiteboard, it popped out as soon as I entered the room.'

'Come again? A Matray what?' enquired Jonathan inquisitively.

'A Matryoshka word is when you find a shorter word hidden within another. The term Matryoshka is taken from the Russian for nesting dolls. There is a Matryoshka in Tomas' full name.'

'What is it you have seen in Adman's name?' asked Tate.

'If you decapitalise the 'A', it is far easier to see.' David walked over to the whiteboard, rewrote the name with a lowercase 'a' and rearranged the letter spacing.

He then circled the second and third words as one.

Tomas(Dead man)

'Well, I'll be damned!' exclaimed Jonathan. Tate and Harriet looked at each other for a split second before Harriet reacted.

'The seventh victim's name has been staring us straight in the face. Good work, DC Morrison. Perhaps the Narcissus' messages aren't as straightforward as we first thought. It seems she has been having some fun with conundrums.'

'So we most probably have a victim,' proclaimed Jonathan, 'and the seventh act of mercy is 'to bury the dead.' All we need now is a location.'

'Sir? The reason I interrupted your meeting?'

'Yes. Sorry, David. What was it?'

'I have a call for you that you should take immediately. It may well be important, and in light of things, I believe it is now all the more consequential.'

'It's the Tate Britain. Apparently, someone has just added a picture to their collection.'

Tate Britain

London, England

97

Not in her wildest dreams would she have imagined how her shift at the gallery would transpire today. Abbie had been a gallery attendant at Tate Britain for a little over 18 months. Having previously worked at the V & A museum, she had jumped at the chance when a vacancy had been advertised at the gallery. She had been over the moon when she had taken the call offering her the position. She could not get over the fact that she would be paid to wander about a gallery and admire some of the nation's most iconic artworks.

Abbie stood at the entrance of Room 31 and the Clore Gallery beyond. The only other access points from the Prints and Drawing Room above and the auditorium below had been secured at the lift and stair entrance. The room before her had been immediately taped off after she had radioed for security and the gallery wing had been cleared of visitors. She paced nervously, not knowing what to do but wait. She looked directly across the room towards the self-portrait of JMW Turner. It was an elegant portrayal less than a metre high in which he had created a half-length front-facing portrait on a dark background. Abbie had always thought that his attire made him look like a character straight out of a Shakespearian film.

Her shift had not started until 2 pm because this evening was a 'Late at the Tate' extended opening. As usual, she had passed through staff security before storing her belongings in the employee lockers. She had collected her two-way radio and had been delighted to hear that her first shift of the day would be attending in Room 8. With the footfall being considerably lighter during the lunch hour, she would be able to appreciate the works of one of her favourite artists, Sir John Everett Millais. She had a soft spot for the works of the pre-Raphaelites, especially Millais' painting of "Ophelia". The work depicts the rejected lover of Shakespeare's Hamlet as she sings moments before drowning in a brook. Abbie would often find herself getting lost for long moments within the beauty of the scene when she was supposed to attend to the visitors.

Her afternoon had continued to play out much like any other day. She had moved around the various rooms and exhibits in rotation along with other gallery attendants. Their role was not to provide security but to supervise the smooth running of the gallery and assist the visitors in any way they could to ensure everyone had a positive experience.

She had just begun a thirty-minute rotation within the rooms of the Clore Gallery and the JMW Turner collection when she had noticed a visitor in a short red skirt enter the exhibit from Room 17. She remembered noticing that the woman had beautifully defined features and the most wonderful silky dark hair. The other thing that stood out at the time was the bright red baby carrier the woman had strapped across her chest. The very same baby carrier that now lay discarded upon the floor between herself and JMW Turner.

Abbie had not paid the woman any more notice than the other half dozen or so visitors wandering around the Turner bequest. That was until she noticed the woman standing to one side in the corner of the gallery. She had continued to observe the woman's movements with a slight sense of trepidation. Over the past couple of days, the Gallery Directors had placed a higher than usual emphasis on security measures. Gallery attendants had been asked to be extra vigilant of all visitors due to the recent exploits of the front page serial killer they were calling the Narcissus. As Abbie had continued to observe the woman's behaviour, she had wondered if she should call security. But just as she was about to do that, she heard a baby's cry emanate from the direction of the visitor. Abbie's anxieties subsided, and her heightened sense of a foreboding situation abated.

She had suddenly realised she may well have been overhasty as the woman dressed in red lifted something from the carrier. It was definitely not a baby. In fact, it looked a bit like a small computer tablet. Perhaps the woman was going to take some pictures. It had become common to see visitors wandering through the rooms and viewing historic works of art through the eye of an iPad. Gone were the days of reminding visitors not to use the flash of the 35mm camera hanging from the strap around their neck.

However, no photographs were captured on the recently removed tablet.

The woman seemed oblivious to Abbie's presence and without turning to check if anyone was watching, she unmindfully held the tablet at arm's length and pushed it to the wall. Abbie stood frozen, unsure of what she should do. However, the training manual did not cover how to proceed when a serial killer places a new acquisition in the gallery.

The woman had moved from the corner as Abbie snapped back into the present moment. She had her finger on the radio button and was about to call security when the woman removed the baby carrier and flung it in the attendant's direction.

'Be a good girl and look after the little one, will you? He's due for a sleep in...' The woman looked at her watch, 'Two hours and forty minutes.' The red baby carrier had landed on the gallery floor a short distance from where Abbie was hesitantly standing in a quandary about what the current situation required her to do.

By now, the woman in the red skirt had walked further into the Clore Gallery and had left in the direction of the stairwell and the emergency exit.

Abbie had looked down at the red carrier at her feet. The sound of baby cries still emanating from within.

Finally, she had engaged the button on her two-way radio.

98

Tate and Harriet had left Thorney Street immediately after the phone call from the director at Tate Britain. They left Jonathan and DS Garrett with the task of locating Tomas De Adman as priority one. He needed to be offered protection even if it would indeed jeopardise their current investigations. They had arranged to remain in two-way contact, as presently neither party was sure what Tate and Harriet would discover at Tate Britain and whether Tomas De Adman was, in fact, the Narcissus' seventh victim.

Founded by sugar magnate Sir Henry Tate in 1893, Tate Britain, formerly the National Gallery of British Art, sits within the City of Westminster upon the site of the former Millbank prison. The gallery is home to the national collection of British art. Its permanent collection includes works by Constable, Gainsborough, Reynold, Stubbs and, in modern times, Bacon, Blake, Hockney and Hirst. Upon his death, JMW Turner bequeathed the majority of his collection to the Nation. The largest collection of his works is still held at the gallery.

With Tate Britain only a few hundred yards further along the north bank of the Thames, they had not given a vehicle a moment's thought and had taken off on foot. With both detectives being physically active due to their sporting pastimes, it did not take long for them to cover the relatively short distance to the gallery.

Tate took the steps at the front of the building two at a time, closely followed by Harriet. As he entered through the revolving door, he removed his ID from his jacket.

'DCI Tate Randall,' he declared, holding his card forward for the security detail to see. 'and DI Harriet Stone,' he expressed as Harriet joined him in the foyer. She stopped behind him, hands on her knees, bent at the waist as she fought to catch her breath. A tall, thin gentleman stepped forward and offered his hand. Not in a handshake but as a gesture in the direction in which he would escort them.

'This way, if you please. My name is Julian Hughes. I am one of the directors.' He led them to the right of the foyer. 'It's just through here in the Turner Gallery.' They followed Mr Hughes, all three walking with a swiftness to their step.

'Any relation?' enquired Tate.

'Yes,' replied Julian, knowing all too well what the question referred to. 'Arthur Hughes was my great, great Grandfather. I also knew your parents. They were still working here when I first started.'

Having passed through two rooms of contemporary art, they were met by a gallery attendant standing irresolutely behind a taped-off entrance. The young woman looked unsettled and nervous.

'This is Abigail Miller. She was the attendant who witnessed the incident.'

'Hi, Abigail. My name is Harriet Stone. I am a Detective Inspector with the Metropolitan CID,' She offered a hand across the security tape. 'My colleague is DCI Tate Randall of the Arts & Antiquities Investigation Department.' Abigail said a demure hello. 'Abigail. Could you tell us in your own words exactly what happened earlier?'

'You can call me Abbie if you like.' She shakily cleared her throat and took a moment to compose herself and think about recounting her experience. 'I had not long been on my rotation in the Clore Gallery when I noticed a pretty looking lady enter the room carrying what I thought was a baby.' She looked down at the discarded baby carrier. Both detectives noted her sideways glance at the object on the gallery floor. 'I didn't think any more of it until I noticed her standing in a blank, pictureless corner of the room. At first, I thought maybe she was sorting out the baby, but then I saw her remove a computer tablet from the carrier, which at that point was strapped across her chest.' Abbie stopped to contain her thoughts once again. 'She then just stuck the tablet to the wall before turning to leave via the emergency exit. But not before she removed the baby carrier and threw it in my direction.'

'Did she say anything?' enquired Harriet.

'She said to look after the baby and that it would need a sleep in a couple of hours or so. I checked to see if there was a baby inside. But there wasn't. I didn't think there would be. Not after the way she hurled the bag across the room.'

'Please think carefully, Abbie. This is important. Is that exactly what she said to you, her exact words?'

Again, the attendant took a moment. 'She said to ensure I look after the baby as he will require a sleep in two hours and forty minutes. Which I thought was a little strange.' Harriet looked briefly at Tate, who nodded silently, meaning he was happy with all that had been said.

'Did the lady say anything else?' Harriet asked.

'No. Nothing at all. She just turned and left. That's when I radioed security, and they came, and we cleared the rooms.'

'Did anyone else touch the bag?'

'No. I don't remember so. I think I was the only one. Just when I checked to make sure there wasn't a baby inside.'

'Thank you, Abbie. You've been great. Do you think you can hang around for a while in case we have any other questions? At some point, we will need to take a statement. Is that OK?' Abbie looked across at the director, who nodded his approval.

Both Harriet and Tate donned sterile nitrile gloves and ducked under the tape. As they approached the discarded baby carrier, Tate bent down and while doing so, he removed a pen from the inside pocket of his jacket. Using the pen as a wand, he lifted the uppermost side of the carrier's opening. As he did so, a baby's cry came from within. Not expecting the sound, he rocked backwards on his heels and needed to steady himself. He looked at Harriet, who was crouched to his side, and once again eased the opening of the bag with the pen. Harriet used the torch function on her phone to light up the interior space.

'There's an MP3 player, probably the source of the baby's cries and what looks to be a box,' declared Harriet. They both looked across at each other. Tate nodded, and Harriet reached with her gloved hand and gently removed the box from the bag. As she warily held it before them, letters written on its surface could easily be seen.

R.I.P   T.J.R

'Well. It is definitely meant for you. One final taunt at the hand of the Narcissus,' stated Harriet as she placed the box on the floor. Tate pocketed the pen and inspected the cardboard outer.

'It looks very much like we have a second coffin,' he said, picking it up and tilting his head to look at the underside. 'I believe the Narcissus is again contriving to lead us towards a final showdown, much like the previous one at Battersea. This cardboard coffin is clearly pointing to her seventh victim and the 'Bury the Dead' act of mercy. It seems she is once again one step ahead, and we are about to discover the location of a seventh body.' Tate carefully eased the lid from the box.

Inside, he discovered something that did not surprise him at all. The box contained a small, partially covered corn dolly. Its face could just be seen above a sandy filling.

'Well, that confirms our thoughts and predictions. Let's hope the picture provides us with a clue to the location of the body.' Tate placed the box on the floor next to the baby carrier and alongside Harriet, they walked towards the corner where the Narcissus had hung the picture.

As they neared the frame upon the wall, the sound of music could be heard. They had not noticed it before, and it seemed to be coming from within the frame. It did not take Tate long to recognise the tune. It was the track Jonathan had mentioned earlier. The final track on the *After the Flood* album by Neptune's Finger. The instrumental entitled 'Rebirth.' The two detectives looked at each other. Each was a little mystified at what they were exactly about to find. As they moved closer to take their first look at the picture, they were both somewhat taken aback. The picture was not simply a picture. It was a video feed playing on a tablet screen. The film appeared to be playing in current time, a clock in the corner of the screen confirming the fact.

The images showed the body of a man lying in a stone sarcophagus. His legs and the majority of his lower torso were covered in sand. As with the corn dolly in the box, his face could easily be seen.

Tate froze.

He could not believe what he was seeing. The face in the sarcophagus was not that of Tomas De Adman.

And the R.I.P eulogy on the cardboard box had not been for Tate Joseph Randall.

It was for Turner Joshua Randall.

99

Tate felt as if someone had just knocked the stuffing out of him. He stood at a loss for words as he stared at the video images. A small stream of sand like that of an hourglass could be seen slowly spilling into the side of the stone sarcophagus. Turner lay in a supine position with his arms folded across his chest. Although he remained still, most probably sedated, it was just possible to see the rise and fall of his chest. This gave Tate a small amount of hope to cling to. His brother was currently still alive.

Harriet had also remained quiet, not knowing quite what to say. No amount of words would ease the angst she knew Tate would be fearing at the sight of his brother's plight. The best she could do was utilise her knowledge, skill and training to uncover the smallest of details that would lead to the location where Turner was being held.

Tate also continued to scrutinise every frame of the video feed to ascertain a lead or at least give them some direction in which to start their search. He needed to remain calm and level-headed if he were to have any chance of finding his brother. For the first time in a matter of minutes, he spoke.

'It appears to be somewhere of Christian or Catholic religion. The embellishments in the background have an appearance similar to those seen in churches throughout the country. It's not a main altar. It may be a smaller side altar, chapel or chancel. Aside from that, there is very little to go on.' Tate remained captivated by the images. He did not look in Harriet's direction. His complete focus was to save his brother. He continued to dissect the room within the image. 'The flow of the sand seems to be coming through the ceiling above. The vaulting is very shallow. Both suggest the altar we are viewing is possibly underground or beneath a large building in some form of crypt, sepulchre or undercroft. It would be useful if we could freeze the image and zoom in on the rear of the altar.'

'Here, let me try,' Harriet proposed, holding her phone forward to gain the maximum resolution possible. She took a sequence of shots before switching to video format and recording a few seconds of footage. Apart from the trickling of sand, there was little movement in the live feed, allowing Harriet to get a decent fixed image of the room. She held the phone between herself and Tate and enlarged the picture as tight as possible. Slowly, she used the tip of a finger to move around the image.

'The golden figures nearest the sarcophagus seem to represent a biblical narrative,' Harriet suggested as she pinched the phone's screen to maximum zoom.

'The lower central one is unquestionably the crucifixion of Christ. It's not quite possible to make out the upper centre piece of the ornamentation as the image is indistinguishable at this focal length and unclear when zoomed. However, there are clearly two golden winged angels on the pillars to each side of the altar. There also appears to be some sort of chair or throne on the left-hand side. Again, it is unclear.'

Tate was suddenly aware that he had no idea how long they had been studying the video feed. He looked at his watch. It had, in fact, only been five minutes. He drew his focus from the picture frame and crossed to where the director and attendant stood.

'Abbie. Do you remember what the time was when the woman told you the baby would need a sleep in 2 hours and 40 minutes?' asked Tate. 'Please take your time to think. It is important for you to be as accurate as you can.'

The gallery attendant took a few moments, just as she had done when previously questioned, before providing her answer. 'My rotation in the Clore Gallery started at 5.30 pm. I had only been here for about ten minutes when I noticed the woman dressed in red entering the room. It all happened quite quickly, so it was about five more minutes before she threw the baby carrier.'

'So, am I right in understanding that it was approximately 5.45 pm when the woman checked her watch before making her statement about the baby's sleep.'

'Yes. That would be about right.'

Tate looked at his watch again while running a calculation through his head. 'It's now 6.27 pm. That's forty-two minutes, give or take, since the Narcissus issued the time cue. That leaves us just under two hours to locate Turner before the sands of time run dry.'

They were both aware of the emphasis of Tate's last sentence. The idiom of time running out either through something reaching an end or a person's death.

'We could do with more eyes on this. The clock is ticking, and we have very little to go on.'

'I totally agree,' replied Harriet.

'Jon and Jane are closest. I will call them and get them here immediately. As soon as we figure out something to go on, I want you and I to be able to leave ASAP. We cannot afford to waste vital minutes.'

'I'll make the call. You focus on the video feed. I will also call Andy and the team at Bethnal Green. I will send him the images from my phone. There is a good chance that George might recognise something. His years on the beat were a path well-trodden. He is no stranger to the boroughs and communities that abound within the capital. If anyone is going to recognise the locality, George is as good a bet as anybody.' Tate agreed with Harriet. They needed every available resource they could get their hands on. 'I will also get Andy to get everyone in the department to make it priority one and nobody to leave until the night is through.'

It had taken Jonathan and Jane Garrett very little time to join Tate and Harriet at the gallery. Before they had left Thorney Street, DS Garrett had passed their ongoing searches over to DC Morrison, informing him to call as soon as he had anything, no matter how trivial it may seem.

Jonathan and Jane could offer little more than their senior officers had already uncovered within the live feed. All four agreed it was worth taking a look from a different perspective.

'Ok. Let's look at what we do know and reconceive the circumstances,' proposed Jonathan. 'The location will all most definitely be within Greater London. If then, we compare the situation with the first series of killings, the Narcissus will once again want to confront you. Therefore, with the time limitation, it can't be a great distance away. She would have given you more time to warrant the travelling distance if it were farther afield. All of the crime scenes have also been within the capital. Therefore, we can safely say the location will likely be in Central London.' The other three detectives agreed with Jonathan's assertion, and Tate was happy to follow his friend's lead.

'All six of the killings during this second campaign have related to both the Acts of Mercy and the Matthew 25 Bible verses.' As Jonathan was postulating, the cogs in Harriet's mind began to turn as she conceived the direction in which the supposition was heading.

'The video feed is unquestionably within a place of worship. The churches of St Matthew within Central London would be a good place to start.'

'Exactly,' confirmed Jonathan.

DS Garrett had also been premeditating the same inference and was scrolling through search results on her phone. 'There are fifteen Churches of St Matthew in Central London. Those closest to Tate Britain are in Westminster, Elephant & Castle, Brixton and Fulham.'

'There is also one close to the station in Bethnal Green. Its proximity might well be enticing to the Narcissus,' declared Harriet.

'There is another slight divergence to consider,' propounded Tate. 'This whole murderous campaign started with the Narcissus stealing Caravaggio's 'St Mary Magdalene in Ecstasy.' We should also consider the Churches of St Mary Magdalene.'

Again, DS Garrett was prompted by her boss's direction with the mention of the Caravaggio and once again searched the internet for answers. 'In this instance, there are seventeen. Again, the closest are Bermondsey, Regent's Park, Paddington and Wandsworth.'

'That's thirty-two possible locations in all. We can't feasibly search that many in the time we have. However, the local community forces in each of the boroughs can. I'll get George onto it immediately. I will ask him to ensure that the local boys are all instructed to approach with caution.' Harriet removed her phone and stepped to one side to make the call.

While they had been speculating on the best approach to begin their search for the video feed's location, Tate had not been able to draw his attention away from the image of his brother lying quiescently in a tomb. A tomb that his brother had no reason to be in. His brother unquestionably had no involvement with the Narcissus case. The only reason for his brother's entombment was Tate himself.

'We can't just sit here and wait for news from the local constabularies,' declared Tate as he paced to-and-fro in front of the video feed. 'The picture was planted a little over an hour ago. The location cannot be that far from here, or she would have risked someone discovering the site. We start close and move outwards. Harriet and I will jump in the Land Rover. Jonathan and Jane, you stay and run things from here. Keep in constant communication. I want to know as and when something happens. If anything changes, call me immediately.' The two officers acknowledged their superior before Tate continued.

'Jane. Which of those churches is in the closest proximity to Tate Britain?'

The Undercroft
London, England

100

He wanted to open his eyes, but each time he tried, his eyelids felt too heavy, and a weary tiredness pulled him back. Occasionally, when his eyelids allowed, he attempted to glimpse the world around him before drifting back into the safety of a dream. But all remained black. Little did he know that when the confines of the dream would eventually release him, it would plunge him straight into his worst nightmare. A terrifying nightmare beyond his wildest imagination.

The Narcissus continued to light the candles as she continued back down the steps. The flame from each candle added further illumination to the church's undercroft. She crossed under the double arches of the vaulted ceiling towards the chantry on the undercroft's south side. Once used as a mortuary chapel to lay out the dead before burial, it was transformed into a reproduction of a medieval chantry in the late 19th century. She passed from the undercroft through the oak door into the outer chantry. Candles lit its entire length. The simplicity of the undercroft's concrete vaulted ceiling and bare tiled floor was in juxtaposition to the splendour of the elaborate decorations of the adjoining room. The chantry's ceiling was a deep royal blue and bejewelled with an encrustation of stars. A succession of arched windows ran the length of the room, separating it from the remainder of the undercroft. Each of its panels was decorated in exquisite tiles or panes of stained glass. Bold colours of the brightest reds, greens and blues. Every surface sparkled in the shimmering light of the candles.

A pair of double doors set into the arch of the vaulted ceiling stood as the entrance to a tiny chapel. Like the outer chantry, they, too, were embellished in the style of the medieval period. A beautifully ornate altar stood before the end wall. A small statue of the chapel's patron saint looked down from above. A sarcophagus lay below. Simple in its construction, it was cut from stone and had none of the elaborate embellishments of the altar and surrounding walls. The body of Turner

Randall lay reposefully within the confines of the tomb. His hands were tied at the wrist and his ankles were similarly restrained. However, his lower body, legs and feet could no longer be seen due to the sand that continued to spill from the ceiling above.

Turner woke. Although his eyes were still closed. Perhaps he was mistaken and he was not awake at all. Confusion encircled his mind. Perhaps he was trapped on the edge of that dream. He tried to open his eyes once more. But still, they remained closed, and the world around him remained in darkness. There was a distinctive smell, but he could not recall where he had encountered it before. A peculiar taste sat upon his tongue. As his senses began to come to life, recognition of the situation began to stir from within. He tried to move both his arms and legs, but they, too, were stuck fast, and he fought to free his restrictions. Turner strained at his eyes once more, but the lids refused to budge. The familiarity of the taste in his mouth returned and he recognised the distinctive odour and taste of adhesive within his mouth and nose. Once more, he overstretched his brow to force his eyes to open, but still, the restrictions held. His mind began to pull the pieces of awareness together and he painted a picture within the blackness. He slowly realised the situation he had awoken to find himself in. Restricted, restrained, trapped and most probably captured.

He began to shout behind the tape, but the words escaped in an unintelligible murmur. He fought against the restraints to his limbs, but they held strong. His breathing was short and shallow. Something was restricting his chest cavity from expanding. He remembered a similar feeling from his childhood when his brother had buried him up to his neck on a beach in Dorset.

Suddenly, light flooded his new world. He felt a second tearing across his eyelid as someone removed what he now realised was tape. More light inundated his vision as he opened a second eye. It took a few moments until his sight adjusted to the increased brightness. A third ripping sensation smarted his face. This time across his mouth and lips. With the release he felt from the removal of his facial restraints, he tried once again to move his limbs. However, a weighty force restricted any movement. He strained to lift his head to gain a greater field of vision but only managed to raise his neck enough to discover the majority of his body buried beneath a large volume of sand. Movement to his side distracted his attention. He glanced sideways and, in doing so, realised he was entrapped in what appeared to be some sort of stone chamber. For a second time, the shadows fluttered with movement.

'Sarah?' he quizzed, unable to see beyond the confines of his tomb. His memory began to unfold from its own restraints. 'Is that you, Sarah?' he enquired again. His recollection of Sarah's unexpected visit being the last thing he remembered before waking.

'Yes.' came the reply in a voice he recognised. 'I hope you are enjoying our little date together.' The shadows grew in the flickering light of the candles as the source of the voice moved ever closer to the sarcophagus.

'Help me please,' begged Turner, still at a loss for some form of understanding to the questions that overwhelmed his mind. A figure appeared from above. A familiar face smiled down upon him. A sudden fearfulness engulfed his thoughts.

'You're not Sarah.' He knew the face but could not place it. Moments passed as memories ran riot in his head to fit a name to the face. From the depths, it came to him.

You're—'

'Yes, Turner. I am the face in the light, the dark in the night.

And together, we shall discover the true righteousness of man.'

City of Westminster
London, England

101

They had not spoken much on the way back to pick up the Land Rover. It was hard for Harriet to find words that were beneficial to the situation and, more specifically, to alleviate the tortures and tribulations Tate would be suffering. Harriet knew all too well what Tate would be going through, having lost her partner to the hands of the Narcissus at the end of the first murderous campaign. Tate himself battled within his head to find the answers, which would inevitably lead to uncovering where Turner was being held. All the while confronting the blame and responsibilities that tormented his conscience. He could not help but hold himself accountable for Turner's abduction.

He turned left onto Horseferry Road. The traffic was relatively light in London terms and the first church they were heading to was only a short distance from Thorney Street. The pavements were already crawling with vampires, ghouls, witches, monsters and zombies. Dozens of miniature terrors in their quest for treats. Each was swinging an orange tub to collect their bounty. Tate did his best to concentrate on other road users and crossing pedestrians, but a hundred other things seemed to be swamping his mind.

'We'll find him,' were the first consoling words Harriet could find to break the silence.

'I know,' responded Tate, 'but will we find him in time?' The nagging dilemma in his head fought to use an alternative wording, but Tate refused to reference the possibility of his brother dying. 'There must be something I am not seeing. It will be staring me straight in the face, but I just can't figure out what it is.' Harriet noticed the first-person singularity that Tate used as he fought the self-blame and shouldered the culpability of finding his brother.

She spoke with re-assurance. 'We both have good teams. I know this will be hard to accept, but I am confident that one of them will spot something that will lead us to Turner's location.'

Tate did not answer immediately as he concentrated on a procession of goblins and trolls as he attempted to make the right turn onto Monck Street.

'I will not be able to face Mum and Dad if—'

He stopped mid-sentence as a recollection relating to his parents popped into his head. Why had it not dawned on him before? It may not have been staring him head-on, but he was now kicking himself for not thinking of it sooner.

He spoke his next thoughts out loud for Harriet to understand. 'Mum and Dad were married at St Matthew's Westminster. It is significant to both Turner and I. Hell, we were both christened there and we were both there for the funerals of our grandparents, for heaven's sake.' Out of the very little they had to go on, both detectives grasped at the ray of optimism.

The bell tower of St Matthew's Church stood tall, directly ahead of them at the end of the street. Tate abandoned the Land Rover on the pavement outside the four-storey narthex of the church, the vehicle's blue lights still flashing. He was out of the driver's door before Harriet could remove the traditional lap belt still fitted to the vintage Landy. Tate entered the church through the main doors, Harriet still a short distance behind. He made no attempt to be inconspicuous and was in no way furtive. He had one objective with the possibility of only one desired outcome. To save his brother before time ran out.

Tate burst through the vestibule doors into the inner sanctum of the church. Much to his surprise and the astonishment of a group of female parishioners gathered around the tables of a flower arranging evening class. Tate stood motionless as Harriet arrived at his shoulder. His eyes swept down one side of the nave, across the high altar and back along the aisles of the opposite side. Nothing whatsoever out of the ordinary revealed itself.

'Good Evening. Welcome to St Matthew's. Is there anything I can help you with?'

Tate continued to survey the spaces to either side of the nave. 'Is there a crypt or vault beneath the church?'

'Unfortunately, there isn't one that we are aware of. If there was, I believe it would have been found during the rebuilding,' replied the pastor.

Harriet stepped forward, producing her ID. 'We are sorry for the intrusion, minister. We are currently investigating an abduction which we are led to believe has a link to a church of St Matthew.'

Tate was still inquisitive and interrupted. 'Have you noticed anything out of the ordinary in the last twenty-four hours?'

'The church would have been locked overnight and members of the congregation and community have been coming and going since morning prayer at 10 am. I am sure somebody would have noticed if something mischievous was happening here in the church.

'Thank you, minister. We are sorry to have disturbed the women of your community,' apologised Harriet, safe in the knowledge that even though the connections with Tate's family were evident, St Matthew's Westminster was not the church they sought.

'One more question if you wouldn't mind, minister,' asked Tate. The pastor opened his hands in acceptance. 'Do you have an open sarcophagus within the church?'

'I am afraid the answer is, once again, No.'

Tate's eagerness waned as his optimism had been met by a number of revelations that he had not been expecting. He had been ardent that the family connections to the church had been favourable. However, his eagerness had caused him to lose sight of the situation. The church of St Matthew in Westminster was not the location they desperately sought. The clock was still ticking and the sand would still be flowing.

But Tate would not give up hope until he had found Turner alive.

102

During their time at the Tate Gallery, Jonathan and DS Garrett continued to view the live feed. At all times, at least one of them was continually watching the screen in case of a new development or the image changing. Apart from the increase in the level of sand, nothing noteworthy had occurred so far. Detective Garrett had taken a statement from the gallery attendant and recorded all that she could remember from her encounter with the Narcissus. The Clore wing of the gallery remained closed and Jonathan took the opportunity to view JMW Turner's other works within the room while he took a break from watching the live feed. He was walking back towards the corner where Jane was standing when the picture nearest him caught his attention.

'I don't bloody believe it,' he exclaimed, his words echoing around the empty gallery.

'What is it?' enquired Jane as she looked up to see Jonathan leaning forward, reading the gallery's exhibit label to the side of a large dark picture. Jonathan continued to study the painting's description before returning his attention to the painting itself. He stood before the picture and took a few steps backwards to gain a better perspective.

'Well?' said Jane.

'The picture is obviously by Turner, as is all of this collection. It is entitled 'The Deluge.' The picture depicts the raging storm, savage seas and the colossal waves of the biblical flood. It's yet another link to Neptune's Finger and their *After the Flood* album.'

Jane sidled over to join Jonathan while keeping one eye on the live feed. 'You don't think we have been drawn to look at the wrong picture,' enquired Jane. 'Perhaps the answers we are looking for lie within the Turner painting. The other picture placement might well have been a pretence to distract our attention. Maybe we have been looking in the wrong direction.' Both detectives continued to survey the picture. Jonathan walked closer so he could inspect the picture's finer detail. Jane watched as Jonathan paid particular attention to one corner of the Turner work.

After examining the area, he turned back to Jane. 'In the dark area of the right-hand foreground, a man locked in shackles can be seen saving a distressed woman from drowning. It could be taken as another connection to the Acts of Mercy. It could be seen as an eighth act. The woman's life is in peril, and despite the man's own tortures, he stops to help her.

It could be written as 'You were in danger, and I saved you.'

'Much in the same way as Tate's tribulations with Turner,' Jane suggested, her attention drawn back to the image on the video feed, her eyes catching the suggestion of movement.

Jonathan continued. 'There doesn't appear to be anything further which may help us discover Turner's location.' Jane did not hear Jonathan's words as her focus had now completely returned to the other picture. A figure had entered the frame.

'Jon,' the only word she had, her eyes transfixed and drawn to the images. Images that were now showing the presence of a woman.

'Jon!' She exclaimed, once again in the hushed tone that was commonplace in a gallery. There was no response. Jonathan was still captivated in the detail of his own entrancing picture. Jane watched as the female stood and looked into the sarcophagus. She looked to be talking, but there was no sound besides the instrumental over-track.

'Jon. The Narcissus is back at the video location,' this time raising her voice above the customary gallery whisper. It had the desired effect and Jonathan immediately re-joined Jane at the other picture.

They watched as the images played out. The image appeared to be no different from when Jonathan had last looked.

'She entered from the right-hand side and appeared to talk to Turner for around 30 seconds before she exited again on the same side,' clarified Jane.

'The sand level has increased considerably since we first viewed the—'

He did not finish the sentence as the Narcissus once again entered the frame. As before, she entered from the right, but this time, she was carrying what looked like an aluminium framework. She placed it upon the open tomb and proceeded to secure it to the stonework with a series of metal clasps. Turner's body could still be seen, but a mesh of two-inch squares now covered the sarcophagus's open top. One end of the covering seemed to be hinged to allow opening. The Narcissus placed a padlock through a hasp and staple to secure the opening section. Finally, she spun the lock's combination dial. All the while, Jonathan could be seen mouthing words whilst his limbs writhed below the surface of the sand, which was now level with the lower parts of his shoulders. Jonathan and Jane continued to watch as the Narcissus leant across the installed mesh and spoke to Turner before once again leaving the camera's field of vision.

'I still think we are missing something, which is probably staring us straight in the face,' stressed Jonathan. 'This is all part of the Narcissus' game. She will want Tate to discover Turner's whereabouts and confront her before the sand buries his brother alive.'

'I am going to give Tate a call and notify him of the changes as he requested,' Jane stated as she removed her phone. No sooner had she done so than it began to ring. Recognising the caller's ID, she answered it immediately and activated the hands-free mode.

'Hi, David. You're on speakerphone. Jonathan is here with me.'

'I've made a discovery. Quite a breakthrough, really,' revealed David, an edge of eagerness in his voice. 'Tom has been looking at the Acts of Mercy and Matthew 25, while I have been looking back at all of the Narcissus' messages that use the lyrics from the Neptune's Finger songs. And I've found something quite interesting hidden within.' The statement captured both Jane's and Jonathan's complete attention.

'I started playing around with the words within each of the groups of lyrics. Sometimes, messages are hidden within certain aspects of a verse. For example, the first words of each line may read as a statement, sentence or message. You find them a lot in role-playing games as secret hidden passwords. This type of puzzle is called an acrostic.'

Jane looked across at Jonathan, who she could see was becoming impatient. 'What did you find, David?'

'Nothing.'

Jonathan tutted and tipped his head.

But David continued. 'So, I tried a different approach by looking at the letters. Again, sometimes, the first or last letters of each line can also spell a word or message or can be rearranged to do so. While playing around with the first letter of each line of the lyrical messages, I discovered several potential words could be formed within the acrostic.'

Jonathan's impatience won over and he could not hold back. 'What is it you found, David? Cut to the chase. We don't have much time.'

'Sorry,' came the reply, 'I do tend to over explain myself from time to time.'

'David!'

'So after a bit of word juggling, I found that the first letters could be rearranged to form the words…

St Mary Magdalene Paddington.'

Jonathan had already unlocked his phone before DC Morrison had completed his sentence. He hit the speed dial button for Tate.

103

Turner continued to take fright as his fear escalated beyond a level that many could ever imagine. He watched as the Narcissus fixed a metal pipe between the ceiling and the sarcophagus where he lay. The sand continued to flow inside the pipe fixture so that no one could restrict or stop its flow. Turner had reached the stage where he knew there was little point in continuing to struggle or attempting to free himself from his restraints. There was no chance of escaping his incarceration. His brother was now his only hope. With his mind in rapturous torment, he still clung to the belief that his involvement was all part of the Narcissus' master plan and a ruse to entice Tate to confront her one final time. Whether he lived or died would be dependent on how swiftly his brother was able to uncover the location in which he was currently being held.

Turner must have closed his eyes for a split second or maybe even a minute or two. For however long, it did not matter. He was again fully alert. He strained his neck to look down. The level of the sand had not increased much if anything at all. Therefore, he could not have been detached for long. However, something was different. At first, he could not place what it was. He used all of his senses to factor in the subtle difference. It was a sound. Or, more specifically, a sound that was no longer there. He strained to lift his chin once more. The flow of sand from the pipe to the sarcophagus had stopped.

The Narcissus appeared at the edge of Turner's peripheral vision before she leant over the encaged sarcophagus.

'Yes, the flow of the sand has stopped. It seems your brother is taking longer than I anticipated to discover our little sacred covert. I would hate for you to be buried alive before his arrival. As brothers, I would wish to grant you a final farewell before the execution of your burial.' Turner's trepidations reignited into an irrational hysteria. The level of the sand may well have stopped just shy of his neck, but the knowing that it would start once again on Tate's arrival bedevilled Turner's psyche.

'Calm yourself. There is no need to panic just yet,' the Narcissus taunted. 'First, I wish you to hear of your brother's adjudgments.' The Narcissus moved to the end of the sarcophagus so that Turner had no need to strain to see her. She looked down at him and smiled. Only his head and neck remained visible above the accumulation of sand.

'It's a real shame. You and Sarah would have made a lovely couple. Such a sweet girl. Definitely, one of the better sides to my split personality.' The Narcissus released a scornful snigger directly into Turner's face.

'You are completely deranged,' hollered Turner in return, 'a psychopathic maniac.'

'And that's the part of me you don't want to mess with.' She gave him a malevolent wink. The surface of the sand could be seen to undulate as Turner once again wrestled to free his limbs from the constraints within. Not so he could cut and run from the Narcissus' capture, but to free himself to get his hands around the neck of the villainous woman who held such malice for his brother. The Narcissus noticed the change in Turner's temperament. He was no longer in fear for his life. He had crossed that line and was now inflamed by a fury within for his brother's nemesis. The hunted clawed at its cage to get at the hunter. The lamb had become the wolf and the Narcissus had witnessed the metamorphosis.

'Ahh... There it is. Eventually, it rises to the surface. The evil that lurks inside all of us. Some are better at caging its rage. However, it fights to escape every man, and eventually, it defeats even the strongest among us. Faith gives way to sin, and the world is corrupted by the evil that men do,' preached the Narcissus in a way that resonated with her belief of being of a higher order. She continued her holier-than-thou discourse. 'Those who act upon the fates of mercy will, in return, receive penance for their sins. Grace and salvation will be granted to those who see the failings of others and act in order to punish the sinners who cannot see past their own misdoings. For we are God's soldiers.'

Turner heard the misconceived pontifications. There was little else he could do in his current predicament. He attempted to turn a deaf ear to the words. He may have no option but to listen to the delusional ramblings, but he could still choose to disregard its inference.

'I have yet to beguile the immorality from within Tate. But maybe we will see the serpent raise its ugly head when he is confronted with the moral choice I intend to offer him. We shall see if there really is such a thing as brotherly love when Tate faces his final judgement. You or I.'

The noise of a door opening in the church above seized the attention of both the captive and the captor. Turner immediately shouted his brother's name. The Narcissus promptly retaped Turner's mouth before he could cry out again and relocked the cage. Both remained motionless as each waited with bated breath for further sounds of movement from above. Turner for a ray of hope that his rescue was imminent and the Narcissus content that the game was still in play and she could once again get the opportunity to face her adversary. She extended an index finger in front of her lips and shushed quietly as she removed a small remote from her pocket. She once again listened for a presence above. The sound of footsteps was just distinguishable. She silenced her hostage for a second time, smiled slyly and pressed the remote.

As before, the sand began to spill into Turner's tomb.

The Church of St Mary Magdalene
Paddington, London, England

104

Local constabularies across the capital had begun to search the churches of St Mary's and St Magdalene's within their districts. Of the five churches checked for the presence of the suspected crime scene, nothing untoward had been found so far.

Tate and Harriet had just exited the Land Rover outside the Church of St Mary Magdalene, Regent's Park when Tate received the call from Jonathan. They immediately jumped back into the Landy while Jonathan continued to explain the circumstances behind the discovery of the location. Tate and Harriet listened through the hands-free mode as they sped west along the A501.

With the blue lights flashing, it took very little time to cover the short distance between the two churches. They abandoned the Land Rover in the parking area to the south of the building and hastened to the vestibule at the western end of the church.

The church of St Mary Magdalene, Paddington, lies on the banks of the Grand Union Canal adjacent to 'Little Venice.' Constructed in the late 19th century, it is considered to be architect George Edmund Street's crowning masterpiece. Its towering red and white spire stands tall as a recognisable landmark above the surrounding neighbourhood. The painted ceiling of the nave and the stained glass of the apse are regarded as some of the most noteworthy examples throughout the capital's churches.

Tate was first through the door, and Harriet followed closely behind. He passed straight through the narthex and onto the rear of the nave, where he was promptly met by a sight he was not expecting. Tate stood stock-still, startled by the inner appearance of the church. Harriet arrived by his side. Scaffolding had been erected along the entire length of the nave's north side, through the transepts and across the chancel before the large stain-glassed apse. The church was undergoing a major internal renovation. The appearance had momentarily flummoxed Tate, but it was not long before he regained his composure, and his eyes began to search the inner space for a door or stairway which would lead to some form of subterranean crypt or undercroft.

'Here!' Harriet cried out, pointing to the opening of a flight of stone steps that appeared to descend below the nave. Tate had not noticed the stairs at first due to an assemblage of scaffolding poles that criss-crossed the opening. Tate joined Harriet at the head of the steps. The flickering of candles and a golden glow emanated from below. The two detectives' eyes traced the curving of the steps as they disappeared into the depths of the cavern. Positioned upon the tread of each step was a small jack-o'-lantern. A single letter had been carved into the flesh of each pumpkin. A candle within created a fiery radiance that flared through each sculpted lantern. The assembled letters spelt out an inviting salutation.

WELCOME TO HELL

'I'll go first. You follow a few steps behind. That way, there is less chance of the Narcissus surprising both of us. Keep your eyes peeled. She will be here. Somewhere. She will want a confrontation,' declared Tate as he took the first step. Each additional step was taken cautiously, each detective anxious about what lay ahead.

They stepped out of the small curving stairwell onto the terracotta tiled floor of the undercroft. The only light came from a corridor of lanterns leading from the foot of the stairs to a large medieval-looking wooden door on the far side. This time, each of the pumpkins was carved with traditional Halloween images. Witches, bats, skulls and numerous depictions of toothy jack-o'-lanterns. Both Tate and Harriet surveyed the room for signs of the Narcissus' presence. Tate had to restrain himself from proceeding hastily in his endeavour to locate his brother before time ran out.

'I don't see anything, do you?' enquired Harriet.

'Not as such,' replied Tate, 'but there are numerous places where she may be hiding. Let's continue but remain vigilant. I'll cross to the door. Once I am there, you join me.' Harriet nodded in agreement and watched as Tate followed the line of lanterns before she also crossed to the far side of the vaulted room. Both detectives checked the expanse of the room that now lay behind them before looking through the leaded windows of the transecting wall to the small chancel beyond.

'The place seems empty. Perhaps she has gone,' suggested Harriet. Tate did not want to think along those lines. If the Narcissus had departed, would that mean they were too late? The undercroft was hauntingly quiet, but if you listened carefully enough, you could just hear the sound of the sand as it fell into the sarcophagus. It confirmed Tate's darkest fear, and he could hold back no longer.

'I'm going in. Turner may not have long.' He eased the door and stepped into the grotto-like chancel. Harriet once again followed his lead. Both were slightly taken aback by the beauty of the small chapel and its medieval decor as they stood facing the narrow double doors that separated the chancel from the chapel's altar. The doors were parted enough to get sight of the sarcophagus beyond. Both detectives wasted no further time, and side by side, they moved towards the doors. They each pushed a leaf of the door to one side and thrust forward into the tiny chapel. Tate instantly crossed to the sarcophagus while Harriet scanned the room for any sign of the Narcissus. Again, she found nothing. There were, however, three recent acquisitions. Three further lanterns, each much larger than those lighting the path. One was placed above the altar, the other two to either side. Each was carved with a single word.

TATE OR TURNER

Turner's eyes looked up. Lost and fearful. The sand was now at a level where the features upon his face were all that remained to be seen. A glint appeared in his eyes upon seeing his brother's face. He had known all along that Tate would arrive in time. He had always been there when Turner had needed him. Right here, right now, he needed him more than ever before.

Tate looked through the wire cage and gave his brother a reassuring smile. 'We're here now, Turner. You no longer need to worry. We will have you out of there before you know it.' Tate returned to his usual calm self despite the situation. He could not show his apprehensions. He knew they had very little time. The sand was still spilling at a steady flow. He looked at the fixings between the cage and the stonework. He did not rattle the wire as he knew it would be futile and did not wish to cause his brother further anguish. He examined the padlock of the opening section before scanning the room for further answers. There was little to be seen aside from the pumpkins, candelabras and the statue of St Mary Magdalene. Tate attempted to raise one corner of the statue, but it was too heavy to move, let alone lift it down. He could not see a way to break the lock or the cage, so he approached the situation from a different angle.

'Harriet. I remember noticing some builder's materials and tools in the outer room. See if you can find something we could get under the pipe to stop or divert the flow of the sand.' Turner began to mumble behind his taped mouth, and Tate returned his attention to his brother. The sand was now above his earline and beginning to reach the corners of Turner's lips and nostrils. 'Look for some form of pipe, too. We need to provide Turner with some sort of breathing system.'

Without a word, Harriet made off in search of possible solutions to aid Turner's inevitable quandary.

Tate again turned back to his brother. 'I've got this. You are going to be fine. We are going to provide you with something to breathe through. Until then, I will leave the tape across your mouth. It will prevent the sand from entering. With each breath through your nose, blow out extra hard. It will help to keep the sand away.' Turner attempted to nod, but his head held fast. 'I need to look for something I can use to reach through the caging and remove the tape when necessary. I will be right back, OK?' Turner's eyes looked desperately at his brother and he blinked twice. Tate took it as a confirmation and turned to search for an improvised solution. In his haste to find his brother, Tate had not noticed the two small prayer desks to the rear of the small chapel. Upon one of the desks lay a traditional prayer scroll. Tate removed the wooden winding stick. He looked up at the statue of St Mary Magdalene and apologised before breaking the stick towards one end.

Harriet arrived back at the altar. She was armed with a short length of copper pipe, a cylinder vacuum cleaner, and an extension lead. Tate was about to ask, but she beat him to it.

'I'm hoping this will suck out the sand faster than it is going in.' she exclaimed.

'Take the motor assembly out of the collection drum so the sand can flow freely onto the floor. It will also save time not having to empty it,' suggested Tate. Harriet took the end of the extension lead back out into the chancery and Tate turned to his brother. 'Turner. Listen carefully. I will gently push the end of this broken stick through the tape across your mouth. After I remove it, I want you to blow out as hard as you can. We need to keep as much sand as possible away from your mouth. I know this won't be easy, but I am then going to carefully insert the end of this copper pipe into your mouth. I want you to grip it as tightly as you can with your lips. When you have done this, I want you to blink twice. If you understand, blink once now.' Turner blinked his panic-stricken eyes. Tate took his cue and proceeded to provide the breathing apparatus as he had just explained.

Harriet reappeared at the head of the sarcophagus. 'Harriet is behind the top of your head. The noise you are about to hear is a vacuum cleaner. She is going to start sucking out the sand around your face. Ok?' Once again, Turner blinked his confirmation. Harriet was poised to start the vacuum's motor when a cacophonous bellowing sounded above.

Tate looked to Harriet, both of whom, without sharing words, knew what the dissonant sound could only mean. Harriet looked at Tate one final time.

'Go. I've got this. Turner will be fine.' She turned on the vacuum motor and placed the nozzle through the cage and into the sand. 'Go,' she demanded a second time. Tate looked at Turner, who blinked once. Tate then diverted his eyes to the sand spilling from the vacuum's motor onto the floor. Happy that the flow seemed faster than that of the sand still entering the sarcophagus, he turned and headed for the stairs and the church above.

The Church of St Mary Magdalene
Paddington, London, England

105

Tate bounded up the stairs, taking the steps two at a time. As he exited the stairwell back into the main church's nave, the pipe organ sounded once more. He scanned the expansive space before him for the source of the sound. As the pipes resonated for a third time, Tate decided the organ had to be in one of the two transepts.

He sprinted down the nave's central aisle past the numerous rows of congregational chairs towards the church's main chancel and altar. As he crossed the transept, the organ's pipes again echoed through the internal sacred space. Tate realised that the source of the sound originated in an area to his right. As he crossed towards the northern transept, the bellow of the organ pipes subsided, and a heckling cackle pierced the air. Tate quickened his stride in the direction from which the laughter had emanated.

He found himself in a small vestry and at the foot of another stone stairwell, which he presumed led to the tower. He listened for any further noises. A muffled rustling sound came from above. The stairs were not only the entrance to the bell tower but also the only exit. If the Narcissus had ascended the tower, there would be no other way down. Was she inviting another confrontation in a similar way to the power station roof of last summer, where before his eyes, she had made a devious escape? He had no choice but to rise to the challenge. The stone steps before him would be his Jacob's Ladder and a passageway to his re-encounter with someone who believed they had a godly power.

Assuming there would be little space within the stairwell to initiate an ambush, Tate once again took the steps two at a time as they spiralled upwards within the confined space of the tower. He slowed his ascent as he reached the bell tower floor and peered cautiously into the space. At first, it appeared to be unoccupied. However, Tate was stupefied when the source of the rustling hopped into view. A pair of jackdaws appeared in a face-off.

Tate cursed himself for such a mistake. His haste to apprehend the Narcissus once and for all had caused him to act without thinking. He had been too keen to confront his nemesis. However, a further set of stairs leading to an upper tower still held the possibility of a showdown. Tate was about to climb the second flight when a clattering from below distracted his attention. He was now faced with a decision. Continue up or head down in the direction of the latest noise. His instincts took over and he again took the steps two at a time as he descended the spiralled stairwell.

As he reemerged from the south transept, he had no need to continue his search. The Narcissus stood facing him on the scaffolding directly across from where he had just exited. It appeared as if she was waiting for his arrival.

'I'm so glad to see you finally made it. You never fail to please, do you, Tate? How's your brother, by the way? I have heard it said that being buried alive is as peaceful as drowning.' She laughed at her witticism.

'It's time to give it up, Lena. This has gone too far. Your actions are beyond control,' Tate demanded, knowing that he needed to keep the Narcissus talking if he was going to take advantage of the situation. As she talked and he listened, Tate began to slowly and discreetly move along sideways parallel to the length of the scaffolding. He purposely did not move closer to the Narcissus as his approach may have unnerved her, and Tate wanted her to remain exactly where she was.

'Oh, my calling has only just begun. There are still legions of sinners who deserve to choose their merciful fate.' Tate could sense that the Narcissus had more to say, so he turned a deaf ear and continued to edge towards the end of the scaffolding nearest to the main exit.

'The cleansing will not happen overnight. Eventually, others will join the cause, and the Earth will be purged of transgressors.'

Tate was more than aware of the Narcissus' heightened intelligence and was conscious that she would scrutinise his every move. He posed a further question to distract her focus. 'What has all this got to do with the stolen Caravaggio?' Tate could foretell the answer but needed a further diversion.

'I was only taking back that which was rightfully mine. It was stolen from my paternal ancestor during the last days of his life. With a significant wounding to his face, he endeavoured to continue his journey northwards along the coast in an attempt to reach Rome once again and receive a papal pardon for the sins he had committed.'

Without notice, Tate had managed to traverse much farther than he had first envisaged, but he still needed to gain farther ground.

'And where is the 'St Mary Magdalene in Ecstasy'?

'You will be pleased to hear that she is safe and in good hands. There are others with instructions for her wellbeing should I not return. Did you not notice our spiritual mother looking down upon Turner? Much like how I now look down upon you as you worm along indiscreetly in the hope of blocking my exit.'

Tate had been foiled, but he seized the moment and travelled the remaining distance to the end of the scaffolding framework in seconds. The Narcissus was momentarily addled with Tate's movements and she edged farther along the platform towards the apse windows. Tate found himself in the exact position he had planned for. He had put himself between the Narcissus and the only accessible exit apart from the tower. Suddenly, without warning, the Narcissus made an unexpected dart towards the altar end of the church.

But Tate was ready.

He stood on the lowest rail of the scaffold and grasped the chest-height horizontal pole with both hands. He crouched back slightly to gain maximum momentum, and in one fluid movement, he leapt upwards, caught hold of the upper safety rail, springing up and through onto the scaffold's upper platform. It was the same dynamic movement he had been practising on the wall at the climbing centre during the previous few weeks.

Without time to stop and think, Tate took off across the platform in the direction of his quarry. He made good ground across the scaffold that ran the entirety of the northern wall. The sound of his feet clattering across the boarding reverberated throughout the church. As he reached the rear of the altar beyond the transept, he stepped up onto the handrail much in the same way that a runner does in a steeple chase and flung himself diagonally across the corner of the scaffolding and made to grapple the Narcissus mid-dive. His forward motion was much more than he had expected. As he tackled the Narcissus at the waist, his continuing momentum unbalanced her and she toppled over the rear safety rail and fell between the rear of the framework and the windows of the apse.

As Tate's dive continued, he held a hand forward, and as his body hit the boarded deck, he stretched to the limit of his reach, and at the final moment, he grasped hold of the Narcissus' wrist. With the weight of his body laid out across the platform, he managed to maintain his grip, and she hung perilously above the altar.

The Narcissus hung, suspended in midair, dangling from the end of

Tate's outstretched arm. His grasp being her only lifeline. She swung facing the stained glass windows of the apse. She looked up and back over her shoulder directly into Tate's eyes as he lay spreadeagled across the platform.

'I've got you,' claimed Tate, 'try to swing your legs back under the scaffolding and get a footing.' The Narcissus just stared as she contemplated the situation. She made no attempt to seek salvation. Her eyes reflected a state of vanquish. Mortality had finally captured her and she was ready to accept her fate.

She spoke serenely, locked in Tate's gaze. 'I do not fear death. I welcome it. Death is not the end of the story. It is just the closing of a chapter. However, my next chapter will be told posthumously.'

Tate could feel the Narcissus' hand gradually slipping from his grip. He tried to re-engage his fingers around her wrist to maintain his hold. Although, it appeared as if the Narcissus was doing little to prevent herself from an eventual fall.

'Lena!' yelled Tate. He thought using her given name may break through her shell of indifference and push past her narcissistic personality so he could engage with her inner self and the person he once knew. But it appeared to be to no avail. The narcissistic persona was too strong and her other selves were now buried too far into her fractured mind. The Narcissus simply smiled. At that moment, Tate knew that there was no stopping the inevitable. The smile on the Narcissus' face slowly began to morph and the evil in her eye began to fade. Tate could sense that she had decided it was time to make her peace and be judged for her mercies.

She looked up to Tate one final time before allowing her fingers to slip from his grasp. As she began to fall, she spread her arms and lowered her head. However, her fall ended abruptly as her torso plunged into a large candelabra hung above the altar. The central prong of the three-pointed sconces pierced her throat, and her arms ensnared on the tapered ends of the left and right sides.

The Narcissus hung crucified from the candelabra. The skin of her back exposed, her blouse having been torn from her body after snagging on the scaffolding during the fall. Her recently completed tattoo, depicting the Seven Acts of Mercy, had become the church's new altarpiece. Her lifeless body slumped from her extended arms in a reverse depiction to that of Jesus on the Cross. She had become her very own masterpiece of the crucifixion.

Her head sat heavily over her chin, but she managed to summon enough strength through gritted determination and pertinacity to turn and lock eyes with Tate one last time. She fought with death to prolong her dying moments, and with her endmost breath, she imparted just four final words.

'My legacy has begun.'

The Church of St Mary Magdalene
Paddington, London, England

106

A camera flash exploded from the far end of the church. Tate looked towards the narthex just as the photographer disappeared towards the exit. Tate had no reason to intervene. There was no longer a need to keep the Narcissus from the public eye.

The story was over.

Brooks pushed the church door to one side and sped onto the riverside lawn. He could not believe what he had just witnessed. He had expected to discover another victim's body after he had received the phone call and instruction from the Narcissus earlier that evening. He could never have envisaged the body he would photograph being that of the Narcissus herself. The setting and the way her body hung in its crucified form above the altar had been gifted to him on a plate. Every tabloid across the globe would be scrambling for the images he held in his camera. He would be able to name his price. Brooks had finally captured that prize winning front page picture he had always longed for.

Tate wasted no time. He did not pursue the photographer. Turner's release was his primary concern. He did not need to check Lena for a pulse. He had witnessed her final breath. He promptly used a fireman's ladder slide to descend from the scaffolding and at pace leapt down the stone stairway to the undercroft. The candles lining the pathway flickered as he swiftly crossed to the chancel. Shadows of the jack-o'-lanterns danced across the vaulted walls and ceilings. As he entered the tiny area before the altar, he immediately sensed something was wrong. No sound came from the vacuum's motor, which meant it had stopped working.

'It started to overheat as it struggled with the density of the sand,' declared Harriet, her hand on the motor's casing, poised to recommence the sand removal as soon as it had cooled sufficiently. 'We were making significant headway before the overheating had begun.'

Tate leant over the sarcophagus and turned his attention to his brother. 'How are you doing? Still hanging in there?' Turner looked back at Tate through tired eyes and blinked twice. The ordeal was now affecting him, not only physically but mentally, too. Tate knew he needed to get Turner out of his current predicament as quickly as possible. Each minute longer would only add to the torture and anguish he would suffer, reliving his ordeal in years to come.

'How's the breathing?' asked Tate. Turner blinked twice, although Tate knew it would not be the easiest thing with the low volume of air in the pipe and the rebreathing of the carbon dioxide that remained in the tube upon each exhalation. Tate needed to act fast. He took the briefest of moments to think about the situation. He could see three possibilities:

Break into the cage.

Stop the flow of the sand.

Remove the padlock.

Whichever he decided, he needed to do it fast.

The cage looked secure, and he hadn't noticed any power tools lying around, which he would need if they were to try and remove the grill. Tate then looked at the galvanised pipe leading up and through the ceiling. He moved to the bottom end of the sarcophagus and gave the pipe a hard shake while pulling it downwards.

'I've already tried that,' proclaimed Harriet, 'it seems to be well and truly secured from above.' Finally, he turned his attention to the padlock. Again, Harriet informed Tate what she had learnt during his absence. 'It is an ultra-modern four pin digital padlock. It has been programmed to allow the user four attempts before locking the mechanism for the next 60 minutes.' Tate looked inquisitively at Harriet. 'I looked it up on the Internet while waiting for the motor to cool. We have three attempts left!' Tate's look now became one of a quizzical nature. 'I only found out about the maximum of four attempts when I tried what I thought was a possible combination, resulting in the digital screen reading '3 more attempts'.'

'What number did you try?' Tate asked as his mind started to run through possible four-digit combinations.'

'6925.' Tate looked at Harriet, puzzled by her answer. She read his expression and explained. 'Matthew 25. The numbers 6 and 9 are the phonetic numbers for the letters M and W. The combination is most probably part of her game. So I have been thinking of various possibilities linking to the Narcissus, the crime scenes and the first—'

She stopped mid-sentence. A look of alarm on her face. 'What happened? Did you confront her? Where is she now?'

'She's gone.' Harriet noticed Tate's turn of phrase.

'Gone?'

'She fell from the scaffolding and was impaled above the main altar.'

For a moment, Harriet did not know how to react. The evil that had plagued their lives for what seemed like an age had been defeated.

The Narcissus was dead.

She was unsure about how that made her feel. Was death a substantial enough sentence for the crimes she had committed, or had she avoided a greater punishment? It would probably take some time and justification to come to terms with the Narcissus' final demise. But for now, her attention had to be on releasing Turner.

Tate checked on his brother again, and the reality of the ongoing situation snapped Harriet back into the now.

'What other combinations or prospective possibilities did you come up with?'

'I went down the date route, the lock being four digits fits the concept of a two-digit day and month or a four-digit year.' Harriet realised the vacuum motor now felt cold to her touch, and she made Turner aware that she would continue extracting the sand. He blinked twice in response. 'Years with a link to the Narcissus enquiry could include the year Caravaggio painted the 'Seven Acts of Mercy' or the year he painted the 'St Mary Magdalene in Ecstasy'. I also came up with the possibility of the year of Caravaggio's death.'

'The year of his death is a strong candidate. The Narcissus has mentioned death more than once and the final act of mercy is 'bury the dead'.'

'What year did he die?'

Tate shrugged. 'I'll need to look it up.' He retrieved his mobile and tapped in a search. 'Google says 1610.'

'What do you think?' enquired Harriet.

'It's as good as any other. Let's give it a try. We do not have time to be over studious. He punched the numbers into the keypad. The red LED screen scrolled. 'You have two attempts remaining.'

'Any other suggestions?' asked Harriet.

Tate thought again for a minute or so. 'Maybe Turner's birth year. And likewise, my birth year. Maybe the 'Seven Acts of Mercy' in phonetic numbers in a similar way to your first suggestion.

'What do you think we should try next?'

Tate pondered the question for a moment. Before responding, he thought about the specifics of the case and the Narcissus' actions of late. 'This all started with the stealing of the 'St Mary Magdalene in Ecstasy', so the date of its conception would be relevant. Although this second killing spree has centred around another Caravaggio work, his 'Seven Acts of Mercy'.'

Tate paused. A thought had just come to him.

'When she fell from the scaffolding, her blouse was ripped from her back. Lena has had a full back tattoo depicting the artwork.'

Again, he stopped. This time to search for a second date.

'Caravaggio painted his work of the 'Seven Acts of Mercy' in 1607.'

Harriet raised her eyes at Tate. 'What do you think? If it's incorrect, we will only have one final attempt.'

'It is as worthy as the other considerations,' declared Tate, who looked over to his brother to get his reaction. However, the response he received was not what he expected. It appeared Turner was attempting to say something through his air pipe and the mouth bindings. The words Turner was trying to express were all but audible and the vacuum's motor did not help the situation. However, Tate could tell his brother was trying his hardest to be understood. He leant in over the cage.

'Do you want me to remove the pipe and tape? The sand level seems to be decreasing.' Turner blinked twice. Tate proceeded to remove the air pipe and binding, which caused Turner to cough and gag. But no sooner had he caught his breath than he wasted no time conveying his thoughts.

'0311,' his voice coarse and raspy from the sandy dust and restrictions of the breathing pipe. He repeated his words to ensure they had been heard correctly.

'0311.'

Tate had heard the number clearly but could not perceive its reasoning.

'What makes you think that's the correct combination?'

Turner cleared his throat once more. 'The 3rd of November,' he croaked. 'Three days after death comes the resurrection.' Tate began to make sense of Turner's supposition. He could see the association between the verses of Matthew 25 and the Acts of Mercy.

Turner continued to hypothesise his thoughts. 'If I am to rise from the dead, it will be on the 3rd day after my entombment. The 3rd of November will be my day of reckoning. 0311 will unlock my tomb so I can rise again.' Tate and Harriet looked at each other, both perplexed by Turner's postulations. 'I've had some time to try and think in a similar way as the Narcissus,' he declared, noticing the other pair's reactions. 'The reverse number is also my birth date. The 11th March.'

Tate could comprehend all that Turner was asserting. It all seemed feasible. 'The day of reckoning precedes the Last Judgement, both are fundamental to the verses of Matthew 25 and both have frequently been referred to by the Narcissus within her chosen passages from the Neptune's Finger album. I think there is a strong possibility that you may well be right,' declared Tate as a final recollection materialised in his memory. 'The live feed screen the Narcissus placed at Tate Britain was playing a loop of the last track from the *After the Flood* album. Its title is 'Rebirth'.'

Turner stared up at his brother and gave his demand. 'Then this is my judgement. My life and my decision. Try the code.' Tate did not need to ask twice; his brother had made that clear. He stepped to the end of the sarcophagus and tapped in the digits.

As he hit the fourth number, the shackle disengaged.

107

Jonathan had booked the table at Flat Iron, Borough, for 8 pm. He had arrived shortly before 7 pm to meet with Tate for a pre-dinner drink. But it was not Tate who arrived for the early aperitif, but Penny. Harriet had also suggested she and Penny could meet at an earlier pre-arranged time before the others were due to show up. It would be another forty minutes before Tate and Harriet appeared together, having had no intention of arriving any sooner. When they finally walked through the restaurant's entrance together, they were pleased to find their friends happily enjoying each other's company at the bar.

Turner hobbled in on crutches shortly after, having discovered upon his liberation from his entombment that the Narcissus had carved the numbers 4 and 6 into the soles of his feet in an identical manner to those of the previous victims. Time would heal the superficial wounds, but he would be scarred in a much deeper way after his ordeal for a far greater time to come. However, he had put on a brave face when invited to come this evening, knowing that Sarah, the woman he had so hoped to begin a new relationship with, had turned out to have been one of the Narcissus' split personalities and obviously would not be joining them. His spirits lifted slightly when the first members of Tate and Harriet's teams began to arrive. He would not be playing his usual spare part after all. Little did he know that as the night drew on, a short Indian lady in a dark green saree would attach herself to him after learning, much to her delight, that Tate had a younger brother.

DS Jane Garrett had arrived shortly after with DCs Tom Chamberlain and David Morrison after meeting earlier at the Anchor pub on Bankside. They appeared in high spirits, having already enjoyed one or two pints of London Pride at their earlier happy hour gathering.

Most of Harriet's team had fallen out of a taxi on Stoney Street, having also started their celebrations at several pubs on Bethnal Green High Street shortly after departing work. George Quinn and Iain Richards arrived separately just as a restaurant host escorted everyone to a long shared table at the restaurant's centre.

With everyone present and currently finding seats at the table, Tate and Harriet chose a pair of chairs opposite each other at the far end. A waiter came with tin cups of complimentary popcorn. He took the group's orders, the majority choosing the signature flat iron steak, whilst a select few indulged in the 8oz Wagyu fillet. Everyone was in high spirits after closing a major case, especially those with closer personal involvement. Individuals from both teams happily mixed, sharing their stories and anecdotes. Moments of loud, raucous laughter erupted around the table as someone shared an amusing tale.

The steaks were delivered along with an abundance of beef dripping chips, bone marrow garlic mash, creamed spinach and fresh green salad. The conversation continued to amplify as members of both teams discovered common ground and shared stories of the drudgery of a detective's daily routine.

While the waiting staff cleared the empty plates and served further drinks, Tate whispered to Harriet that he should say a few words. She agreed and was happy for him to take the podium.

Sitting at the opposite end of the table, Jonathan noticed his friend as Tate stood to address those present. He raised his glass and chinked a discarded knife across its rim.

'Hush now people. The *Grand Fromage* appears to have something he wishes to share with us all.' His announcement had the desired effect and the babble and chatter subsided. Everyone around the table turned their attention to the senior officer.

Tate raised a glass.

'I would like to thank you all for your continued commitment, support and work ethic. It does not go unnoticed, and each of you is as vital as the next in every investigation we are tasked with.'

'Hear, hear!' shouted Jake Evans, raising his bottle of lager.

'We would not be sitting here today, knowing that we have successfully closed a major investigation and prevented further bloodshed, without your contributions and dedication to the cause.'

'And double time pay for extended hours,' quipped Greg Thompson, saluting his pint glass with George.

'Remember, we still have a painting to recover, but for now, the next round of drinks is on the London Metropolitan police force. An escalation of cheering and applause encircled the table and Tate retook his seat opposite Harriet.

They had foiled one of London's most dangerous serial killers of recent years.

Tate looked down the length of the table and Harriet followed his gaze. 'It appears we have a great team,' he declared, raising his glass to Harriet. She, too, raised hers.

'I think we do,' she said, chinking Tate's glass.

Little did they know that they would all be working alongside each other again in the not too distant future.

108

London's art community rejoiced at the headline news that the Narcissus' murderous campaign had come to an end. One story was featured across the front pages worldwide, and the photographer got his payday and five minutes of fame.

Art collectors could once again be safe in the knowledge that they could purchase a high-profile painting, knowing full well that they would not end up being the subject of somebody's macabre murderscape.

The ghouls of Halloween had finished their trick or treating for another year and the city was preparing for its next big event. In just two days, fires would be lit and firework displays would light up the capital in celebration of the anniversary of Guy Fawkes's plot to blow up the parliament buildings.

Two men, side by side, made their way down Charing Cross Road. Both men were dressed in the finest tailored suits. Each suit the blood red of a cardinal's cassock. Much like the cardinal's cassock symbolising a willingness to die for his faith, the two men dressed in red were willing to be arrested for the cause and what they had been asked to do. One of the men wore a large-brimmed hat, and the other moved alongside his companion in an electric wheelchair. They parted ways as the pair approached the intersection with William IV Street and the Edith Cavell Memorial. Each gent attracted sufficient attention from the commuters and tourists to signify their cause. Their attire was lavish enough to captivate and allure the curiosity of the crowds as they continued their journeys.

As the sound of Big Ben signalled the 10th hour of the morning, each man made his way to the entrance of a gallery. The gentleman in the wheelchair approached the Getty entrance of the National Gallery and the gent on foot, the entrance to the National Portrait Gallery in the building to the rear.

The gent in the large red hat joined the queue at the main entrance of the Portrait Gallery. The visitors waited as the doors had yet to be opened.

The smartly dressed gent in the electric wheelchair entered the National Gallery at the disabled entrance and swiftly made his way through the Anneburg Court to the central lifts. He exited on the second level straight into the Central Hall. Knowing his final destination, he wasted no time as he traversed his pre-planned route through Rooms- 39, 38, 36 and 37 before entering the Julia and Hans Rausing Room.

As soon as the Portrait Gallery opened its doors, the other gent passed through the entrance and security checks along with the other early visitors. Like his colleague at the other gallery, he headed straight to the main lifts, for the room he sought was on the third level. When the lift doors parted, the gent stepped out onto the landing behind the other visitors. As the crowd separated in the various directions of the gallery rooms, the gent set off in the direction of Room 18, passing through Rooms- 13,15,16 and 17.

Over at the other gallery, the gent manoeuvred the wheelchair around Room 32, stopping frequently in front of a painting to make as if the picture warranted further perusal. However, his attention was firmly fixed on the movements of the gallery attendant. The gent patiently moved from picture to picture but did not shift his focus from the attendant. He had just manoeuvred his chair before the 'Marriage at Cana' by Mattia Preti when the attendant crossed the length of the room and disappeared into an adjoining gallery.

He saw his opportunity and took advantage of the attendant's absence. He negotiated the electric chair across the room toward the gallery's Caravaggio paintings. He checked for the presence of the attendant once more before standing and walking to the rear of the chair. Hidden behind a false backing, he removed a frame. Then, before any of the other visitors were aware, he pushed the pre-glued frame to the wall in a gap between two of the paintings. The 'St Mary Magdalene in Ecstasy' was finally where it rightfully belonged. It was hung in a public gallery for the masses to view alongside other great masterpieces by the genius that was Caravaggio.

At the very exact moment in the Portrait Gallery, the other man in red removed his large brimmed hat. He retrieved a far smaller frame from the interior of the hat's crown, and when he was confident others in the room were not looking, he too pressed his pre-glued frame to the gallery's wall.

The pencil sketch of Maddalena Antognetti, drawn by Caravaggio while she slept, now hung in a location it duly deserved amongst the other exquisite pencil sketches of the National Portrait Gallery.

The hanging of the pair of pictures was not just a daring act but a moment of awe and wonder that would become part of the Narcissus legacy and draw the lineage of a long-established family to a close.

Lena's death in the church of St Mary Magdalene would end the long and distinguished bloodline of Caravaggio.

Pio Monte Della Misericordia

Naples, Italy

Epilogue

The priest knelt before the altar, his thoughts lost in a blissful reverie. He blessed himself with the sign of the cross, his eyes drawn to the picture above the altar. The artist's representation of each merciful act held him in its grasp, offering a sanctuary for his contemplations. As each day drew to a close, he would find solace in the picture, feeling a deep connection to it whilst reflecting on his own judgements and perceptions.

Amid his deliberations, the young woman he had met only weeks earlier emerged at the forefront of his memories. His mind wandered back to the conversations they had shared, their mutual adoration for the picture and his wonderment at the discovery of her lineage to Caravaggio. He pondered the woman's whereabouts and recent circumstances and wondered if their paths were destined to cross again.

Father Salvatore went about the remainder of his chores, the only sound being the gentle chiming of the bell marking the end of another day. He looked forward to a quiet evening in his quarters, savouring a simple meal of pancetta and gnocchi.

Before he departed, he checked on Father Giuseppe in the vestry. The aged priest was peacefully asleep and Father Salvatore decided not to disturb him. As he turned to leave, his eyes were drawn to the row of wooden pigeon holes on the far wall. To his surprise, the one with his initials held a single envelope.

Father Salvatore turned the envelope in his hands, curious of its sender. He paid particular attention to the postal marks, notably the postal origin stamp. Two words in deep blue could easily be seen: GREAT BRITAIN. The beginnings of a subtle smile crept from the corner of the priest's lips. He tentatively eased the seal on the envelope and removed the contents.

The first was a letter on a single sheet of elegant writing paper. The words were written in a graceful, refined hand.

Dearest Father Salvatore,

If you are reading this, my mercies have been judged and I am now jubilant in eternal life.

As my forefather before me, I wish to offer my support to your brotherhood's cause. As you know, I am the last of a bloodline, so I wish for the Pio Monte Della Misericordia to become my sole beneficiary. I know you will use this gift wisely to further the fraternity's work. It was a pleasure to have known you, if only for the shortest of times.

Lena

The smile did not materialise. Tears filled the corners of the priest's eyes. His frail hands trembled as he shuffled the second sheet of paper forward. It was folded in two.

Father Salvatore's wavering hands endeavoured to unfold the banker's draft and as he parted the two folds of the cheque, he could no longer restrain the tears from welling. He bowed his head in desolation and gently whispered...

'Che Dio sia con te.'

'May God be with you.'

Matthew 2:35-46

The Seven Acts of Mercy

[35] 'For I was hungry and you gave me something to eat, I was thirsty and you gave me something to drink, I was a stranger and you invited me in, [36] I needed clothes and you clothed me, I was sick and you looked after me, I was in prison and you came to visit me.'

[37] Then the righteous will answer him, 'Lord, when did we see you hungry and feed you, or thirsty and give you something to drink? [38] When did we see you a stranger and invite you in, or needing clothes and clothe you? [39] When did we see you sick or in prison and go to visit you?'

[40] The King will reply, 'Truly I tell you, whatever you did for one of the least of these brothers and sisters of mine, you did for me.'

[41] Then he will say to those on his left, 'Depart from me, you who are cursed, into the eternal fire prepared for the devil and his angels. [42] For I was hungry and you gave me nothing to eat, I was thirsty and you gave me nothing to drink, [43] I was a stranger and you did not invite me in, I needed clothes and you did not clothe me, I was sick and in prison and you did not look after me.'

[44] They also will answer, 'Lord, when did we see you hungry or thirsty or a stranger or needing clothes or sick or in prison, and did not help you?'

[45] He will reply, 'Truly I tell you, whatever you did not do for one of the least of these, you did not do for me.'

[46] 'Then they will go away to eternal punishment, but the righteous to eternal life.'

Messages from the Author

NARCISSUS has received a remarkable reception from both my local community and those further afield. The response and feedback have been overwhelming and humbling. I cannot thank my readers enough.

The challenge of producing a second book within twelve months was initially daunting. However, the continued support, encouragement, and optimism of everyone I have encountered along the journey has inspirited every newly written page.

Thank you to those who have escorted NARCISSUS II along its creative path.

Carlos, Carla, and the staff at Five Senses Café for their ever-joyful welcome and for expressing the mini caffeine bombs that fuel my imagination. *Obrigado.*

Will and the staff at SMS PC Repair for ensuring the technology does what it should and who are always on hand when it decides to do something it shouldn't.

Gilly at Tink Ink for providing an in-depth insight into the world of tattoo artistry and ensuring my narrative is on the mark.

Marie at Foto Finish for creating a fantastic series of advertising and promotional material.

Stevie at Chard Bookshop for promoting and stocking an endless supply of NARCISSUS for my hometown readers.

Lee at Lee Mitchell Photography for the arduous task of capturing an image of me smiling.

Keith and Karolina at Michael Terence Publishing, without whose knowledge, guidance, and support there would be only words and pages.

My new copyeditor, Suzanne, whose patience, diligence, meticulousness, and assiduity have refined my circumlocutive sentences.

And not forgetting my father, Brian, for affording me the opportunity to follow my aspirations and championing each chapter during our daily eventide readings.

Available worldwide from Amazon
and all good bookstores

———————————

www.mtp.agency

www.facebook.com/mtp.agency

@mtp_agency

Milton Keynes UK
Ingram Content Group UK Ltd.
UKHW031158251124
451529UK00004B/405